Thornbear

By

Michael G. Manning

Cover by Amalia Chitulescu
Editing by Grace Bryan Butler and Thys Dry
© 2014 by Michael G. Manning
ISBN: 978-1502893390

Printed in the United States of America.

For more information about the Mageborn series check out the author's Facebook page:

https://www.facebook.com/MagebornAuthor

You can also find interesting discussions and information at the Mageborn forums or the Mageborn Wiki:

http://www.illenielsdoom.com/

http://magebornwiki.com/index.php/Main_Page

Chapter 1

"Your move," said Matthew Illeniel, barely concealing his glee.

Gram looked at the chessboard between them. He knew it was a lost cause, but then it almost always was when he sat down at the table with his closest friend. Matthew was a year older, which gave him a predictable advantage, but it was more than that. Gram knew that even if he were the older of the two, he would be losing most of their games. Everyone in the Illeniel family was good at chess.

Not that Gram was a bad player. He could hold his own with many older players, as his mother had started teaching him the game at a young age. Lady Rose Thornbear was the best chess player in Castle Cameron, with the possible exception of the Count himself. Their games were the subject of great interest and speculation among the castle staff whenever they held one in the great hall.

Lady Rose was his mother, and the Count di' Cameron was Matthew's father, but while Matthew had definitely inherited his father's formidable talent for the game, Gram would probably never approach his esteemed mother's prowess. He took more after his own father, Dorian Thornbear.

Gram reached out and laid his king on its side, the universal gesture of resignation. "It's your game," he confessed.

Matthew frowned, "You still had options."

"Not when you get that look on your face," answered Gram.

"Did you see it?" asked Matthew.

"Nope."

"Then how do you know I would have won?"

Gram sighed, "That's the point, Matt. I didn't see it. At all. You're too good. You should play Mother instead."

Matthew rubbed his chin thoughtfully, secretly pleased with the compliment. "You think I'm ready for her?"

"No," said Gram frankly. "She would grind you into dust, but at least you would learn something. You aren't going to get any better playing me."

"Perhaps I'm playing to do *you* the service of allowing you to improve," said Matthew slyly.

Gram laughed, "Ha! You just like an easy win. We both know I'm probably as good as I'm ever going to get. It just isn't in me. Even *Conall* is starting to win games against me now, and he's only eleven."

Conall was Matthew's younger brother by five years, and while he hadn't yet shown signs of magical ability like Matthew and Moira, he had definitely inherited Mordecai Illeniel's sharp wit. Irene, the youngest of the Illeniel children, was the only one Gram could still beat reliably, and she was only nine.

Matthew frowned. Despite Gram's jovial tone it bothered him to hear his friend give up on the hope of improving. "So you don't think you'll ever get better?"

"It isn't the end of the world," responded Gram.

"Isn't it?" countered Matthew. "We're only *now* coming into our own. We're young. Dad says we're supposed to be testing the limits, but you're admitting defeat before we even enter the race."

Most of the time Gram no longer felt the twinge of pain he once had whenever others mentioned their fathers, but this conversation seemed to bring the past closer to him, and he felt the sting once more. "You're a wizard, Matt, just like your father. You don't have any limits. Mere mortals like myself have to live by different rules. I'm only cut out for one thing, and the last thing *my* father did was forbid me to follow in his footsteps and do that very thing."

"I really don't think he meant it that way," observed Matthew, more subdued now. He didn't like the suggestion that wizards didn't have the same issues that other people did, but that wasn't an argument his friend needed just then.

"Well Mother does, and her opinion is the only one that counts," said Gram bitterly. "It's not as if we can ask my dad what he meant."

"You won't be a minor forever," said Matthew, the light of rebellion in his eyes.

Gram sighed, "I'm already past the age at which I should have started training. My father was at weapons training by the time he was twelve."

"You poor old man," said Matthew. "Already over the hill at the tender age of fifteen. Stop whining. You've already learned much of what you need; you're an excellent rider, a passable shot with a bow, and you're a far better swordsman than I am."

Matthew, unlike Gram, had been given frequent lessons in the use of a sword, both by Sir Harold and by his mother, the Countess. While Mordecai hadn't felt it particularly important for him to learn such skills, as the Count had never been trained in the sword himself, Matthew's mother had felt differently. Matthew had shared what he had been taught with Gram, sparring privately with him, despite Lady Rose's injunction. Even with such second-hand teaching, Gram Thornbear had learned quickly and his natural talent had given him an advantage over Matthew almost from their first sparring match.

"I appreciate the compliment," said Gram, "but playing at swords with you isn't going to give me enough skill to become a passable man-at-arms someday, much less a knight."

"Maybe if you approached Captain Draper or …"

"He won't go against her wishes," interrupted Gram. "I've tried before." Draper was the guard captain for Castle Cameron.

"What if…"

"Just drop it!" growled Gram. "It's not your problem!" Standing, he stepped away from the table. "I need some air," he declared as he headed to the door. He was gone before his friend could say anything else.

***

It was a warm day, almost too warm, but for the breeze whistling through the trees as Gram rode through the woods that encircled Castle Cameron. The sunshine was too cheerful for his mood, though, so he sought the darker shade of the forest rather than following more traveled trails or the open glens.

He had brought his bow with him, though he had no real expectation of using it. He had come on a whim, seeking solitude. Without hounds or huntsmen, his chances of spotting game were slim. He merely wanted the quiet that only the forest could provide.

The limbs were low and riding beneath them had become difficult so he dismounted and led his horse, a calm mare named 'Pebble'. Her name was based more on her placid nature than upon her relative size. She was one of the many horses in the Count di' Cameron's stable, but Gram frequently chose her when he decided to ride. She wasn't the fastest of horses, but she was rock steady. Somehow he felt a kinship to her because of that.

Gram stopped. The trees were close and the air still. Despite the bright mid-morning sun, it was almost dark in the dense cover. He gave Pebble's lead a quick loop over a small branch to keep her from wandering. The limb wasn't big enough to give her any trouble if she made a serious attempt to escape, but that wasn't the point. She knew as well as he did how such things worked. With hardly a glance at him she began to crop the sparse grass within reach of the tree.

Reaching across her back Gram pulled his quarterstaff from where it was tied next to his bow. The six-foot rod of solid oak felt comforting in his hands. He had brought it, not from any particular need for protection, but rather as an outlet. Moving a good distance from Pebble, he made note of the trees and limbs around him and took a deep breath.

He shut his eyes and straightened his back, smelling the air as he filled his lungs. Wood and bark, decomposing leaves and musty earth, those were the scents that predominated. They helped him to clear his mind as he held the staff in front of him, one end planted in the dirt while the other pointed toward the sky. In his mind he could see the trees around him, remembering what he had seen before he closed his eyes.

Motionless, he remained that way for an unmeasured time until at last his body felt the moment had come. Without warning he shifted, and the stillness was replaced with a rush of explosive speed. The staff in front of him vanished, disappearing into a blur of grey and brown as his arms acted to guide it around him in a complex play of movement. It passed the low hanging branches without striking them; and while it was a lengthy piece of wood, it never quite struck the saplings that encroached on his space.

Gram danced with the flow of the wood, letting its momentum pull him along. His eyes were no longer closed, but wide instead, taking in all the light around him. He turned and stepped, moving forward and then back, now to one side and then to the other. The quarterstaff never stopped. As he went, it passed over his back and then across his front, coming to rest under one arm here and then rebounding in a reversal of motion.

Gram moved, but the world around him was untouched.

After a time, sweat began to bead on his brow, a result of his focused exertion. A strong wind came up from an unexpected direction, cooling him and bringing new smells; sunshine, clean air, and… leather. It held the acrid tang of leather and sweat, along with a hint of steel.

He stopped, going still. Searching the dim brush around him Gram's eyes found nothing, but he knew someone was there. He saw no one, and heard even less, but the shifting wind had given away the presence of another.

"Who's there?" he called in a clear voice.

"It's just yer adorin' audience," came the answer in sarcastic tones.

The direction the sound came from matched the wind's brief change, but Gram still saw no one. Glancing higher, his sharp eyes finally found a bulky shadow in the limbs above where he had been looking. "I see you now," he announced.

"If ye'd seen me, ye should have left half an hour ago, ye witless prick!" argued the voice. With a sigh of exasperation the shadow unfolded, dropping a leafy bough that had broken up his outline.

As the figure stretched out Gram caught sight of a long limbed bow, sending a momentary surge of adrenaline through him. *Was the stranger preparing to shoot?* His fear proved unfounded however, as the man's face came into the light, and he recognized him as Chad Grayson, the master huntsman for the Count di' Cameron.

Easing the bow over one shoulder, the hunter climbed easily downward, swinging from the lowest branch to drop lightly to the forest floor. He was in his mid-thirties but moved with the fluidity of a younger man. He gave Gram a sour look. "I been settin' in that damned tree over an hour before you showed up. I'd have had a fat doe by now if ye hadn't come along and started thrashin' about like a wounded goat caught in a briar patch!"

Gram stared at him, replaying the man's colorful language in his head. *A wounded goat in... what?* He had never spent much time with the older man and wasn't really sure how he should react.

"Begging your pardon, Master Grayson, but you do recognize me don't you?" asked Gram, just to make sure the hunter knew whom he was addressing.

"Of course I do! Ye're Lady Rose's doltish *get*! My eyes haven't gone, nor yet my memory," spat out the irritated ranger.

Doltish get... Gram rolled the words over in his mind while his blood began to rise. 'Get' was an infrequently used term for offspring and it was typically reserved for livestock in his experience. Being an aristocrat by birth, he wasn't much used to being verbally assaulted, and he had never been exposed to a master of invective such as Chad Grayson. "Did I hear that correctly?" he said, still having trouble believing his ears. "Did you just refer to me as 'Rose's doltish get'?"

The huntsman was already pacing the area, muttering to himself, complaining that the deer would likely change to different trails after Gram's exercise routine. "What? No!" he answered. "I said *Lady* Rose's doltish get. I hain't forgotten my manners now."

"You'll take that back, scoundrel, else I'll make you eat those words," returned Gram in a low voice.

Chad hadn't even bothered to look at him as he walked. "*Scoundrel?*" he said, repeating Gram's insult scornfully. "Did ye learn to cuss while suppin' on yer momma's teat? I've heard better from young lads still waitin' to lose their fuzz."

Gram lost it, swinging the staff in a low arc meant to strike the other man's backside. It missed when the older man seemed to stumble and fall forward. Chad recovered and stood back up quickly, turning to look at Gram with innocent eyes. "Did you feel a breeze just now?" he questioned.

"You'll feel more than that if you don't apologize!" snapped Gram, gripping his staff for another swing.

Chad stopped and gave him a chilling stare, glancing down first and letting his gaze travel upward, stopping when he reached Gram's eyes. The hunter was a slender man with a rangy build, but even at just fifteen Gram stood as tall as the hunter and he certainly outweighed him.

"An' you think you're man enough to make me?" asked the hunter.

Gram's blood was boiling, and he answered with his staff, snapping the end forward with blinding speed.

Chad caught it in one palm, the heavy wood landing with a brutal smack against his flesh. Clenching that hand and catching Gram's collar in his other, the lean hunter fell backward and brought one leg up to strike the teenager in his stomach, simultaneously pulling as he kicked upward, he flipped the younger man over to land hard on his back.

Gram never let go of his weapon, even as he twisted, trying to roll over and regain his feet. The huntsman moved around him, holding the other end of the oaken weapon and forcing Gram's arm into an awkward position across his body. Before he could untangle himself, the other man was behind him, pulling the heavy wood upward with both hands until it was close to choking off the young lord's windpipe.

Gram managed to get both hands on the staff, holding the wood away from his throat, but the woodsman had a far better position. Chad had his knee against the younger man's back as he leaned backward, pulling hard on the weapon.

"Just give up and lie still, ye big dope and maybe I won't have to hurt ye!" muttered the hunter.

Furious, Gram refused to give up even though the staff was now pressing hard against his throat. His face turned red as his hands pulled downward, straining against the pressure. With a loud crack the staff broke and Chad fell backward still holding the two pieces.

Gram leapt up and turned, aiming a kick at the older man who had fallen behind him.

Rolling quickly, Chad avoided the blow and caught hold of Gram's ankle with both hands. Holding tightly to prevent another kick, he used his legs to knock the teen's other leg out from under him. The two of them wrestled on the ground for a long minute until the hunter managed to get behind the young lord and slip him into a headlock.

Gram's chin was down, and he was only getting stronger as his rage grew. Pulling at the hunter's wrist with one hand he could feel the older man's arm beginning to give way. *I'll crush his bones!*

He grew still when he felt cold steel against the back of his neck.

"I suggest you calm yerself down, *boy!*" grated the hunter.

"You wouldn't dare," said Gram.

"Don't test me, lad," answered Chad, "or I'll leave you cold on the ground. I ain't takin' a beating from some young buck that's still wet behind the ears."

"If you kill me, they'll hang you," suggested Gram.

"Not if they don't ever find your body, an' if I thought for a minute that they would, I'd be gone long before they did. Now, do ye still want to wager yer life?"

Gram was silent for a long moment before replying, "You're a coward for pulling a knife on me."

"Ye think I give a shit? If I recall ye took not one, but two swings at me with that damn big stick o' yours before I was forced to defend meself," answered Chad. "Now make up yer mind. Do I leave you on the ground, or will ye calm down and act like you've got some sense?"

Taking a deep breath, Gram tried to relax. "Alright, you win."

"Ye're not going to change your mind once I let you up?" asked Chad, maintaining his grip.

"You can't really be sure of anything I say while you have a blade to my neck," noted Gram.

"Are ye suggestin' that your word's no good, boy?" said the hunter. "Yer father wouldn't be pleased."

"I'm under duress," said Gram. "But maybe a woodsman like you wouldn't understand honor."

The edge of the blade dug into the nape of his neck, sending a trickle of blood across his shoulder and down his chest. "Careful lad, now's not the time fer insults. I understand fine, but there'd be no ransom or parole if knights couldn't be expected to honor a surrender."

Gram was momentarily perplexed. He hadn't expected the hunter to be aware of the finer points of chivalry. "You plan on ransoming me?"

"Nah, I just want yer word that the fight's over. It's like parole but I don't keep you prisoner we just go our separate ways, and nobody has to get hurt."

The teen let his muscles go limp. "Very well, I surrender. Let me up, and this fight is done, you have my word."

The blade vanished, and the weight on his back disappeared as the hunter released him and stepped away quickly. Gram stood, wiping at the blood on his neck.

"You should still apologize for your lack of respect," he declared, careful to keep his tone neutral.

"Where I come from boys are taught to respect their elders," returned Chad. "An' I don't apologize fer tellin' the truth."

"You insulted me," insisted Gram.

"I called ye someone's doltish get. That ain't an insult boy, it's colorful language, an' what's more—it's true," Chad informed him with a mocking smile.

Gram gritted his teeth, "And what if I said you were a spotted whoreson?"

"I'd say you need to learn to cuss. Even if'n ye knew how, it wouldn't bother me none. A man's got to learn to control his temper. Yer own dear father knew that. He never let words provoke him to a fight, somethin' you'd do well to learn."

A surge of anger made Gram step forward. He wanted to throttle the arrogant hunter, "Don't you dare bring my father into this!"

Grayson leapt back and rolled, pulling his bow up from the ground. Gram felt a light breeze beside his cheek and found himself staring down the shaft of a nocked and drawn arrow. "I done warned ye boy. Threaten me again an' I'll have ta find a new place to live."

Gram stopped and tried again to calm himself. "I won't forget this, villain. That's twice you've threatened to kill me."

Chad relaxed the bow and un-nocked his arrow, putting it back in his quiver. He bent to gather the rest of his kit from the ground and started to leave. "I don't give a damn, boy."

Turning to leave as well, Gram spotted an arrow imbedded in the trunk of a small sapling that had been behind and slightly to the right of his head, causing his eyes to go wide. He hadn't noticed the shot when the hunter had first reclaimed his bow a moment before.

"Keep it boy. Let it be a lesson to ye," came the woodsman's voice, already hidden by the thick forest. "Learn some sense an' mebbe one o' these days we can talk."

Leading Pebble back the way they had come, Gram returned home. By the time he got there, his anger had disappeared, to be replaced by an uneasy feeling of embarrassment and shame.

I'm not fit to bear the Thornbear name. Maybe mother is right, he thought to himself.

Chapter 2

From atop one of the statues that decorated the entryway into the main keep, came a voice, "Where are you going?" Glancing up, Gram spotted a small cloth bear, stuffed with rags and patched so many times that the toy's original cloth was impossible to determine. It was one of Moira's oldest and most intelligent magical companions.

"None of your business," he answered in a surly tone. Anything he told the bear would be relayed to her creator. He had nothing against Matthew's sister, indeed she was one of his close friends, but he wasn't interested in making his embarrassment known to anyone.

Moira Illeniel was Matthew Illeniel's twin sister, as far as most knew, but in reality she was adopted. Most thought that she and Matthew shared the same birthday, but she had actually been born over a thousand years before her brother. Her mother had been the last Centyr archmage, and her father, ironically, had been named Mordecai Illeniel, just as her adopted father was. Technically, Moira was her brother's many times removed great aunt.

Matthew didn't like being reminded of that.

Being a child of the Centyr lineage, she had inherited the same gifts her mother had possessed; namely, the ability to create intelligent magical minds, or anima as they were more properly called. Grace had been the first she had created, having given her teddy bear life as a not-quite-so-imaginary friend.

A soft thump heralded the bear's drop from the statue to land on the flagstones behind him. "It isn't like you to be so unsociable," said Grace, ambling along slightly behind him.

Gram clenched his jaw and picked up his pace, moving along the corridor and deeper into the castle. He really didn't want to talk to anyone and the bear was struggling to keep up now. Rounding a corner, he deftly avoided two servers carrying a large tureen of hot soup.

He realized almost instantly that an accident was about to ensue. Turning and ducking, he caught the small bear, lifting her as she followed him around the corner and neatly whisking her out of the way of the servers' feet.

"Whoo!" cried Grace in alarm as he snatched her up.

"How do you manage to make so much noise without having proper lungs?" he questioned aloud.

Grace's head turned toward his face, and somehow he could tell her button eyes were focusing on his. "You saved me!" she announced. "How gallant."

Embarrassed, he tried to shush her, "Don't be so loud. I only saved you a bath in hot soup. I doubt it would have done more than make you smell bad."

The servers were watching them curiously, but as soon as he met their eyes they ducked their heads respectfully and continued on their way. Like everyone else in Cameron Castle they were well familiar with Moira's small companions. Talking bears were no novelty for them.

"The triviality of the consequence in no way diminishes the chivalry of your rescue," replied the bear. Although she had no eyelashes, Gram could almost feel her batting them at him as she spoke.

Tucking her into the crook of his arm, he gave up on leaving her behind and resumed his course. "Shouldn't you be watching Irene or something similar?" he questioned.

"Irene is nine now, so she doesn't need as much minding anymore. Besides, why do you think I wander so much? Whenever I stay at home, Penny or Lilly put me to watching the children. I love them, but even a bear needs adult conversation now and then," she complained.

"What about Moira?"

"She stays pretty busy…" noted Grace, letting the sentence trail off.

It was obvious she felt she wasn't getting the attention she deserved, but at the same time she didn't want to speak ill of her creator in front of someone else. Gram decided to change the subject, "Are you implying that mine is 'adult' conversation?"

"You are much older than I am," pointed out the bear.

"Point taken, milady," admitted Gram. He hadn't really thought about that fact. Grace had been created only a few years past, sometime after Moira had begun to develop her abilities. It was easy to forget since the stuffed animal seemed to have a very mature personality. "I fear that not many consider my conversation worth seeking."

She patted his arm lightly. "I think I can sympathize with your problem."

His dark mood lightened a bit as a hint of a smile crept onto his lips. He caught it before it became a laugh. "I never realized how much I had in common with a stuffed bear, but it makes sense now," he observed. "I'm dressed and groomed, taken out to be viewed, but not allowed to make decisions for myself or take any real action."

Grace nodded, "At least you get some attention, many hardly notice me at all—and then there's my other limitation."

"What's that?" he asked.

"I can only go a day or two before she has to refresh my energy; any longer and I'll simply cease to exist."

"I have to eat to live," countered Gram.

"But you can eat a great variety of things, from a great variety of places. I can receive my sustenance from only one source," explained Grace.

Gram frowned, "Couldn't Matthew or another wizard renew you?"

The little bear shook her head, "Only a Centyr wizard can do it, and only the one who created the animus, otherwise my personality would be distorted."

"I never knew," admitted the teen. "If you ran out though, couldn't Moira just bring you back?" He mimed an imaginary display of magic by waving his hands.

The bear gave him a hard look. "If you died and Gareth Gaelyn made a new 'Gram', and somehow they brought it to life, would it be you?"

"No," said Gram immediately. "It would be a different body, but Moira could reanimate your body."

Grace clucked at him reproachfully, "This isn't really my body, Gram." She gestured with her short arms to indicate her plump cloth body as she continued, "I just wear it because it's what Moira likes, just like you wear clothes. My real form is pure aythar, and if it fades I'm gone forever."

Gram stared at her for a moment, mildly shocked. He hadn't really given the nature of her existence much thought. In fact, he had never really considered her at all, or any of Moira's other small retinue of magical creations. Some came and went quickly, temporary and barely intelligent. Others lasted a few months before she let them lapse, but only Grace had remained. She had been the first of Moira's intelligent magical companions and the only one whom she had never allowed to fade.

What must it be like to live completely at the whim of another, with the potential to die not from malice, but just from simple forgetfulness? It made Gram's own situation seem far better by comparison. His mind went still for a moment considering the implications before he realized he had been staring at her awkwardly for some time.

"It isn't polite to stare at a lady so, young lord," remonstrated Grace in a coquettish voice to break the clumsy silence.

He coughed, "I'm sorry. I was just wondering…" He let the sentence falter, unsure what to say next, he was no expert at dissembling; a quality he had been told he inherited from his father. He didn't want to admit that he had been pitying her the nature of her existence.

"Wondering…?" she prompted.

Given enough time, his brain eventually produced an acceptable response, "About your true form, what you look like underneath the cloth and buttons."

Grace covered the line of yarn that served to indicate her mouth with one stuffed paw, "Master Gram, how bold of you! Are you asking to see me without my clothes?"

"What?" blurted Gram, already turning red. "No!"

**

That evening Chad Grayson was at the Muddy Pig, sitting in a corner of the main room, nursing a dram of whiskey. He was there most evenings, the huntsman was fond of his drink, but unlike most evenings his expression was dour and uninviting.

During the daytime many mistook his sharp tongue and quick reprimands to mean that he was unsociable. His given vocation did keep him in the woods for long periods of time after all. 'They' couldn't be more wrong however, for once the sun went down and the tavern filled with people his more colorful side came to the fore.

He drank perhaps too much, though it varied considerably with his mood. Tonight he drank with the air of a man who had found his proper vocation, with seriousness and a distinct lack of small talk. The waitresses and other patrons avoided him. They had seen his darker moods on occasion in the past and knew better than to disturb him on such an evening.

Cyhan had never been one to exercise such caution. Entering the room he spent a long pause scanning the crowd before selecting his table. He sat across from Chad in the dark corner, signaling to the barmaid with one hand that he'd have a pint of brown ale.

"Piss off," ordered Chad before the massive warrior had even fully settled into his seat.

Cyhan ignored the remark as he watched one of the hostesses bringing his pint over. He accepted the heavy wooden mug from her, nodding to indicate his thanks. He had never been overly expressive.

Chad lifted his own mug, his arm swaying as he called to the server, "Hey! Darlin', I'm out."

The young woman, Danae, gave him a concerned look. "Haven't you had enough for a while?"

"Not yet, lass, not yet," answered the woodsman. He glanced over at Cyhan as he sat back down, "Stop givin' me that look. Ye can keep yer opinions to yerself."

Cyhan took a long swallow from his mug, giving the hunter only a quick glance over the rim. He said nothing.

"Ahhh, 'm just tryin' to make up for a spectacularly shitty day," explained Chad.

Danae returned and filled his mug, pouring brown ale from a clay pitcher.

"That ain't what I was drinkin' lass, an' ye know it," noted the hunter.

"You've had enough of McDaniel's whiskey," she told him. "You really shouldn't be drinking beer either."

Joe McDaniel was the owner of the Muddy Pig and the first man to introduce distilled spirits to Cameron and Lancaster. The whiskey he produced was still 'rough' by his own estimation, but it was quite popular with the locals.

"Beer just sobers me up," complained the hunter.

The statement might have been a boast coming from someone else, but Cyhan had seen the proof of it before. It took wine or strong spirits to overcome the master huntsman's tolerance for alcohol. More than once he had watched the man grow sober after an hour or two of beer. Chad and the tavern owner, Joe, were much alike in that regard. Few men were fool enough to engage either of them in a drinking contest.

"Well it's all you'll be getting for a while," said Danae.

Chad glared at her as she walked away, swearing under his breath. Drunk and angry as Chad was, Cyhan noted that the hunter's eyes never left the gentle sway of her hips. Not until she had rounded the bar and passed from sight.

Cyhan snorted quietly.

The hunter looked at him, "You can jus' shut up. I'll stop lookin' when I'm dead." After a moment he added, "She ain't that much younger'n me, anyway."

The knight gave him a solid stare, then lifted his mug for a long pull.

"Go fuck yerself," stated Chad quietly in response, lifting his own mug. Out of habit he used his right hand to grab the handle and winced automatically when his bruised bones sent shivers of pain through the alcohol induced haze. He switched the mug to his left hand.

The big warrior's raised eyebrow was question enough.

"Ah…," sighed the hunter. "I hurt it today. Got in a pissin' match with young Master Gram. The lil' prick took a swing at me, an' I made the mistake o' trying to catch his staff."

Cyhan put his mug down, furrowing his brows.

"Nah, the boy started it," said Chad. "Came out and stomped all over a spot I'd been layin' at, waiting for a fat doe. Not that he knew that, but the boy's got no sense o' proper manners!"

The warrior waited as the hunter paused in his story.

"Well, I'll admit, I was pretty irritated, and a little hung-over, but the boy's got an awful short temper; nothing like his dad at all. Dorian was practically docile when he was a lad. He never even got in fights with the other boys, and he damn sure never took a swing at someone without good cause." Chad looked over at Cyhan to gauge his companion's reaction.

"It wouldn't ha' come to that," argued Chad, "if the lad had had the least bit o' respect or the slightest bit of patience. The boy was awful damn tetchy." He paused for a moment, taking another sip of his ale. "An' he sure don't know how to take a joke—or cuss worth a damn."

Cyhan raised both eyebrows.

"I called him 'Rose's doltish get'," related the hunter, chuckling a little as he spoke. "What can I say?

I was inspired. My da' always said not to hide yer gifts."

The Knight of Stone brought his hand up to his face, passing it over his eyes, and then up to smooth his forehead before running it back through his hair. Then he lifted his hand and waved at Danae to bring them more ale. He could tell it would be a long tale.

"I kinda wanted to forget about the whole thing," said Chad, "but I guess if you insist, I'll tell you about it. I almost bit off more'n I could chew. It was damn foolish really."

Cyhan nodded, and Chad launched into an abbreviated version of his encounter with Dorian's son, leaving the story more or less unembellished. Chad wasn't one to color his stories, whether to boast or to sugarcoat. At the end, he came close to admitting his embarrassment.

"I never meant to let it get that far, but the boy's damn strong, an' he really does have a bad temper. Big as he is, ye expect him to be strong fer his age," said Chad, slurring the words faintly. "But normally they ain't *that* strong, or quick. He damn near broke my hand, and then he came close to pullin' my arm outta its socket when I had him in a choke."

The old knight coughed, muttering something before taking another pull on his mug.

"Yeah, I know," said Chad, acknowledging the sentiment even though he hadn't heard the words. "I shoulda' expected it an' jus' left the boy alone. But by the time I got inta' it, it was too late, an' I'll be damned if I take a beatin' from some kid what ain't even wet his sword yet, if ye take my meanin'. Shit, that boy was so mad he mighta' killed me. He'd lost his head, and I ain't exactly young anymore."

"You should stop being an asshole, then," suggested Cyhan, speaking his first clear words since taking his seat. "Sounds like your body can't afford to pay the tab for your mouth any longer."

The hunter stared at him without expression before laughing. "You should know!"

"If Rose would listen to reason, it probably wouldn't have been a problem," commented the quiet warrior. "He'd be training already, and you would have probably been more careful with your words."

"Sometimes I think ye only come in this place to try an' piss me off," responded Chad.

The large warrior broke into a frightening smile, "Why do you think I usually sit next to you?"

"I figured it was my good looks," said the hunter with a chuckle.

Cyhan glanced up, noting Danae's eyes on Chad's back from across the room. "Maybe I was wrong; the maid is definitely watching you closely. She might have an eye for you after all."

Chad looked over his shoulder, nodding at the younger woman before turning back. "Nah, she's just worried about me."

"That usually indicates something," said Cyhan.

"She's not my type anyway," said the hunter already sobering up.

Cyhan lifted an eyebrow once more.

Chad grinned, "Girl's got a mouth on her. Ye should hear her cuss."

The irony of that left Cyhan laughing for a long while.

Chapter 3

A few days later Moira encountered Gram in one of the halls not long after the morning meal. "Gram!" she called. "I wanted to catch you before you ran off somewhere or got busy."

Busy? he thought, *as if I am ever really busy.* Then another thought occurred to him, "Whatever Grace said, that is not what I meant!"

Moira paused, "Grace? What do you mean?"

Gram's face felt hot, but he hoped it didn't show. "She didn't say anything to you?"

The young wizard frowned, "I talked to her this morning. Was there some message she was supposed to give me?"

"Err, no," said Gram, fumbling to figure a way to gracefully erase his blunder. "Not really, don't worry about it."

Moira smiled wickedly, "Did she overhear something she shouldn't have?"

"No, I—uh—I don't think so."

Moira Illeniel pursed her lips into a brief pout, "Well if she did, she didn't repeat any of it. Despite what some think, she isn't a gossip, or a spy. She speaks her mind, but she doesn't eavesdrop for me."

"What did you want to talk about?" said Gram, hoping to leave the subject.

His friend narrowed her eyes, "It's a girl isn't it?"

"What?!"

"I knew it!" she declared.

"No! It isn't a girl. I—just stop!" he told her.

She watched him carefully for a moment, "No, I suppose not. But *if* there were to be someone, you should come talk to me."

"I'm not interested in anyone," he responded immediately. "And why would I talk to you about it anyway?"

Moira sighed, "So I could give you advice, and find out what she thinks, or maybe even help you avoid making mistakes."

Exasperated, Gram started walking, "If this is all you wanted to tell me, then you should have saved your breath."

"Matthew wanted to ask you about something," she replied.

"About what?"

"Who knows?" she answered. "He hardly talks to me at all. He's always cooped up in his workshop. It's a miracle he gets any sun."

"You could have told me that from the beginning," complained Gram.

"It wouldn't have been as much fun," she admitted with a smirk.

"Do you know where he is now?"

Her eyes unfocused for a second before she replied, "In the workshop again, as usual."

Gram thanked her and left, heading toward the entry hall. There were two workshops now; the old one that had once been the Matthew's grandfather's smithy, and the more secluded one beside the Count's secret mountain home. Mordecai had switched to working in the shop beside his home over the past few years, and Matthew had begun using the older shop in the castle yard. He claimed it was so that he would have his own space, but Gram knew it was more for privacy. Matthew's father was sometimes too overbearing when it came to safety.

He found his friend there, sitting at a table and scratching something into a heavy leather-bound journal. Glancing at it from across the room, Gram wasn't surprised that he couldn't decipher it. His eyes were more than sharp enough, but Matthew's handwriting was famously deplorable. That, along with the fact that most of what he was writing was in a different language, punctuated by strange symbols, made it impossible to guess at its meaning.

"Hey," he said, announcing himself.

Matthew grunted, acknowledging Gram's arrival without looking up. He continued to scribble in the journal.

He looks just like his dad, noted Gram mentally, for probably the hundredth time. He knew his friend well enough to know that he was in the middle of something important, or he would have set the book aside already. Leaving Matthew to finish whatever he was doing, he wandered over to the right side of the room where a long shelf beneath a window held a collection of oddities.

Most of the objects there were odds and ends that Mordecai, or in some cases Matthew, had created as amusements. Gram picked up one of his favorites, two wooden balls that, while physically unconnected, were nevertheless incapable of moving more than a foot and a half apart. They were heavy, roughly a pound each when held in the hand, but as soon as you released one it would hover in the air, as though weightless.

Gram placed them in the air in front of himself and began gently batting at them with a small paddle. The first ball flew away in one direction until it reached the end of its invisible tether. At that point it jerked the other ball into motion, and they began circling one another while drifting at half the speed of the original. Stepping around them, Gram struck one hard, causing it to fly violently in the other direction, yanking its partner out of its previous path.

He distracted himself in that fashion for several minutes, until he heard Matthew's voice, "You ought to keep those. They were always your favorite." The two of them had frequently shared the odd toys that Matthew received.

"Didn't your dad give you these?" asked Gram.

"Nah, I made those. One of my first projects. I can make more," explained his friend.

Gram was sorely tempted. "Thanks, but I think we've both outgrown 'em."

"Screw you then," said Matthew with a half-grin. "I was going to make another set immediately. I still like to mess with a lot of that junk."

"Fine, I'll take them," announced Gram. "If only to make you work more." He caught one of the balls in his hand and watched the other spin in circles around it for a moment, and then he stopped it as well and put both of them in the pocket of his waistcoat. "What did you want?" he asked.

Matthew's face became more serious, "About the other day…"

"Forget it," said Gram. "I was just cross."

"Yeah, I understand, but I had an idea…," said his friend.

Gram gave Matt a sidelong look.

"…about what you said the other day…" began the young wizard. Matthew's arms moved as he spoke, always seeming to be in danger of knocking something over, though they never quite did. "…about how you thought a wizard could do anything…"

Gram shook his head, "Well, I know that wasn't quite true…"

"That's not it," interrupted Matt. "It got me to thinking about you—and your dad."

"And?"

"Well, Dad always said your father was a stoic. It was a kind of miracle he ever managed to form the earthbond to begin with, but somehow he did. But that's not what I'm wondering. Your mother was normal, so it's anyone's guess whether you're a stoic like your dad, or whether you have some emittance like your mother."

As usual, Matthew was beginning the conversation in the middle of what had probably been a long chain of thought. It didn't help that although Gram had grown up around wizards, he didn't really understand magic, much less what 'emittance' was. Gram didn't bother asking for an explanation, he'd been down that road before. "I'm assuming you have a point here," he said instead.

"We should find out whether you're a stoic or not, and if not, how much emittance and capacitance you possess," continued Matthew.

"I don't have a damned clue what you're talking about."

"Whether or not you can use magic," said Matthew.

"I'm not a wizard," reminded Gram.

Matt shook his head, "That's not what I mean. There's more to it than that. There's a lot of variation, even among ordinary people. Some, like your dad, are almost completely dead to aythar, while most others have varying degrees of emittance and capacitance. For example, Marcus Lancaster had a normal, low capacitance, but he had a rather high emittance, which made him an ideal channeler for Millicenth."

"I wish you could hear yourself," commented Gram.

"Would you like to know what it's like to be a wizard, for just a minute?"

That caught Gram's attention, "You can do that?"

"Maybe," shrugged his friend. "If you aren't a stoic…mostly I want to know for a project."

"What project?" asked Gram suspiciously. He could tell by the way Matthew's eyes shifted suddenly that he was planning something that might lead to trouble.

"Your sword."

He gave Matthew a strange look, "What sword?"

"Your dad's sword," replied Matt with a smug look.

"The one in Albamarl, on display?" Gram was referring to his father's longsword. That sword had originally belonged to his grandfather, whom he had inherited his name from, and was one of the first swords Mordecai had enchanted. The main chapterhouse for the Order of the Thorn kept it on display in the capital. They had asked Lady Rose to gift them with the broken great sword, Thorn, but she had refused to relinquish it for sentimental reasons.

"Nope. Thorn, the broken one…"

"Whatever you're thinking, it's a stupid idea. I've had thoughts about secretly buying a sword, but she would never let that pass. She keeps it on the wall in her bedroom, in plain view. If I tried to sneak it out, she would know immediately…"

Matthew waved his hands dismissively, "I've already thought about that. She can't do anything if she doesn't know it's gone."

"She's going to know, Matt! She looks at it every time she thinks of him. I wouldn't be surprised to find out she was taking it off the wall and sleeping with it. She's obsessed."

"Wizards can do anything, remember?"

Gram made a sour face, "I'm sorry. I was exaggerating, but there's no way…"

"There is a way."

"How?"

Matt grinned, "You signal me the next time you all leave, like at dinnertime maybe. I'll skip the meal, pretend I'm sick, and then I'll sneak into her room and grab the sword. I'll leave an illusion on the wall so she won't…"

"Not good enough," countered Gram. "I told you, she touches it sometimes. She may even take it down."

"Let me finish," said Matthew reproachfully. "I'll bring it back here and create a close copy. It won't be perfect, but with a bit of illusion attached, I can produce something she can touch and that will look exactly like the original. I'll sneak in again and replace the simple illusion with the copy, and then she'll never know the difference. All we need is a full twenty-four hours."

Gram was doubtful, "I think she probably touches it almost every day."

Matt nodded, "That's fine. I'll make sure the illusion has a tactile component. It will be alright so long as she doesn't try to take it off the wall, at least until I get the copy in its place."

"So, assuming that your plan works, and I don't wind up locked away for the rest of my youth, what does your magical testing have to do with any of this?" asked Gram.

"You know the Sun-swords?" asked Matthew.

"Yeah…"

"Well, your dad couldn't use them, because he was a stoic. I need to know whether you're the same, otherwise I might make a sword you can't use," explained the young wizard.

"It's broken," reminded Gram. "You have to fix it first. Do you even know how to enchant a sword?"

"Are you kidding?" said Matt with a slightly wounded expression. "How long have you known me? I'm not just going to fix it, I'm going to make it into something worthy of your legend!"

"You mean my father's legend," corrected Gram.

"No, I mean *yours*," reaffirmed Matt. "It's going to be something fit for your father's memory and strong enough to match your deeds as well."

Gram stared at his friend, transfixed. The words, coming from anyone else, would have been an obvious attempt at mockery, but he could see the sincerity in Matthew's face. He felt a whirl of emotions rising within himself, things he didn't want to deal with in front of his friend. He started for the door. "You're crazy."

Matthew caught him by the shoulders. "I'm dead, damned serious."

Gram was growing more irritated, in part because his friend never seemed to clue in on when it was time to let go of something, and also because he secretly wanted to believe him. "What's the point, Matt? Warriors, knights, protectors, whatever you want to call them, they aren't needed anymore! The Knights of Stone, they don't have the earthbond anymore. The Order of the Thorn, they don't either. Do you know why? Because they're obsolete! The good guys won, it's over. We're all living happily ever after.

"The dark gods are gone, the shining gods dismissed, the Queen protects us from the capital, and she's got wizards to see her will done. There won't be any more wars, and if there are, your father will crush them. There's no need for men to carry steel anymore." Gram's speech was one that he'd heard in various forms on many occasions from his mother. He'd hated hearing it then, but he used it now defensively.

"I don't think so," said Matthew. "I've heard too many stories, and I'm sure you've heard them too— like when they sent assassins to kill my parents while they were visiting the old king. If it weren't for your

35

dad, both of my parents would be dead now, and that's just one occasion. And that wasn't gods or wizards, it was just ordinary men. No one is perfect, no one is safe, not completely, that's why there are knights, that's why there are soldiers! And you, you could be the greatest knight ever!"

"Damnitt, just shut up!"

"No," said Matthew. "I won't. I don't care how stupid it sounds, it's true! You wish you could be a wizard, don't you? I've heard your remarks, don't think I didn't notice. But you know what? Sometimes I wish I could be you!"

That brought Gram up short. "You what?"

"I said, 'Sometimes I wish I could be you'," repeated Matthew.

"You really are an idiot then."

"You just can't see yourself the way everyone else does. Me, Conall, all the boys in the castle, hell even the adults, they all see it! The only thing you *aren't* is a wizard."

Gram gave his friend a blank stare.

"You're the perfect son of the perfect knight and your mother is the most accomplished noblewoman in the entire kingdom. You dance better than anyone in the keep, your penmanship is immaculate, your archery is flawless, your riding—I could go on. You're the best at everything you do, and people know it. They can see it. Even when you walk, your balance is so good it makes me feel like I'm just stumbling along."

"I'm not even close to being able to beat you at chess," noted Gram.

"As if anyone cares about that," said Matthew. "Watch this." Reaching over he picked up a wooden mallet from the worktable, and without warning he threw it at his friend's face.

Gram caught it in midair, "What's that about?"

Matthew gave him a lopsided grin, "If you did that to me I'd have a nasty bruise."

"You always have those shields up."

"The point is, *I* wouldn't have caught it, and even accounting for my own clumsiness, most other people wouldn't have either. But I *knew* you would," responded the young wizard.

"There's nothing magic about catching a hammer."

"Someday, someone is probably going to throw something much worse than that at me, or someone we care about, and I'm hoping that you are there to catch it." As he finished Matthew turned red, feeling embarrassed.

Gram didn't answer. He was dealing with his own embarrassment. His first instinct was to make a joke of things, or to poke fun at his friend's sentiments, but something stopped him. After a while he replied, "Alright. What do you want me to do?"

"First we test you, to see if you're a stoic or not. If not, I can try to show you what it's like to use aythar," answered Matthew before adding, "Hold out your hand."

Gram stretched out his hand, and Matthew took it with his own.

"I'm going to try channeling some of my aythar into you," he explained. "If you're a stoic, you won't feel anything, but if you're not, you'll start to feel a

37

sort of warmth, almost like heat. Tell me if that happens."

A few seconds passed, and Gram felt his hand heating up as something like liquid warmth began to flow from his arm into the center of his being. Startled, he spoke up, "I feel it!"

"That's good," said Matt. "Don't let go. I'm going to see if I can gauge your emittance and capacitance."

"Why is that good?" asked Gram. "Doesn't that mean I'm not immune to magic the way my father was?"

"He wasn't *immune* to magic," corrected Matthew. "He was personally immutable in certain ways, but most physical applications still affected him normally." The look on Gram's face told him that his explanation was wasted. "Anyway, no, for my purpose this is good. It means that some of the fancier things I'd like to do with your father's sword will be possible."

"Such as?"

"Let me concentrate. Tell me if your hand starts to burn, or if you feel like you're going to explode."

"What?!"

"Trust me."

"Fine," said Gram. He waited as the warmth continued to grow and he began to have a tingling sensation throughout his body. After a couple of minutes, his hand began to feel as though it were on fire. "It's starting to get painful."

"Just your hand, or all of you?" asked Matthew.

"Just the hand," replied Gram. The pain in his hand receded after that, but the tingling throughout his body continued to grow. Eventually he began to feel as though his entire body was vibrating with energy. He felt strong and quick, more so than ever before.

"Are you still doing alright?" questioned his friend.

"Yeah, but I feel really good, like I could run a hundred miles and not be tired," said Gram.

A quarter of an hour passed, and the sensation continued to build. "You still alright?" said Matthew, a worried look on his face.

"I feel wonderful!" boomed Gram, "Don't stop!"

Matthew kept it up for another ten minutes before releasing his friend's hand. "That's enough."

"Why did you stop?"

"Too dangerous. Whatever your capacitance is, it's obviously very high, or you're unable to judge how close you are to your limit," answered Matthew.

Gram laughed, "It doesn't feel dangerous. I don't think I've ever felt this good in my entire life." His voice sounded louder than usual even to his own ears, but his mood was too good to worry about it.

Matthew appeared anxious. "It's definitely unusual. Your emittance is very low, which is normal for most non-mages, but your capacitance is very high, like a wizard's."

"I'm not even sure what those two terms you keep using mean," admitted Gram. "Is it good or bad?"

Matthew shrugged, "I'm not sure. Heck, we don't even know what normal is. No one has ever studied the capacitance of normal people, it might not be that unusual, though I somehow doubt that."

"But what does it *mean?*" asked Gram, with extra emphasis.

"Well, you can think of it like a wine bottle," said Matthew, using the same analogy his father had years before. "The wine in the bottle is aythar, the magic, the energy that we all use. The mouth of the bottle is your emittance, it determines how fast the wine can flow into or out of the bottle. Your capacitance is how big the body of the bottle is, how much wine it can hold.

"Your emittance was very low, probably typical for a regular person, but your capacitance was very high, too high to safely test like this. I stopped because I was starting to get tired, and I was beginning to worry that we might go too far," explained Matthew.

"What happens if you go too far?"

Matthew lifted his shoulders again, "I dunno. You might catch fire, or explode, or lose your mind. It would probably be similar to what happens when one of my dad's iron bombs is broken."

That didn't sound good. "Oh," said Gram.

"Now that I know your relative abilities, I can start planning out the sword's enchantment," offered his friend.

Gram nodded, "So I'm guessing you want me to go then?" He knew Matthew too well. His friend was already ready to return to his solitude so that he could start working on his project.

Matthew smiled.

"How long will I feel like this?" asked Gram. His body felt incredibly light, as though he were floating above the ground.

"A few hours, or possibly a few days," said Matthew, already looking down at his journal, his mind starting to drift. "Just be careful. It's sort of like when someone gets an earthbond, except that this will wear off as the extra aythar dwindles away."

Gram nodded before crossing to the door. He reached out for the handle, and then things went to hell. Pulling gently, he was astounded when the door handle came away in his hand. The door itself shot back and struck the wall, rebounding to hang loosely in its frame. The sudden lack of resistance caused Gram to lose his balance, and he reached out to catch a low hanging beam to steady himself. Somehow his arm over shot its mark though and instead of his hand catching the beam, his forearm went through it.

Pain shot through his arm, and he finished falling forward. He almost caught himself, but he stopped before his reflexes could cause any more trouble. He forced himself to remain still until after he had settled firmly onto the floor.

"Holy shit!" exclaimed Matthew from across the room. "Stay still!"

I figured that out already, thought Gram. In the back of his mind, he could remember a cold day, years and years past. His father had been training a newly minted Knight of Stone. *"Imagine that everything is made of paper. Move slowly and touch everything as if you think it will fall apart. You'll start to adjust in a day or two."*

Matthew was examining the ceiling crossbeam that been broken. Wide-eyed, he glanced down, "Do you hurt anywhere?"

"My arm," said Gram. The limb in question was bent at an impossible angle and blood was dripping from several cuts. A long piece of something jagged and white was poking through the skin.

"Oh, damn!"

"We're going to have to call your dad," said Gram, remembering the first time that Matthew's father had had to fix a broken arm for him.

His friend stared into his eyes for a long moment while his mind struggled to process the situation. "No," he said at last. "I can fix it. If we call him, he's going to ask a lot of questions."

"Do you know how?"

"Well, I'm nowhere near as good at it, but I can fix a bone and seal the skin," said Matthew. "I think the rest will heal on its own. Dad tried to teach us as much as he could about healing."

"Are you sure?" asked Gram uncertainly. "I don't want to be crippled."

Matthew's confidence was gradually returning. "Yeah, I'm sure, and if I'm wrong, we can get Moira to look at it in a day or two. She's got a better touch with this sort of thing."

"And if she mucks it up too?"

Matthew gave him a wild look, "Then we'll make you a *new* arm, a magic arm, forged from the finest steel and enchanted to have the strength of a dozen men!"

"Oh lord," groaned Gram. "Kill me first. Just do what you can."

"Alright," said Matthew, biting his lip as he started using his senses to sort out what he would do first. "This is going to hurt."

"It didn't hurt when your dad did it," responded Gram with a mild sense of alarm.

"Yeah," nodded his friend. "He knows how to block the nerves to stop the pain. I still haven't mastered that part."

"Why not?!"

"It isn't as if I get people to practice on every day," said Matthew defensively. "...and some people seem to have an instinctive feel for it—unlike me," he admitted.

"Shit," said Gram.

It hurt a lot more than he expected, but Gram didn't make much noise, keeping his teeth clenched and his mouth closed to muffle his involuntary grunts and cries. It took all his will to keep himself still until Matthew was done.

Thornbear

Chapter 4

Lady Rose Thornbear sat in the front anteroom of the family apartments she shared with her son, Gram and her daughter, Carissa. It was early, the sort of early that even morning people regard as rather extreme, but for Rose it wasn't unusual.

She sipped at her tea carefully, to avoid burning her lips. Some preferred to take their first tea near a window, to enjoy the morning sun, but she never bothered. The sky had barely begun to lighten with the first false dawn when she rose each day; there would be nothing to see. By the time the sun made its full appearance, she would have already finished her tea, dressed, and begun whatever tasks awaited her.

"Morning, Mother," Gram said quietly as he entered the room.

He had come back late the night before, after she had taken to her bed, and now he was leaving before the dawn. That struck her as odd.

"Good morning, sweet son of mine," she replied. "Where are you headed so early?"

"I thought I'd take a morning ride," he said after an almost imperceptible moment of hesitation.

Her expression never wavered, but Rose's attention focused sharply on her son then. His prevarication was unusual, and it brought the rest of her mind away from its casual thoughts. *Why is he lying?*

She had come to make certain allowances for his age. He was fifteen after all. Unlike most teenagers though, he had yet to try to hide much from his mother. He had inherited an abnormally strong streak of honesty from his father, which was probably for the best, since he was a terrible liar.

It wouldn't have mattered, though. Few people managed to slip a lie past Rose's scrutiny.

"Give your mother a hug before you leave then," she told him. "I may not see you for the rest of the day."

Gram stopped and turned back, changing direction with a faint jerk in his step.

He was hoping to get past me without getting too close, she realized, setting her cup on an end table as she rose to embrace him. Her son put one arm around her, keeping his right side away from her.

She let him escape the hug, but his action had told her where to look. As he stepped away again, she took note of the bruising near his right wrist, almost hidden by his shirt cuff. Now that she knew what to look for, she also noted that the hand itself seemed to have some swelling.

He was in a fight.

Her mind leapt into action then, reviewing the past day, and then the day before that. Before he had gotten more than a few feet distant, she had narrowed down the window of time in which his injury could have occurred. *Yesterday, after midmorning, that was the last time I saw him,* she thought, marking the time. *He was off to see Matthew.*

She had seen the other boy later, and he had been fine. He wouldn't have come away unmarked if he had been in a fight with Gram. She knew that for certain, wizard or not. It had to have been someone else, sometime after that. Mentally she reviewed everyone she had seen at the evening meal the day before.

Gram's left hand was on the handle when she finally spoke, "Do I need to be concerned about Master Grayson?" Her son twitched as the name left her lips.

"Pardon?" he replied innocently.

His reaction had already confirmed her suspicion. "Don't play dumb, people might start to believe the act," she responded, letting her irritation begin to show. She regretted the harsh words immediately, but didn't let her weakness show. "I merely want to know if you need help with whatever you've gotten into. Do I need to do something about Master Grayson? Should I be concerned about your injury?"

Gram's face fell visibly. He had long ago learned it was nearly impossible to hide anything from his mother's keen eyes, and he had known the moment she stopped him before he left that there was a good chance she would figure out he had been hurt. The fact that she had opened with Chad Grayson's name was surprising, but he had grown accustomed to her deductions. He didn't even bother trying to understand how she had made that connection.

"No, Mother, I don't want you to do anything about Master Grayson," he answered, letting his bitterness show.

"Watch your tone," she warned.

"Why bother, Mother? I could never hide anything from your intellect!" he shot back, letting his voice rise.

Rose's face was calm, featureless, a sure sign that he had roused her ire. "You might not want to bother to try fooling me, but if you don't learn to control your emotions, you will someday find your enemies using them against you."

"And that's important, right Mother?! The entire world is full of nothing but enemies? Do you ever listen to yourself? Is that how you like living, continually fearful, constantly watching the shadows?" Gram's face had gone red, and he had thrown caution to the wind. In his short fifteen years, he had never spoken to her that way, now that he had crossed the line, he felt he might as well speak his mind.

Her eyes narrowed, "Yes! It is important, very important in the world of politics, the world of diplomacy! Someday you'll be the *Hightower.* Do you realize what that means?"

The Hightower was the most important of Lady Rose's titles, inherited from her father even though her own last name was now Thornbear. In function, it meant she was in charge of the city guard for the city of Albamarl as well as being primarily responsible for logistics and supply to the entire army of Lothion.

"Of course I do! That's all I hear from you and the tutors! And yet I hear nothing about learning to use a sword! Don't you think the man in charge of so many soldiers should be taught at least the rudiments of swordplay?"

"Are you suggesting that I would do a better job of it if I trained with a sword?" she asked coldly.

"Certainly not. You're already far too perfect, Mother," he replied sarcastically, "but even

Grandfather trained as a soldier before he came of age." He was referring to her father.

"And look what good it did him," she spat, her fury beginning to erode her calm façade. "He was poisoned! His skill with a sword did nothing for him when the assassins came to finish the job! The finest weapon you will ever possess, is the one inside your thick skull."

"I'm not like you, Mother, don't you understand? I will never think like you do. I can't, no one can. As smart as you are, when will you realize that I am *not* a genius like you? I can't read people's minds the way you do, or play chess the way you do. The whole world is a game board for you, and you're always three moves ahead, but someday you'll be gone, and I'll be left. And when I screw it up, which I *will,* the only thing that will be between me and a bad end, is going to be this!" He punctuated his statement by raising his clenched fist.

A low growl came from Rose. "You will not grow up brawling and bleeding. That's not what I want for you, and I promised your father as much."

"I don't care!" shouted Gram. "He's dead! This is *my* life to live!" Unable to contain himself any longer he pulled the door open and stepped out, slamming it behind him. His strength was still greater than normal, and it was all he could do to keep from breaking it.

Once he had gone, Rose spent a long time staring at the door. Her face was wet and her normally organized mind was a tempest of raw emotions.

***

He was almost to the stables when he crossed paths with Cyhan in the castle yard. Gram was moving with frantic energy evident in every stride. Whatever Matthew had done to him the day before still hadn't dissipated, and though he tried to move slowly and gently it still gave his movements an element of violent energy.

"Whoa! Where are you headed so early this morning, young Thornbear?" asked the large warrior as Gram passed.

He stopped for the briefest of moments, struggling to rein in his anger. "I feel like a ride," he answered curtly before continuing onward.

Cyhan's hand reached out, as if he meant to place it against the younger man's chest, but Gram was no longer there. Moving almost too quickly to be believed, Gram sidestepped and pivoted, neatly avoiding the hand in his path and putting him beyond it. He kept walking.

"I'm not in a mood for delays this morning, *Sir* Cyhan," he said, using a distinctly unpleasant emphasis on the knight's honorific.

"We need to talk," said the older man.

"This isn't the time," said Gram, fighting to contain his frustration. *Did she send him to talk to me?* he wondered. *Surely not, I came straight here.*

"The sun isn't even up yet," observed Cyhan.

Gram had to stop to undo the latch on the gate that led into the interior of the stables. The momentary pause allowed the other man to catch up to him, and as he started to open the gate he felt Cyhan's hand on his shoulder. Rolling his shoulder down, he spun, swatting the other man's hand away with his injured arm. At least that's what he had intended to do.

Despite his injury, his arm moved far faster than he desired, and what had been meant as a brush off became a rapid swing. If his forearm had connected, the pain would have been memorable, but somehow Cyhan wasn't quite there. The knight moved almost leisurely as he stepped to one side and took his torso out of Gram's reach.

"Easy boy," he said calmly. "You're gonna hurt yourself."

"Sorry," said Gram, chagrined by his unintentional attack. "I didn't mean to do that."

Cyhan's eyes were steady as he watched the young noble. The older warrior's imperturbable demeanor often gave the impression that somewhere inside, his heart and other vital organs had been carved of stone. "I know that," he answered, "but as you are right now, it's easy to make mistakes. You need to relax. Move slowly."

"I'm not drunk," argued Gram.

"Did you break that arm?"

Startled by the question, Gram stared at him suspiciously. Though he was only fifteen he was nearly eye to eye with the man. "My arm's fine."

"Really?" said Cyhan, reaching toward Gram's right forearm.

He jerked the limb back, almost striking the gate with his elbow in his haste. "It's just a bruise," he said, looking away.

"Who did this to you?"

"It was an accident."

"Not the arm, the bond," clarified Cyhan.

"What?"

"How many men do you think I've trained? I know the signs when I see them. You look like you're about to vibrate out of your skin. You can barely keep yourself still. Let me see that arm. You probably broke it and didn't even realize."

"I don't have a bond," stated Gram truthfully. As far as he knew, no one had an earthbond anymore. Even Cyhan had eventually given his up when the side effects began to catch up to him.

Cyhan considered and discarded several courses of action in the span of a few seconds. He didn't want to make the situation worse, or spook the young man into hurting himself further. That left him with only one option. Words.

"I know what you're feeling," he said slowly. "I've been there. Right now, your body is so full of power and strength that you feel like the world itself isn't as real as you are. It's always that way, until you get used to it. But what you may not realize is that the power can cause you to hurt yourself. Your muscles could rip themselves completely apart if you don't stay calm."

"I don't have a bond," repeated Gram.

"Show me the arm."

Gram stared at the knight, uncertain. Cyhan's face was calm, and he exuded an aura of implacability, the kind of certainty that made him difficult to argue with. His once dark hair was now a mixture of dark and grey, which only served to reinforce the iron in his dark brown eyes. Gram carefully began to roll up his sleeve.

He expected a hiss or an intake of breath, even a whistle of amazement, but Cyhan just studied the swollen limb without a word. Gram's forearm was an ugly black and blue, and the swelling had doubled its size, making the skin look shiny in the early dawn light.

"Fingers work? Make a fist," ordered the knight.

Gram did as he was told, doing his best to ignore the pain.

"Turn your hand at the wrist," commanded the older man, demonstrating by twisting his own fist back and forth.

That hurt even more, but Gram managed it anyway.

Cyhan's eyes narrowed, "The bones are whole, but you broke it not long ago, didn't you? Who fixed it, the same one who gave you the bond?"

Gram closed his mouth.

Cyhan almost smiled at that. The look of silent determination on Gram's face reminded him so much of Dorian just then. *Stubborn, just like his father.* "You need to get someone who knows what they're doing to look at that arm. As it is now, it will take weeks for you to recover proper use of it, assuming you don't wind up with some permanent damage. I'd recommend Elaine or the Count."

The younger man grew more stone-faced.

Cyhan was well-versed in the silent language of stubborn men. Some had accused him of inventing it. "If you didn't want them to know, then you shouldn't have fucked up your arm. Come see me after you get one of them to look at it."

Gram's face flickered with uncertainty.

"I'd recommend the Count. He might not tell your mother, if you ask him nicely. Elaine might offer the same, assuming you feel like riding to Arundel, but she could talk the horns off a goat. Either way, if I don't see you this afternoon, looking much improved, I'll take the matter to the Count myself. Understood?"

"Yes sir." Gram took a step back toward the keep.

"Gram," said the knight.

"Yes sir?"

"Don't forget, right now the world is made of glass, and that includes your body. Anything other than the most gentle of touches will break something," reminded Cyhan.

"Yes sir."

"Find me after lunch—or I'll find you." The words carried a not-so-subtle hint.

Gram could feel the warrior's eyes following him until he had reached the main door to the keep. His first impression as he replayed the encounter was one of unease, but as he thought it over he came to realize that he felt relieved on some level. The older man's confident competence had settled his nerves, and while he didn't look forward to seeing him later the solidity of the command gave him a reassuring feeling of certainty.

He didn't press me about the details either. Cyhan's behavior was a stark contrast to his mother's. She only stopped asking questions when she had extracted every bit of information from him.

Chapter 4

For perhaps the millionth time, he wondered silently what things might have been like if his father had lived.

Thornbear

Chapter 5

Ascending the stairs that led to the living quarters within the keep, Gram's head was trying to work out his best option. He wanted to talk to Matthew before going to the Count, but that was unlikely to happen. He knew his friend well enough to know that he had probably stayed up until the wee hours of the morning working on his project. Matthew was unlikely to rise before the sun stood high in the sky.

He stopped in the hall that led to the Count's apartments. There was a guard stationed outside the door that led to the foyer, but that didn't worry him. Being a frequent visitor, he was unlikely to even be questioned. What caught his attention was a small stuffed bear coming in the opposite direction.

"Good morning, my champion," Grace said to him as she approached. In a smaller voice she added, "You don't want to go in there right now," as she passed by.

Gram turned and followed the bear until they had gone around the corner and left the view of the day guard. "What's going on?" he asked her.

"Your mother is visiting the Countess and she looked to be in as foul a mood as I've ever seen," said Grace. "You wouldn't know anything about that, would you?"

"Well..." he drew the word out with an embarrassed expression.

"I thought so," said the small bear reproachfully. "What did you do?"

"She thinks I've been fighting with the chief huntsman," he began, unsure what to tell her. He felt trapped. It would be impossible for him to see the Count without encountering his mother again, and if she saw his arm...

Grace looked at him doubtfully, somehow conveying her disbelief despite the limitations of her features.

"... and I lost my temper when she questioned me. I may have said some things I shouldn't have," he admitted.

"Oooh," Grace said in a pained voice, then she asked "*Did* you get in a fight with the master huntsman?" It was a good question. Rose Thornbear had a reputation for being uncomfortably discerning.

Gram shrugged, "Well, yeah, but that isn't how I got this." He gestured at his swollen arm.

The bear put one stuffed paw in front of her yarn mouth. "Oh my," she said worriedly.

Shit, thought Gram, *I didn't mean to show her that. Why do I keep talking to her?* "It was an accident. I was hoping to see the Count. I thought maybe he could fix it before Mother gets a look at it."

"You should see him anyway," advised the bear. "I don't know a lot about wounds, but if that is as bad as it looks, I think it's more important than upsetting Lady Rose."

"I'll figure something else out," said Gram, moving to go down the stairs. He was pretty sure he'd rather lose the arm than face his mother again.

"No!" protested Grace. "This is serious. I'll go tell him myself if you don't come back here!"

Reaching down with one long arm, Gram plucked her up from the ground. "Then I suppose you'll have to come with me."

"Kidnapping? You are no true knight to treat a lady so! Villain! Cad! Unhand me," she declaimed as loudly as her voice would allow.

"Shhh!" said Gram desperately as he descended the stairs. "You're going to attract attention."

"I have no other recourse, since you have taken me captive," responded the bear in a dramatic voice. "You have left me no other weapon with which to defend my virtue!"

The young man stopped on the stairs, cocking his head to one side, bemused. "Your virtue? Seriously? Where do you get this stuff, Grace?"

Grace became uncertain, "Well, that's what they say in the stories."

Gram laughed, "You've been reading Moira's romance novels?" He and Matthew had both teased her about the books she had been reading recently, though neither of them thought to consider the fact that she had gotten the books from the Count's own collection.

"Perhaps…"

"Well I am neither a knight nor a villain, and I have neither a horse to carry you away nor a dungeon vile to keep you in, so you'll just have to accompany me for a while until I sort this out," he told her frankly.

The little bear stared at him for a moment, "There might be another way, if you'll trust me."

"You have an idea?"

"Let me go back. I'll fetch Moira to you, and she can look at your arm. She's almost as good a healer as Elaine or even Mordecai himself," suggested Grace, ending on a proud note.

Gram thought about it, "You won't tell anyone?"

"Just my mistress."

"Don't tell her 'til she's almost here. She might blow it otherwise," said Gram.

The bear nodded, "I will have to tell her something, though, or she won't come."

"Just tell her it's a private emergency. Tell her I'll be grateful if she will help, but that you don't know what's wrong," Gram told her.

"That's a lie," said Grace disapprovingly.

"Well, reword it however you have to, you know what I mean," he answered, frustrated.

"I can do that," she agreed.

"I'll wait at Matthew's workshop, in the courtyard," added Gram as she began to leave. "Someone might think it odd if they see me hiding in the stairwell."

Grace nodded, and then she was gone.

***

"What's all the mystery about?" asked Moira as she stepped into the workshop, glancing around curiously.

The old courtyard workshop technically belonged to Mordecai, but it had become Matthew's private domain over the years. It had become so by mutual accord between the twins and was now an accomplished fact. She had no real interest in crafting or enchanting, and he had no desire to have his sister clutter up the place. It was a sign of the distance that had grown between the two siblings as they drew closer to adulthood.

Still, Moira couldn't help but look around with a certain amount of interest, both from a barely hidden desire to irk her brother, as well as simple interest. She was surprised to find that Gram was waiting there alone. Somehow that fact made her slightly apprehensive.

"This," said Gram, sliding up his sleeve to draw her attention.

The arm was badly swollen, a fact she might have noticed despite his sleeve, but she had long ago made a habit of keeping her mental focus away from the areas hidden by clothing, particularly with regard to boys. It wasn't something that her father or any other wizard had drilled into her, just a simple result of her natural unobtrusiveness.

She gave an involuntary gasp at the sight of it, and then again as her magesight explored the wound in more detail. Moira was empathic in the entirely normal way that many people are, and just seeing such a painful injury evoked a complementary pain within her. "How did you do that?" she asked after regaining her internal composure.

"I accidentally broke the ceiling beam," said Gram nonchalantly, pointing to indicate the damaged area.

Her eyes went wide, "Huh?" After a moment they narrowed as her mind grew suspicious.

Gram shrugged, "I didn't know my own strength."

"Sure," she answered in a tone that gave no doubt about her lack of credulity. "Is that why your mother is so mad?"

"Not exactly," said Gram. "She hasn't seen most of it. I'd kind of rather she didn't see the rest."

She looked at him with eyes that were growing wider, "You want me to try and fix that?"

He nodded.

She shook her head, "You should really let my dad look at that, or Elaine, but she's in Arundel right now. I wouldn't know where to start…"

Moira had learned to heal simple cuts and scrapes from her father, and he had even had her help with some of the farmers' injured livestock, to give her a feel for more serious problems, but she had never dealt with anything so serious on a fellow human being. The idea scared her. She took a step back.

"Please!" begged Gram. "If my mother sees this, she'll kill me."

"My father…"

"…would have to tell my mother," interrupted Gram.

"She's already madder than anything I've ever seen," said Moira. "I don't think it would be any worse."

"Believe me, it could be worse."

"Who did that to you?" she asked.

"The ceiling beam," said Gram. "I wasn't lying."

"Matthew has something to do with it then," she postulated.

Gram was no good at deception, but he didn't intend to expose his friend's part. "Maybe—look, I don't want to tell anyone about this, or drag anyone else into it. Will you just do what you can? Please?"

"Only if you tell me what you two are plotting," she insisted, crossing her arms stubbornly.

"Will you promise not to tell anyone?"

Moira hesitated; while she had always been something of a free-spirit, she still had a good measure of caution in her. In the end, her curiosity took precedence over prudence. "Alright, I promise."

Gram slowly filled her in. He barely mentioned his fight with Chad Grayson, spending most of his time discussing Matthew's idea to steal his father's sword and remake it. That was what really interested him, so much so that he explained the manner in which he received his injury almost incidentally. He finished by relating his encounter with Cyhan so that she would understand his reason for urgency.

"That's why your aythar is so bright," commented Moira. "You're still holding onto what Matt gave you; that might help."

"Why?"

"You will probably heal faster while you have some extra aythar," she explained, "unless I make it worse."

The two of them exchanged worried glances, and then Gram tried to reassure her, "You can do it."

She could read his uncertainty as well as her own, but she pushed her fears aside and focused on the swollen arm, letting her focus tighten and descend, drawing her awareness into the bruised and damaged flesh.

The bones are strong and whole, but I can see where they were joined, she thought. *He did that right, but some of these vessels were just sealed, without even attempting to pair them up with their matching severed halves.* She could also see a lot of blood had infiltrated the tissues and been left there.

Eventually the body would reabsorb it, but it would take time. The unrepaired blood vessels would be a bigger problem. They were the real cause for the excessive swelling; the circulation in his arm was inadequate. Over time his body would probably replace the vessels, growing new ones to compensate, but it might take a year or more to fully recover.

Most of her knowledge was purely theoretical, the result of lectures from her father. The fact that he had been able to *show* her the inner workings of the body without actually needing to cut anyone open had also been a great advantage. Still, she had never done more than fix very minor wounds in people and a broken leg or two in local sheep.

She had also never worked on a wound that had been undisturbed for a day or so.

Quietly, she formulated a plan, though her stomach began to flutter with uneasiness as she considered it. *Make a cut and coax the old blood out first...* There were other things that needed to be connected, other channels that carried fluids besides blood. Her father had had a name for them, but her mind failed to present it when requested. *No matter, I don't need to know their name to stitch them together.*

She began.

Gram stiffened despite himself, and then several sharp pains forced a raspy cry from his lips.

Moira looked at him in chagrin, she had forgotten to do something about the pain. "I'm sorry! Wait I can make that part better."

Like her brother, she was having trouble remembering which nerve controlled sensation in the arm. *But if I do all of them it will probably cover it.* She located the nerves in the shoulder and followed them back mentally, until they reached the spine. *There.*

Gram collapsed. He could control his neck and everything above, but his arms, legs, everything else— it was gone. "What have you done to me?" he cried in alarm.

Moira responded with a few words that were definitely not lady-like. *Crap, I didn't mean to block that much.* After a moment she attempted to reassure him, "I blocked more than I meant to, but that's alright. You can still breathe, otherwise you wouldn't have been able to say anything, and your heart is still beating, so I think you'll be fine."

"Fine?! What if you stop my heart next?!" The loss of mobility had robbed Gram of his composure, and he began to panic, twisting his head forcefully back and forth as he attempted to reassert control over his body.

"You'll need to be still," said Moira, trying to soothe him with the same soft tones she had often heard her mother use with Irene when she was little.

Her voice had the opposite effect though, making Gram even more fearful. "Undo it! Let me go,

Moira!" His voice was loud, as if he might be ready to start yelling for help.

Unsure what else to do, she placed her hand over his mouth, pushing his head back down. *"Shibal,"* she said, exerting her will and attempting to put him to sleep. However, his necklace, the same type that everyone in Castle Cameron wore, prevented her magic from affecting his mind directly.

Gram's teeth bit down painfully on the meat of her hand, and she jerked it back before slapping him reflexively. "Stop that!" she exclaimed before immediately changing course. "Oh, I'm sorry, Gram. I didn't mean to do that!"

"Just let me have my body back!"

"Sorry, I can't do that. Just relax, I'll fix this." Unclasping the chain around his neck, she repeated her spell, *"Shibal."*

Fighting to move, Gram felt her power smothering his consciousness, his eyes closed even as he struggled, and darkness overcame him.

Chapter 6

Gram waited outside the great hall after the noon meal was finished. He had eaten at one of the low tables, hoping to avoid his mother. She had spotted him, of that he had no doubt, though she gave no sign of it as she nibbled on her food at the high table. She didn't call out to him or otherwise attempt to force him to his customary seat. No, that would have created a commotion, something she would never do. She would wait, like a spider, biding its time. He would have to face her eventually, and she knew it.

The thought sent a cold trickle of sweat down the back of his neck. He loved his mother. In the main, she was warm and kind, incredibly sweet and intuitive, despite her fierce intelligence. But when she faced an enemy, she was implacable, cold, and calculating. Gram had seen it before, mostly in her political dealings, but now he felt an echo of the fear those opponents must have experienced.

He had never spoken to her that way before, never rebelled so openly. She had had little occasion to punish him in the past, not since he was a small child, and that had been different. Now he was nearly a man, and he feared that he had broken something with her that could not be repaired.

Cyhan walked through the doorway and passed him without even a glance. He turned in the hall and headed for the entry hall that would lead him outside. Gram followed without a word.

Once outside, they headed for the main gate, which led into the walled town of Washbrook. Gram moved up to walk beside the older warrior once they had left the castle environs. Cyhan didn't say anything until they had walked a hundred yards or more, but then he turned and stopped.

"Let me see it," he said without preamble.

Gram drew back his sleeve to display his forearm. The swelling had eased considerably, and the color had improved dramatically. The blacks and purples were mostly gone, replaced by yellow and faint brown patches. A small, faint, silver line marked the inside of the arm where, for some reason, Moira had opened the skin and then resealed it.

It ached when he clenched his fist, but the pain was much less pronounced than it had been that morning. Then, it had throbbed and burned constantly, whether he moved it or not, while now he almost didn't feel it when it was at rest.

"Looks a lot better," noted Cyhan. "The Count?"

"Moira," answered Gram. Giving her name reminded him of his confusion and worry when he had first awakened after her treatment. He still wasn't happy about her bedside manner, but he couldn't fault her results. He hoped he never had to ask her for healing again, though. The paralysis had been a terrifying experience.

The knight grunted, then spoke, "Not bad—the girl has come a long way. She did a much better job than her brother, at least."

"It wasn't his fault," argued Gram, suddenly angry. He didn't like it when people made judgments about his closest friend.

"He's the one who gave you the bond though, isn't he?" countered Cyhan.

"I don't have a bond," said Gram.

"You're handling it better today, but you still show the signs," said the veteran knight.

Gram shook his head, "No, really, he was only testing me, and Moira thinks I just got overloaded with magic… or something." He knew she had said 'aythar', but he wasn't sure if that was a term for energy, or magic, or both, so he stuck with 'magic'.

Cyhan gave him a look that seemed to pierce straight through him. In some ways it reminded him of his mother's gaze, for he could tell the warrior knew much more about him than would ordinarily be assumed from just a short glance, yet it felt different. His mother's eyes dissected the world, and though he knew she loved him, there was always something disconcerting about the knowledge she gleaned. Cyhan's eyes held something different; a quiet stillness, and a deep knowledge that coexisted with an overwhelming sense of confident masculinity.

Just a look, and Gram knew that the other man understood him, not because of any clever deductions, but rather because the old warrior knew men, he knew soldiers, and he had trained countless young men to be warriors. Cyhan had been a boy on the cusp of manhood once, and even more important, he had been much like Gram.

"I don't know much about magic," said Cyhan, "but I can help you."

"They said this was just temporary," explained Gram. "It probably won't last more than a day or two."

The big man gave an almost inaudible grunt.

"So, it would probably be a waste of your time," continued the teen.

Cyhan raised one eyebrow, silently challenging Gram's statement.

He knew then—Cyhan was offering something far greater than just a bit of advice. The realization washed over him like a cool wave, calming his spirit. The frustration that had burned within him for so long bubbled up for a moment, threatening to overwhelm him and making his eyes water, and then it passed. "Are you offering to train me?" The question felt stupid for some reason, but he had to be sure.

"Yeah—I suppose I am," said the older man, with no hint of a smile.

"What about my mother?"

"I'm not offering to train her," said Cyhan flatly.

"She's made it clear to everyone that she doesn't want me trained as a knight," clarified Gram.

Cyhan chuffed, "I've sworn no oath to your mother."

"What about the Count?"

"He's given me leave to use my own judgment, and he's never given any command where you're concerned anyway. You should be more worried about what the training will be like," said the older man.

Gram hesitated a second, but only to formulate his response, his resolve was already set, "Can we start now?"

Too young to know fear, thought Cyhan. "Follow me. From now on, while you are training, you will only speak when I give you permission or in response to a direct question. You will call me 'Zaihair' or 'Sir'. Do you understand?"

"Yes sir," responded Gram immediately.

They walked a short distance, heading toward the outer wall of Washbrook. Gram assumed it was because Cyhan intended to lead him back to the woods outside the small town. After a time, he posed a question to his new teacher, "What does the term Zaihair mea..."

He never finished the question. Cyhan's eyes flashed a warning that rendered him mute.

"I'm not your friend any longer, boy," said the big man with a warning growl. "You speak only when I permit it, forget again and I'll reinforce the message with pain." He stopped there, watching the younger man.

Gram almost answered, instinctively feeling the need to say 'yes sir', but he held himself back, sensing the warning in Cyhan's eyes.

The older man waited, and then smiled faintly, "Good. You aren't stupid enough to mistake a pause for a question. Do you understand?"

"Yes sir."

They walked on until they had left the town far behind. They stopped short of the forest itself as Cyhan indicated a smooth grassy area in the clearing that served as a border between a farmer's field and the start of the woods. "Sit," he commanded.

Gram did so, and Cyhan began to circle him, stopping when he was behind the young man, just out of his peripheral vision.

Time passed and he said nothing. Gram began to itch. Sweat was slowly beading on his skin in the hot afternoon sun, and small flies were swarming about him. They weren't biting flies, but they did land on him occasionally, walking about on his skin before taking off again. He swatted at them.

"Be still," ordered the man standing behind him.

The words carried a warning, and Gram ceased his movements. The itching grew in intensity, made far more unbearable by the knowledge that he wasn't supposed to move. Gritting his teeth, he held himself motionless. *This is a test,* he told himself. *I can handle this.*

An hour passed, and then perhaps another. It was difficult to be sure, only the movement of the sun gave him any indication of how long he had been sitting there. His legs hurt and his butt had gone numb. Gram was regretting his choice of sitting positions already, but he kept himself still. He itched everywhere, and his eyes searched the grass before him desperately for anything that might allow him some distraction.

Even his hair began to bother him. Faint breezes would shift it at times; and while that was normally a pleasant experience, now it maddened him. The movement tickled his ears and neck, which he knew he must not scratch. Over time his itching seemed to move, being most intense in one area and then later moving to another, but it never disappeared or relented.

It was the longest afternoon of his short life, stretching out before and behind him like the road to eternity. He began to fear it would never end. *Time has stopped. It should be nightfall by now,* he thought. *Maybe he intends to keep me here even then.*

And then he heard a voice, "Stand up. It's time to go in."

His body twitched, eager to do just that, but his mind hesitated. *Maybe I imagined it?* It took him a moment to decide the command had been real. He stood and almost fell when he tried to take to his feet. Pain, followed by tingling and numbness, engulfed his lower body. A low groan escaped his lips, but Cyhan ignored the sound.

His teacher watched him for a minute before beginning to walk. Gram stumbled along in his wake. As they passed through the gate into the castle yard, Cyhan spoke again, "Zaihair is a word from my home. The simplest translation would be 'teacher' or 'master', but the most precise, is 'life-holder'."

Gram made no reply.

"When we pass through the door, your training is over for the day and you may behave as you normally would, but you will not ask me about today. Tomorrow you will meet me again after the noon meal, and your training will begin again."

Gram said nothing then, but once they had passed through the main door he finally spoke, "Thank you, sir."

***

"Your arm looks better," said Grace the next day. She was addressing him from a table in one of the side corridors that led away from the main hall. He had just finished breakfast.

"Thanks," said Gram, pausing since it was obvious that she intended to come with him. He lifted her when she got closer. Just a year or two previously, he might have been too self-conscious to be seen in public with a stuffed animal, but he wasn't worried about such things as much anymore.

She cast an appraising eye on the fading bruises. "She did a good job," she noted with a certain pride.

"She did," he agreed. Inwardly he winced whenever he remembered the paralysis she had inflicted on him before rendering him unconscious.

"She gave her brother a bad time about not having paid enough attention when the Count was teaching them the basics of healing, but I don't think he paid her much heed," commented the small bear. "He's been very involved in some new project. He's hardly been eating." She watched the young man's face as she spoke.

Gram was familiar with the technique, for his mother was a master of it. "Please don't," he told her.

"Don't what?" she asked innocently.

"Feed me information just so you can watch me for clues. I may not be as clever as some, but it gets really old, especially when your mother is like mine," he answered somewhat bitterly.

"Sorry," said Grace honestly.

"I just wish people would say what they mean, nothing more and nothing less," he continued. "Mother is probably the world's greatest adept at the art of conversation. She truly enjoys it, but it just makes me tired."

She waited a moment before replying, "You're right. I didn't consider your feelings."

Gram felt bad for making such a fuss over it then, "I shouldn't be so touchy."

"I like to talk," she said sincerely, "but I will try to be more straightforward with you."

"It's alright," he told her. "Just ask me what you want to know."

"What's Matthew working on?"

"Are *you* asking, or are you asking for Moira?"

"For myself," she said promptly. "I'm just curious. I won't betray your confidence."

He gave her a long stare. "It's something private, and it's important to me."

"Fair enough."

"I have a question for you, though," he said then.

Grace perked up, "Certainly."

"Why are you so interested in me?"

A dozen replies ran through the magical construct's mind, but she discarded them all. They were facetious stories, artful lies. She knew he wouldn't accept them. If she was going to continue talking to him, she would have to be forthright, even if it was painful. "Loneliness," she said simply. "Not many people are kind enough to talk to me, or take me seriously."

Gram started to interject, but she rushed to finish, "No, wait. I'm not speaking ill of anyone, but Moira only has so many hours in the day. She spends a lot of time with me, but the rest of the time I really have no one to converse with. People tend to ignore me, or avoid me when they think I may be spying on my mistress' behalf."

He mulled her words over for a minute, "You don't have any friends." It was a statement, not a question.

"Just Moira," she answered.

"How about me?" he asked.

Her button eyes were incapable of tears, but emotion swept over her nonetheless. Gently she hugged his neck. "Thank you," she said. "That's two then; you, and Moira."

She dropped from his shoulder and left him at the next doorway, waving a simple good-bye.

The rest of his day was uneventful, though he looked forward to seeing Cyhan that afternoon. Unfortunately, his 'training' consisted of more of the same treatment as the day before. Sit, be still, don't talk. He felt certain he would go mad before they were done.

Chapter 7

Gram sat in his customary place at the high table for dinner that evening, which was beside Matthew and Conall at the right end of the table. The high table itself was quite long, over twenty feet, and Rose Thornbear sat near the center beside the Countess, Penelope Illeniel. Consequently, he didn't have to worry about making conversation with his mother.

"Have you thought about my plan?" asked Matthew in a conspiratorial tone.

"No."

Matthew sighed, "I'm almost finished with the diagramming, but I can't start on the actual work until we get it."

"Mother isn't really happy with me right now, Matt," began Gram. "This isn't a good time to piss her off even more."

"There's never going to be a good time," said the young wizard. "Besides, she won't even know."

"Can't you just make a new sword?"

Matthew blinked, surprised at the suggestion. "I could, but that's not the point."

"What sword?" whispered Conall, enthusiastically leaning toward Gram.

Gram looked at the younger boy, unsure what to say, "Uhh…"

Matthew leaned in front of him, "Mind your own business, turd-burglar. It's one of *my* projects, so dust off."

Conall made a face before answering in a high pitched voice, "It's one of my projects!"

Gram was still reviewing the previous remarks, "Turd-burglar?"

"He's always stealing my stuff," said Matthew, by way of explanation.

"What project?" asked Moira innocently, leaning in from across the table.

"None of yours," warned Matthew. "I was just telling the turd-burglar to stay out of my things."

"You better stop calling me that!" growled Conall.

"Turd-burglar," said Gram again, talking to himself. "That doesn't make much sense."

Matthew glared at his brother, "Or what? You'll tell Mom? You're such a little snitch."

"Stop it, Matt!" said Moira, raising her voice. "You don't have to be so mean."

Gram had an epiphany just as Moira was threatening her brother, "Oh, I see, turd-burglar, you mean because he's always stealing your *shit!*" He said it with a half laugh and some emphasis on the last word. Unfortunately, everyone had fallen silent as Moira finished her admonishment.

The entire table glanced at Gram as he gleefully pronounced the word 'shit'.

Rose watched as her son turned crimson, but Gram refused to meet her eyes.

***

She was waiting for him when he returned to the family apartment that evening. "Gram."

His mother's voice startled him. He had been expecting it, but he had somehow hoped that she would let the conversation go for a few more days before she forced it.

"Yes, Mother," he answered dutifully, standing a bit straighter. He kept himself stiff, almost as though he were a soldier standing at attention.

"Please, Son, I need to tell you a few things. Don't be so…" she didn't quite finish with 'formal' before he interrupted.

"I'm sorry, Mother. Please forgive me," interjected her son. He didn't meet her eyes, but he couldn't help noticing that she seemed tired, perhaps even worn. It wasn't something he expected to see.

She shook her head, "No, Gram, that isn't what I wanted…"

"I know I was wrong, Mother. I apologize," he responded curtly. He was angry again, though he couldn't name the reason. He hoped that by capitulating immediately she would keep the lecture short and let him take his rest.

Rose sighed. *He's so impatient and so angry,* she thought. *Have I been so cruel to my son?* "I'm leaving for the capital," she said, moving to the heart of the matter before he could rush the conversation further.

That brought her son up short. Gram stared at her, questions in his eyes.

"The Queen needs me, and there are matters that I have put aside for too long. I will be gone for an extended period," she told him.

"How long?" he asked.

"Six months at least," she responded, "but thanks to the World Road I will be able to visit regularly without too much trouble. The question is whether you wish to come with me or stay here."

He found himself studying the stones beneath his feet, in the rare spots where they weren't covered by soft rugs. "What about Carissa?" His sister was nine now and already in bed, but she was the first thing to spring to mind.

"I considered leaving her here, under the Countess' care, but I dislike the thought of being separated from her for so long," admitted Rose. "I will take her with me, but you're of an age to decide for yourself. What would you rather do?"

Something in her eyes made him hesitate. Her voice was calm, but he could see a hidden sadness in her features. She hoped he would choose to go with them, but there was nothing he wanted less. He also wanted to see where Cyhan's training would lead.

"My friends are here…"

She nodded, dipping her head, as if in acquiescence of some defeat. "I understand, Gram."

"I've been before," he added, struggling with a feeling of guilt.

She rose and stepped closer, "It's alright, Son. I really do understand. I was young once, hard as it may be to believe. There are things for you to learn in Albamarl, but there may be more important priorities for you here."

He stiffened for a second. Did she know about his training with Cyhan?

Rose put her arms around her son.

He hugged her back, feeling his anger drain away, to be replaced with an unnamed sadness. She felt small, fragile. Though she was tall for a woman, she now had to tilt her head to hug him. For most of his life she had towered over him, powerful, strong, and infallible. He had seen respect, admiration, and sometimes fear in everyone she interacted with, but now he saw her in a new light. For a moment she was just a small, frail, human being.

The revelation shook the foundation of his being. For the first time, he knew the deeper existential fear that every person gains as they begin to face adulthood. "I'm sorry, Momma," he told her, wishing then that he could give up his new knowledge. He didn't want to grow up. Not if it meant he had to live in a world where she was mortal, fallible... vulnerable.

"What's wrong?"

It was Carissa's voice. She stood in the doorway, watching them with worried eyes.

"Come here," said Rose, opening her arms to welcome her daughter to join them. She held both her children for a while, and then she explained to Carissa that her brother would be staying in Cameron without them.

***

The next day was quiet. His mother and sister were occupied with their packing, though she didn't plan to leave for another two days. Matthew was still busy with his preparations, so much so that Gram couldn't even find him to tell him that stealing the sword hilt would be easy…assuming that his mother didn't take it with her.

He spent a couple of hours riding, simply to ease his boredom. He didn't look forward to his training that afternoon, since the only thing he ever got to do was sit still and learn to enjoy being bitten by insects.

Cyhan led him to the same place after lunch. He gestured to the same spot with a long slender rod. No explanation was necessary. Gram sat and grew still.

This was his third day of sitting. He had learned from his first experience to make sure he took a comfortable position in the beginning, since he wouldn't be permitted to shift about or adjust his seating. Cross-legged seemed to work best, but his ass would still go numb. He knew that when he was allowed to stand later, his legs would throb, and his knees would scream. The ache his lower back would acquire wasn't anything to sneer at either. They were unfamiliar sensations for someone of his age.

There's some trick to this, he thought as the first hour drew to a close. *Maybe he's waiting for me to protest, to refuse to sit any longer. He can't seriously want to spend four or five hours watching me sit here silently.* He couldn't see his teacher, but he knew Cyhan was there, standing behind him, somewhere beyond the edge of his peripheral vision.

Maybe I'm failing by sitting here. Maybe I'm supposed to refuse, to show my determination.

He tried to stand, feeling his legs falter from lack of blood flow, then he fell reeling, a sharp pain blossoming across his lower back. Rolling over he saw his mentor standing there, rod in hand.

He hit me!

Adrenaline surged through him, and despite the numbness and tingling, he surged to his feet. The energy that Matthew had given him had faded over the past two days, but he still felt uncommonly fast. "Stop," he ordered his teacher.

The older man watched him with dead eyes and then moved to the right. Gram flinched, preparing to dodge the next strike, but he only succeeded in putting himself in the path of the next blow, which came from his right. This one was to the side of his head.

"Sit," commanded Cyhan.

"What is wrong with..." began Gram, but a new blow caught him on the back of the neck and the pain stole the words from his lips. He lost his temper then, feeling his blood begin to rage. He leapt up again and moved to one side, hoping to gain enough ground to escape his tormentor's strikes until he could gather his wits.

Two more blows sent him to the ground, and he felt blood trickling down from his scalp. Before he could recover, he felt the tip of the rod against his throat. "Stay down, boy. Don't even think of baring your teeth at me."

Gram swallowed, looking up at the warrior from the corner of his eye. He was face down on the ground, and he could taste dirt and blood in his mouth. He opened his mouth to speak but paused when he felt the pressure on his throat increase.

"I haven't given you permission to speak."

Gram froze, closing his mouth. Something in his teacher's voice told him he would regret it if he chose

83

to rebel any further. *He wouldn't kill me,* said his rational mind, but his gut was telling him something entirely different.

"Take your position; sit and be silent."

He did as he was told, not even daring to wipe the blood from his face as it dripped into one eye.

"Today was your first mistake, so I will give you some advice. Stop thinking. This isn't a game or a riddle. I'm not waiting for you to figure out some hidden meaning. I'm not here to teach you to think."

They spent the rest of the afternoon repeating the same lesson from the two previous days. The blood on Gram's face dried and cracked, making his face itch even more than before. At some point close to the end of their usual period, his teacher spoke again.

"You may ask me questions now."

"Why do you want me to be still?" asked Gram.

The wooden rod in Cyhan's hand twitched, rising. "Have you forgotten your first instruction?"

The younger man felt a cold chill. "Zaihair!" he blurted out.

The other man nodded, "Repeat your question."

"Why do you want me to be still, Zaihair?"

"Because you needed to learn," said the old knight. "Find a better question."

He had spent most of the afternoon doing nothing else. Sorting through them quickly, Gram picked another, "I've seen you training knights in the castle yard, Zaihair, but I have never seen you make them do this. Why are you making me sit when they don't?"

"Better," said Cyhan. "I am teaching you more than how to wield a sword, or wear armor. I owe a debt

84

to your father, and I have no son of my own, so I intend to teach you *Zan-zei*. The first step is learning stillness."

"What is 'zan-z-eye'?" asked Gram, pronouncing the word as carefully as he could.

"It means, 'the unnamed path'," explained Cyhan. "One more question, and then we are done for today."

I have a hundred questions! Gram thought furiously before settling on one, "How will sitting still make me a better fighter, Zaihair?"

"Stillness alone will not do anything for you, but you must learn it before you can understand movement," began his teacher. "Silence, of the body and mind, will make you aware of the world. When you become completely still, your body will vanish, only then can you observe your opponent, become your opponent. To do that, you must defeat yourself first."

What is that supposed to mean?!

"Rise. It is time to return."

Thornbear

Chapter 8

A large hand gripped his shoulder, forcing him to pause before he got too close to the horse. "Wait Gram, go slowly. Give them a second to know you're there," said his father.

He looked up at his dad, uncertain. He just wanted to get closer, to touch them. Surely that couldn't be wrong?

Dorian smiled, teeth showing beneath his thick mustache. "You're still small; if you go scurrying in at your normal speed, you'll startle them. They don't want to hurt you, but if you scare them, you could get stepped on or worse." His eyes flicked to the large stallion in one of the stalls at the end. "Stay away from that one, though. He's not too friendly."

Gram eased forward, going slowly now. Reaching out with one hand, he lightly stroked the horse's brown coat. "There… there," he chanted, repeating the words he had heard his father say many times before, "there's a sweet girl."

"Do you like that one?" asked his father.

He nodded, looking up again. The smell of leather and sweat passed by his nose, along with the acrid tang of metal. They were smells he had long ago come to associate with his father.

"She's younger than you," revealed Dorian.

Gram looked at him in surprise. The mare was enormous to his young eyes. She didn't look like a child; her size was close to that of the other horses. "Really?"

"She's just a yearling."

"How old is that?"

Dorian laughed, "She's a little over a year old."

"Can I ride her?" asked Gram hopefully.

His father shook his head, "I'm afraid not, Son. Though she looks big, she's not ready yet. She has to grow some more, and her bones have to harden. She's still too soft. You can ride her mother, though." He pointed at a larger mare, one that was looking in on them, her head passing over the gate that separated the stable from the outer corral.

"What's her name?"

"The mother is called 'Star', she used to belong to the Queen's father, but the Count bought her years ago," explained Dorian.

"No, *her* name," repeated Gram, petting the yearling to make his question clearer.

Dorian smiled, "Well, that's what I brought you here for—it seems no one has given her a name she likes yet."

"Why?"

"I don't know, but I think it might be because we're all too *old*. She might like a name better if it came from someone young." Dorian brought out a strangely formed brush with large teeth and began to move it in wide circular, sweeping motions. "This is a curry comb," he explained. "You have to be careful with it, just use it to loosen up the dirt in her coat." Putting the brush in his son's hand, he demonstrated by moving Gram's hand over the yearling's side.

"Do you think I'm young enough to name her?" asked the five year old.

"Maybe," said Dorian as he let go of his son's hand, watching carefully to make sure that the boy kept his movements smooth and gentle. "There's only one way to find out."

Gram stopped, glancing at his father and then back at the young filly. "Pebble," he told her confidently. "Do you like that?" He spoke to her seriously, with all the gravity that only a child can feel when addressing such a creature.

The horse looked at him from one large brown eye, her ears pricked forward at the sound of his voice. Bending her neck, she blew suddenly, her warm breath tickling his ear and neck, and then she nudged his head with her muzzle.

"She likes it!" said Gram excitedly, looking upward for his father's approval.

"Oh no!" exclaimed Dorian in mock chagrin. "I was afraid that would happen."

Gram frowned, "Why?"

"Well, that means you'll have to take care of her from now on. She's chosen you. It's a heavy burden for a boy of your age."

"I don't mind," declared Gram. "I can do it!"

Dorian studied him carefully for a while, as if thinking deeply. "Very well," he said at last, "I guess there's no help for it. Let me show you the other brushes then. This one is called a 'dandy' brush…"

"Wait," said Gram, suddenly unsure.

"What, Son?" asked his father.

Looking down at his hands Gram realized he wasn't five, not anymore. He was bigger, far too large, he was fifteen. Clarity washed over him, and sadness replaced his former wonder. Looking at his father, he felt tears start in his eyes, "You're dead."

As soon as he said the words, he knew it was a mistake. He shouldn't have said them, he had violated the rules. The dream was over. Dorian looked at him sadly.

"How is your mother?" asked his father. "And little Carissa? Are they well?" His body was changing, growing harder, crystalline.

"They're fine," said Gram hurriedly. "But we miss you."

"I know, Son." Dorian's arms and legs were different now, alien, composed of what seemed to be pure diamond. Even his eyes were changing now.

"I love you, Dad. Please don't go," whispered Gram desperately.

"I love you too," said his father. Long blades were growing from his arms. He backed away to leave more space between them, his body was sharp and dangerous. "Give you mother and sister my love." A mist rose from the ground, and the world grew hazy.

Gram woke from his slumber and clenched his stomach, fighting to suppress the involuntary sobs that his dream had evoked. Drawing deep breaths he relaxed, though in his mind he struggled to hold onto the last wisps of his vision. Awake he felt again the loss, but even worse, he could no longer see his father. The face in his mind wasn't truly from his memory, it was the face in a portrait. A painting his mother had had done of the two of them, before his death.

Chapter 8

He was no longer sure he could remember his father's real face anymore, except in the dream—maybe.

Gram Thornbear sat up in his bed. In the next room he could hear his mother moving already, preparing for her trip. He stood and crossed to the small bookcase on the other side of his room. Drawing out a dusty book on geography, he opened it, cautious to avoid letting its contents spill. Years ago he had hollowed the interior of the book, once he was certain that his tutors would no longer expect him to refer to its contents. He had created a round space, just large enough to hold the fist-sized ruby that was all that remained of Dorian Thornbear.

In the dim early dawn light the stone seemed to almost glow from within, though he was sure it was his imagination. He held it in his hand, trying to recall his father's face again. A faint warmth against his palm eased the ache he felt in his heart.

Putting the stone away, he closed the book and replaced it on the shelf. He had never shown the stone to anyone, though he couldn't say why. His mother and sister deserved to see it as much as he did, but he never considered telling them about it. It was his. His mother had her memories, her children, and the broken sword. Carissa couldn't remember their father at all.

But this was his birthright. The image of his father's face might fade from his waking mind, but the red stone was physical, it was real. No matter how his memories faded, the ruby heart would always stand as proof that his father truly had existed.

Gram left the room feeling calmer. He would help his mother finish her packing and loading, and later the three of them would make their sad goodbye's.

***

Two days later Matthew was standing beside him in Rose Thornbear's bedroom. They were looking at the broken sword on the wall.

It was big. Thorn, before it had been broken, had been six feet in length, from the pommel to the tip of the blade. The piece on the wall was the hilt, quillons, and a foot and a half of the blade itself. Most of the actual blade that remained was the ricasso, an unsharpened region just beyond the quillons that could be gripped when necessary for certain maneuvers, such as when the fighting was too close to effectively swing the sword in the usual manner. The ricasso ended with two triangular flukes that served as a type of smaller hand guard; beyond that the blade was double edged.

All in all, the piece on the wall was almost half the original length. Matthew looked at Gram, "Well?"

"What?"

"Are you going to take it down?"

"You're the one who wants to remake it," reminded Gram.

"But it belongs to you," Matthew pointed out.

"It belongs to my mother," Gram remarked.

"You're the heir," said Matthew.

"So?"

"It wouldn't be right for me to take it down," said his friend. "It would be like…"

"…stealing?" finished Gram.

"Yeah, sort of," agreed Matthew. "It's symbolic. He was your father, so you should take it down, and then hand it to me."

Gram snorted, "If I didn't know better, Matt, I'd say that you were superstitious."

The young wizard gave him an exasperated look. "My father slew most of the gods, I don't think it's possible for me to be superstitious."

"Sentimental then, like my Nana," said Gram. Nana was his name for Elise Thornbear, his grandmother.

Matthew grinned briefly, "Alright, I'll accept that. We have been looking up at this sword for years after all."

Since his friend had given up the argument, Gram decided there was nothing left to do but take the sword down. Carefully, he gripped Thorn by the ricasso and lifted it away from the hooks that supported it on the wall. Shifting his grip, he put both hands on the hilt and held it reverently, close to his chest, with the blade pointing downward. He closed his eyes for a moment, letting the feel of its weight settle in both his hands and his mind.

Matthew waited patiently, not wanting to interrupt his friend's reverie. When Gram opened his eyes again, Matthew held out his hands for the weapon.

Gram started to hand it over, but then paused. "You said you'd make a duplicate, but when you finish, what will Thorn itself look like? We can't hang the mended sword back on the wall."

"We could just leave the duplicate there," observed Matthew.

"That wouldn't be right."

Matthew smiled then, "I knew you would say that. Don't worry. It will look exactly the same as it did before."

"I thought you were going to fix it?"

"I am."

"But…"

Matthew grew serious. "This was once one of the finest enchanted weapons Dad ever crafted, but it will be even better when I'm done. It will be like nothing done before. Trust me."

Gram handed him the sword. "The rest is down here."

"The rest?"

"Yeah, they went back and collected the other pieces after everything calmed down," said Gram. "She keeps the rest in this case." He pulled out a slender wooden box and opened it. Inside were four pieces of the shattered blade.

Matthew pursed his lips pensively. "I suppose I can make copies of those too. I never knew they recovered the rest of it."

"If you don't want to use them that's fine," replied Gram.

"No, I'd rather use it all, since it's here."

"Does it make any difference?" asked Gram. "I mean, does using the already magicked steel make it better or easier?"

The young wizard shook his head. "No, there's really no magic left in it. When it shattered, the enchantment was ruined. This is just steel now."

"Then why do you want to use it?"

Matthew's blue eyes stared into his, "You know why."

Gram nodded, "Yeah."

Matthew unfolded a leather sack that he had brought with him, opening the top to slide the pieces of the sword into it. When he had finished, he folded it back up and put it into a pocket in his coat.

"Was that one of those magical pouches your father makes?"

Matthew grinned again, "Nope. Something new."

"Like how?"

"Dad's are a variation on a magical portal. They open into a storage container the he has hidden somewhere else. Mine doesn't have a container hidden anywhere. It actually opens into a small pocket dimension…"

"Stop," said Gram.

His friend's face fell. "But it's really important, because I'm going to use the same principles in part of the enchantment…"

"And I still won't understand," said Gram.

Matthew closed his mouth, but Gram could see the words still rolling around in his friend's head, bottled up behind his lips. The thought made him want to laugh, and eventually he relented. "Fine, tell me anyway, but don't expect me to remember any of it."

"Sure you will," began Matthew immediately. "It's really simple, at least in function… the math behind it is pretty hairy, which is probably why no one has done it before. The basic principle relies on the fact that we are actually surrounded by an unknown number of dimensions, beyond the three we normally think of, and they pass through an even greater number of parallel worlds..."

Gram nodded now and then as he walked his friend back to his workshop. It hardly mattered, though. Matthew didn't have many people to talk to about his projects, and he kept up a constant stream of exposition as they traveled, barely noticing whether Gram responded or not.

He's just making it all clear in his own mind, thought Gram. For his own part, he was thinking forward to his afternoon with Cyhan, wondering whether he would finally progress to something beyond sitting still and being eaten by insects.

***

His afternoon with the big warrior was turning out to be a disappointment. The only difference so far was that instead of his usual wooden rod Cyhan had brought a collection of slender reeds, bound into a rod-like shape. He gave no explanation for the change.

Gram had been sitting in place for more than an hour when it happened.

Recently, he had begun to slip away while he sat in place, not in the usual manner; his instructor always sensed if he started to fall asleep. This was different. He would focus on his discomforts, the pain in his legs, the itching of his skin, and they would begin to fade.

It was rather like staring at a spot on a wall until you found you could no longer see it without looking away. Sometimes it seemed as though his body was vanishing, but the experience wasn't frightening as one might expect; it was peaceful instead.

He was there again, fading away into non-existence, when he felt a change. It wasn't a noise exactly, but there was movement. His teacher was always standing quietly behind him, Cyhan might have been a tree for all the motion he made while his student sat on the ground. He was moving now, though.

The bundle of reeds struck hard against the side of Gram's neck, sending a sharp, stinging pain thrumming through his body. Certain it was another strange test, Gram held perfectly still, ignoring the injury.

"That was an example," came the older man's voice from behind. "From now on, I will occasionally strike at you. When I do, you can move, either to block or dodge, but only then. If you move when I am not swinging, I will punish you. Do you have any questions?"

"Yes, Zaihair."

"Ask then."

"How will you punish me if I move at the wrong time?"

He could almost hear the smile in Cyhan's voice as he answered, "By striking you as I just did."

Of course, thought Gram. His extra speed and strength had faded over the last two days, and he no longer felt any stronger or faster than normal. He suspected he would be wishing that he was before too much more time passed.

The thought of an impending blow ruined Gram's concentration. His sense of disappearing while he sat was no longer evident. He missed Cyhan's first strike fifteen minutes later and took a stinging blow to his right arm. Tightening his resolve, he focused his concentration, trying to detect any movement or noise behind himself. He missed every attack. Even worse, he began to flinch at imagined attacks, which provoked more punishment.

An hour later he had a wonderful collection of welts and marks on his skin. His teacher took pity on him then, for the attacks stopped, though he never told Gram that he could relax. Two hours passed without incident, and Gram eventually gave up trying to detect attacks, there were none coming. A while longer and his mind relaxed and his body began to disappear again, giving him some respite from his aches and pains.

He felt the next attack coming.

What it was that tipped him off he couldn't have said, but he knew it was coming. Jerking his head to one side and twisting, he caught the next strike by artfully blocking it with his face.

The pain made him fall sideways, but there were no further swings, even though he had left his proper position.

The knight was silent for a minute, as Gram collected himself and sat back up. "That was good."

What? Gram was surprised, unable to understand what was good about being struck in the face. By dodging, he had made the attack worse.

"We're done for today," said his teacher. "Remember what you felt. You'll need it tomorrow."

Thornbear

Chapter 9

The next morning Gram began to realize how lonely living by himself could be. His mother's early morning habits were such that it felt strange to wake and not find her drinking her tea. The family apartments were too quiet, almost stagnant, especially without Carissa. Her youthful enthusiasm generally served to lighten the atmosphere.

Now there was no atmosphere, just an empty home.

Never one to dwell on such things, Gram dressed quickly and left. His mornings were quiet, until it was time to meet his tutor, so he decided to do something he hadn't done in a while. He went to observe the exercise yard.

It was a place he had learned to avoid. Not because he wasn't allowed to watch, but simply because it often worsened his mood. Today the young soldiers were out drilling with wooden swords, hacking and pounding on the pells. Captain Draper circled the area, watching his men and offering advice where it was needed, while Sir Cyhan led a smaller group in more individual exercises to one side of the field.

Cyhan was the only knight who still resided in Castle Cameron. The others had gone to join the Queen's new Order of the Thorn years past. That might change soon, though. The Count hadn't shown much interest in increasing his military force by replacing his lost knights, but Sir Cyhan had convinced him that a few were necessary, if only because they were required if the Queen ever called for a levy.

Consequently, Sir Cyhan spent his mornings working with the most promising of the young soldiers, improving their skills and observing their potential. It was rumored that he would choose two to serve him as squires soon, which was a sure sign of their eventual elevation to knighthood.

Four of them practiced with him, wearing heavy mail and carrying heavy wooden weapons. Cyhan was in his fifties now, but he still moved like a predator among them. What it was that set him apart was hard to define. He was strong and quick, but he conserved his movements in a way that his young charges didn't. They were learning, though, with the endless energy of youth. What they lacked in skill, they made up for with enthusiasm.

Perry Draper, the son of the guard captain, was probably the most promising of the lot. Even Gram's untrained eyes could see that. He moved with natural athleticism, and he was always the first to master whatever Cyhan taught them.

He's sure to be picked for squire, thought Gram.

"It is unusual to see you here, Master Thornbear," said a familiar voice.

Glancing over, Gram saw Lynarralla had joined him. She was an odd girl, with silver hair and brilliant blue eyes. Her ears, when they managed to peak out from her hair, were softly pointed. She was the first of the She'Har children, and she lived with the Count's family as a sort of fosterling, to learn the ways of humankind. Physically she looked to be a young woman of fifteen or sixteen years, but in reality she was only four years old. Her kind were born with all the knowledge that human children took years to acquire.

"I was bored," said Gram, affecting disinterest, not that he needed to have bothered. Lynarralla's social acuity was poor, she was the complete opposite of his mother in that regard. "What brings you out here this morning?"

"The Countess," she replied, her eyes flickering to one side to draw his attention to a new entrant on the field.

Penelope Illeniel and her daughter Irene were approaching from one side, moving toward Cyhan and his special "class". They paused for a moment, and Irene left her, walking over to join Gram and Lynarralla.

"Hello Gram," said the youngest of the Illeniel children. Irene was nine, and unlike her siblings she strongly favored her mother, with soft brown hair and dark eyes.

"Hi Rennie," he replied, calling her by her nickname. The Countess disapproved of the name, but everyone close to Irene called her that anyway—when her mother wasn't within earshot.

She smiled at him, "It's been very boring since Carissa left, but at least you're still here."

Gram's sister was her closest friend. "I haven't heard from them yet, but I bet she's missing you, too."

The girl nodded, "Did you come to watch Momma?" It was obvious from the Countess' attire that she intended to get some exercise; she wore a heavily padded arming doublet and carried a wooden shield and practice sword.

"Only by chance," he admitted. "I didn't have anything else to do."

Out on the field Cyhan gave the Countess a short bow and then presented his students to her. Afterward they took turns sparring with her, one after another and then two at a time. Despite her smaller size she handily defeated her opponents.

One of them, Perry, offered a suggestion of some sort, but Gram couldn't hear his words from where he stood. The Countess nodded, and Cyhan smiled while the others formed a circle around them. It appeared that they were going to face one another.

It started casually, as if they were simply playing at combat. Penelope Illeniel circled her opponent in a counterclockwise direction, forcing him to turn. She tested his reactions now and then and each time found him ready for her.

She remained on the offence, advancing on him now, trying to force him to shift his stance, to give up ground, but the big man stubbornly held his position. He moved with an economy of motion, never overextending himself, content to defend without counterattacking.

The Countess stepped up her attack, moving ever faster, her heavy wooden sword beginning to blur with speed. Despite that, Cyhan never seemed to hurry; his sword was always where it needed to be before her attacks could land.

Gram watched with fascination. He had seen the knight sparring before, but he fought differently now, cautiously. When he fought with his students, he never seemed to display that sort of focus. That alone told

Gram that even though he seemed to be treating the fight casually, he was in reality taking it far more seriously.

The Countess grew impatient and her sword-arm sped up, her strikes cracking sharply against Cyhan's sword. She was moving faster than seemed humanly possible, and her strength was hard to be believed. The big man was being visibly moved by the shock of her blows.

Still, she failed to penetrate his defense.

"I thought the Countess gave up the earthbond," noted Gram. Penelope's speed was definitely beyond normal.

Lynarralla nodded, "She did, but the Count gave her one of the dragons. They can amplify their owner's speed and strength in much the same way."

He raised his eyebrows in surprise. The dragons that Mordecai Illeniel had created were already the topic of many rumors and debates. He had given the first to the Queen of Lothion, Ariadne Lancaster. Most agreed that he had created more than one, but no one knew how many exactly, or whether he had given them to anyone yet.

The faster the Countess moved the slower Cyhan seemed. He seemed almost catatonic, staring at his opponent with dead eyes that seemed to pass straight through her, yet whenever her sword came close, his was there to meet it. At times she moved so quickly that Gram couldn't tell what she was doing. He found it easier to watch Cyhan's weapon, for wherever it went, his opponent's blade was bound to arrive.

How is he doing that?

Eventually her attack faltered, and the Countess took a step back. Her foot slipped on the uneven ground and she staggered.

Cyhan moved then, stepping forward to take advantage of her weakness, but instead of moving in the direction she had taken, he slipped to the right, swinging his weapon high. Gram thought his move foolish until the Countess leapt into his path. She had feigned her slip and feinted to draw him out, but he had made his attack upon the place where she was going, rather than where she had pretended to be moving.

Even so, her reflexes were far beyond human, she ducked the blade at the last second and then high-stepped with her left leg, to avoid his simultaneous trip, something Gram hadn't even noticed. Then she crumpled, flying back and collapsing, for the bottom edge of Cyhan's shield had slammed into her stomach. Before she could recover, he was on her, wooden sword tip at her throat.

Penelope held up one hand to indicate her surrender, for she didn't have the wind to answer verbally. Coughing and choking, it was a minute before she was able to accept his hand and take her feet again.

"I do not understand," said Lynarralla. "He should not have won."

Gram had seen Cyhan best the Countess before, but that had been when neither of them had the earthbond. This was the first time he had seen her fight as she had in the past, with magically enhanced speed and senses. Even having watched it with his own eyes, it was hard to believe. "I don't think he's ever lost," said Gram.

Irene tugged on his sleeve, "He did once."

"Huh?" he glanced down at the girl, surprised.

"He did lose," she repeated, "At least once anyway. My dad said that your dad beat him."

Gram hadn't heard that story, but then he supposed there were many stories that he hadn't heard. Occasionally the Count would talk about his father, or he would hear the songs that minstrels had made, but he knew there were many things he didn't know. His mother only spoke of Dorian to remember his kindness, or his honor. She never spoke of his fighting prowess.

Most of the other people who knew his father were afraid to mention him in Gram's presence, probably for fear of awakening old wounds.

I knew he was a great warrior, but could he have really done that? He had just seen Cyhan accomplish something that shouldn't have been possible. No normal human should have been able to defeat someone magically enhanced the way the Countess was, especially considering that she was a brilliant swordswoman even without the magic.

***

"No, don't sit. Stand up," said Cyhan.

He did as he was told, curious as to why he was suddenly being allowed to stand. He wouldn't complain, though, standing in one spot for four or five hours would be a lot less uncomfortable than sitting for the same period.

The big man brought out a long strip of dark wool, "This will cover your eyes."

Gram frowned, he knew better than to speak.

"Ask," ordered his teacher.

"Why the blindfold?"

"Your eyes will interfere, distract you from what you must learn," answered the knight.

"But I haven't learned anything yet, Zaihair!" blurted Gram, letting his frustration show. Then he closed his mouth, clenching his jaw to keep from saying more.

Cyhan almost smiled, "Go ahead. Finish what you want to say."

Gram struggled for a moment. The past week had taught him to conserve his words. He never got many with Cyhan, so he had begun to think carefully before wasting any. "Why won't you teach me to fight?"

"Like the ones I teach in the training yard?"

"Yes, Zaihair."

Cyhan grinned, and it was a frightening expression on his normally still face, feral and full of implied threat. "You think you're better than they are, boy?"

Gram felt his blood rising, "Yes, sir."

"You aren't. If I put you in an arming doublet and handed you a sword, you would learn, and you might learn enough to beat them, or most others, but you would always be limited by *this*," his mentor punctuated the sentence by jabbing his finger into Gram's arm. "You watched my sparring match with the Countess today?"

"Yes, Zaihair."

"Then you have seen what I am trying to teach you. Now put the blindfold on." He waited while Gram tied the wool around his head, covering his eyes. Then he continued, "Today will be similar to yesterday. You will stand here without moving or speaking. If I strike at you, you may move or attempt to block the attack. If you move when I am not attacking, I will punish you."

The afternoon passed slowly. Gram was struck twice, both times because he had moved to avoid an imaginary attack. It was only after several hours that Cyhan finally attacked, and he utterly failed to detect it. Gram's mind was focused on trying to detect an attack, and it kept him from regaining the kind of composure he had had the day before.

When Cyhan eventually called a halt, Gram was disappointed. He had not managed to avoid a single attack.

The next day was similar, but more boring. Cyhan gave him the same rules but never attacked, not even once. Gram was punished three times for avoiding attacks that weren't real.

The third day he gave up. Unable to see and bored by the knowledge that Cyhan wasn't likely to attack at all, he found himself relaxing. The wind was gentle, and the only sounds were those of the grass and the occasional lowing of cows in the distance. As had happened before when he was sitting, he felt as if his body was fading away, becoming transparent. He no longer existed at all.

He felt the bundle of reeds coming, and he moved before they reached him.

The thrill of victory he felt at that small accomplishment destroyed his state of mind. He waited, but his teacher said nothing. *At least tell me I did something right!* Cyhan's silence made him angry.

The next attack left a stinging welt across the back of his legs.

The rest of his day passed without any further attacks, but he began to get a sense of what Cyhan was teaching him. The week that followed was similar. Each day Cyhan would blindfold him, and then he would wait. After enough time had passed, Gram would find himself slipping into a sort of trance, a place within his mind where his self no longer held sway. If an attack came during those times, he could avoid it, but he usually lost the feeling afterward.

His teacher would attack again if he missed, but once he had struck his student, he would stop, sometimes waiting hours before swinging at him again.

Gram began to understand the pattern behind it. Cyhan knew that once he had struck him, he had lost the proper frame of mind. He was waiting in the hope that Gram would regain it. If Gram avoided an attack he rewarded him by attacking again.

After the second week Gram began to avoid more than one blow before losing the proper state of mind.

During the third week he had his breakthrough.

He dodged the first attack without losing his calm. A second attack came minutes later, and he moved away from that one as well. The third attack came without pause, and he ducked under it. The fourth and fifth blows followed without interruption, and soon

Gram found himself in constant motion, stepping forward and back, now left and then right.

Some of the blows hit him anyway, but he felt them coming. When Cyhan suddenly stopped he became still. An hour passed, and when the next blow came he moved again, neatly avoiding it.

They repeated that cycle several more times, and when the day ended Cyhan gave him one word, "Good."

The next day he told Gram to leave the blindfold off.

This should be much easier, he thought, but he couldn't have been more wrong.

Cyhan stood behind him, never entering his field of vision, much as he had when Gram had been sitting. Gram struggled to regain the feeling he had had before, but without the blindfold he found his eyes constantly drawn to any motion. The grass, trees in the distance, even the movement of the clouds served to distract him. When his teacher attacked, he failed to avoid it.

It was days more before he began to have the same success he had had with the blindfold on. He initially tried closing his eyes, but Cyhan forbade it, wanting him to learn to maintain the proper state of mind even while his eyes flooded his head with unnecessary information. When he began to succeed with his eyes open, Cyhan moved into view, letting his student see him.

That completely destroyed Gram's focus.

"Don't close your eyes," warned Cyhan, when Gram again tried closing them.

Even when Gram regained the proper composure, he found it more difficult to avoid Cyhan's blows when he could see them. A week later Cyhan told him, "Stop looking at my eyes."

"Why, Zaihair?"

"The eyes lie. Watch my center, where my balance is. A feint begins with the eyes, or sometimes the weapon, or a leg, but my center will be moving in the direction I am truly going," explained the big man.

Gram tried, but no matter how hard he tried, it was easier said than done. In fact, over the next month he began to realize that when it came to the lessons that Cyhan was giving him, trying harder frequently led to more failure. The key was relaxing his conscious mind and letting his body act with as little intervention as possible. It made mistakes, but those were corrected by repetition and painful reminders given by Cyhan's bundle of reeds.

The weeks passed, and he grew less frustrated as he began to realize what he was learning. It wasn't something he could put into words, in fact words only interfered. He finally understood, to some degree, that the reason Cyhan spoke so little was because his most important lessons were not merely difficult to discuss, they were actually antithetical to the spoken word.

Summer was coming to a close, and Gram had been studying with the old warrior for more than two months when Cyhan finally handed him a wooden practice sword. "Why am I handing this to you now?" he asked.

It was uncommon for him to ask his student questions, but Gram understood the lesson now. "It's like the blindfold," he said simply.

Cyhan nodded and they began, proving his answer correct almost immediately. Having a weapon in his hands disrupted his ability to reach the proper state of mind. He began to try to think ahead, to anticipate his opponent, or even to counterattack. The result led him to begin receiving many more welts on his arms and legs again, just as he had when the blindfold had been removed.

This time, however, he knew what he had to learn, and he did his best to prevent his conscious desires from interfering. Within a few days he was showing noticeable improvement.

Gram had a warm feeling of accomplishment at the end of that week. It was almost the last day of summer, and he had finally reached a point where he could block or avoid most of Cyhan's attacks without losing the proper state of mind.

His training was over for the day, and as they crossed the castle yard Gram's main thought was to wonder what would be served at the evening meal. A flash of green caught his eye, and glancing up, he saw an unfamiliar woman looking out from one of the small windows in the upper keep.

A young woman, close to my age, he noted mentally. She had dark hair and eyes, and she seemed to be watching him with intense interest. As soon as he met her gaze, though, she disappeared from view. *I wonder who that was.*

Thornbear

Chapter 10

His curiosity was satisfied during the evening meal. He had arrived at the normal time, and the hall fell quiet soon afterward. A small bell was rung, and everyone rose to stand beside their chairs as the Count and Countess entered the hall. Normally they took their seats immediately after that, with no preamble and little delay, but today they paused.

Mordecai Illeniel held up his hand before speaking, "Before we begin our meal, my wife would like to introduce our newest arrival and guest."

Penelope nodded and gestured behind her. A young woman entered from the doorway behind them and took a position next to the countess. The Countess raised her voice then, "This is Lady Alyssa, daughter and heir to the Baron of Conradt in northern Gododdin. Her mother has asked us to foster her over the winter, and the Count and I were pleased to accept her offer. Please show her the same courtesy you would to any guest and make her feel as welcome as possible."

Moira waved then, gesturing toward their guest, urging her to take a place beside her at the high table. Gram noticed the change in seating at that point. His sister Carissa's place at the table, which had been vacant for the past two months, now had Irene standing behind it, while Irene's seat beside Moira's chair was empty. Lady Alyssa moved to stand there, taking Moira's hand with a grateful smile.

The Count and Countess took their seats, and everyone else sat thereafter; the evening meal had begun.

"When did you hear that we were getting a visitor?" asked Gram, leaning closer to Matthew.

His friend shrugged, "I dunno." He seemed unfazed by the new face at the table.

Conall spoke up instead, "Mother told us she was coming a while ago. Matt just doesn't pay much attention."

"Nobody asked your opinion, turd-burglar," responded Matthew before taking his first spoonful of the soup.

Gram glanced at the young woman who had just taken her seat directly across from him. She was still engrossed in conversation with Moira, but her eyes flicked to him momentarily, registering his presence. He felt awkward then, uncertain whether to interrupt them to introduce himself or to wait. He compromised by looking down at his soup bowl, to avoid making eye contact until she was introduced.

Act normally and hold your conversation with others until introduced. Make eye contact then, and try to make your smile as friendly as possible. He could hear his mother's voice in his mind, lecturing him once again on proper etiquette. Inevitably, he remembered more than was really helpful. *No, not like that. You look like you're in pain, Son.* She had gone to great lengths to get him to produce a natural looking smile after that, but it was to no avail. Every time he attempted it, his face contorted, giving him the look of someone with an affliction.

His ears picked up Moira's voice then, "…these are my brothers, Conall and Matthew—of course you have already met Irene. The handsome fellow beside Matt is Gram Thornbear, son of Lady Rose Thornbear… he's also the heir to the Hightower estate in Albamarl…"

Gram took his cue, looking their guest in the eye and standing to offer his hand across the table. *Always offer your hand to a lady,* his mother had said, *except when being introduced across a table, then it is more acceptable to wait rather than reach across the serving dishes.*

Lady Alyssa took his hand graciously and rewarded him with a smile, followed by a friendly laugh as he awkwardly retrieved his arm and sat down again. Matthew watched him with an amused look, starting to laugh as well, but then choked on his soup. His coughing drew attention away from Gram and dispelled the strange air at the table. Moira began to berate him for his table manners and Conall joined in gleefully.

Gram glanced back at Alyssa and found her looking directly at him, rather than paying attention to the banter amongst the Illeniel siblings. She smiled as their eyes met, and he felt his face grow warm. He attempted to smile in return, but his sudden self-consciousness ruined the expression, and he knew he had only succeeded in looking ridiculous. He took refuge in studying his soup.

As he began ferrying the hot liquid from the bowl to his lips, his mind brought back her image. Alyssa was young, younger than he had realized, which probably explained her being seated next to Moira rather than beside the Countess. Her hair was so dark as to seem almost black, and her eyes were a deep brown. Somehow her features reminded him of Cyhan, though unlike the knight, her skin was a light olive tone, where his complexion was dusky.

"Gram!" Moira's voice cut sharply through the fog in his mind.

"Excuse me?" he answered, startled.

"Alyssa was talking to you. Didn't you hear her?"

He looked into those dark eyes again before focusing on her hair instead. *Avoid the eyes, they make it too hard to talk,* he told himself. "Pardon me, Lady Alyssa, I didn't mean to give offense," he told her.

"No, it's quite alright," she answered. "Please, call me Alyssa."

"Certainly," he replied, watching her dark tresses slide as her head moved. The candlelight seemed to cling to them. "I would appreciate it if you would do the same."

"I was just asking if your father was Sir Dorian," she said, repeating the question he had missed before.

"Ahhh, yes, I think so," he responded.

"You aren't sure?" chuckled Matthew, elbowing him.

Gram could feel his blush returning, "Well, no, of course I'm sure... I mean yes!"

Moira frowned at her brother, "Matt, don't tease him. You know what he meant."

"I just didn't want Lady Alyssa to think he was uncertain of his parentage," protested Matthew. He couldn't help but grin slightly as he did so.

Chapter 10

Fortunately the next serving tray arrived then and distracted them for a moment. Gram managed to stay out of the conversation after that.

***

Gram decided to check on his friend's progress with the sword. He and Matthew hadn't talked much recently, and he was beginning to get worried that something might have gone wrong with the project.

A small form darted out from the statuary in the front hall, a form he immediately recognized. "Good evening, Grace," he said, pausing and giving her a completely unnecessary bow. "Have you been well?"

Her face was incapable of many expressions, but he could hear the smile in her voice as she replied, "Very well, thank you, Master Thornbear."

He lifted her, letting her ride on his shoulder as he walked.

"Where are you off to?" she asked.

"I thought I'd visit Matt in his workshop," he replied honestly.

"You never did tell me what his project involved," she noted.

He nodded, "You're right."

The bear gave an audible sigh, which made Gram wonder how she made such sounds since she had no lungs. *Or how she talks at all, for that matter,* he told himself.

"Well, if you won't talk about that, tell me what you think of our new guest, Lady Alyssa," she enjoined him.

He lifted his brows, "I had no idea she was coming. She was a surprise."

"She's very beautiful," noted Grace, stating the obvious for Gram's benefit.

"She wasn't unattractive," he responded noncommittally.

Grace watched his features. "She was very elegant, not to mention graceful, when she settled into the quarters that the Countess set aside for her. The men were falling all over themselves to do her the favor of carrying her things. She seems to have a lot of allure for a girl her age."

"Girl?" said Gram curiously. "How old is she?"

"Moira told me that Alyssa had just turned sixteen before she left Gododdin," answered the stuffed animal.

Gram chuffed at that, "Then she's hardly a girl anymore." *And she's only a few months older than me,* he noted silently. Sixteen was also the age at which most people began to treat you as an adult, although in Lothion children were still considered under the rule of their parents until they reached the age of nineteen.

"That's true," said Grace, "in fact, her mother probably sent her here hoping she might catch some young lordling's eye. The Count and Countess can introduce her into polite society, allowing her to begin the search for an appropriate husband."

He laughed, "You mean Matthew? I don't think he's very interested in her. She would have done better in the capital."

"But Cameron is much closer to Gododdin, which has to be a factor in any parent's mind," reminded

Grace. "Plus, it is well known that the Count is probably the most powerful figure in Lothion's politics, aside from the Queen herself."

"Mother says our good Count has made himself a political hermit; if he has any potential sway, he is no longer using it," lectured Gram. The words surprised him. He hadn't realized how deeply his mother's lessons had sunk in.

"There are other eligible young men in Castle Cameron besides Matthew Illeniel," Grace told him.

Perry Draper maybe, thought Gram. *He'll be knighted most likely. George Prathion might be a possibility, as well. He's only a little older and he's close by.* "Yeah, I suppose you're right," he admitted, missing her point entirely.

She tapped his shoulder, "I'll leave you here. I'd rather not go all the way to the workshop, so as to avoid walking back."

"Sure thing, milady," he said, depositing her on the stone cobbles with a mock bow. "It wouldn't do to get dirt from the yard on your delicate paws."

"Why thank you, milord," she replied, covering her mouth with one paw and doing her best to affect a coquettish look. Gram laughed and turned away.

He stepped across the threshold and crossed the yard, but the workshop was still locked. Matthew had enspelled it to prevent anyone other than him from opening the door, so Gram waited. He knew his friend would be along shortly. Matthew had been spending most of his evenings in the shop.

Sure enough, Matthew appeared within a quarter of an hour. He gave Gram a wary look as he approached. "It isn't ready yet."

"You've been at it for a while now," observed Gram. "They say your dad did the original enchantment in less than a day."

Matthew glared at him, "This is a bit more complicated than what he did." He didn't open the door.

"Aren't you going inside?" asked Gram.

"It isn't ready for you to see it." He looked distinctly uncomfortable.

Gram sighed, "I'm not going to be able to see the magic anyway. I just want to see what the blade looks like."

"It doesn't look like much of anything yet," said the young wizard.

"Let me in," Gram insisted.

Matthew held up his hands, "I'd rather you wait, Gram. It doesn't look like you're expecting yet, and I don't want you to get upset."

Gram's eyes narrowed. "What did you do to it?" he hissed. "Let me see it."

"Will you calm down? People can see us out here," cautioned his friend.

"Then let's go inside, Matt!" said Gram with some emphasis.

"Fine, but you have to promise to keep your head."

Gram knew better than that, "I'm not promising anything until you show me what you've done."

Matthew didn't argue any further, he opened the door and let his friend inside before he could get any more upset. Once the door had closed behind them, he paused to say a few words in Lycian, the ancient tongue used by wizards when casting spells.

"What was that?"

"Just a precaution," said the young wizard. *To keep people from hearing anything if you start yelling,* he thought to himself. "It's over here in this case." He brought out a long wooden box, bound and reinforced with iron. There were no visible locks, but he had enchanted it to ensure that no one else could open it. He lifted the lid and waited while Gram took a look at the interior.

"Where's Thorn?"

"That's it," said Matthew. "I haven't finished assembling it yet."

"Assembling?" said Gram quietly. His throat seemed to have gone dry. The interior of the box held a vast collection of tiny pieces of metal, most of them smaller than the nail on the end of his pinky finger. "It's not a puzzle, Matt. Swords are supposed to be forged, not *assembled.*"

"Well, this one is different," said his friend.

My life is over, thought Gram, feeling a cold sweat beading on his forehead. *There's no way she can forgive this. I can't even forgive me for this.* "What have you done?" he moaned. "I can't show this to my mother. She'll have me exiled!"

"Now, Gram, that's an exaggeration," said his friend soothingly. "Besides, you don't have to worry. No matter how this turns out you, still have the duplicate on the wall. She'll never even know if we don't put the original back."

"I'll know!" shouted Gram, beginning to panic. "Do you think I can hide something like this from her? I can't! I'm a terrible liar, and she can read me like a book. Even if I *could* keep it a secret, I couldn't bear it. It would kill me!" He ran his hands through his hair, tugging at it as if he were considering pulling it out by the roots. "I'm dead."

Matthew patted his shoulder. "You aren't dead. So far everything is going according to plan, it's just taking me longer than I anticipated."

Gram shrugged off his friend's gesture, "This was your plan?! To cut it up into a thousand-thousand little pieces? If you had told me that, I would *never* have agreed to this!"

The wizard nodded, "Well, that's why I didn't tell you, of course, but just wait till it's finished. You'll never be able to tell when you look at it."

"I very much doubt that."

"Look," said Matthew, reaching down and holding up two nearly identical pieces of metal. Holding them together with his fingers, he mumbled a few words and then handed them to Gram. "Can you tell where they are joined?"

Gram's eyes were sharp, but he couldn't find a seam. "No," he admitted grudgingly.

"This will be like that, times a million," explained Matthew. "Trust me."

"How much longer before it's finished?" said Gram, daring to hope that his friend could do what he said.

"Three or four months at least," said Matthew.

"Months?!" exclaimed Gram. "You realize my mother is bound to visit within that time, or even finish and return for good. How long do you think I can fool her?"

His friend gave him a stubborn look. "You'll thank me when this is over, and no matter what happens, I swear to you that this will be worth it."

"I'll be the world's happiest man, living alone, just me and my fantastic sword—in *Dunbar*!"

Matthew rubbed his chin, imitating his father who frequently rubbed his beard when he was thinking. "You know, my friend, you are learning faster than I expected. I think you'll master the art of sarcasm soon if you keep progressing at this rate."

Gram growled and struggled to keep from pummeling his friend.

Thornbear

Chapter 11

The next morning Gram took Pebble out for a ride. His tutor had left to return home for a month, and that left him with an abundance of free time between breakfast and lunch each day. He didn't mind, though, geography and history were not something he would miss. When he was younger he had also been forced to spend his afternoons learning arithmetic and studying literature, but Rose had relented on the math front once he had demonstrated enough skill to balance an account book.

Literature was something she had hoped he would grow to love, but by the time he was fourteen she had finally given up on that as well. History and geography were non-negotiable, however, as she felt no nobleman could get by without both knowledge of where his enemies and allies lived and an intimate understanding of everything that had gone before.

He was looking forward to a month without supervision.

Pebble tossed her head, looking back at him sideways from one of her big brown eyes.

"I don't care," he told her blithely, leaving the reins slack and letting her have her head. "You're in charge today, Pebble.

Pebble chuffed loudly, blowing out a lungful of air and easing to the right. She meandered easily, taking a comfortable pace that wouldn't tire her and stopping frequently to munch on particularly sweet looking patches of clover or grass.

Gram leaned back and watched the world slowly pass. The sky was blue and the air still warm with the last of summer's heat. It would begin to get cool in a few more weeks, but for now it was perfect. White clouds drifted by, undisturbed in their course by anything other than the occasional hawk flying across the vaulted skies.

His horse had been wandering across a wide pasture, following a short wicker fence that was more of a suggestion than a real border. The grass grew taller close to the places where the posts were set, and Pebble took her time stopping at each to nibble at the tender greenery.

It was a moment before he became aware of the noise that was disturbing his peaceful reverie. *What was that?* Now that he was listening, he heard nothing. He pulled on Pebble's reins, so that she would stop, and the gentle mare patiently waited while he listened.

There. It was a grunt, followed by a deeper sound, coming from his left. That direction led away from the farmer's cot and into a vast pasture, one only interrupted by a thin stream that wandered through it. Gram gave a tug on the reins, nudged Pebble with his heels, and the mare began walking, heading to the left.

A loud bleating noise helped him to identify the source of the original sound. *One of the farmer's sheep must be in trouble.* He urged Pebble forward, and she increased her pace. Soon he could hear the light burbling of the stream. *It must have fallen into the brook.*

The land rose gently in front of him, disguising the fact that the stream bank was close by, but Gram was familiar with the area. He slowed Pebble down before they reached the edge. The small stream had cut the earth away there, leaving a steep bank that led down on this side, before gently sloping up on the other. An unsuspecting animal, particularly one moving at a run, might easily slip and hurt itself there.

Dismounting, he dropped the reins, giving Pebble a familiar look. "Pretend I just tied them to a stump," he told her.

She gave him a steady look that he took to indicate agreement. She wouldn't wander far. The grass was tall, and she had plenty to occupy her anyway.

Gram waded through the waist high grass until he could look over the edge. Sure enough a large ewe was there, lying on a large boulder. From the look of things he guessed she had stumbled over the edge and tumbled down the five or six feet to land on the hard stone. It was a bit of bad luck since such a short drop probably wouldn't have injured her if she hadn't landed badly.

Damn stupid sheep, he thought. *She should know this pasture well enough to remember where the stream is.*

There were plenty of easy places to walk down, so he had little difficulty reaching her. The ewe was bleating at him regularly now, crying in pain and fear. "Easy girl," he told her. "Just rest easy, we'll have you safe in a minute. Let me see where you're hurt." Carefully, he lifted her body so that he could slide her away from the rock, checking first to make certain she wasn't caught somehow.

There was blood on the stone, but her legs were free, so he eased her away to set her on the smooth ground beside the water. He examined her there, feeling her legs to see if they were broken. "You might have broken something when you fell," he suggested aloud, talking softly to calm her. "Don't worry, though. If you can't walk, I can carry you home. We'll make sure you're alright." *Unless the bone's come through, the farmer will probably put you down if that's the case.*

Her legs seemed intact, and he found no broken bones, but the blood puzzled him. The wind shifted, blowing in his face. It had been at his back before. Pebble gave a loud whinny, sounding fearful.

"Hold on, Pebble!" he called, hoping his mare wouldn't turn skittish and leave him to walk. "I'll be back up there in a second." Searching through the thick wool for the source of the blood he found three long gashes.

That's the problem, he noted silently, *her muscle's torn.* His subconscious mind was nagging at him then, trying to tell him something, but he couldn't quite bring the thought fully into the light of his consciousness.

The light flickered, a shadow passing across the sun for a split second.

Gram dropped down on all fours above the ewe and then rolled to the left across the damp sand as a giant cat sailed through the air above him. He had acted without thought, before his mind could even register the meaning of the signs, the claw marks on the ewe,

Pebble's warning when the wind shifted, or the change in light. His body had moved on its own.

The panther looked to weigh almost as much as he did, a monster that was probably over a hundred and fifty pounds. It had landed gracefully, twisting before it had even reached the ground, preparing to spring again.

Shit!

He had brought a falchion with him, but it was tied to Pebble's saddle. All he had on him was his belt knife, a four inch straight bladed item better suited for minor tasks. The cat was in the air before he could gather his wits to draw it.

He was still on the ground when the cat sprang, so it was impossible to drop beneath it and he was nowhere near fast enough to push himself up and over it. Instead he rolled back to his right, and he almost made it, but the panther lashed out with one paw, catching the side of his head as it passed. The curved claws caught in the skin of his cheek, and the beast twisted, using the attachment to arrest its motion and swing its body around to reach him.

The other foreleg was moving toward his head, and once it had him between the two he knew the rear legs would come up to rake his belly.

Gram's conscious mind wasn't operating, though. Like his body, it was nowhere near fast enough to process everything that was happening in time to make good choices. His answers came from the empty place, the place where he ceased to exist.

He caught the paw that was ripping through his face with his right hand, gripping it tightly as he continued to roll, drawing the cat with him. Its other foreleg hit the sand as it desperately sought to maintain its balance, but he was having none of that. The momentum of his roll pulled it off balance, and his left arm circled around the beast as it twisted beneath him in the sand.

It was strong. If he had been thinking, his mind would have told him that pound for pound cats are much stronger than humans, but that thought would have done little more than slow him down.

Tightening his arm, he pulled the panther into a headlock, his elbow close against its bottom jaw. The cat screamed as he clung to it, keeping its head in the clench. Driving forward with powerful legs, it forced him up, despite the fact that it had to lift both their bodies. Unable to control its movement, he fell, and the beast's body twisted with incredible flexibility. Claws ripped into his trousers as it thrashed, but he held on.

It surged up again, trying to throw him off, but this time he used his own legs to aid its push, and they both left the ground for a moment, to fall a few feet closer to the water's edge. As they flew, he brought his feet up and wrapped his legs around the cat's muscular mid-body, just ahead of its rear limbs.

Now it could no longer twist its lower body to rake him with its hind legs, and the cat began to thrash violently within his arms, making it difficult to hold on. Gram managed to bring his right arm up, using it to lock his left forearm in place. Using all four of his limbs to grapple the panther, he was no longer able to control their movement. The cat's mouth was snapping and yowling as it struggled, trying to move its head enough to get a bite on him.

The bite is the worst. Those jaws are strong enough to break bones or anything else that comes between them, said his inner voice, choosing that moment to speak up.

He ignored it, and as the cat pushed away from the ground again he tried to aid its motion, twisting his torso to throw it off balance. The two of them rolled into the water.

Gram took a deep breath before his head went under the green water. The cat wasn't happy about their abrupt bath, and it redoubled its efforts to shake him off, but he wasn't letting up. He could feel the muscles rippling beneath the skin of the panther's neck as he tightened his headlock. As hard as he tried, he couldn't get the position or the leverage to crush its throat, but then, he no longer needed too.

It fought him as he kept it under, using his weight to keep them both from surfacing. It was kicking wildly, but the soft mud gave it little to push against. They sank deeper into the water and farther from the shore.

His head was pounding, and there were spots in his vision. How long he had held on he couldn't be sure, but his lungs were screaming for air. He had gotten a good lungful of air before they went in, and he thought the cat had sucked in some water already, but he couldn't be sure. It still struggled. Clenching his teeth, he refused to give up, until at last the great cat's body relaxed, going limp in the water.

Letting go, he got his head above the surface just as he lost control, choking as he got a little water in with his first breath. He flailed for a moment, fighting to orient himself as he stood in the soft mud. He was only seven feet from the shore, and he was standing in water that came up to his chest. The cat floated beside him.

Coughing and hacking he reached out with one hand to push its head beneath the water. *Just to be sure.* He remained there for several moments, clearing his lungs and catching his breath before he began making his way to the shore. He drew the lifeless body of the drowned cat along with him, rolling it onto the sand bar before climbing out himself.

Gram was shaking from a combination of the wind on his wet skin and the aftereffects of adrenaline. Exhausted, he lay down on his back. He stared up at the sky, wondering at its crystalline blue color, interrupted only by impossibly white clouds. He breathed deeply.

I'm alive.

He heard steps coming through the grass, but he didn't bother rising. Whoever it was wouldn't be a threat. Still, he was surprised when he saw Chad Grayson's face appear above the grass on the opposite side of the brook.

"It's a bit too late in the season to be swimming," remarked the hunter as he saw Gram's wet and bedraggled form.

Gram chuckled and then, unable to help himself, he fell to laughing loudly. It felt good after such a close brush with death.

"I can see it's no use tryin' to give ye advice. Ye're touched," added Chad. His eyes had picked out the form of the big cat and now they were searching the ground around Gram. He noted the wounded ewe lying close by. "I been lookin' fer that pussy."

Gram laughed harder at that. It was a minute or more before he finally managed to calm himself. "You're welcome to it. It's certainly done me no good."

"Hang on, I'll be right there," said the huntsman before he disappeared back into the tall grass. Gram could hear him moving south for a short distance until he found a narrower place to cross the stream. A few minutes later he had joined the young man, none the worse for his crossing, other than wet boots.

"Ye're a right mess," observed Chad.

Gram nodded. "Heh, I bet."

The hunter leaned in, using his hand to tilt Gram's face to one side. He hissed when he saw the claw marks there. "Oooh, that's gonna leave a mark, boy. Someone'll need to sew that up fer ye."

"Got any thread?" asked Gram.

"Ye don't want me doin' it. Needs to be cleaned first anyway."

"They always said panthers don't attack people, that they look for easier prey," Gram wondered, sitting up.

"Usually they don't," agreed the hunter. "But last year we didn't get much rain, and then we followed it with a cold winter."

"Huh?" Gram couldn't seem to form a better sentence for his question just then.

"Food," explained Chad. "The bigger predators, wolves and such, they've had it hard cuz of a lack of small game. This one had taken to raiding farms. It managed to kill the Adams' milk cow two weeks back. He was huntin' Mr. McDermott's sheep today. You jus' had the misfortune of tryin' to steal his lunch."

"Is that why you're here?"

"Yeh, I was hopin' te ketch him layin' up after his next kill. Never thought it would be you."

"Me either."

"Yer damn lucky to be alive. Like ye say, they don' often attack people, but when they do, it's nothin' to laugh about. What did ye kill him with?"

Gram held up two shaky hands. "I never got a chance to pull my knife."

Chad let out a long whistle. "Damn, boy! My hat's off to ye," he said, though he didn't actually doff his cap.

Gram stood. He was mostly recovered from the effects of his fight, and he felt uncommonly good, other than a faint pain burning the skin along the left side of his face. "Do you want the cat?" he asked.

"Nah, that's yer kill, boy," said the hunter.

Gram thought for a moment, "Well, I'd like to get this ewe back to her owner. Would you mind taking the panther back for me? You can keep whatever you want from it." His ears picked up the sound of riders coming from the distance.

"I can probably do that fer ye," said the hunter with a nod. Taking out his knife, he gutted the cat by the water's edge. He did it with practiced ease and within minutes he had field dressed the animal and had wrapped it in a wide cloth before draping it across his shoulders.

Gram watched with admiration for his skill. "Listen, Master Grayson, about our fight…"

The hunter focused on him then, meeting his eyes, "Yeh?"

"I'd like to apologize. I shouldn't have lost my temper…"

"…that's fine, boy," interrupted the huntsman. "No harm done, though I appreciate that ye've thought on it." He began walking back along the edge of the stream, heading toward his previous crossing point. "One o' these days you'll have to come out with me. Mebbe I'll teach ye a thing or two." He disappeared from view after that.

Gram stared after him bemused. *He's harder to figure out than Sir Cyhan.* The ewe took the opportunity to issue another loud series of bleats.

"I'm coming, girl," said Gram reassuringly. Kneeling, he slipped his arms beneath her shoulder and hindquarters. She was heavy, but he thought he could manage her weight. The farmer's cot was only a half-mile to the east of him. He felt sure he could carry her at least that far.

Putting her across Pebble's back would be even easier, but he would have to tie her in place and he worried that he might injure her more by putting her in such a position. First he had to get her up the embankment and onto level ground, though.

His muscles grew taut as he slowly straightened his knees to lift her, keeping her body close against his chest. The ewe's weight was considerably greater than he had anticipated. "Damn girl, there's more to you than just wool," he noted in a soothing voice. The ewe began to kick with her forelegs, threatening his equilibrium, but he kept talking until she settled down quietly.

She must weigh as much as most grown men, he thought, eyeing the steep slope. There was no help for it, though. He began making his way up, the muscles in his calves and thighs protesting as he took the incline. Almost—the top was close, but it was too steep for him to carry her up it. He would have to lift her over his head to get her onto the level grass above before following. There was no way to make it while carrying her as he was, the sand kept sliding out from under his feet.

He tried.

Lifting a couple of hundred pounds straight overhead was no easy task even in normal circumstances, but with a living, moving sheep, it was nigh impossible. He did it anyway, ignoring the strain in his back and shoulders. She was almost over the top when the sand collapsed beneath him. He caught her as they fell, but her weight knocked the wind from him as he landed on the soft ground.

"Damnitt!" he swore, once he could finally get a good lungful of air. He never thought of giving up, though. Instead he was considering how much farther he would have to carry her if he followed the stream until he found an easier place to get her out.

"Need some assistance?" It was a woman's voice.

Two figures had appeared, rising above the top of the embankment, both were on horseback. It was Lady

Alyssa and Perry Draper. She wore a bright blue riding dress while he was accoutered in mail and a brown doublet.

Out for a ride, and he's serving as her escort through the dangerous farmland, thought Gram uncharitably. He chided himself for that, especially considering his own recent predicament. *Well, perhaps it is a little dangerous.*

"Nah," said Gram in a droll voice. "I was just enjoying the scenery."

She laughed, but her smile vanished when she caught sight of the right side of his face. "There's blood all over you. Stay put, I'll come help you."

Perry had been silent so far, but he protested at that idea. "You can't, Lady Alyssa, you'll ruin your dress."

"Then you go down there and help them up," she told him angrily.

He eyed the mud and sand, knowing it would be a serious chore to clean his armor if he got into the muck. His other option would be to remove it first, which would make the work of getting the ewe up the bank easier. "I'd rather not leave you here, unprotected."

She stared at him, "Honestly, Perry, how dangerous do you think this pasture is?"

Gram had been watching them while he gathered his strength for another attempt. What amazed him most was her initial offer to climb down in her dress. It had been her first suggestion, before even considering having her companion help. *She's obviously used to doing things herself,* he observed. "Actually, I was just attacked by a panther," he announced, thinking to reinforce Perry's argument.

In the past Perry had always gotten along with Gram, despite an undercurrent of envy that ran between them. They were similar in many respects, despite their differences in station and the fact that Perry would likely someday be a knight. Today, however, was different. Today Alyssa was with them.

"A panther?" scoffed the captain's son. "Do you seriously expect us to believe that?"

At that moment, Gram couldn't have cared less, "Well… yeah."

"And where is this dangerous beast now?" asked Perry. "I suppose you'll tell me it ran off."

"No," said Gram, shaking his head. "It's dead. I drowned it in the brook."

Perry looked at him unbelievingly, "Where's the body then?"

Gram was growing angry now. "Are you calling me a liar, Perry?" he growled. "I didn't roll around in the dirt down here just to impress *you*."

"I'm just suggesting that perhaps you got dirty playing with your girlfriend…" began Perry.

Alyssa stopped him before things got out of hand, "Perry! Do you have any rope?"

The question interrupted the argument better than any protest could have. "What?" he said, pausing for a moment. "No…"

"Why don't you ride back and get some? We can use it to make a sling, to get the ewe out," she suggested.

"What if there's a panther?" he said sarcastically.

"Weren't you convinced that there wasn't?" she asked, glaring at him. "And if there was one, then Gram has already dispatched it."

Perry could feel her anger, and he knew then that he wasn't improving his reputation with her. Rather than make things worse, he nodded. "You're right. We should focus on the problem rather than argue about make believe."

She dismounted as he was speaking, and before he could ask she answered him, "I'll wait here." Her eyes dared him to argue with her.

"Very well," he said at last. "I'll be back shortly."

As soon as he had passed from sight, she spoke to Gram, "I'm sorry. I didn't realize he was such a jackass."

Gram's brows went up in surprise at her invective. Obviously there were some things about Lady Alyssa that went beyond the normal definition of 'ladylike'. "He's not normally like that," said Gram, but he stopped himself before giving a reason for Perry's behavior. He was working hard to rein in his temper.

Alyssa was undoing the laces on her sleeves.

"What are you doing?" he asked her.

"Well, one thing he was right about is my dress. If I try to help you, I'll ruin it," she said simply.

"So…"

She grinned at him, "So I'm taking it off." Her hands were working at the laces in the back now. Fortunately the riding dress wasn't as complicated as some of the fancier dresses ladies sometimes wore. She soon had it loosened up enough to begin shucking it off over her head.

Gram was stunned, torn between the desire to watch her undress and extreme embarrassment. Shaking off his paralysis, he turned around.

A minute later her voice called to him. "You can't get her up here that way, turn around and hand her up to me."

Peeking over one shoulder he saw her lying down on the grass above. She was clad in white underclothes that covered her from shoulders to knees, her arms outstretched toward him. "I thought you were waiting for Perry to come back with a rope."

"Don't be silly," she told him. "Between the two of us we can get her up and back home before he's even halfway back."

"But…"

"Are you going to hand her up or not?"

"She's very heavy, Lady Alyssa. You won't be able to hold her," he replied, beginning to think in more practical terms since there was obviously no dissuading her. "Perhaps if we walk down that way…"

"Just hand her up," she insisted.

Thinking he was certain to wind up falling with a ewe on top of him again, he nevertheless worked his way back up the sandy slope. At the steepest point, close to the top, he lifted the now struggling ewe. Alyssa caught its head and shoulders in her hands and began to pull, allowing him to push from farther down, behind the hindquarters. Once the sheep was halfway up she caught it around the middle and took it from him dragging it up and over the edge.

As she did he couldn't help but note the lean muscles moving under her skin. She wasn't overlarge, but her slim figure disguised a surprisingly athletic physique. Obviously Alyssa got more heavy exercise than most of the women Gram was familiar with in Cameron Castle.

Free of his burden, he clambered over the embankment and joined her. He found her already examining the ewe's wound. "This looks ugly," she announced, "but the bones are whole. She'll probably be fine if the wound doesn't turn sour."

She sounded a lot like his grandmother. Elise Thornbear was an expert herbalist and an old veteran at patching up wounded men. She didn't have to do as much of it any more, the wizards of Cameron Castle fixed most serious wounds before she was needed these days.

"I think the shepherd's cot is over that way," he said, pointing to indicate the direction. "Thank you for helping me." He kept his eyes down, focused on the ewe. The damp ground had soiled Alyssa's thin shift, and parts of it were now disturbingly semi-transparent.

She watched his face, staring at him with deep brown eyes. "We can probably keep her atop your horse if we walk on either side and hold her."

"It will be simpler if I just carry her," he responded. "You should wait for Perry. It will give you time to put your dress back on too."

"I'm not putting it back on over this," she said, using her hands to indicate her soiled chest. The movement served to draw his eyes there, and his face began to grow hot. "I'll have to take this off before I put the dress on," she continued, well aware of his inner turmoil.

"Let me get started before you do that," said Gram hastily, averting his eyes again.

As he turned his head, she got a much closer look at the right side of his face. "Wait, let me look at your face," she told him.

"It's fine."

"No, it isn't," she said with authority. "Hold still." She had already taken hold of his chin with one hand and was leaning close. "It's bleeding still, and those gashes are deep. You're going to have some serious scarring if this isn't sewn up properly. We need to clean it before it starts to dry."

"Grandmother can take care of it when I get back," he told her.

She stood and took him by the hand, pulling him along. "Let's wash it in the stream. It will be much easier if we do it now."

He gestured weakly at the ewe, "What about…"

"…she's not going anywhere," she said firmly.

She didn't release his hand until they reached the stream, a fact he was inordinately aware of.

When she let him go he leaned down at the water's edge.

"Not there," she said sharply. "Farther out, where the water's moving. It will be cleaner." Without waiting she took his hand again and led him into the water. "Ooh!" The cold water stole her breath for a moment.

Gram laughed, "Didn't think it was that deep did you?"

She smirked at him before replying, "No. Come here." Teeth chattering, she grabbed his ear and pulled him out farther, until the water was up to his chest. She pushed down on his head to get it under the water.

Being taller and stronger he could have resisted, but he didn't. After he came back up she kept his face close to the water while she splashed it again. "This is going to hurt a little," she warned, using her fingers to lightly rub the torn skin. "I have to get the dirt out."

It hurt considerably more than 'a little', but he kept that to himself, hissing softly only when he absolutely couldn't keep quiet.

"That wasn't so bad was it?" she asked as they waded out.

"No," he replied, trying to sound truthful. "Ah!" he exclaimed as he looked down at her.

The water had done predictable things to her underclothes, and the cold had had other effects. "Don't be such a prude," she told him, ignoring his embarrassment. She climbed up the embankment without looking back.

Despite himself he studied her as she went, long limbs helped to emphasize her healthy muscle tone. To distract himself he brought his hands and shirt up to dab at his face.

"Don't touch it," she warned from above. "Your shirt is already ruined. Just let it bleed for a while. I'll sew it up after we deliver your ewe."

Grimacing he let go of the shirt and followed her up. Once there he wasted no time scooping up the wounded ewe, lifting her as gently as he could.

Alyssa watched him silently, her dark eyes inscrutable. She gathered up her horse's reins and then walked her over to do the same with Pebble. "I'll lead the horses. Which way is it again?"

"Just follow me," he said hurriedly. He was certain it would drive him mad if he had to watch her walking ahead of him.

Chapter 12

It took them almost a half an hour to reach the shepherd's cot, and when they got there Alyssa waited some distance back to avoid being seen in her current state. Apparently she did have some sense of propriety, at least when it came to people other than Gram. His mind didn't examine that fact too closely. He was too busy trying to keep his mind away from mental images of her.

Alan McDermott was none too happy when he saw the condition of his sheep, but he was grateful to Gram for bringing her to him. "Thank you, milord," he said sincerely.

"I'm not a lord," corrected Gram. "Someday perhaps, but not yet."

"No matter, good master. You're a true nobleman for bringin' me Nelly back," replied the shepherd.

"Nelly?"

"Aye, that's her name," said the man.

He left shortly after that, returning to where Alyssa waited. "I thought you might have gotten your dress back on by now," he commented.

She smiled, "Not until my things dry. They're thin, though, so it shouldn't take too long."

I know all too well how thin they are! "If someone sees us there will be terrible rumors," he cautioned.

"Let's walk a while," she told him. "The horses will make it less likely someone will see me. We can find a sunnier spot, and after I dry I can put the dress back on."

The entire field was sunny, so Gram wasn't entirely sure what a 'sunnier' spot would look like, but he kept his doubts to himself. They walked beside the horses for a half an hour before she broke the silence.

"You don't talk much do you?"

"Not often," he agreed.

"Why not?"

"There are not many things I need to say. I've never been one to talk just for the sake of filling up time," he answered.

She didn't comment, and they walked a bit farther, until they reached a slightly more sheltered hollow. The ground rose slightly around them, making them less visible in the distance. Alyssa stopped and began rummaging through one of her saddlebags. After a minute she brought out a leather roll and began unwrapping it. Within was a collection of curved needles, cloth, and string; everything needed for wound dressing.

"Why do you have all that?" he asked, curious.

"Habit," she replied. "My Nana taught me when I was young, and I've always believed in being prepared. Back home we had to do a lot of doctoring after the war."

She would have been a child back then, thought Gram, *what sort of childhood did she have?*

Alyssa walked in circles for a minute to flatten the grass in a small area before sitting down. "Come," she said, "Sit here."

Gram hesitated, "You look drier. Why don't you put your dress back on first?"

"This way the worst thing that happens is I get blood on my underclothes. I prefer that to my dress," she reasoned. "Don't worry, I don't bite."

He sat, reluctantly, assuming a cross-legged position. He could feel Pebble's eyes on him, faintly disapproving, or maybe that was his guilty conscience playing tricks on him.

She leaned close, examining the torn skin and he became acutely aware of her nearness. *Beautiful ears,* he noted silently, mentally tracing the line of her jaw and examining the smooth olive skin of her neck. Warm breath touched his cheek, and his heart began to pound. *Why am I reacting like this?* he wondered. He had never had such an extreme response to any other woman getting close to him.

He already knew the answer, though, even if he couldn't put it into words.

"Close your eyes," she ordered. "It will be easier if you aren't trying to watch the needle—for both of us."

She knows, he thought, alarmed. He knew he'd die of shame if she told anyone else what an infatuated fool he was.

"Relax," she said softly, then the needle bit into his skin.

He flinched as the pain brought his mind back to his more immediate concerns.

She paused, thoughtful. "This won't work. Here, do you mind lying down?" She smoothed her lap, indicating he should put the uninjured side of his face there.

His mind went blank and he did as she asked. It was a comfortable position, and it allowed her an easier time working with his cheek. He stared out at the grass, ignoring her warmth. The pain of the needle stole his breath, and he fought to keep from yelling.

Minutes passed with agonizing slowness as she delicately stitched his face, working her way from the end of each tear until she had completely closed it. There were two long gashes and one smaller one that passed through his right eyebrow. It had narrowly missed his eye. That one hurt the worst.

It might have been an hour before she finished, it felt more like days. Gram was exhausted from the effort of trying to remain silent. He had mostly succeeded, though he had let out the occasional grunt or yelp when it got particularly bad. Alyssa's hands were stained with blood, he noted, as she packed away her needle and thread. It was probably safe for him to move now, but she said nothing, and he stayed silent. Now that the pain was over, he was loath to move from his peaceful place.

"Close your eyes. It's alright to rest a while," she whispered.

And so he did, content.

She watched him sleep, observing his chest rising and falling slowly, until she was sure he was unconscious. Then she waited a while longer, before finally resting her hand lightly on his chest. It was an innocent gesture, unless one were to look at her eyes. There was no innocence in them. Gently she traced his chest, feeling the muscles there and admiring the contours of his body.

Eventually her legs went numb, and she woke him, unable to take the discomfort any longer.

He gave her a worried look as he came to, "I'm sorry. How long have I…?"

"Not long," she said reassuringly, gracing him with a smile.

He sat up, edging away, suddenly aware of her femininity once more. He stood and offered her his hand, "Let me help you up."

She took it, staggering as her legs began to come to life once more. She held onto his hand longer than was strictly necessary, studying his face boldly with no attempt to disguise her interest.

Time seemed to stop, except for the thumping drum in his chest, but he held her gaze.

Alyssa tilted her head, shifting her eyes. "Not a bad job, if I do say so myself."

Gram released her hand quickly, realizing that she had merely been studying her handiwork. He turned away to hide the flush in his cheeks. "Thank you," he said, and then he walked farther away. "You should put your dress on, and then I'll ride back with you."

She watched him, a faint smile on her lips. "Certainly." Then she circled her horse, to put its bulk between them before slipping the bottom of her dress over her head. She managed to get her head almost to the neck before it caught. Her arms were straight above her head, stuck in the sleeves, while part of the dress was caught around her hips.

She began a strange hopping dance as she wiggled and shook, trying to get the dress to slide down and into place.

Unfortunately Gram saw none of it; he had positioned himself a goodly distance away and had put his back to her. Several minutes later she called him, "It's safe now. Help me with the laces would you?"

Gram grimaced and then winced when the expression pulled at the stitches in his face. It was much more sensitive since she had done her work, and it made his face feel tight. He helped her with the laces as best he could. Fortunately he had some experience, from assisting his sister, Carissa, on many occasions.

"You have surprisingly deft hands for such a womanly task," she observed as he worked, though her eyes were on his face rather than his hands.

"My mother and sister," he supplied, failing to find any more words to explain himself.

After that they remounted and turned the horse's heads back toward Castle Cameron. They set a moderate pace, and it took an hour to reach the gate leading into Washbrook. The guard called out to those inside when he saw them approaching. Apparently Perry had passed the word for them to be on the lookout for their return.

Gram waved and they rode through without stopping, following the single lane road that passed through Washbrook and led to the much bigger gatehouse that guarded the entry to Cameron Castle. They were met there by Captain Draper and several guardsmen.

"We were worried for your safety, Lady Alyssa," he told the young woman before turning to Gram. "Lady Thornbear is waiting for you. We gave her the news that you had been injured." Lady Thornbear referred to his grandmother, Elise Thornbear. She had retained the title after his grandfather and namesake's death. To avoid confusion, his mother was referred to as Lady Rose, or on formal occasions, as Lady Hightower, in deference to her title.

"Thank you, Captain," he replied. "Please have someone tell her I will join her shortly, once I've cleaned up a bit."

"She said to tell you to come directly, rather than wait, Master Gram," Captain Draper informed him.

Gram sighed. "Very well… I'll just take Pebble to the stable."

"I can take her for you, sir," volunteered one of the guardsmen, "and Lady Alyssa's mount as well."

"You are most kind," she told the man, dismounting and handing him the reins. "Has Perry returned?"

"Not yet, milady," answered the captain. "My son returned earlier when he couldn't find you. He left again, along with several guardsmen. They're still out searching for you."

"Please give them my apologies for the inconvenience when they return," she responded before holding her hand out to Gram. "Would you escort me in, Master Gram?"

He had just finished dismounting himself, and her request caught him off-guard. He hastily handed his reins to one of the guards and then offered her his arm. Together they walked toward the main keep. Several thoughts passed through his mind, but he couldn't find the words to put to them, so he remained silent.

Once they had gone inside, he gave her an apologetic glance, "I'm afraid I must leave you here. Thank you for your kindness." He touched his stitches as he spoke.

"In spite of its unusual nature, I enjoyed our time," she said demurely, averting her eyes. Now that she was within the castle she seemed to take on a different air. Gone were the bold direct stares and her daring personality. "They said that Lady Thornbear wanted you, but I was told your mother was away."

"My grandmother," he explained.

She nodded. "I have not met her yet. Would it be acceptable for me to come with you?"

The question surprised him. He had expected she would want to retire immediately, to clean up and repair the damage their adventure had had on her appearance. Few ladies would be willing to embrace a new social encounter without preparing first. He wondered what his grandmother would think. While she was very traditional, like his mother, she also valued practicality above all else.

"If you wish," he replied. "It would be my pleasure to introduce you." Something stirred within him, a warmth at the thought of her coming with him.

Elise Thornbear had moved to Cameron Castle several years previously, after her son Dorian, and her close friend, Queen Genevieve, had died. With Genevieve's death she had had no compelling reason to stay in the capital any longer, while her daughter-in-law and grandchildren were in Cameron. It had been a simple decision to move. She now lived quietly in a modest apartment that the Count had given her.

Gram saw her frequently, she sat at the high table at the evening meals, but she endeavored not to bother much beyond that. She had visited his mother no more than once a week while she was in residence, but now that Rose was in the capital, she had asked Gram to visit her instead. He had done so, once and sometimes twice a week.

Today was different, of course; she wanted to inspect his wounds, however minor they might be.

Frances, his grandmother's main attendant and companion, opened the door when he knocked, "Oh Gram!" she said gladly when she saw him. "Come in, Elise has been worried about you." The older woman had served his grandmother for many years, and she and Elise were on familiar terms now, which included Gram as well.

She paused when she saw Alyssa. "Oh, you brought Lady Alyssa with you! Forgive my poor manners, milady. Please come inside. Make yourself comfortable while I fetch Lady Thornbear." Frances had reverted to more formal speech on seeing the visitor. She waved her hand to indicate the chairs arranged artfully around the sitting room.

They had just sat down when Elise entered the room, looking anxious. She had appeared before Frances had even left the room. It was clear she had been worried. "Gram, let me look at you. They told me you were hurt."

"It's just a scratch, grandmother," he reassured her.

"Let me judge that," she said waspishly, then she glanced at his companion. "Pardon my rudeness, Lady Alyssa, I hadn't expected company."

"No offense taken, Lady Thornbear. Please forgive my presumptuousness for intruding at such a time," responded Alyssa, dropping into a respectful curtsey.

That'll get you points with her, thought Gram, admiring her etiquette. *Even mother couldn't fault that response.*

Elise nodded, already turning Gram's chin in her hands. "Who did these stitches?" she asked sternly.

"Well… uh," Gram spluttered.

"I did, Lady Thornbear," answered Alyssa promptly.

His grandmother's eyes focused on her, as if seeing her for the first time. "Very fine work," she complimented. "Who taught you?"

"Nan—my grandmother," responded Alyssa, correcting herself.

"Give your gran my compliments. She was an excellent teacher," noted Elise clinically. "These are probably as good as what I could have managed," she admitted. "Are you hurt anywhere else?"

"Just scratches," said Gram.

"Let me see."

He looked down with obvious embarrassment.

"Speak up!" snapped Elise.

"My thigh, but it's nothing to worry about," he told her.

His grandmother bent carefully, eyeing his ripped trousers. "Take off your pants."

"Grandmother," he said emphatically, looking toward Alyssa.

"Anyone who can do stitches like that should have no fear of seeing a naked man," noted Elise. One glance at her grandson's face changed her mind, though. "Oh. I see," she responded neutrally. "Step into the other room then."

Once he had some privacy, Gram removed his trousers and Elise cleaned the scratches with something that burned. After a moment she decided that he didn't need more stitches and she settled for applying a thin paste before dressing it with clean cloth. She let him dress himself, and then they rejoined the others.

Elise took Alyssa's hand. "I'm happy to meet you, Lady Alyssa," she said. "Please excuse my brevity before."

"I understand completely, Lady Thornbear," replied the younger woman. "Call me Alyssa if you would. I am honored to make your acquaintance."

"Certainly, call me Elise then," replied his grandmother. "Frances, would you mind making tea for us?"

Frances left and the two women fell to talking. Elise began by asking pointed questions, "Why didn't you check for other wounds?"

"It was a lapse on my part," admitted Alyssa. "I noted the torn fabric, but he was walking without difficulty, and we had a ewe to return. I forgot to double check it afterward when I did the stitches."

"Hmm," said the old woman. "Understandable, but try to do better in the future. Men will hide wounds sometimes, unless you are direct with them. What does your grandmother recommend to keep the wound from going bad?"

"Horse reed if it's a shallow cut, or fen lilly if you need to pack a deeper wound," responded Alyssa immediately.

Elise nodded, "Good. Horse reed is toxic in larger wounds. I hadn't heard of using fen lilly, though."

The two women grew more involved in their conversation, leaving Gram to himself. A quarter hour had passed when Elise finally addressed him directly, "Gram, you look bored. Would you mind if I kept your friend for a while? I'm sure you aren't interested in this conversation."

He nodded gratefully, "I do have something to do." Glancing at Alyssa he added, "You will forgive me for leaving you?"

Alyssa nodded, smiling. "Your grandmother is delightful, Gram. I would love to stay and talk with her."

Freed from responsibility, he rose and exited. As he passed through the door he could hear them talking again already.

"Your features remind me slightly of the people from the Southern Desert," Elise was asking.

He only heard the beginning of Alyssa's answer as the door closed, "One of my grandparents came…"

Gram hurried down the hall. He had missed the noon meal, and he was late for his meeting with Sir Cyhan.

Chapter 13

He encountered Perry in the castle yard before he could get to his meeting place.

"Where did you go?" demanded the captain's son. His face was flustered, and he gave off an angry air. He hadn't enjoyed searching for them.

"We returned the sheep," said Gram calmly.

"I checked the farmer's cot," returned Perry. "You weren't there."

"Did you bother asking the farmer, or did you just ride by when you didn't see the horses? He would have told you which direction we went," said Gram, meeting Perry's gaze evenly.

"You sent me on a fool's errand, and made haste to avoid me," accused Perry.

"I didn't ask you for rope." Gram's voice held an unspoken threat.

Two other young men, Robert Lethy and Sam Withers, spotted them and crossed the yard to join them. They were close friends of Perry's, as well as being among Cyhan's promising group of squire candidates.

"You found him!" exclaimed Robert energetically as they approached. "We rode all over looking for you, Gram." Robert was naturally gregarious, though he and Gram weren't particularly close.

Perry looked over at his friends. "I was just asking him if he ever found that panther."

"Panther?" asked Sam.

Perry grinned, "Yeah, Gram said he was attacked by a big cat after he found the injured ewe." Apparently he hadn't bothered to tell them that part of the story before.

"Attacked?" questioned Sam. "My Da says they won't attack a grown man, too risky."

"It mighta' been sick, or starvin'," suggested Robert.

Before Gram could respond, Perry spoke, "Gram killed it too, didn't you?"

"Yeah," he said flatly. He knew his story would sound unbelievable. Perry was clearly trying to make him look like a liar, but his mind wouldn't supply him with the words that would settle the situation.

"What did you kill it with?" asked Robert, honestly curious. "Did you have a bow with you?" He paused when Gram didn't respond, then he added incredulously, "Was it a spear?"

"I…"

"He was barehanded!" announced Perry.

"What?!" Sam's voice was stunned.

"It sprang at me by the stream, and I managed to roll into the water with it. I held my breath until it quit moving," said Gram. It sounded crazy to his own ears, but it was the truth.

As preposterous as his story was, the two young men looked as though were prepared to believe him. Gram had never been known to brag or make up stories.

"Where is it?" asked Robert enthusiastically. "I want to see it!"

"Well, I don't have…"

"...he lost it in the water, fellows," said Perry, talking from the side of his mouth, as though he were hinting that they should pretend to believe something clearly untrue. Gram bristled at him.

"I never said that," he insisted. "Chad Grayson showed up before you got there. I let him take the body back."

"And I'm sure he'll back up your story," said Perry, "though he'll probably have 'lost' it by then."

"Are you calling me a liar, Perry?" challenged Gram. Sam and Robert both took a step back from the two of them.

"Of course, not," said Perry derisively. "If I suggested that you paid the huntsman to back up a false story, you'd probably challenge me. Then I'd be shamed for thrashing the noble, but *untrained* young Thornbear."

"Oh I doubt young Master Gram would tell anyone if ye wanted to keep it private, Perry," said the voice of Chad Grayson. He had approached unnoticed. "He was kind enough to keep my name clean after he and I had our differences. I'd be wary, though. The boy is monstrously strong. If he gets his hands on ye, he'll likely break somethin' 'afore ye get free agin. Ye should see what he did ta' me cat!"

All four of them looked at him in surprise.

Chad gestured at the gatehouse, "It's over there if ye want ta look. I'm takin' it to the tanner's in a bit, so ye don't have too long."

"You really did drown it?" said Sam in amazement.

Gram nodded, "Yeah."

"Ye should be more careful with yer words, young Draper," admonished the hunter.

The captain's son knew he had made a mistake, and he admitted it immediately, "Sorry Master Grayson, the fault is mine." His eyes said something completely different when they met Gram's, though.

The four of them left the hunter and went to look at the big cat. Gram was headed in that direction anyway.

"Look at the size o' that pussy!" exclaimed Robert, which caused him and Sam both to laugh. It was stretched out on a heavy table inside the wall near the gate. One of the guards told them that they were planning to weigh it, although he was already betting that it was over two hundred pounds.

Gram stood apart, with Perry.

"No hard feelings?" he asked the other, offering his hand.

Perry met his eyes and then took it, "Yeah. Sorry for what I said." His grip was firmer than it needed to be.

Gram tightened his own hand in response, "In future, if you feel the need, Master Grayson was telling the truth. I'd meet you someplace private, and we could keep it between us, no matter how it turned out."

Perry tensed, but then the anger drained out of his eyes. "I believe you, but it's alright. I was being an ass. I don't know what came over me."

Gram knew exactly what had come over him, and after his morning with Alyssa he could better understand Perry's feelings. "She turned my brains to mush too," said Gram.

The captain's son frowned momentarily, then smiled faintly, "May the better man win." He moved to join the others.

Gram left them then, hoping Cyhan wouldn't be too angry when he met up with him. He was already almost an hour late.

***

Cyhan had already heard about the search for them, and he seemed unbothered by the delay. He showed more interest in Gram's stitches. "Those look well done."

"My grandmother seemed impressed too," Gram told him.

"The girl has more to her than most. You will still have scars, though. You won't be quite as pretty anymore."

Is he teasing me? Gram wasn't sure. The big man had never made any attempts at humor before. "I wasn't too worried about it," he replied neutrally.

"Let one of the wizards see it," suggested Cyhan. "They could close it, and you wouldn't have to bother with the stitches. The scars would be smaller too."

It was something that had occurred to Gram already, but he had discarded the idea without giving it much consideration, though he wasn't sure why. He raised a hand to his cheek, pensive. "It doesn't feel right," he admitted. "I'd rather keep them."

The old veteran's eyes watched him, and Gram worried for a moment. Would he think Gram was being vain? Some young men would treasure scars as badges of honor, something to brag about around the fire at night. He might also think Gram was being unnecessarily sentimental. Gram waited to see what the old knight would say.

Cyhan studied him silently for a moment longer and then looked away, rising to his feet. "Let's get started. I'll avoid your face 'til it's finished healing." And that was it.

Gram felt a sense of relief. He never knew what his teacher was thinking, but he could feel a certain kinship. Cyhan understood, and he accepted. He rarely gave praise of any sort, but his acceptance was more than enough.

That evening Gram saw Alyssa again, sitting in her now customary seat across from him at the table. She shared a knowing glance with him before spending most of the meal chatting with Moira. For his part, Gram tried to focus on his food, but he found himself staring at her without consciously meaning too. He returned his eyes to his food, but as soon as he stopped thinking about it, his eyes would return to her.

She's going to think you're strange, he told himself. Just then she looked up and met his eyes.

"Gram," she said, leaning forward so she could keep her voice lower. "Who's that fellow sitting beside the Count? They introduced me before, but it was hard to remember everyone's names."

"Ahh," Gram struggled for a moment, trying to recover from his embarrassment. "That's Sir Cyhan." His answer seemed inordinately brief, but his mind refused to offer him a more eloquent response.

"He looks different—and dangerous," she remarked.

"He's from the South," explained Gram. "That's why his skin is darker, and as for dangerous—well, he's probably the most skilled knight in Lothion."

"More skilled than Dorian Thornbear?" she asked lightly.

Gram frowned, thinking on what Irene had said to him before, then he looked down, "I don't know, honestly. Sometimes I struggle just to remember my father's face."

"I'm sorry," she said regretfully. "That was thoughtless of me."

He nodded and returned to his food, unsure how to respond. The rest of the meal was filled with an awkward silence that seemed to hover over him.

When he left the great hall, the familiar form of a certain stuffed bear met him just outside the door. It was crowded with people, so he scooped the bear up and carried her with him.

"Hello Gram," said Grace cheerfully.

"You're going to get stepped on like that," he cautioned.

"It's the only place I can be sure to find you," she said, there was a pout in her voice.

"I'm betting you heard about today," he postulated.

"You're brighter than you look," she teased. "Though that was a pretty easy guess. What happened?"

He gave her a brief, almost mechanical description of the events of the day. She seemed very unsatisfied.

"That's it? What about Lady Alyssa? What did you think of her? She's very beautiful. Did your grandmother like her? Why didn't you get someone to heal your face? You're keeping the stitches because of her, aren't you?" The questions were coming in rapid fire succession from the small bear.

Gram gaped at her, trying to sort through the verbal barrage. "I can't answer all that at once," he said at last.

"You like her, don't you?" asked Grace, settling on the most important question first.

Gram's first reaction was a flat denial, but then he changed his mind, "I don't know. I've just met her."

Grace accepted that, though it was obvious she had her own opinion. "I think she fancies you," she observed.

"What?" he said, slightly alarmed. "There's no reason to think that."

"Not from the way *you* tell the story," replied Grace, "but I can read through the bland details."

"Then enlighten me o' sage," he remarked, making a weak attempt at sarcasm.

"Listen well then, poor supplicant," she began, taking on the challenge with relish. "First, the lady sent her companion away, rather than returning to the castle herself, or leaving you to your task alone. Second, she suggested leaving the shepherd's home, so that she could spirit you away to a hidden location…"

"… now wait!" interrupted Gram. "She didn't 'spirit me away'. She was just walking to let the sun dry her dress." He had left out the details concerning her removal of the dress. That had been too much for him to explain.

"Then why did she want to stop in such a hard to find place?"

"So no one would see her..." he offered.

"...because she wanted to be alone with you," substituted Grace.

"No, she didn't want to be seen changing!" he blurted out. "It wasn't anything like that."

The bear stared at him, somehow managing to convey her shock and surprise, "She didn't want what? I think you left something out of your story. Did you do something—inappropriate?"

"N—no!" he stammered.

"Do explain."

They had already reached his door, so he took her inside to make sure no one heard them. "Will you promise to keep this to yourself?"

She nodded, "So long as you didn't do anything terrible."

"Of course not, listen..." He gave her a more complete retelling of his story, leaving out only his thoughts at the time. There was no need to let her know how much he had been affected by the sight of Alyssa's half-clad form.

"Oh Gram," she said when he had finished.

"What?" he asked nervously.

"I hope your mother likes her," said the bear.

"I just met her!" he protested.

"Well she's already left her mark on you, quite literally in this case," noted Grace, indicating his wounded face.

"The panther did this," he countered.

"But you're keeping the stitches," returned Grace. "That says enough." She got up to leave.

"You won't tell anyone, right? About the dress and..." he said, sounding desperate.

"No, your secret is safe with me, but I'm keeping an eye on that girl," she responded primly.

He held the door for her since she was far too short to manage it by herself. "Thank you, Grace."

"Just don't do anything you'll regret," she replied, and then she was gone.

Chapter 14

Matthew met Gram at breakfast and asked him to follow him to the workshop. Once they were alone, he gave him a conspiratorial grin.

"Is it finished?"

"No," said the young wizard.

Gram's face fell, "Well, why are you smiling then?"

Matthew sighed, "You certainly aren't easy to please."

"I just want to have it back in place before Mother gets back!"

"And then what?" asked Matthew.

"Then I can breathe easy, that's what."

"Well, it doesn't make much sense if I repair Thorn, or improve it, if it's just going to sit on a wall, looking as if it's still broken. Does it?" asked Matthew, obviously leading toward something.

"I figured I'd cross that bridge only when necessary," admitted Gram.

"When would that be?"

"After I've come of age?" suggested Gram. "Or better yet, after she dies—of old age, of course! I'd never wish my mother dead."

Matthew tilted his head to one side, "You do realize your mother is only in her late thirties? You might be approaching old age yourself before she passes."

Gram rolled his eyes, "And I'm sure you have a better idea."

"Yeah, but eventually you will have to assert yourself."

Gram had done that once already, and he still felt guilty for it. He wasn't sure if he wanted to hurt his mother any further. "I won't have any rights to assert until I come of age anyway."

Matthew nodded, "The good news is I might have a way to get you by until then."

"What is it?"

"A tattoo," announced his friend, grinning from ear to ear as if he had just said the cleverest thing in the world.

"I can't get a tattoo!" protested Gram. "I'd have to hide it, and you know how well I hide things," then he paused. "Wait, what good is a tattoo going to do me?"

"An excellent question, my young friend," said Matthew slickly, trying to sound as if he were a sly tinker selling his wares.

"I'm barely a year younger than you," pointed out Gram.

"That's not the point," said Matthew, growing exasperated.

"Well, it kinda is, since we're both technically young…"

"Listen," interrupted Matthew seriously. "This would be a magical tattoo, an enchantment permanently engraved on living flesh."

Gram winced at the combination of 'engraved' and 'living flesh', it sounded terribly painful. "I'm already pretty well marked up these days," he said, directing Matthew's attention to his face. "I'm not sure I need any more scars."

"It won't be scars. It'll be a real tattoo, but I can make sure it isn't visible, except when you use it," said Matthew.

"You still haven't told me what it would do."

"It will let you call Thorn, whenever you need it."

He stared at his friend blankly for a moment. "You mean I'd have to yell for it?"

Matthew shook his head, "No, no, you would just touch the tattoo and will it to come to you."

"Will it?"

"It's like thinking, but with emphasis. You would infuse a tiny bit of aythar into the symbols, and the enchantment would activate, causing Thorn to translate to you."

"I'm not a wizard, Matt. I can't infuse things," he said before adding a moment later, "And I'm not quite sure what you mean by 'translate'. Is this something like a teleportation circle?"

Matthew was growing even more excited. "Yes you can! That's why I tested you before. This is similar to the Sun-Swords. Your father couldn't use one, but you can. It only takes a tiny amount to start it, the enchantment does the rest. As for the word 'translate', I sort of took to using that to differentiate my new technique from teleportation. For most purposes it's the same thing, but instead of moving the sword from one place to another, it will be moving from one dimension to another. In fact, the sword will use translation for much more than just that; when you give it different commands, translation will be the method used to bring the extra material to you. A teleportation circle, or even a permanent portal would be totally incapable of handling such a task, but using this method…"

Gram began waving his hands, desperate to stop his friend before he drowned under the weight of arcane jargon. "You lost me after, 'for most purposes it's the same thing'. Did you say 'commands'?"

"Yes."

"What commands?"

"I haven't sorted all that out yet, can we just stay focused on the tattoo for now?"

"You're the one who went off about dimensions and portals," said Gram dourly.

Matthew pulled out a sheet of fine vellum. It was marked with a strange pattern and dotted with odd symbols. "This is the schema. Hold out your arm, and I'll transfer it to your skin."

"How much is this going to hurt?" Gram was still a bit wary after his previous experiences with healing at the twins' hands.

"Not at all," said Matthew immediately. "The painful part is when we turn it into an actual tattoo. This is just so I'll have a guide to follow on your skin."

"I feel much better now," said Gram dryly. "You promise it won't be visible?"

"Definitely," assured his friend. "That's what these symbols here are for." He pointed to one edge of the pattern. Then he flipped the vellum over, placing the pattern against Gram's arm.

"Won't it be backwards?"

Matthew sighed, "C'mon, Gram. I'm not stupid. I reversed it already, so it'll be the right way around." Then he pursed his lips, putting on a thoughtful face.

"What?"

"I was just thinking how funny it would be if I had reversed it."

"What would happen then?"

"The first time you tried to use it, you'd be translated into the null dimension that stores the sword, instead of the other way around. You'd be trapped in an empty featureless blackness—probably for eternity."

Gram started to pull away, "Forget it, I don't..."

Matthew started laughing, "Relax, I was joking."

He stared at his friend suspiciously, "What would really happen then?"

The young wizard shrugged, "I dunno. It probably just wouldn't work."

"But you're *sure* that it will work, and that it's the right way around. Right?"

"Definitely," said Matthew, his light brown hair falling down, almost covering his eyes. "I tested it myself." Smoothing the vellum once more, he muttered a few words, and Gram felt a tingling on the skin of his right forearm. When Matthew pulled it away, he could see that it was now blank, and the symbols had transferred neatly onto his skin. "Now we need to make it permanent."

"How are you going to—ow!" Gram felt a sharp pain, as if a horsefly had bitten his arm.

Matthew gave him a grim look, "I know it hurts. That was just one spot. I can do this quickly or a little at a time."

"Make it quick then," answered Gram stoically.

"The only downside is that it hurts a *lot* if I do it quickly, and you'll have to hold still."

"Give me a few minutes then," said Gram. "I want to try something." He settled himself and grew still, trying to recapture the feeling that he sought when training. It had grown much easier with constant practice over the past months. The emptiness settled over him almost as soon as he sought it, and he felt his sense of self fade away. "Alright, I'm ready," he said, but it seemed almost as if someone else were speaking.

Matthew closed his eyes and concentrated, and then Gram's arm was on fire. The pain was intense, and it continued, as what felt like a burning ember traced the pattern on his arm. Gram watched his skin with a sense of detachment. He felt the pain, but it was a sensation without meaning or urgency.

The process was finished in what was probably only a minute or two, and then Matthew looked at his friend, curious. "Damn, Gram, you never even flinched."

Gram blinked at him, and then his thinking mind returned, the one that had all the words. "That hurt pretty badly," he admitted.

"I wouldn't have known it by looking at you."

"It's a trick I learned from Cyhan. Should we test it now?"

Matthew nodded, "One sec, I have to set it up." Without bothering to explain, he brought out what appeared to be the same sword they had borrowed a couple of months ago. It was still broken, but at least it was no longer in thousands of tiny pieces. He held it up, seemed to touch something, and then the weapon disappeared.

"Where did it go?"

"Somewhere—else, another dimension," said the wizard. "Now you should be able to call it to you, and it will translate into your hand, no matter where you are. Try it."

"What do I do?" asked Gram. The tattoo on his arm had vanished, though the skin where it had been was raw and bleeding in places. He could almost see the pattern within the irritated area.

"Imagine yourself pushing energy into the area where the tattoo is. Think of the sword in your hand at the same time," instructed Matthew.

It took several tries before Gram managed to coordinate his thoughts and the image of the sword in his mind, but when he did, it happened naturally, as if the sword had been in his hand all along.

"Now reverse it," said Matthew. "Pull energy from the tattoo and imagine the sword vanishing."

That was harder, but he eventually got it. He practiced calling the sword several more times, growing more excited each time. "This is amazing, Matt!"

"Just wait until I finish the sword," said his friend smugly.

"How much is done now?"

"Well, that part, and it's no longer in thousands of pieces."

"That's all? You've had it for months!"

Matthew shrugged, "It's taking a lot longer than I expected, but so far everything is working as I hoped.

I had to break it down first, and since you were worried about your mother, the first form I finished was this one."

"First form?"

"The broken sword," said Matthew. "So you could make it look like it used to—this form."

"It's going to have different forms? Like what?"

"The next one will be its original unbroken form," said his friend. "After that... let me surprise you."

Gram looked at him with dawning respect. He had worried that his friend might not be able to deliver what he promised, but now he was beginning to believe. He also suspected that Matt's potential as an enchanter was greater than anyone realized. "Did your father teach you this enchantment?"

"He taught me everything he knows, but this is something new—I think. I don't know what the ancients knew, but I believe this is completely novel. Translation is very different, and what I'm going to do with it, with your sword, well, I'm sure that's never been done before." There was a quiet pride in the young wizard's voice.

Chapter 15

"You're ready," said Cyhan. It was two days since Gram had gotten his invisible tattoo.

He looked at his teacher, but since he hadn't been given permission to speak he waited silently.

"Go ahead," said the older man. "You can speak freely for a while. You're going to have some questions."

"Ready for what, Zaihair?"

"To start attacking, or at least trying to."

Up until that point, Gram had been doing nothing other than trying to keep himself in the proper frame of mind to detect and avoid incoming attacks. Still, he was mildly disappointed. He had hoped he might get to train in armor, or with a shield at least. Fighting with nothing more than a stick in an open field was hardly a realistic way to learn the sort of craft he would need someday.

Cyhan read the lack of enthusiasm in his features. "What were you expecting?"

"When will I start learning to be a knight?"

"What does that mean?"

"You know, armor training, heavy weapons, the lance. The others—they're learning how to care for their armor, how to bear the weight, how to use a shield. You haven't even discussed any of it with me," explained Gram.

"I'm not teaching you to be a knight," said Cyhan. "You'll learn some of that later, and the rest you can learn from anyone. I'm teaching you something far more important."

Gram's face was clouded with frustration. "What's that?"

Cyhan showed his teeth in a feral grin. It was a frightening expression on the old warrior's face, full of enthusiastic menace. "I'm teaching you to survive, boy, to survive and win. You can learn *dressage* from any cavalryman. I will teach you to kill, whether it's with a sword, a spear, or your bare hands. You can fancy it up any way you like afterwards."

He stared at his instructor stubbornly, "I don't intend to be an assassin."

"Just what do you think a knight is, boy?"

He straightened up, thinking of his father, remembering him and everything his mother had said about him. "A knight protects. He serves his lord honorably, and he protects the weak."

"I'm going to kill your little sister, *boy*. How are you going to protect her?" said the big man, an evil gleam in his eye.

Gram knew it was meant as a hypothetical, but hearing the words coming from Cyhan sent chills down his spine. "I wouldn't let you."

"No. You'll cut my fucking head off, or something equally permanent. Anything less and your sister is dead. You're thinking like a soldier, you just want to take orders and fight in a unit. Or maybe you want to be a commander and lead your men to glorious battle on the field, but I'm here to tell you that's bullshit.

"There's nothing glorious about war, or battle. It's kill or be killed. You might study tactics and learn to be a great commander, but that's up *here,*" Cyhan pointed at his head. "First you have to survive, and that means understanding how fighting works, and how not to get killed. That's what I'm teaching you. You'll have to learn the rest from someone else."

Gram frowned.

"Let me start at the beginning," said Cyhan, drawing a deep breath. "There are three types of fighters: men who fight with their bodies, those who fight with their minds, and those who fight with their hearts.

"Most people fight with their bodies. That's simply part of being alive. Soldiers train to learn obedience, to survive. The smarter ones learn to fight with their minds, to plan the battle and lead their men to victory. Some men, though, the crazy ones, they fight with their hearts. Your father was one of those.

"Those sorts are dangerous, because they'll do anything to win, including throwing their lives away just to cut your liver out. That's how your father beat me that day, in case you were wondering."

It felt as though the world stopped for a moment, and Gram stared at him.

"See this cut?" The old knight traced a scar that ran across the bridge of his nose and along one cheek. "Your father did that. I was trying to kill the Count, and he got in the way. He fought me sword to sword, but he wasn't quite good enough. He knew it, and I knew it, but rather than accept it, he took a sword to the gut, just so he could break my blade. I got this scar from his backswing."

"But he died years later, at the World Road…" said Gram.

"Yeah, his armor saved him the day we fought, but he didn't know it would. I saw it in his eyes. He didn't care. He took what he thought would be a deathblow just to stop me. That's the kind of man your father was.

Cyhan paused for a moment and then stepped closer, jabbing his index finger into Gram's chest, "But that's *not* what I'm teaching you. You're already like him. You were born fighting with your heart. That's why you nearly hurt Master Grayson that day, because you didn't have the sense to give up when you should have, and someday, that shit is going to get you killed. Someday you're going to throw your life away for something you think is more important."

"Then what are you teaching me?"

"The unnamed path, boy," growled Cyhan. "I'm teaching you to be perfect. I owe it to your father. He showed me what I lacked; now I'm going to make sure you're good enough that you never have to throw your life away to win. If you die in battle, it won't be because you weren't good enough to beat someone, even someone like me."

Gram was stunned, but as his mind processed the older man's words, a new question appeared in his mind. "What did you lack?"

"A heart," said the big man, his voice pitched almost too low to hear.

Their training ended there for the day. They both knew there would be no way to focus after that discussion. Gram found himself replaying the conversation in his mind, over and over, and it was hard to sleep that night.

***

The next day Gram was at lunch when Moira addressed him directly, "Are you looking forward to the Winter's Dawn?"

That caught him completely off-guard. Winter's Dawn was the name of the traditional harvest festival in Washbrook. In the past it had been a celebration to honor Millicenth, the Lady of the Evening Star, but these days it continued as a way to celebrate the end of the summer's labors. It was an event put on by the people of the town, featuring a bonfire, hot cider, music, and lots of dancing. It was also one of Gram's favorite times of the year.

"I hadn't even given it a thought, really," he admitted to her. Alyssa watched him carefully as he replied.

Matthew chimed in then, "At least this year we'll be old enough to drink." The year before the twins hadn't been quite sixteen yet.

"I still won't be," groused Gram, his birthday would come the week after the festival.

"Not to worry," said Matthew. "You have friends in high places."

Gram wasn't sure he wanted to risk it, but he didn't want to appear timid in front of Alyssa, so he settled for remaining silent.

"What is your festival like?" asked Lady Alyssa, directing her question primarily at Moira.

Moira took to the subject happily, "They build a big bonfire in the middle of the town, in front of the tavern. Usually Joe McDaniel, that's the tavern owner, will have a stage set up outside the Muddy Pig, and musicians perform throughout the day and late into the night. People gather to drink hot cider, mulled wine, and share the music. There will be dancing and story tellers…"

"…and sweets!" interjected Irene from beside her sister. "They set up stands with caramel apples and pies."

"One of the old woodworkers, Master Anderson, sells toys," added Conall.

Matthew nodded, "That used to be my favorite thing. He makes them all year long, using his scraps and leftovers."

"Is this part of a formal event?" questioned Alyssa. "Will we have to dress for a ball, or will we be able to mingle at the festival?"

"Oh no," said Moira. "Our parents have kept it separate. They were both raised as commoners, and they always say that it would be a shame to ruin the festival by mixing it with a formal occasion. That way they can join in the festival like everyone else."

"We have a formal Winter's Ball two weeks after the festival, but it isn't nearly as much fun. It's a lot smaller, and we hold it here in the great hall," said Gram, finally speaking up again.

"Is it too stuffy?" wondered Alyssa.

Gram nodded, "Those with some rank or station dress in their finest. Duke Roland, from Lancaster, usually attends, as well as the Baron of Arundel and his family, but overall it's much quieter."

"Do you dance?" she asked, her eyes challenging him.

Gram smiled, "I do." Lady Rose had seen to that, not that it had been a hardship for him. Of all the things she insisted that he learn as a future nobleman, dancing was the most pleasant. Being naturally active, he found it to be a lot of fun, and he seemed to have a talent for it. That was one reason he enjoyed the festival more than the formal ball.

At the Winter's Dawn, the dancing tended to focus on peasant and country dances. Those were typically much more energetic and wild, with fast tempos and strong beats. The ball, by contrast, mainly featured staid court dances that, while beautiful, focused on slower, statelier patterns.

As he thought about it, his mind imagined what Alyssa might look like in a ball gown, or what it would be like to dance with her. He realized that perhaps the problem with the ball had been his age and his lack of a partner who truly interested him. In the past it had mainly been an occasion for him to dance with older women and relatives.

Moira broke in then, "What's that look about, Gram?" She grinned as if she thought she might know what he was daydreaming about.

Before he could answer, a ringing caught everyone's attention, and the Count stood up. Mordecai Illeniel held a gold goblet in one hand, and he surveyed the room as he waited for everyone to grow quiet.

After the room had gone still, he spoke into the silence, "As most of you know, Sir Cyhan has been our only knight for some years now, but at my urging he has finally decided to take a squire. In fact, after some consideration he has chosen to take not one, but two squires!"

The announcement brought a positive chorus of affirmations from the room, and those who hadn't already taken hold of their cups did so.

The Count continued, "My congratulations go to Perry Draper, the son of our accomplished guard captain, as well as to Robert Lethy. You are both following a long tradition of honorable service and hopefully, someday, if you work hard enough, you may find yourselves as knights. I call a toast!"

Cups were raised and cries of 'hear, hear!' rang out. Perry and Robert were both urged to their feet and forced to make long bows while those nearest pounded their backs. Sir Cyhan rose and true to his nature gave what was probably the briefest speech in the history of such occasions, but Gram heard none of it.

He stared at his plate, his appetite gone. The flavor of his food had turned to ash. Looking around, he was grateful that everyone's eyes were elsewhere, for it would have been taken poorly if anyone had seen the sour expression on his face. Wrestling his emotions under control, he raised his cup to his lips and put on a false smile.

Gram made it through the rest of the meal without embarrassing himself, but he did catch a few people glancing at him, sympathetic looks on their faces. Everyone knew of his mother's prohibition, and while he knew they meant well, the knowledge of their pity only made him feel worse.

He found Cyhan waiting for him as he left the hall.

"I won't be there today," said the knight. "We'll resume tomorrow."

Gram nodded, unsure if his voice would work. Feeling numb he turned away, heading for the stairs. He wanted only to reach the privacy of his room, to escape.

I knew this was coming, he told himself. *Why am I letting it bother me so much?*

He stopped, having nearly walked over someone in his path. He started to apologize, and then he recognized who he had walked into. "I'm sorry, Irene."

The Count's younger daughter looked up at him. She was carrying Moira's bear, Grace in her arms. "Don't you think it's wonderful for Perry?" said the girl, oblivious to his inner torment.

"Of course," he said mechanically. "I'm very happy for him."

"He'll make a good knight someday," she continued. "But I wonder if Robert is a good choice. He's always so silly."

It struck Gram as ironic hearing the nine year old call someone who was so much older, 'silly', but she was right in that regard. Robert Lethy was not only good natured, but very fond of pranks and pratfalls.

While trying to gracefully get past Irene, Gram caught sight of Perry leaving the hall, but what really drew his eye was Alyssa. She was standing close to the captain's son, hand on his arm, talking animatedly to him as they walked out together.

Jealousy reared up, an ugly beast in his heart, teaching Gram yet another harsh lesson about himself. For a moment he wanted nothing other than to destroy Perry Draper, to humiliate him. It was a petty thought, and a new one for him. Seeing it, Gram was amazed at his own pettiness, yet despite knowing it was wrong, he felt it anyway.

Alyssa looked up then, catching his eye, and she smiled at him for a brief moment before returning her attention to the newly made squire.

"Excuse me, Rennie," said Gram to the little girl still chatting away at him. "I need to hurry." Slipping around her, he made his way quickly back to his apartment, not stopping until he had closed himself into his bedroom.

Drawing a familiar book from the shelf, he took the red stone in his hand before sitting on his bed. A long time passed while he sat there, seeking to banish the bitter jealousy in his heart, but he failed in the end. Staring at the ruby, he could only wonder what his father would have thought of him then. His mother had told him many times of his father's kindness, describing him as a man with a boundless, gentle soul.

Father, I wish I could be like you. It felt as though the stone pulsed in his hand, and a faint warmth spread through him. Eventually, he slept.

Chapter 16

The next day he found Chad Grayson waiting for him at the customary place where he usually met Sir Cyhan. Gram stared at him curiously, unsure what to say.

"He asked me to meet ye today," said the hunter.

The new squires need him, thought Gram. "I don't need a babysitter," he told the lean ranger.

"An I ain't paid to be one," returned Chad. "Follow me. If ye can keep from bein' a snot, I might teach you somethin'."

The older man led him across the field and onto the verge of the woods. "We'll start here," he said abruptly. "What do ye see here?" He pointed at the dry grass that bordered the forest.

"Grass," said Gram.

"Anything else?"

He stared closer, straightening after a moment, "There's some dirt under the grass."

"Ye were born ta be a smart ass weren't ye?"

Gram took a deep breath, forcing himself to relax. It wasn't the hunter's fault he was in a bad mood, or that his teacher had dumped him in favor of his squires. He might as well find out what the man was trying to show him. "What do you see?"

"There's a rabbit warren close by," said the hunter. "See the grass there, where it's been nibbled back. That's the way they chew at it."

"Could have been a sheep."

"Nah, they crop it close to the ground—like this," Chad demonstrated by tearing off the majority of the grass, leaving only a small portion an inch above the dirt. "Plus, if ye look there, ye can see some rabbit scat."

Gram was no woodsman, but he wasn't a complete stranger to the wild either. "Might be deer scat."

"The size is different, and the shape. Deer scat is generally darker, and a little more scattered, cuz it's falling from a greater height. It's a bit more oval too."

The hunter led him into the forest then, stopping frequently to draw his attention to important signs. Despite himself, Gram was fascinated by the things the man saw in, what to him had been, featureless underbrush. As the afternoon passed into evening and they began to head back, he found himself with a new question, though.

"Why are you showing me this stuff?"

"I figured I'd give ya a chance at avoiding the next panther that wanted to snack on ye," answered the hunter.

"That's probably pretty unlikely," said Gram.

"Yeah, that's true," replied Chad, "but then there's bears, and wolves, and men."

"Men?"

"That's what he asked me ta teach ye, to track men."

While that sounded like a useful skill, it wasn't the sort of thing Gram had expected, nor did he understand the purpose of showing him animal scat in the wilderness if tracking people was the goal. "You've been showing me animal signs all day…"

The hunter spat on the ground, then pressed his soft boot into it. "Do ye see a track there?"

He stared at the spot. It was damp and the grass had been bent, but it was already rebounding. There was nothing resembling a boot mark. "No," he admitted.

"Right," said Chad. "Cuz there ain't one, and I was deliberately pressin' hard. In the real world a visible print is uncommon, so what you have to learn first, is to see what's already there. Once you know what you should see, the differences begin to stand out. It's like a giant book, but there're no words ta follow. The story reveals itself through a hunnerd different indirect clues, an' what you're lookin' for is what *isn't* there."

Gram frowned.

"Ye learn animal signs first, so you don' mistake them. Ye learn to read the ground, to spot changes in leaf litter, in the way grass is bent, and ye have to know if that's cuz a deer passed, or a man. Sometimes just looking at one place won't tell ye, but if you know how to tell a game trail ye can figure out what's what."

"So I have to learn deer to track people…"

"You have ta learn *everythin'* to track anythin' is what I'm sayin'"

***

Cyhan was there the next day. "Ask," was the only word he gave in greeting.

"Why the hunter?"

"I was busy, and he has much to teach."

"I don't want to be a hunter," Gram stated.

"How many men do you think he killed during the war with Gododdin?" said the big man suddenly.

"I don't know."

"Many," answered the knight. "More than any other besides the Count himself."

Gram's eyes widened, "Really?"

The veteran ignored his question, asking another of his own, "How do you think he did that?"

"With his bow?" said Gram uncertainly.

Cyhan nodded. "The archers killed several times as many as were slain by swords, and he was chief among them."

"He didn't teach me anything about archery, though."

The old warrior paused, then answered, "He will. He has much to teach, treat what he offers as a gift."

"Were you taught to track?"

The big man nodded again. "Yes, but my teacher was not as skilled. Consider yourself lucky."

After that his training with Cyhan changed again. That day he put away the reeds and began barehanded. Gram thought that might indicate an easier day, but it was far from the truth. He collected a number of interesting bruises as the day wore on.

The tone of their sessions was changing as well. Cyhan no longer remained entirely silent; he began using demonstrations, along with short explanations.

"You have learned silence," he told Gram, "and that's good, for silence is at the center of zan-zei. Now we begin to train your body and your mind."

Gram understood enough to wonder at that statement. "Won't that interfere?"

Cyhan's face softened faintly, a sure sign that he had asked a good question. "Yes, and no. You will have to work hard to retain what you've learned, to keep the silence within. The silence is the animal, the unthinking part of you. It understands the world far better than your waking mind does, but in order for you to fight men, you must train your body. First I show you, then you practice what you've seen until your muscles remember it. Then your mind must forget, and allow the silence to control the flow."

"It sounds like going backward and then forward again."

"Exactly, now pay attention, there are four basic arm-locks you must learn…"

The week progressed with more of the same. Hours filled with demonstrations and practice, endless repetition, and then they would stop. Gram would come prepared to learn more, but Cyhan might only ask him to sit again, or stand, meditating on silence, until his body faded from his awareness.

Another week passed, and his teacher began to bring different weapons with him. One day it might be maces, or flails, the next day it would be the staff, or a great sword. In each case, as soon as Gram felt he had begun to get a feel for something, Cyhan would change the routine. They wore heavy mail on some occasions and nothing but simple clothes the next.

The constant change was sometimes stressful, but whenever Gram became frustrated, his teacher would stop, and then Gram would be made to meditate again.

Overall it was the most bizarre sort of training Gram could imagine.

"You never let me master anything," he complained one day, during one of the rare moments that his teacher allowed him to speak freely.

"Mastery is an illusion that only serves to get you killed."

"So I'd be better off if I never learned anything then," said Gram sarcastically.

"I have fought for most of my life, and I have seen many 'masters'. They are no different than anyone else, and they often die at the hand of someone who had never picked up a blade before. Mastery breeds confidence, and confidence leads to arrogance. You must learn enough to be confident, no matter what your weapon, or the place or time, but every fight must be treated as if it were the first, and last, fight of your life.

"When I met your father, he was already a master swordsman, and his skill was always greater than mine with a blade, yet he rarely got the upper hand when we sparred. Do you know why?"

Gram was surprised to hear the knight admit to any sort of inferiority, but he had learned enough to have a 'feeling' for the answer, though he couldn't articulate it. He struggled for a minute before answering, "Because of the sword."

"Yes. He fought with the sword. He had been trained his entire life, to fight with it, and he was brilliant. But battle is about more than a sword, and you must learn to fight with more, the entire *world* is your weapon."

Even the mild criticism of his father irritated him, but the annoyance was tempered by Cyhan's compliment. Gram had never heard Cyhan use the word 'brilliant' in any context ever before. He might say 'good' on rare occasions, but they were very rare. Normally, praise from the old veteran took the form of a neutral expression that indicated you might not be completely hopeless.

When they finished that day, he waited until they were walking back and asked a new question. "Did you like my father?"

Cyhan didn't answer at first, taking a half a minute to think. "Not at first."

"But you did later?"

"I thought he was a fool, but later I learned to respect him. It was years before I knew why I disliked him."

They were almost to the keep before he clarified the remark. "I disliked him because he still believed, in right and wrong, in goodness—and evil. I had given up on people, I lived only to satisfy my honor, sacrificing everything for a rigid code."

"Did you change your mind?"

Cyhan sighed, "Not until the very end. He had to die before I learned the lesson he was teaching."

"Are you trying to teach that to me?" asked Gram, embarrassed even as he asked the question.

The old warrior laughed, "Ha! No, that's not something I can teach, nor do you need to learn it. You're much like him. I'm just trying to make you a better fighter."

"Than him?"

"Than me," finished the big man.

Thornbear

Chapter 17

The weeks rolled by and Gram found himself completely absorbed by what he was learning. Most afternoons he spent with Cyhan, who made certain that every training session was different in some way. Although the constant change had bothered Gram at first, he began to grow comfortable with it, enjoying the challenge of adapting to new rules and situations. His relationship with Chad Grayson changed too.

He began to spend some of his mornings with the hunter, roaming the land around Castle Cameron. He quickly discovered that despite the woodsman's proclivity for drinking he preferred to be up early, very early, though he had an interesting explanation for it.

"Shhh," he told Gram one morning. "Ye're too fuckin' loud."

"Is there something close?"

"No, ye're just aggravatin' me hangover. Why do ye think I like huntin'?"

Gram hadn't given it any thought, so he replied, "I just assumed you liked nature." He kept his voice barely above a whisper.

"Well, yeah, but another part of it is because people are so damn loud. Out here all I have to deal with are overenthusiastic songbirds. Some o' those bastards really piss me off." He paused as a lark broke the silence, as if to illustrate his point. Chad grimaced.

Gram found himself struggling to contain a laugh.

"Ye think I'm jokin'? I'm dead fuckin' serious, boy," said the hunter with a deadpan expression. "The only bright spot is that if I get really pissed off I can kill somethin'. Back in the castle if I get too aggravated and kill someone they'd put me chains. Out here, if I murder somethin' I can take it back and like as not the cook will give me a fuckin' medal."

Gram gave up and began to chortle.

"Stop it boy!" said the hunter as he began to laugh as well. "Ye're makin' me laugh now, and it's gonna make my head explode."

***

The Winter's Dawn festival arrived but for the first time he could remember, Gram wasn't particularly looking forward to it. It was an interruption. He had grown to enjoy his training sessions and the preparations for the festival disrupted that for several days prior to it, and would probably prevent him from training for a few days after as well.

He dressed in some of his best clothes, a fine blue doublet with complementary leggings and soft black boots. He had never lacked for a good wardrobe. The belt he wore was ornamented with silver fittings and a matching black scabbard for his feast knife. A silver chain was the only jewelry he wore, and it complemented the blue of the doublet.

"Even mother would be pleased," he noted aloud, thinking of how she would have fussed over him if she had been there.

A glance in the mirror showed him that his hair was a bit wild, but he didn't care for the latest fashion, which was to oil it. He preferred it loose rather than in wet-looking ringlets.

I don't have anyone to impress anyway, he thought.

He hadn't seen Alyssa much of late, other than at mealtimes. He had spotted her once or twice, walking with Perry Draper. Each time she had caught his eye, smiling and seeming as if she were trying to communicate with him purely through her gaze, but then she would return her attention to Perry and he would be left wondering if he had imagined it.

Gram went into Washbrook in the early afternoon and sampled some of the sweets that were being sold. While he was walking he encountered Matthew and the two of them soon made their way over to the stage near the Muddy Pig. There was already music in the air, but they were there to hear the story tellers. Some of the best from across the region would be there, weaving their tales and amusing captivated crowds.

The two friends had always sought the story tellers first, once they were old enough to be allowed to roam freely anyway. The tales told would range from the oldest, retellings of legendary events and heroes of history, to the more recent, such as stories about the Count, or Dorian Thornbear.

It was probably for that reason that Mordecai Illeniel rarely showed himself at the event until the evening's music and dancing had taken over the foreground. Some of the tales embarrassed him, others saddened him, and on occasion they simply pissed him off. He had told Gram and his own children many times not to believe most of what they heard.

Still, it was an attraction no young person could resist. One year they had had a famous story teller from the capital come, and Moira had been fascinated to hear a tale involving her namesake, Moira Centyr, during the war with Balinthor. The fact that the story involved her true mother, born over a thousand years before, made it a tale of particular interest to her.

This year most of the story tellers were locals, from Lancaster or Washbrook, and the boys had already heard their stories many times before. They listened anyway, enjoying them again and committing the details to memory.

As evening fell the musicians began to gather by the stage and rather than competing from separate corners of the village as they did during the day, they began taking turns, playing old songs and new alike. The bonfire was lit and Joe McDaniel's began to sell libations to those sitting at the benches and tables set up near his tavern.

The area around the bonfire was cleared and the music grew louder as people began to dance. Only the most confident of dancers came out in the beginning, but as the drinks flowed, more and more people joined in the merriment. When enough people had taken to their feet, a call went up for a song called 'The Dunny Drover', a popular song with a traditional dance all its own.

They lined up in rows, men and women facing one another, and the air was soon full of the sound of stomping feet as they reinforced the beat of the song with their steps. Even Matthew, who wasn't overly fond of dancing joined in for that one.

After that dance was done, the music changed, someone had asked for a jig. Some of the dancers retired to their seats, leaving the floor open for those with the energy and skill required for the fast paced and complicated dances. Most of those were the young, but some, like Joe McDaniel's himself, were older, spry veterans.

Gram's eyes were searching, hoping to find one of the village lasses that danced well. Daisy Wellham would have been his first choice, for she was a girl with quick feet and a strong sense of rhythm, but someone else found him before he spotted her.

"There you are," came Alyssa's voice, sounding from behind him.

"Well, hullo yourself," said Gram, gracing her with a smile. He was in a fine mood, a natural product of the dancing he had done already.

"You told me you dance, as I recall," she said, a challenging glint in her eye.

"I do, and have done," he replied confidently. "I was just searching for an able partner." He let his eyes drift past her, scanning the crowd for Daisy once more.

Alyssa narrowed her eyes, "Do you take me so lightly, Master Thornbear?"

He grinned widely, showing more teeth than usual. This was *his* place, and when it came to dancing he felt none of his normal shyness. "Begging your pardon, *Lady* Alyssa," he responded, adding the honorific since she had used his, "I meant no offense, but this is 'Rolly's Jig' they are playing. I'll need a very competent partner to make it interesting."

She arched one brow, "Perhaps I could offer myself…"

He laughed, enjoying the competitive look on her face. He already knew she wanted the dance, but he couldn't help but needles her a bit more. "This is no waltz or courtly pavan. I would not wish to force you beyond your capacity." His eyes glimmered with mirth as he spoke.

"I'll take your challenge, Gram, and pay you back threefold for your discourtesy," she shot back, slipping her hand into his. There was a smile in her voice.

Pulling her close he stepped into the rhythm and spun her out before the words had left her lips. She didn't falter, though, her feet matched his own and soon they were cutting the ground in sharp patterns, dancing and treading in time with the music. Her head tilted, admiring him as they worked together and he returned the look.

He quickly discovered that his partner was no novice when it came to music and movement. The jig was soon over and a strathspey followed right after, but Alyssa never missed a beat. She rolled and flowed with the song like moonlight on the top of a stream. She whispered in his ear as the dance brought her into his arms once again, "You'll pay for what you said before."

Her breath sent a shiver down his spine, but he didn't lose time with the beat. When the next opportunity came he replied in similar fashion, "You're welcome to try."

An hour passed as they danced, oblivious to the envious stares of some in the crowd. The air grew hot as their bodies warmed with the constant and frenetic motion, but neither of them asked to rest or retire.

The tradition amongst the musicians was to play until everyone had surrendered, unable to continue with the fast paced reels. Couples danced until they could no longer continue, and once everyone had taken their seats the players would relent and change to a slower melody, allowing the more moderate dancers to return.

After the first hour had passed, Gram and Alyssa were still dancing. Most of the other couples had admitted defeat, but the two of them refused to give way. Robert Lethy and Daisy were the last remaining, but even they were flagging, their mincing steps beginning to slow. Eventually they left the floor.

"It appears we have vanquished our foes," said Gram as she came close again.

Alyssa met his gaze with smoldering eyes, "I still have one opponent left." Heat radiated from her like a stove and her face was flushed. Neither of them were damp, they were soaked, sweating heavily despite the crispness of the early fall air.

Something in her voice set a fire within him, a new blaze he had never encountered before. The smell of her made him ache, and he knew he wanted her in a way that was far from innocent. Breathing hard, he kept dancing, knowing that once he stopped she would likely be gone.

"Then I'll have you dancing until you beg me to stop," he replied.

Minutes passed and the crowd clapped, keeping time as one by one the musicians gave up and stopped playing, fingers tired and aching. Only when the last one stopped playing and Joe McDaniel came forward did they finally give in.

"For the sake of the sanity, let it be!" shouted Joe, stepping out with two large tankards. "You two have made yer point!" The crowd laughed and cheered, letting the clapping come to an end while Gram spun Alyssa around one final time and then caught her up in his arms.

Breathless, she buried her face against his neck as he carried her to the benches where Matthew and Moira waited, watching them with open admiration. Joe was following them with the tankards, pleasing the crowd as he announced a free round of drinks as a prize for their performance.

Alyssa was heavier than he expected, a product of the athletic musculature of her slender frame. She felt hot in his arms but he kept her body close, refusing to surrender their contact until he reached the benches. As he walked he could feel her lips against his throat, soft and warm, whether they were there by chance or deliberation he wasn't sure. His imagination told him she was kissing him there, her tongue darting out to taste the salt on his skin. It had to be his imagination.

The sharp thrill of her teeth on his skin ended his internal debate.

Not yet being sixteen, Gram had had little experience of women, though he had come to accept the youthful urges that came with maturity. He had felt passion before, briefly, when looking at some of the young women of the village, and he had seen it returned more than once, but he had never considered acting on it. His upbringing had taught him not to abuse women of lower station, for that was what it would surely be if he were to tup one of them. He knew well that he could only marry a woman of the proper class and dalliances with others would be a cruelty and something that could leave him with bastards.

But Alyssa was no commoner, and she was fully knowledgeable of his circumstances, as well as her own.

Lust rose in him like a raging beast, a force more powerful than he had ever imagined it could be, blotting out all other thoughts. He lowered her gently to her seat with hands that were barely restrained from doing far more, his eyes roving to places where he dared not allow his hands to wander. She returned the look with such avidity it might have been scandalous if someone had seen it, her tongue darting out to moisten her lips.

That almost sent him beyond reason. He was leaning close, not having straightened back up yet, and for a moment he felt the urge to kiss her. To press her back against the table and…

"…Gram!" said Matthew again. "Are you going deaf?"

He glanced at his friend with a combination of guilt and annoyance. "Sorry, what?"

Matthew held up the tankards that Joe McDaniel's had passed to him. "Take these, I'm not going to hold them forever."

Moira glanced at her brother before rolling her eyes, amazed at his obliviousness. "You two were amazing out there!" she said to return the air to normal.

Gram nodded as Alyssa replied, "Thank you."

Taking the heavy flagon from Matthew he lifted it and began to pour it down his throat, as if the cool ale could satisfy the intensity of his thirst. His eyes never left Alyssa, though. She was sipping her own tankard and making small talk already, but her gaze returned to him frequently. Eventually she brought the conversation back to him.

"Are you enjoying the festival, milord?" she asked Gram, her features taunting him.

"I doubt I have ever known a better one," he responded.

Robert Lethy came by then, smiling to congratulate them. "I thought my heart was going to burst from my chest!" he announced. "I don't know how you managed to keep going for so long!"

Daisy was still beside him, looking friendly, but her expression hid a mild jealousy. She had never expected to lose her best dance partner, or to be bested by a newcomer. "You dance very well, Lady Alyssa. Your endurance is hard to credit."

"Thank you. I owe some of it to the strength and ardor of my partner..." she answered before giving Gram a very direct look, "...but the women of my family are known for their stamina."

Daisy's cheeks colored at the barely veiled message, but Robert laughed. Perry walked up beside him, swaying slightly. He had taken one too many cups while watching the two of them dance. "Perhaps the lady would give me the pleasure of a dance now that the music has slowed to a pace better suited for us poor mortals," said the captain's son.

He attempted to sound charming, but his words came off as slightly petulant.

"I have hardly rested but I believe I could manage," Alyssa responded. She held out her hand and let him pull her to her feet.

Gram glared daggers at him, but held his tongue, and then Moira jumped in to distract him. "I wouldn't mind a quick sorte onto the dance battlefield myself," she complained before coughing to get his attention.

He took the hint and led her out to dance. The music was slow now, a stately pavan and though Moira was an excellent dancer his attention followed Alyssa as she turned and danced with Perry.

"I don't think you have anything to worry about," Moira told him reassuringly.

"What do you mean?"

She gave him a knowing smile, "I thought at first she might fancy Perry, but she's been watching you since the day she came. Even when he took her for walks she was always looking around, trying to spot you."

"He took her for walks?"

Moira nodded, "He's been courting her since she arrived, and until tonight you didn't show any sign of interest."

Moira was almost like a sister to him, so he didn't bother trying to deny his feelings, instead he asked, "If he's been courting her for that long then it sounds as though I *should* worry."

She shook her head, "If your mother had seen the look she gave you when you were sitting down a moment ago, she would have had her locked in the dungeon."

"We don't have a dungeon."

"Lady Rose would have had one 'specially made," said Moira primly.

He laughed, his head feeling lighter from the ale. The dance was ending so he let go of her hands. "I'll see if I can give mother something to *really* worry about."

Moira winked at him as she retired to the benches and Gram tapped Perry on the shoulder.

"Mind if I have the next dance?" he asked.

Alyssa smiled at him, but Perry was less than pleased. "You've had her to yourself for long enough, let someone else have a turn," he replied, slurring the words slightly.

"I think the lady can decide that for herself," said Gram, a menacing note in his voice.

Perry released her, adrenaline causing him to sober. He faced Gram as his face began to turn crimson. "Are you trying to test me, pretty boy?"

A red demon rose in Gram's chest, filling him with rage but before he could respond Perry stumbled. The captain's son stepped back, trying to regain his balance but Alyssa caught his arm. Though she tried to help him he lost complete control and fell to the ground. Unfortunately he twisted as went and rather than landing on his rear Perry fell awkwardly on his shoulder. His arm made an audible 'pop' as it came out its socket and the young man screamed in pain.

Gram watched him fall, first with amusement and then puzzlement. While it might have looked to most observers as if the other man had simply taken a drunken tumble, he had seen otherwise. Perry had lifted his foot, about to advance, when Alyssa had tapped the sole of his boot with her toe, making him think he had stepped on something. When he had stumbled her 'assistance' had served not only to ensure he lost his balance, but to twist his arm into the position that had resulted in his injury.

No one else seemed to have realized the truth, though, including Perry.

"Someone help him," called Alyssa, soliciting the aid of several men from the crowd. "I think he may have had too much to drink," she suggested. Robert Lethy organized them and soon they were escorting poor Perry home.

After they had left, she looked at Gram. "I believe you wanted another dance?"

"I think I did," said Gram, giving her a shallow bow. Taking one of her hands in his he placed his other on her waist, guiding her into the start of a graceful waltz. "I saw what you did," he said quietly.

"Really?"

"Really."

"And what did you think?"

"Most impressive," he said, studying her face. There was confidence there, residing alongside something else—desire.

"I can be very direct when I decide on something," she told him, "and things were about to get out of hand anyway. I think things ended better this way."

"And you decided you really wanted a dance?" suggested Gram, slipping his hand farther down than was strictly within the bounds of propriety and pulling her close.

"Perhaps," she replied, sliding the hand on his shoulder closer, to stroke the side of his neck with her fingers.

Chapter 18

Gram lay awake that night, staring at the ceiling of his room. Despite rising early and having a long day he couldn't rest. He had danced until his legs had turned to jelly. So much so that he had felt certain he would collapse upon reaching his bed, but once there he couldn't relax. His mind was filled with visions of the woman he spent the evening dancing with.

He would start to drift, and then the memory of her scent came to him, a glimpse of her hair, or her smoldering eyes. The thoughts were so pervasive he began to consider getting out of bed altogether. It was obvious he couldn't sleep.

The knock on the outer door was so faint he thought for a second he had imagined it. Then it came again and he leapt from the bed. *Surely not!* he thought, hurrying to the front room that held the outer door.

Before he reached the door he remembered his nakedness and quickly darted back to his room to slip a long nightshirt over his head. Unable to delay any longer he ran back to the door and opened it quickly.

She stood close to the door, illuminated only by the magical globes that, at this hour, gave only a mild light to prevent people from stumbling in the dark. Without a word he stood aside and let her in, never questioning her reason for appearing so late.

Alyssa held a long cloak around herself, clutching it close to her neck, but she opened it to embrace him as soon as he had closed the door. Beneath it she wore only a thin nightgown, erasing any doubts he might have had about her intentions.

They came together in a desperate rush, and Gram could think of nothing else for the next few minutes, nothing besides her warm lips and burning hands. His heart was pounding and his body burned with feverish heat as he gripped her waist and lifted her, her legs twining around him. Their lips never parted as he walked her to his room.

She drew back, breathless as she stared down into his eyes, and then he tossed her lightly onto the bed he had vacated moments ago. He paused, wondering at his own audacity, but she couldn't wait. Reaching up, she took the collar of his nightshirt and pulled him down, uttering only a single word, "Please…"

He destroyed his shirt before he could get out of it and her nightgown nearly suffered a similar fate, but she solved the problem by simply pulling it up and then sliding her arms free, until the garment covered little more than it would if it had been a sash.

It was the first time he had lain with a woman, but his body knew the basics, and when he stumbled for a moment her hands guided him the rest of the way, urging him on.

Within a short span of minutes he grew close to the conclusion he so desperately needed.

"Wait, Gram!" she said insistently. "Stop, not yet." She used her hands to push his hips away.

"By all the dead gods, please tell me you're not serious," he pleaded, a pained expression on his face.

She smiled, the moonlight from the window showing him pearly teeth. "Are you so eager for children then?"

"Not particularly," he moaned, "but at present I am more than willing to take the risk."

Alyssa put her finger to his lips, "Let me teach you. There are other ways." And then she shifted, sliding down to do something he had never considered. He froze and then groaned.

"If you do that…" he began, hoping to warn her, but she knew already what she was about.

The world ended, and Gram was reborn. When he returned to his senses he looked at her in amazement. "I never expected that… how did you know…?"

"I have sisters, and the women in my family share their secrets. Are you alright? You seem dazed," she told him with a teasing smile.

He growled and slid his arms beneath her legs before lifting her into the air, eliciting a surprised yelp from her. "What are you doing?" she exclaimed as he placed her back against the wall.

"Finding out if the reverse works as well for you," he answered. He let her cries serve as his guide from there.

Some unknown time later they rested, gazing at one another in the dim light from the window. "I didn't know men did things like that," she said, a curious note in her voice.

"Was it unpleasant?"

"No," she said shaking her head, "far from it."

He smiled, kissing her once more, "Are you tired?"

"No," she answered, pulling him closer.

"Neither am I."
"I can already tell."

***

Gram was wide awake as the sun dawned over Cameron Castle. Paradoxically, he felt full of energy, even though he hadn't slept.

As the night had drawn to a close and morning approached, he and Alyssa had finally ended their tryst, not because they were ready to, but for fear of discovery. He had ventured out and scouted the halls to make sure they were clear before she had made a stealthy retreat back to the room that she was supposed to have slept in.

Since then he had spent the last hour waiting for the sun, eager for breakfast. While he felt little fatigue he knew with some certainty that he would be able to devour whatever fare was brought out for the first meal of the day. In his mind's eye he imagined himself as lord of the castle, pounding the table with his fist, "Bring me a roast boar!"

The idea made him laugh, then he mentally corrected himself, *No make that two roast boars.*

At that point he realized he was grinning like an idiot, over what was arguably a not-very-funny mental image. *That's not really what I'm grinning about, though.* He was grinning because he knew he would see Alyssa at the table shortly.

"Lady Alyssa," he mused aloud, before repeating her name several more times, experimenting with its pronunciation. *I am thoroughly besotted.*

The hour passed with excruciating slowness, but eventually he found himself in the feast hall again, searching the crowd even before he reached his seat. She wasn't there yet, but she appeared soon after he sat down.

As she sat across from him, he couldn't help but notice the dark circles under her eyes, complimented by a mischievous grin. He wondered if he looked as good.

"Good morning, Gram," said Matthew as he sat beside him. "Are you tired?"

"Why!?" he replied, startled at his friend's sharp observation. *It couldn't have been his magical sight could it? No, that's impossible; their real beds are a hundred miles from here.*

Alyssa was giggling at his overreaction as Matthew gave him a strange look before explaining, "Because you danced like a madman for half the night?"

Moira leaned over, "Your eyes do look tired. Did you sleep well?"

"Fitfully," admitted Gram, trying to cover his embarrassment, "but I feel better than ever oddly enough, probably better than I've ever felt in my life." He risked a look at Alyssa as he said the last part.

"Me too," she said, entering the conversation. "I was up and down all night, but I feel very well today somehow."

Conall spoke up then, "What's that smell?"

"I was wondering that too," added Matthew, "but I didn't want to bring it up."

Comprehension slowly dawned on Gram, but he restrained himself before giving in to the urge to sniff his shirt. "I don't smell anything," he told them, feigning disinterest.

"It might be something from the kitchen," suggested Alyssa.

"Not unless they're serving sour milk," declared Conall.

Matthew leaned closer to his friend, "I think it might be you, Gram."

Moira glared at her brother, disapproving, "You have the manners of a goat! You shouldn't call someone out if you think that."

Matthew shrugged, "It's not a big deal. He was sweating a lot last night. A little water should cure it. It's not even that bad of a smell—almost pleasant really."

Alyssa choked momentarily.

"If you like the smell of dog vomit," piped Conall.

"Conall!" That was Moira, furious with her youngest brother now.

Rather than face more scrutiny, Gram lifted his bowl and finished the contents. He wanted more but that could wait. "I'll head to the baths." Alyssa gave him a subdued smile as he left.

***

After a thorough washing he returned to his room. He had considered going in search of Master Grayson, but then he remembered that the hunter had been thoroughly soused the night before. He was unlikely to want to go out. In fact, as the morning wore on

Gram realized he was beginning to suffer from his lack of sleep.

A nap was definitely in order.

He found Alyssa waiting in his room.

Shocked, amazed, and pleasantly surprised, he managed to articulate none of that, letting his hands and lips speak for him instead.

"Aren't you tired?" Alyssa's own eyes were fatigued, but a new fire was kindling in them already.

"I was. Want to take a nap with me?"

Several frantic minutes later she observed, "You don't seem to be napping."

It was an hour before they both were settled enough to finally rest, and then he heard the noon bell ring. He was desperate for sleep, but food was an even greater need at that point. He had only gotten a half bowl of porridge earlier. Sitting up, Gram began to struggle into his clothes.

"You can't honestly be planning to get up." For her own part, Alyssa was quite happy to bury herself deeper into the pillows.

He sat staring into space for a while, attempting to formulate a thought. "I might starve to death. I haven't eaten since yesterday afternoon."

"You had some porridge this morning."

Gram laughed. "That wasn't enough to last me more than a half an hour. Besides, if we both miss the meal someone might get suspicious."

"Bring me something back?"

"I'll try to slip a sausage out for you."

She gasped, giving him a look of mock alarm, "Please Master Thornbear, have mercy on a poor girl!"

He gave an evil laugh as he left.

***

Moira had some questions for him when he got to the table, "Have you seen Alyssa?"

A dozen things ran through his head and he considered his reply. The most important being that if Moira decided to make a serious search, her magical vision would turn up Alyssa's location within a matter of minutes. He had seen both her and her brother do as much before on several occasions. His mind tried to create a plausible fiction, but eventually he gave up.

"I saw her at breakfast."

She nodded. "I thought she'd find me after that, but she went to the bathhouse and then she disappeared."

"Why are you asking me anyway?"

"Well, you two seem to be much closer now," said Moira, giving him a mischievous grin.

He could feel the blood rushing to his face.

"Plus, I've searched the castle with my magesight and couldn't find her," she continued.

Matthew jumped in then, "So you think she's hiding in Gram's room!? And you yell at me for poor manners!"

I'm going to die, thought Gram, his heart pounding. He stared wildly at the two of them, his eyes moving back and forth.

"I never said that!" protested Moira, glaring at her brother, "but you just did, idiot!"

"Why would you think she was in there?" asked Irene.

"Lady Rose had Father install privacy screens," explained her oldest brother.

Irene was still confused. "What's that?" she asked. Gram was wondering the same thing, but he was afraid to ask anything at the moment.

"It's a weak shield to block magesight, like they have at the palace in Albamarl. Gram's grandmother has them around her apartments too. Those are the only two places we can't see into—well, unless we broke the screens, but then Dad would be very cross," said Matthew. "You'll see what I mean when your magesight awakens someday."

"Oh," said Irene.

Gram had been listening to the new information intently. Mother had never told him about having privacy screens, not that he would have cared before the events of the previous evening.

"She probably just went riding," suggested Matthew.

"Yeah," agreed Moira, "but she could have asked me. I would have gone with her."

Putting his head down, Gram focused on his food. He was still ravenous and the best thing he could think to do was to avoid the conversation altogether. A bead of sweat ran down his temple, and he hoped no one would ask him why he was sweating. *If they ask I tell them it's hot in here,* he repeated to himself. He was a terrible liar but he thought that if he worked at it he might manage a simple one if he had the answer ready.

Fortunately, they never asked.

***

"Can I have the day off?"

Cyhan gave him a blank stare before eventually replying, "Why?"

Gram had returned to his room briefly already, but then he had remembered he was supposed to meet his teacher. He had told Alyssa he would try to beg off and then hurried to meet Cyhan.

"I haven't slept in almost a day and a half. I'm half dead." It was easy to be honest with the warrior, since he never asked questions beyond what might be important to the present.

"This is a good opportunity then," said the big man with an evil expression. "You will learn two things today."

His student didn't ask. Gram knew his teacher would explain if he felt it necessary.

This time he did, "One, that a fight never comes when you are ready, and two, that neglecting the proper care of your body is always a poor choice."

By the time Gram returned to the castle that evening his body ached from head to toe. They had fought barehanded, a choice he suspected that his teacher had made solely for the purpose of allowing him better control of how and where he inflicted bruises upon his poor student.

Alyssa wasn't in his room when he returned, so he didn't see her until he went to the great hall for dinner. The look of disappointment on her face when he saw her told him that she had been unhappy with his failure to return, but of course they couldn't talk about it openly at the table. Her expression changed when she saw the state he was in.

His legs trembled as he carefully lowered himself onto his seat, wincing as he discovered a new bruise.

"Are you alright?" asked Alyssa with some concern.

"I took a fall this afternoon."

Matthew stared at him, "Have you been fighting?"

"I just took a fall, that's it," said Gram stubbornly, refusing to look at his friend.

Matthew leaned in, whispering, "I can see your bruises, including the ones your clothing hides. So can my sister. Who did this?"

"It was Perry wasn't it," said Moira angrily, leaning across the table and keeping her voice low. "It's not fair. He trains every day and now he's bullying you just because he likes the same girl that…"

"I said, I took a fall! Leave it alone," growled Gram loudly. Then he lowered his voice, noting the curious stares from the adults farther down the table, "No one is bullying me."

"We can't help you if you don't talk to us," said Moira, her eyes were growing moist.

Alyssa was afraid Moira might make a scene, so she intervened. "Let him be. He's a man. He'll tell us if he wants our help."

Matthew clapped him on the shoulder, sending another sharp pain through him. "Just say the word and I'll make them pay dearly."

"I don't want, or need, protecting!" Gram was angry now, though he felt a certain pride in what Alyssa had just said.

The table fell silent after that, for which Gram was grateful. When he was finished he returned to his room, wasting no time in finding his bed. He slept as the dead, falling into blackness unsullied by dreams.

He awoke hours later, confused and wondering at the time. A warm body slid close and he felt Alyssa's arm move across his chest. "How?"

"You left the door unlatched."

With one hand he drew a lock of her hair across his lips, enjoying the scent. "A wise move it seems."

"You should rest more."

"What time is it?"

"Midnight. I waited until I was sure the twins had gone home before sneaking in," she explained.

"Then I've had enough rest."

She didn't protest as he made his meaning clear. Neither of them slept after that.

Chapter 19

The next two weeks were the happiest of his life as Gram fell into a new routine. Most mornings he spent with Chad, learning to track or improving his archery, the afternoons were spent with Cyhan, and he would sleep immediately after the evening meal.

The nights belonged to Alyssa.

She would wait until most were asleep before padding quietly to his door, moving like a ghost. He made sure it was never locked or barred, and once she was inside the next five hours were theirs alone; a quiet paradise of darkness and soft kisses.

Only a few days remained before the formal Winter Ball. Lady Alyssa was rising reluctantly from the bed to dress while he watched appreciatively. She had taken to bringing a simple dress with her, so that if she did encounter someone in the hall during her return it wouldn't seem quite so suspicious. She kept an extra in his wardrobe as well.

She looked at Gram, a speculative expression on her face, "How far do you suppose the wizard's special vision lets them see?"

"Worried one of the twins might wake up before you sneak back one morning?" asked Gram.

"No, I was listening when they told you about your mother's special privacy screens. Besides, their actual beds are far from here. Aren't they?"

He levered himself up on his elbows. "How did you know that?"

"Moira mentioned it once," she answered. "I had already noticed that their supposed apartments seemed rather stagnant and unused."

That surprised him. The Illeniels were exceedingly cautious about letting that information out. Before the Count's final battle with Mal'goroth no one had known, aside from a very few close friends and confidants. Even afterward, the people who had taken refuge through their magical portal were never told where the Illeniel family's true home was located and they had been strongly discouraged from ever discussing the matter.

Being a foreigner he had assumed she would be ignorant of the matter, and Moira of all people would know better than to answer that question.

Then again, they have become close friends, he decided.

"I probably shouldn't have said anything," she said, interrupting his thoughts.

He blinked, "No, it's fine. It's just something we aren't supposed to talk about."

"Oh," she replied, somewhat startled. "I'm sorry. I didn't mean to pry."

"Don't worry," he reassured her. "I know you didn't."

"You don't have to tell me about it. I know you trust me already."

In fact he hadn't intended to go any further with the conversation, but now that she had said that, he felt an impulse to show her just how much he *did* trust her. "It's over a hundred miles to the west of here, close to the source of the Glenmae River, in the Elentirs."

She frowned. "I just told you not to tell me."

He grabbed her arm, pulling her back down onto the bed so he could lean over and kiss her. "I know. I just wanted to make sure you realized, just how much I trust you."

Her eyes began to grow wet.

"I love you, Alyssa."

"Stop, you shouldn't say that. You hardly know me," she protested.

He looked deep into her eyes, until it felt as if he was seeing beyond them, into her soul. There was pain there, a deeper hurt that he couldn't understand, but he felt it nonetheless. He could also see the desperate need that she kept so well hidden, the need for him.

"I know you well enough, Alyssa Conradt. I can see the depth of you, your quiet strength and your secret vulnerability. Someday you will explain them to me, but for now, it's enough that I love you, completely and unreservedly, and not just because you're the first woman I have ever lain with."

The words caused her eyes to fill, and tears began to spill onto her cheeks. "I knew you were a virgin, but you have yet to ask me…"

"Ask what?"

"About my lack—in that regard."

He had noticed the lack of blood after their first night together, but had decided it was none of his concern. His grandmother had once told him her own story, something she had never even told his father. He was not fool enough to think that a maidenhead, or lack thereof, indicated worth or value. "So long as you love only me, I care not for what came before."

"Stop. No—I don't deserve this. I'm not worthy of your love." Her quiet tears became sobs.

"Why are you crying?" He was utterly confused.

"Because I *do* love you, and I shouldn't!" She was clutching him now, with all the strength in her arms. "I've never felt like this before, not for anyone."

"That's good," he said, smiling and stroking her hair. "Because once Mother returns, I'd like to introduce you to her. And then I'll petition your father for your hand in marriage…if you're willing."

"No, Gram! No, no, no, no, no… you can't do that. You don't understand."

"I understand love, and you're the only one for me. How complicated can it be?"

She pushed him away, putting some space between them. "I was raped. Do you understand now?"

He felt an instant of rage, but there was no proper target for his anger, so he suppressed it. "Who did that to you?"

"One of my father's friends, a trusted retainer," she admitted. "He threatened me if I were to tell, and I already knew my future would be ruined."

"He's never been punished?"

She shook her head, "No. I never told. He came to my room more than once."

The fire within Gram's heart was threatening to become an inferno. "When was this?"

"I was twelve, and he plagued me until I was almost fourteen."

"Where is he now?"

"Dead."

"You said he wasn't punished."

She had withdrawn further, standing across the room from him now, close to the door. "It was a freak accident, a fall from a horse."

"His death should have been far more painful."

Alyssa started to leave.

"Where are you going?"

"Away."

He leapt up from the bed, crossing the room to bar her path. "Why?"

"What do you mean why? You can't love me, Gram. I'm not fit for you. Your mother will understand that, even if you're too thick-headed to admit it. The last few weeks should have already shown you the truth. I might as well be a whore, except I'm too wanton to ask for payment."

"Shut up," he told her gently. "My grandmother was a whore, and I know full well that you aren't one. Not only that, but I love my gran very much, just as my grandfather did. Don't blame yourself for what someone else did to you."

Her eyes were wide. "Your grandmother was... what?!"

He took a few minutes to tell her the story of his grandmother and the man he had been named after, including her near-tragic attempt to assassinate his grandfather.

"That's an incredible story," she admitted when he had finished.

"Then you should understand. I am a Thornbear. Nothing will stop my love for you, and you will only do us both harm if you attempt to forestall it." He lifted her chin with his fingers, and when he lowered his lips to hers, she returned his kiss.

"I want to believe you."

"You should know by now, it's nearly impossible for me to lie successfully," he told her.

She nodded, unable to speak, her throat closed. "Mmhmm."

Some women were ugly when they cried, but Gram couldn't help but find her beautiful. "Will you marry me, Alyssa?"

"Your mother will never allow that."

"Yes she will."

"No she won't."

"Fine. If she approves and your father consents, will you marry me?"

"It will never happen."

"Let me worry about that. If they do, will you?"

She dried her cheeks with her sleeve, but the tears kept falling. "Yes," she said at last. "Now stop asking me." Then she ducked around him, beating a hasty retreat to the outer door. She was gone before he could recover. In her haste she failed to notice the button eyes watching her from the end of the hall.

Gram was left with a feeling of triumph and sorrow. He still couldn't understand her reluctance, but he was determined. He would overcome any obstacle to ensure their happiness.

***

"What?" asked Chad.

"Why don't you show me how you shot so fast that day?"

"What day?"

"The day we got in the fight."

Chad sighed, "That ain't somethin' to be teachin' ye."

"Why not?"

"Cuz it will just ruin you. Ye have a fine eye and a steady hand with the bow but ye're not goin' to be that sort of bowman."

Gram stared at him curiously, waiting for a better explanation.

"Listen, you ain't got the time fer it. I know ye're wantin' to be a knight and ye're already a noble. That sort of shootin' requires devotion. Ye can't just learn it an then remember it a year later when ye want. It takes daily practice to maintain. It's just like rangin' marks for battlefield archers."

That was something he had shown Gram, along with an explanation of why it wasn't something he should bother practicing. He had set up targets across a field, marking distances from fifty yards out to as far as two hundred. The hunter hadn't hit the distant targets, but his arrows had come close as he launched them in parabolic arcs. He was able to switch to any given range and adjust his shot to drop the arrow within feet of it, if not directly on the target.

Gram's shots had been far more random in how close they arrived. The smallest change in the angle of the shot could alter the distance the arrow traveled by fifty yards or more.

The archer had explained that for professional archers, 'ranging' was one of the most important types of practice, for it allowed them to shoot with their peers and drop volleys of arrows at the correct distance to hit oncoming troops.

"But it's also something you have to practice every week. Your body changes, yer bow changes, and ye have to stay in tune with 'em to maintain the ability to properly range yer shot. Stick to close target shooting, forty yards or less. Those skills keep much longer."

The idea that some skills required constant practice simply to maintain them at a functional level, was a new concept to Gram. Apparently it also applied to speed shooting.

"Look," said Chad. "I'll show ye, slowly."

Holding his bow forward with one hand, he reached back and pulled two arrows from the quiver, holding them between his fingers. He put the nock of one to the string, but he held it still without shooting. There was something odd about the position of his hand.

"Your hand is backwards," said Gram, curious.

"Yeh," said the hunter, "and the arrow is on the same side of the bow stave as me hand is."

Ordinarily the shaft would be placed on the opposite side, so that the tension created by the draw would hold it flush against the bow. The way Chad was holding it now made no sense.

"Won't it slip away to the side?"

"Not with my hand reversed, it keeps the tension on it the other way," explained the older man. "I can nock it much faster this way, and after the first draw I can have the second on the string and away so fast ye'll hardly know it was there."

"It seems sort of clumsy, though."

"It is, if ye don't practice it and if ye try it fer anythin' over twenty or thirty yards ye'll just be wastin' yer arrows. Those shots require a steady hand and careful aim. Also if ye get used to shootin' like this, and ye don't keep up your regular practice it can spoil yer form."

"So I shouldn't bother…"

"…Unless ye're planning to devote yer life to the bow it ain't worth it," finished Chad. "Stick to straight shots an' a three finger draw. Engrave that on yer heart and when ye need it, yer body'll know what to do, without gettin' confused."

Thornbear

Chapter 20

A small form caught his attention a few minutes before the noon meal.

"Hello, Grace."

"Can I talk to you for a minute?" asked the bear.

It wasn't her usual casual greeting, so Gram stopped and looked at her curiously. Lifting her, he answered, "Sure."

"In private?"

"It's almost time for lunch."

"It won't take too long, but I don't want anyone to overhear," she said seriously.

He took her outside, to give them some distance from anyone else. "What's wrong?"

"I saw something this morning, by accident, and it has me a little worried."

His body tensed. "What did you see?"

"You know, I don't really sleep. So I was walking…"

"…and?"

"I saw Alyssa leaving your apartment."

"Did you tell anyone?"

She shook her head, "No, but I don't think your mother will be happy if she…"

"It's none of her business!"

"You're her son."

"That doesn't give her leave to control my life," said Gram.

"What if something happens? If you are caught her reputation will be ruined. What if she gets pregnant?"

"I don't care, Grace. I'm going to marry her."

"You hardly know her. What of her parents?"

"They will give us their blessing."

"How do you know that?" she asked him.

"Because they have to, and if they don't…" Gram's face took on a stubborn look, "…they have to."

"But…"

"I love her, Grace. Nothing will keep me from her." He stared at the small bear intently, "Are you going to tell?"

She struggled with the decision for a moment and then at last she responded, "No." *I can't think of anyone to tell that it wouldn't make this worse.*

"Thank you." With that he set her down gently and went back inside. It was time to eat.

***

Matthew wanted to talk to him after the evening meal.

"Will this be quick?" asked Gram.

"You have somewhere to be?" asked his friend, grinning. He knew that neither of them had any obligations.

Yes, I need to get some sleep. If he went to bed as soon as possible he would have at most five or six hours to sleep before midnight. "No," he said with a sigh of resignation. "I'm just tired."

"I just wanted to tell you that the tattoo won't work right now."

"Why not?"

"The sword isn't in the dimensional pocket. I have it out, in my shop. I'm working on the next phase," explained the young wizard.

"Shouldn't it just teleport from wherever?"

"No. Because it isn't teleportation. It's translation. It isn't really moving when you activate the tattoo enchantment, it's translating from the other dimension to this one, so it won't work if it's already in this dimension."

"What happens if I try to do it while it's here?"

Matthew shrugged, "I'm not sure. Maybe nothing, but it might ruin the tattoo, or worse."

"Worse?"

"Imagine your arm being translated into the empty pocket dimension—without you."

Gram swore, "Shit! Every time I think you might be doing the right thing you have to scare me again."

"It's just a hypothetical."

"Well you can keep your hypotheticals!"

"Just don't mess with it until I tell you I've finished," reiterated his friend.

***

That night Gram woke, sensing another figure in the room. Opening his eyes, he saw the slender figure of a woman leaning over the bed. Her hand was outstretched, as she prepared to stroke his brow.

Reaching up, he caught her hand in his own, bringing it to his lips.

"Gram? Are you awake?"

He froze. It was his mother's voice. Eyes wide he stared at the figure, beginning to see the subtle differences. His mother was taller for one, and her hair was piled on top of her head, braided into some mysterious design. Alyssa's would have been loose, falling over her shoulders.

"Mother?"

"I'm back," she told him. "I didn't want to miss the Winter Ball."

His mind was awhirl. "Where's Carissa?"

"In bed," said Rose. "She was tired and I didn't intend on us arriving home so late."

"What time is it?" His heart was pounding in his chest. Alyssa might appear at any moment.

"Only nine," she answered. "I was surprised to find you asleep already."

"I was tired." *There's still time. I have to warn her.*

"I can only imagine what you must have been up to these past months while we were away," said his mother with a smile in her voice. She leaned close to kiss his forehead.

No, you can't, he told himself silently, horrified at the thought of his mother even suggesting it.

"I won't keep you up. I'm going to bed, the unpacking can wait until tomorrow," she added.

He sat up. "Actually, I'm glad you woke me. Matthew wanted to show me something. I only meant to take a quick nap."

"Don't be out long then, sensible people should be finding their beds by now." She straightened up and left the room. Nine was already late for his mother, who normally retired shortly after eight each evening.

Gram rose and dressed quickly in a loose tunic and trousers and then added a pair of soft cloth shoes. Heading to the front room he slipped out the door and into the hall. He passed two servers before rounding the corner to find Grace waiting for him near the door to Alyssa's rooms.

"Going somewhere?" she asked.

"I don't have time to talk," said Gram, preparing to knock.

"Don't," warned Grace. "Moira's inside. Keep walking before she wonders why you've stopped outside the door."

He reacted instantly, dropping his arm and moving on. Grace followed him. He scooped her up as he walked. "I need to warn her…"

"…that your mother is home?" said Grace, finishing his sentence for him. "Moira's done that already."

"She knows? You said you wouldn't tell anyone!" he hissed.

"I didn't. She doesn't. And may I add, how rude! You libidinous paramour, do you think me so unreliable?" said Grace, reacting with umbrage.

"Libidinny…what?"

The bear had her paws on her hips, "Would you prefer 'oversexed suitor'?"

Gram gaped at her for a moment. "You have to stop reading those books."

"That is not an appropriate response."

He blew out a lungful of air, "I'm sorry. I should not have doubted you."

"Apology accepted, my lascivious libertine. Perhaps there is hope for you yet."

"You have a plan?"

"I meant for your manners," said Grace. "You don't need to worry about the other. Moira has already told her about your mother's return."

"But you just said…"

"Don't be dense," replied Grace, exasperated. "It's news, women talk."

"Oh." A sense of relief washed over him. "Do you think she noticed me outside the room?"

"Definitely. Her magesight is very keen and you were only twenty feet from them so she most certainly not only noticed your presence but knew your identity."

He groaned.

"Relax. She most likely thought you came to confess your undying affection for Lady Alyssa."

"But I didn't."

"Because you lost your nerve," she patted his cheek. "Such a shy boy."

He gave the bear on his shoulder a sour look. "That's ridiculous. Why would she believe something like that?"

"Because she reads the same books I do."

"People don't really do things like that, though," insisted Gram.

Grace put one paw over her eyes. "It might surprise you to learn this, my scandalous swain, but many people do express their endearments for one another *before* taking off their clothes."

He colored at that, but held his peace. Gram's face took on a look of concentration.

"What are you…" she started to ask.

"Wait," he said, holding up one hand. "Give me a minute."

"For what?"

"I'm working on a response."

She waited patiently while he thought. Eventually he responded, "That was unfair, you—truculent teddy."

Grace chuckled, "That was terrible. I am neither of those things. If you're going to give me a name with a "t", for the sake of alliteration, then at least use a girl's name, something like "Tamarah", or perhaps "Tiffany". I will never be a "Teddy". Where did you get the word truculent from anyway?"

"Despite your low opinion of my wits, I do have an excellent vocabulary," he replied. "Remember who my mother is."

"*You* should have remembered that before you let that minx into your bed," observed Grace pointedly.

***

The next morning Gram's mother was already up, sipping her tea when he left his room. She studied his face as he entered.

"What happened to your face?" Setting the tea aside, she rose and examined him. "What terrible scars. How did this happen?"

He was forced to relate the story, though he omitted all of the questionable details. Carissa joined them before he had finished and he had to begin again. Neither of them were happy by the time he had finished.

"Why didn't you let the Count heal you?" asked Rose. "He might have kept the scarring to a minimum."

"Grandmother said the stitches were very well done."

"That isn't an answer, Son."

"Not many fight a panther barehanded and survive," he told her.

"Youthful vanity?" exclaimed Rose. "You thought a good story was worth being disfigured?"

He sighed, "I'm not disfigured, Mother." The scars made three rough lines across his face, marking his cheek, with one of them scoring a line through his eyebrow.

She threw up her hands, a dramatic gesture she would never have made if they had been in public. "Just like your father! Sometimes I wonder if you got anything from me at all."

Chapter 21

Two days had passed, and Gram was going quietly insane. He had stopped going out with Chad Grayson in the mornings, mostly because he was hoping to see Alyssa. He haunted the halls and corridors of Castle Cameron hoping to run into her, but his luck had abandoned him. She hadn't shown up for meals in the great hall. Claiming a sudden illness, she had Moira bringing food to her in her room.

"Why are you so interested?" Moira asked him after he pestered her for what was probably the fifth time, hoping for information about Alyssa.

"I just want to make sure she's alright," he said defensively.

She gave him a sly smile. "I'll just bet you do."

"Is she sick or not?"

"She isn't feeling well," affirmed Moira, "but I have it on good authority that she will be present at the ball tonight."

"So, she's just pretending to be sick."

"Where is your couth?" She frowned at him.

"I just don't understand why she's gone into hiding."

She sighed. "Maybe she's nervous about meeting your mother."

Gram was stricken with panic, "She said that?!"

"No, but your reaction is telling."

His mouth gaped, closed, and then fell open once more.

"Ordinarily you would have said, 'Why is she nervous?', or something like that, but your immediate acceptance, coupled with shock and fear…," she let her statement trail off, staring at him. Then she smiled, "Congratulations, you sly devil. And she never gave me the faintest hint either! I should have known, though, she's been giving Perry nary a glance since the Winter's Dawn Festival."

"By all the dead gods, someone save me from women!" he swore.

"I won't tell anyone," she whispered. "Have you kissed her yet?"

Gram choked, but Grace joined them then and took pity on him. "Shame on you, Moira! You know a true gentleman would never discuss such things."

Moira focused on her small companion, "Ooh! I should have known! You were in on it weren't you? How dare you hide things from me!"

"Run Gram!" cried Grace, pretending to struggle as her creator snatched her up. "I can't hold her for long. Save yourself!"

"Shhh!" ordered Moira. "You're making a scene."

Gram took the bear at her word, though, and beat a hasty retreat, escaping before Moira could ask him any more questions.

***

"What do you think?"

"About what?" said Gram, teasing. He already knew exactly what his sister was referring to.

Her blue eyes widened, "The dress!"

He gave her an astonished glance, as if he had just seen her for the first time. She was clad in a light blue gown with long sleeves decorated by white embroidery. Her hair had been elaborately braided by their mother's expert hands and it was ornamented with a delicate silver tiara featuring a brilliant topaz. She looked every inch her mother's daughter.

"Aren't you too young for the ball?"

"You know very well that I turned ten last month," she chided.

He had not forgotten. "My, my!" he exclaimed. "Ten, now… please forgive your poor brother. It pains me to remember my dear sister's ever advancing maturity."

"You will have to work harder. I can't take care of you forever," she told him seriously. "One day soon I will be a married woman, and you will be left to fend for yourself."

"Never!" he protested. "I will defend your honor so vigorously that none will dare to court my sweet little sister."

"Poor Brother," she said, pityingly. "You'll never find a wife if you dote on your sister too much."

He laughed, "You really think I'm helpless don't you?"

"With girls—yes, but don't worry, someday I will find a good one for you." She paused. "But only after I'm married, of course."

I might surprise you, he thought, but he kept it to himself. "Do you need help with the laces?" he asked, knowing that was what she was waiting for.

She nodded, "Mother's working on her hair."

He helped her lace the sleeves. "This will be your first ball."

"Do I look too young?"

Forever, he thought sadly. *You'll never be old enough to me.* But he didn't tell her that. Instead he reassured her, "You look very much a lady now."

"Will anyone want to dance with me?" Behind the mature façade his sister was secretly nervous and uncertain.

"They had better!" he growled, making a fist. She giggled and then he added, "Of course, then I'll have to beat up the ones that ask."

"Then you'll have to beat them all up," she countered rationally, "those that ask and those that don't!"

He looked at the ceiling and struck a dramatic pose, "It's a heavy curse our father has left to me."

"Do you think he would be proud of me?" she asked. The topic of their father was one of great curiosity for his sister. She was too young to remember him, or to suffer the same sadness that he and their mother did. He was careful never to let her see how painful such questions were, though, for fear she might stop asking.

"He would," was as much as he could say before his throat closed, so he hugged her to cover his reaction.

Rose entered then, pretending she had no just been listening. "Are you both ready?"

They nodded and together they left, but not before her sharp eyes noted the small piece of ribbon that had fallen between the bed and Gram's bedside table. It wasn't a color that she remembered her daughter having worn before, but she pushed the information to one side, like so many other things, to be considered at another time.

***

The great hall had been transformed for the ball. Gone were the massive trestle tables from the center area. Some had been kept, to provide a place for drinks and small treats, but the majority had been removed. The elevated area that normally held the high table had been converted into a stage where the musicians had set up their instruments, and the air was already filled with light music.

People mingled in small groups around the room. Some of them were not even nobility; the Countess made a point of inviting some of the more prosperous citizens of Washbrook. Roland, the Duke of Lancaster was present, along with his wife, Melanie they had brought with them number of important members of their household as well. The Baron of Arundel, Walter Prathion was there as well, with his wife, Rebecca and both of their grown children, George and Elaine.

There were a few from Malvern and Trent, along with visitors from Surencia, in Gododdin, but none of them interested Gram in the least. His eyes scanned the crowd with only one goal.

Where is she?

"Take your sister around for introductions," said Rose. "I need to say hello to the duchess." By 'duchess' she was referring to Roland's wife Melanie, who was already deeply engaged in conversation with Penelope Illeniel. Like the Countess, Melanie Lancaster had come from common stock, so she naturally gravitated to Penny for advice in social settings.

Gram did as he was told, leading Carissa to meet various personages. She already knew those from Cameron and the town of Washbrook, but she was a newcomer to some of the nobility.

"This is Lord Eric, son of the Count of Malvern," said Gram, introducing her to a young nobleman close to his own age. "May I present my sister Carissa?"

The Count himself was in poor health, but his son had taken over handling the affairs of Malvern. Given his age and unmarried status he was expected to attend every possible social event in Lothion. He greeted the two of them amiably, having been acquainted with Gram years before. Gram felt a certain kinship to Eric, primarily due to the similarity in their ages and the expectations that would someday fall to them.

"A pleasure to meet you young lady," returned Eric, bowing to the young girl with a flourish and hovering over her hand for an instant without quite touching his lips to her skin.

"Charmed," said Carissa.

"And this fine gentleman beside him is Lord Stephen Balistair," continued Gram, introducing the Earl. It was a mark of his loyalty to Lothion that Stephen Balistair had taken up the cause against the usurper during the Duke of Tremont's uprising years before. His father, the previous Earl, had been one of Tremont's supporters until Dorian Thornbear had removed the man's head at the order of Ariadne Lancaster.

Gram had been uncertain whether his sister remembered everything that Rose had taught her regarding each of the guests but she dispelled his doubt when they moved on a few minutes later. "He seems nice," she said, "despite what happened."

Gram nodded, "He stayed loyal throughout. He came with us when we fled the capital."

"And who is this remarkable treasure on your arm?" came a voice from behind.

Turning at once Gram was relieved to finally see Alyssa. Keeping his composure, he answered, "Lady Alyssa, you look lovely this evening. This is my sister, Carissa. Carissa this is Lady Alyssa Conradt, daughter of Baron Conradt, from Gododdin."

"Very nice to meet you," said Carissa.

"I'd like to thank you," responded Alyssa. "I'm told that the seat I've been sitting in is yours."

"Mother put me there originally so I could keep an eye on Gram," teased the young girl. "I hope the task hasn't been too much trouble for you."

Alyssa laughed, "I worried at first. He seemed so depressed when I first sat across from him. I only learned later that it was because he was mourning your absence."

Gram was, as always, amazed at his young sister's ability to charm adults. *She really is growing up to be like Mother.* The musicians began to play for the first dance of the evening, and Lord Eric came over quickly, offering his hand to Carissa.

"Might I prevail upon the lady to grace me with a dance?" asked the young count.

"I'd be delighted," answered Carissa, before glancing at Alyssa. "Would you mind taking charge of my brother for a while? I wouldn't want to abandon him otherwise."

Alyssa smiled, "I will do my best." After the two of them stepped away she looked at Gram. "Your sister is amazing. How old did you say she was?"

"Ten, but you'd never know it to hear her talk."

"She seems very precocious. One wonders that you two are related at all."

"She takes after our mother. I'm sure you'll meet her before long."

"I'm told that your lady mother is a formidable woman," said Alyssa.

"You don't know the half of it yet," he agreed. "Would you care for a trip around the dance floor?"

She held out her hand. "I thought you'd never ask."

The two of them danced, making their way across the floor with graceful steps. For a short time Gram forgot his worries and cares, content merely to follow the music. Alyssa's hand was warm in his and it was a struggle to avoid staring at her too much.

"I've missed you the past few days," he told her. "You had me terribly worried."

"I needed to recover. Our last conversation was unexpected," she replied. Her smile was light, but her eyes still hid a deep pain.

"I meant every word," said Gram.

"Sometimes the world has a way of making our decisions for us, despite our best intentions."

Looking over her shoulder, Gram spotted Perry Draper. He wasn't dancing. He stood along one wall, talking to Moira and Robert Lethy and casting dark glares in Gram's direction.

Alyssa followed Gram's eyes and winced when she realized he was looking at Perry. "I spoke with him a few minutes ago," she began.

"Oh," said Gram neutrally.

"He wasn't happy. I told him that I no longer fancied his company."

"You did before?"

"He tried to woo me when I first arrived, and I was not altogether against the idea initially," she admitted.

She had never spoken of Perry's attempts to court her, but Gram wasn't worried. "That must have been hard. What changed your mind regarding him?"

"I met someone else," she answered, giving Gram a mischievous smile.

"Poor Perry," sympathized Gram. "If I were to fall from such heights I doubt my heart would survive. This new someone must be terribly happy, though."

"He does seem so," she agreed.

The song was ending then, but Gram couldn't bear to part with her for another partner, and so they danced again, and again. Eventually fate intervened and Gram was forced to relinquish her for a while.

"May I cut in?" A hand was on his shoulder.

Stifling his annoyance, Gram looked back, only to find the Count di' Cameron standing there. "Of course, my lord."

Mordecai smiled at him. "Forgive me, Gram. My lady-wife has been beset by a swarm of admirers, and I, set adrift, could not bear to witness your monopoly of dear Lady Alyssa's charms."

Gram ruefully accepted his defeat and moved away, to find his mother waiting there. "Are you enjoying the ball, Mother?"

"Of course," she replied looking at him with one brow raised, "though not as much as some."

"She is a delightful dance partner."

"Then I shall have to meet her. I am told she has shown some interest in you."

"I would not go so far as to speak for her, but I have found considerable joy in her company," Gram admitted, working hard to conceal his anxiety. *She has to like her, she must.*

"She is quite beautiful." observed Rose. "I cannot help but notice her olive complexion, though, an unusual thing from one so far north."

"One of her relatives is from the Southern Desert," explained Gram.

"I thought she bore a faint resemblance to Sir Cyhan," said his mother. "That would make sense then."

The thought surprised Gram, for he had never considered any similarity between the two. She certainly had nothing of Cyhan's rugged features, but there was something in the eyes...

"It must come from John's side," continued Rose. "I've met Marie before, and there was no hint of it in her features."

"Marie?"

"Conradt," said Rose with a nod, "her mother."

His mother knew her mother. *Why am I not surprised?* "You met her mother?"

"When I was younger, yes. She had not married yet. She was from Albamarl originally; her father was a minor knight in service to the Airedales."

"How long ago was this?"

"Twenty years," she said immediately, and then added. "I must seem very old to you."

Twenty years, and she probably remembers every detail. "Do you know much about her father?"

His mother looked at him, her eyes shifting from their gaze on the past to focus on the present. Gram affected a calm appearance as he watched the girl dance, but his stance held a certain tension. He was nervous—and he had just asked a question about the young lady's parentage. "The Conradt Barony is a very old one in Gododdin, but they have come down in the world since the time of King Valerius."

The change in Gram's posture answered her question, so she decided to go easy on her son.

"Still, she would be a suitable match for almost any young man in Lothion," she added.

He relaxed a bit. "Would you like me to introduce you, since she arrived after you left?"

"That's very thoughtful of you."

He waited until the song had finished and then caught her just as Mordecai was taking his leave of her. "Might I borrow you for a while?"

She smiled and took his arm, letting him guide her toward Lady Rose. "I'm nervous."

"Don't be," he told her. "She can smell fear."

Alyssa laughed, "That's terrible. You shouldn't speak of your mother so."

He smoothed his face, but gave her a knowing wink. They were within earshot now. "Mother, it is my pleasure to introduce Lady Alyssa Conradt. Alyssa, this is my mother, Lady Rose Thornbear."

Alyssa curtsied, bowing her head deeply, "Lady Rose, it is an honor to meet you."

Rose stepped closer, returning the gesture before taking both of Alyssa's hands in her own. "Please be at ease. I am happy to make your acquaintance. The Countess and my son have both spoken highly of you."

"They are too kind," demurred Alyssa.

"I think not. I also owe you a debt for your treatment of Gram's injuries. Elise tells me that your needlework is as fine as any she has seen," said Rose.

Alyssa blushed.

"Tell me, how is Marie?"

Alyssa hesitated, taken unaware by the question, "She is well, milady."

"You take after her a bit," added Rose, "but you must favor your father more."

"I didn't realize you knew my mother," admitted Alyssa.

"She never mentioned me?" Rose's eyes were calm, but Gram recognized his mother's expression. She was analyzing her opponent. "I thought I made a bigger impression. Well, no matter, perhaps she didn't realize I lived in Cameron now. You will have to send her my greetings when you return."

"I will indeed, milady," said Alyssa. "Though I may be slightly cross with her for neglecting to tell me about such a good friend."

"Don't worry about it, dear," answered Rose. "Marie was always a little forgetful. I'll tease her about it in my next letter."

"I would be happy to take it with me when I return," offered Alyssa.

"Thank you," said Rose. "Tell me, does your mother still sing? She used to have such a lovely voice."

Why is she doing this? Her words were friendly, but Gram knew his mother was testing her. He fought to control his frustration.

"She does," said Alyssa warily.

"She told me you had an even greater gift," said Rose. "Is that true?"

"I would not be so bold as to call it a gift, Lady Rose," said Alyssa, "but I have some skill in that direction. I am sure I could not compare to my mother."

Gram could sense a change in Alyssa. She had been growing tenser, but at the mention of singing she had relaxed. "I didn't know you sang," he said, breaking in.

"You never asked," she countered, smiling.

"Would you honor us with a song?" suggested Rose.

"I wouldn't want to disrupt the dancing."

"Nonsense," said Rose. "I'll speak to the Countess; everyone would be pleased to hear a new voice. Come with me." And with that she led Alyssa away, heading in the direction of Penelope Illeniel.

Gram was left staring after them. *What just happened? Did we win?* He wasn't certain.

"You really like her don't you?" said Carissa, returning to his side.

He winced, "Is it obvious?"

"If I can tell, then Momma must be scared to death," she replied.

"Scared?" Gram laughed, his mother was only human, but he couldn't imagine her being frightened by any woman. She was more intelligent than anyone he could think of, and high society was her battleground of choice.

"If you get married you might leave," added his sister. "Wouldn't you be scared?"

He hadn't looked at it in that light. Gram looked at his sister again, seeing her in a new light. Not only was she more mature than he would have wished, she was too smart for her own good. *Just like Mother,* he thought. "Are you scared?" he asked her.

She tilted her head up, "Not yet. I think I might like her, but it's too soon to tell. If I decide she's a good match for my brother, *then* I'll be a little scared."

"And if you don't like her?"

"Then you have nothing to worry about." His sister bared her teeth in a most unladylike fashion, her hand curled into a claw. She completed the gesture with a cat-like hiss. "I'm a Thornbear too!"

Gram almost choked then, amused and touched at the same time. "I pity your foes," he said in mock seriousness.

"You wouldn't need to pity them. If they hurt you, I would find them, and they probably wouldn't survive the experience." Carissa patted his hand affectionately.

"You are going to be a real terror someday," he told her.

A hush grew as the Countess took the 'stage' in front of the musicians. "If you will listen closely, Lady Alyssa has graciously accepted a request for a song. Please give her your undivided attention." With that Penelope Illeniel stepped down and Alyssa took her place.

She blinked at the crowd as all eyes turned on her. If she were nervous, it wasn't visible. She smiled and then turned to the musicians, making sure they knew the music for her song. Then she faced the hall once more and waited, letting the music reach the proper point before joining it with her voice.

She was singing a song that Gram had only heard once before, when a talented band of troubadours had stopped at Cameron Castle on their way to Surencia. The musical accompaniment was a delicate piece, primarily played on the harp, but the central theme of the song involved a heavy drum beat, followed by a prolonged silence.

The reason the song was rarely performed was because it required a powerful voice and a range spanning more than three octaves. It was known as the 'Aria Adamant'; a lengthy song that spanned the joy of two lovers and followed them until their tragic deaths in the middle of a war between ancient Dunbar and Gododdin. Some claimed it was based on a historical account, but even the historians knew not whether it had any basis in fact, only that there had been a war.

When she began to sing Gram realized that it didn't matter. Fact or fable, the truth of the two lovers rolled across the still room as her voice took command of the empty space. No one moved, and some even stopped breathing, for fear of missing even the smallest part of the song's opening.

Even her breathing contributed, providing dramatic pauses after long melodic passages. It felt as though every person in the room was in limbo when she stopped, fearful she might not continue—but she did. The war began, and the drums came in, providing a counterpoint to her song. Her voice deepened, dipping lower than Gram thought possible for such a slender woman, only to rise again as the song reached its violent crescendo.

The drums ended and their hearts stopped with them, until her voice returned, rising from the ashes of war like the sun over a long dead battlefield. It brought with it the hope of the lovers, finding one another on the field, to share their last moments, before the tragic end.

As the last notes died away and silence filled the room Gram could hear stifled sobs, but they were quickly drowned out as cheers rose up with loud applause. There were few dry eyes in the room and Alyssa herself appeared to have been moved by the song, her eyes glistening and her brow damp from the effort of her singing.

Chapter 22

It was a few minutes before everyone recovered from the effects of the song, but the musicians began to play again and soon people began to dance. Those that weren't dancing could only speak of her performance and Alyssa was soon being shuttled from one group to the next, accepting their congratulations and casting the occasional apologetic glance in Gram's direction.

He only smiled. He was happier than he could remember ever being.

"What did you think?" he asked his mother when she returned to him.

Rose lifted both brows in honest admiration, "She far outshines her mother's singing."

"Do you like her?" he asked, hopeful.

"I hardly know her," she answered, "but there's no doubting her beauty and talent. I do still have questions, but time will answer them."

Gram had hoped for more, but he knew better than to press.

Rose watched him and then added, "You're smitten aren't you?"

He lowered his eyes, "Hopelessly."

"Then I sincerely hope that she is everything she seems. I won't forgive her if she breaks your heart. Would you be willing to grant your mother a dance?"

He agreed and they stepped out on the floor, mother and son, dancing a slow and stately pavan. It lasted for nearly ten minutes and when it was over Rose kissed his cheek.

"Thank you, Gram," she said then. "I hope you realize how proud I am of you."

"I do, Mother," he answered, embarrassed.

After that he left his sister with their mother and began making his way around the room, hoping to be reunited with Alyssa. He passed close to Perry and Robert Lethy during his journey, and they called out to him.

"She has the voice of a goddess!" enthused Robert. "You are a lucky man, Gram."

"How so?" he asked.

"Don't play dumb! She's had eyes for no one else these past few weeks. Every man in the castle is dying of envy now!" said Robert, punching Perry in the arm. "Isn't that right, Perry?"

Perry's face lit with an angry fire. He answered with a simple, "Yeah."

"I'd better get moving, fellows," said Gram, excusing himself.

Before he could get away, Perry leaned close, "I hope you enjoy your whore. I certainly did."

Gram stopped, feeling as though he had been doused with cold water. His mind replayed the words for him, but he couldn't believe they were real. "What did you say to me?"

"You heard me."

The music was still playing, but Gram could no longer hear it. His vision had narrowed to a dark red tunnel, with only one man at its center, Perry Draper.

"You going to start a scene in the middle of the ball, Gram?" sneered Perry. "Wouldn't Mommy be disappointed in you then?"

"No," he said, barely able to speak. "I'm going to fucking kill you." Taking a step forward he shoved his antagonist so suddenly that Perry flew backward, crashing into Robert before falling to the floor.

He leapt up, swinging at Gram with a wild roundhouse.

A small step and a turn and the blow passed, only the inside of Perry's arm struck Gram's shoulder. Close now, his fist came up, and with his knuckles pointed he rammed them into the soft spot just below his opponent's sternum. Perry folded and collapsed in front of him. Gram followed with a solid kick to the face, regretting for a moment that he wore only soft ball shoes rather than his usual riding boots.

Blood spattered the floor as Perry's nose erupted like a red fountain.

People, men in the main, were closing on him from every direction.

Most fights between young men involve a lot of shouting and posturing, and frequently the combatants wait to be 'held back' by their friends, allowing the situation to be contained without losing face. Gram had no such intention.

Sir Cyhan stood less than ten feet away, but he made no move to interfere.

Robert Lethy put a hand on Gram's shoulder, and immediately found himself flying.

Reaching down Gram pulled Perry back up, and then drove him to the floor again with a powerful downward strike. The squire landed and regained enough sense to begin scrabbling, trying to get some distance between them.

Lord Eric and Lord Stephen were moving forward, but Cyhan cautioned them, "I wouldn't do that if I were you."

They ignored him, and Eric flung himself forward, attempting a flying tackle while Stephen approached from the other side to help catch them both afterward.

Gram stepped forward and spun, driving an elbow into Eric's face and sending him to the floor before continuing into a stomp-kick that ended with Lord Stephen falling backward, clutching his mid-section.

"I warned you," noted Cyhan, but no one was listening.

Gram was advancing on Perry now. The other man had regained his feet and fear was written on his face. Desperate, he drew his feast knife, holding it before him, but Gram was undeterred.

Someone screamed as they saw Gram lunge forward, heedless of the knife, but it missed him. Gram had deflected his opponent's wrist, knocking the knife hand upward as he stepped in close. He slipped his arm into Perry's, folding it at the elbow and forcing his antagonist into a tight arm-lock.

He spun then, twisting the arm around to drive the knife and the hand wielding it into Perry's unprotected stomach.

Or at least he tried to do so.

Cyhan's hand caught his shoulder before his spin started, robbing him of the necessary momentum. "That's enough."

Still enraged, Gram released his opponent and relaxed his knees, dropping a foot before sending a fist at his teacher's stomach.

Cyhan half-stepped to the side and clubbed Gram hard in the side of the head. "I said that's enough!"

Gram stared at him, his face blank and uncomprehending, and then he became aware of himself again. Scrambling to his feet he ducked his head, "Yes, Zaihair."

Mordecai Illeniel arrived then. He glanced at the blood on the floor and then at the mess that Perry's face had become. "Can someone explain to me why you two felt the need to attempt to destroy my peace of mind and ruin a perfectly good ball?"

"I think he broke my ribs," gasped Lord Stephen, trying and failing to rise from where he had fallen.

The Count stared at him blankly for a moment. "They're cracked. Hold still." Leaning over he closed his eyes and placed a hand on Stephen's side. The injured lord began to breathe easier after a moment. "There, that's better, though you're still going to have a nasty bruise. Someone get this man a tankard of ale. Help him up!"

People rushed to obey as Mordecai turned to Lord Eric, but that worthy waved him away.

"It's fine," said Eric, holding one hand to his face. "Just swollen."

Mordecai looked at Gram, who was now red with shame. "Gram, would you like to explain why you tried to rearrange Perry here, as well as why you went so far as to assault my guests?"

Gram stared at the Count, his mind frantically rushing to find an acceptable answer. The truth was impossible. He refused to repeat Perry's lie in front of so many people, or in front of anyone for that matter. It was the sort of lie that would immediately become rumor, and whether there was any truth to it or not would be irrelevant. Just the suggestion would damage her reputation.

His mouth opened but nothing came out, his brain had completely seized up.

Exasperated, Mordecai turned to Perry, "Perhaps you would like to explain what happened that so enraged young Gram here? Or why you felt so threatened that you drew steel in my hall?"

Most of Perry's face was obscured by a large rag, which he was now using to staunch the blood coming from his broken nose. Only his eyes were fully visible, but they were expressive, ranging first to the Count and then back to Gram. He knew the impact his words would have if they were repeated in front of the entire assemblage.

He had wanted to hurt Gram, and by extension Alyssa, but even he didn't want to hurt her that much. Nor did he want to be seen as a jealous, petty, ex-lover that would do something so spiteful. No one would win if he repeated his statement now.

And Gram would probably hunt him down and kill him later; at least that is what his ex-friend's eyes were silently warning him. The past few minutes had taught him a new level of fear for Gram Thornbear.

"It was personal, Your Excellency," answered Perry at last.

Mordecai looked back at Gram, "Is that true?"

He nodded, "Yes, sir."

"The next time the two of you have a 'personal' matter, please refrain from attempting to resolve it in a public space. Your quarrel has not only spoiled the mood of one of my favorite events, but you have physically wounded some of my guests. Do you understand how serious this matter is?"

They both nodded, keeping their eyes down and replying with 'yes sirs'.

"Is your quarrel done?"

Despite his previous rage, Gram's head had cooled considerably and his anger was somewhat mollified by the fact that Perry had refused to divulge his hateful remark to the crowd. He couldn't forgive Perry yet, but he had repaid him for the insult. Still, he waited for the other boy to answer first.

"Yes, milord," said Perry.

"Yes, sir," agreed Gram.

"Captain Draper," barked the Count.

"Yes, my lord!" responded the guard captain, who was now standing close by with several men at arms. The look he was giving his son was one of extreme disappointment.

"Take these two fools and lock them up. I don't want them running loose until I decide what to do with them," said Mordecai.

The captain hesitated.

"What, Captain?"

"Where, my lord? We have no dungeon."

Mordecai smiled, "I know the perfect place."

***

The hours passed slowly beneath the castle. Both Gram and Perry had heard of the Iron Heart Chamber, but neither had ever seen it before. It was the place that Mordecai had once imprisoned Karenth the Just, the now-dead god of justice.

The trip down to it had been frightening enough, for the Count had built the chamber deep beneath the castle. The long trip, down, down, through long narrow corridors of stone, had been disturbing. They could almost feel the weight of all that earth pressing down on their heads and shoulders.

It was a place no man could hope to escape from, should his jailor fail to return with the key. It had been built to hold a god.

"How long do you think the Count will keep us here?" asked Perry after an hour had passed, his voice thick and nasal because of the damage to his nose. It was the first time either of them had spoken since being imprisoned.

Gram only glared at him, refusing to speak to his enemy.

An unknown period of time passed, perhaps an hour, possibly more, when Perry spoke again, "Look, I'm sorry."

"Why?"

Perry looked away, "That wasn't me. It wasn't the me that I wanted to be. It was petty and cruel…"

"No," interrupted Gram. "Why would you try to hurt her? Can you hate someone so much for rejecting you?"

The captain's son struggled with his emotions before answering, "It wasn't so much about her, as it was *you*. I loved her, or I thought I did, but really it was you I wanted to hurt."

"What did I ever do to you?"

"Nothing," said Perry bitterly. "You didn't have to. It was who you were, who you are."

"That's a piss poor reason for being an ass. I thought of you as a friend."

"Yeah, it is, but that's the size of it. My whole life I've been compared to you. When we were little I looked up to you. You were always faster, stronger, quicker, but I thought if I just stayed close enough I could be like you. Then we got older and I realized that I'd never be like you. No matter how hard I worked people would always say, 'He's good, but just imagine, if Gram were allowed to train'."

Gram stared at Perry as though he'd grown a second head. In his wildest dreams he'd never imagined that anyone would be jealous of him. "*You*, were jealous of *me*? You have everything I ever wanted!"

"Such as?"

"You're a squire, someday they'll make a knight of you!"

"So? Someday you'll take your title and they'll dub you a knight as well."

"As a formality, maybe, that's not what I want," argued Gram.

"You're still more popular with the ladies, always were."

"Why did you lie like that? If you wanted to insult me, why bring her into it?"

Perry studied Gram's face, considering his words. The wrong response might result in his death. He already felt a powerful remorse for what he had done, but he couldn't mend things by being truthful now. "Not everyone has your strength, Gram. Deep down, I'm just a weak and pathetic man."

"Just shut up," barked Gram. "I'm sick of your whining. I'm not going to pity you."

"I truly am sorry," said Perry. "If Sir Cyhan doesn't strip me of my duty as his squire I will renounce it myself. I'm not worthy to be a knight."

"Do you want me to bloody your nose again?" threatened Gram.

"I'm being honest."

"Someday they're going to talk about last night, and it'll look pretty damn sad if the man I beat up is some broken has-been," said Gram.

"Huh?" Perry was confused.

"I'm saying you'd better finish what you started. If you want to make this right then you'll damn well make a man of yourself. Become a knight, and make them sing your songs someday."

"And how does that make things better for you, exactly?"

"At the very least, I'll be the man that once beat the shit out of the great Sir Perry. That's enough for me." Gram smiled weakly.

Perry laughed but stopped abruptly as his nose began to bleed again. Tilting his head back he kept the rag against it until it stopped. "It isn't fair," he said after a while.

"What isn't?"

"That I should be trained as a knight while Dorian Thornbear's son is left to waste."

Thornbear

Chapter 23

It was late afternoon the following day when they were finally released. Hungry and thirsty, Gram returned to his family's apartment to face his mother's wrath.

She wasn't there, but his grandmother and sister were waiting for him.

Carissa embraced him immediately, squeezing him tightly within her small arms. "Sorry for making you worry," he told her.

"At least you're thinking along the right lines," commented Elise Thornbear as she watched them.

"Sorry, Nana," said Gram.

"Come here," the older woman told him. She held him at arm's length, examining him visually. "Did you get hurt at all?"

"Only my pride."

"Bah," she replied, "that's no hurt at all then."

"I've let you down."

"If you tell your mother this I'll deny it, but I can't say I'm entirely displeased," admitted the old woman.

Gram was flabbergasted.

"Don't give me that look, child. You're too much like your grandfather."

"Which one?" asked Carissa aloud.

"Both of them!" answered Elise. "Take your pick. Duncan Hightower was almost as big a fool as my husband when he was young."

"What about Father?" said Carissa.

Elise laughed, "My son was a timid boy. He never got into fights."

"Timid?" Gram had certainly never heard his father described like that.

"Yes," sighed Elise. "My son was sweet to a fault. His father thought there was something wrong with him. He never hurt a soul, or even raised his hand to anyone, when he was growing up. Even in training he restrained himself, lest he hurt someone else."

"But…"

She waved her hands, "Yes, yes, I know what you've probably heard. Your father was a great warrior, and the world is sorrier for his loss, but until Devon Tremont tried to kill his best friend, he never laid hands on another in anger."

"And even then it was not Devon who received his first blow," said Rose, standing in the doorway.

Elise was startled, but then she chuckled, "I had forgotten about that."

"What? Forgotten about what, Nana?" asked Carissa.

"It was your mother," said Elise.

Gram stared at her in shock.

"He was about to kill Devon Tremont, but your mother interfered, or so they told me. I wasn't there," explained Elise.

"But it wasn't a hard hit—was it Mother?" said Gram, looking to his mother for reassurance.

"He split my lip, but it wasn't intentional. I surprised him and he caught me with a backhanded swing before he knew it was me," Rose told them. "He felt guilty for that for years after."

"In any case," said Elise, "they'll all be more careful now. It's been time and time enough since people learned to be wary of the Thornbears."

Rose frowned at Elise in disapproval, "May I speak to you privately for a moment?" The two women went into Gram's room and closed the door.

His sister hugged him again before asking, "Why did you do it?"

Gram looked into her trusting blue eyes and felt ashamed, but he tried to hide it with a casual smile. "I told you before the dance, remember?"

"Told me what?"

"That I'd beat anyone that didn't ask you for a dance, as well as anyone that *did* dance with you," he reminded.

Carissa thought about it a moment. In point of fact, Perry had not asked her to dance, while she had danced with both Lord Eric and Lord Stephen. All three of them had been injured during Gram's brawl. She knew he was joking, but she went along with it anyway, patting his hand softly. "I had forgotten!" she exclaimed in mock seriousness. "I shall have to be very careful to whom I show my favor in the future."

Elise stepped out of his bedroom, and Rose called to him. "Gram, come here please." He went inside, and she shut the door behind him.

"You realize that you've shamed the entire family, don't you? This is no laughing matter," lectured his mother.

"I do."

"I've had to apologize to Lord Eric and Lord Stephen, something you will also be doing immediately after we finish here. I will have to send expensive presents to their households to make up for your insult."

"I'm sorry, Mother."

"Would you like to explain what possessed you to attack Captain Draper's son in the middle of a formal ball?" Her voice was calm, but he could sense the anger beneath her calm veneer.

"No, Mother, I won't."

Her eyes flashed, a warning he knew better than to ignore. "Why not?"

"I won't repeat lies, even to mitigate my actions."

"So, you think you're protecting someone. Is that it?"

He gave a faint nod.

"Alyssa came by, hoping to see you," said Rose, changing course. "We had a lovely chat."

His face went pale.

"Don't worry. I said nothing untoward to her. She seemed genuinely concerned for you," she reassured him. "Did she have anything to do with your brawl?"

Gram held perfectly still, afraid to move, or even breathe.

Rose narrowed her eyes, "Perhaps it had something to do with this?" Throwing open the door to his wardrobe she pulled out the plain dress that Alyssa had left there. She held it tightly in one fist, her arm shaking with anger.

"Did you think I wouldn't find out?!" she barked at him. "Did you?!"

He stared back, unable to find the words.

"Answer me!" shouted Rose. Her hand shot out and slapped him, hard.

"Please, Mother, it isn't what you think…"

"Isn't it? Do you realize that I knew before I found this dress? This was just the most blatant evidence. Your every word and action has screamed the truth for all to see." Turning, she snatched up the piece of ribbon from where it lay on the floor. "This isn't your sister's, by the way.

"Who else knows?" she continued. "Was that why you attacked young Master Draper? Had you discovered his previous dilly-dallying's with your leman?"

"That's a lie!" said Gram, raising his voice.

"Ah! There's the rowdy tough who beat a young man so badly he thought you might kill him."

"That isn't how it was," protested Gram.

"That's exactly how it was! Only a bully and a coward would beat a man after he's down. That poor boy never had a chance! You beat him half-to-death to cover your own guilt!" she accused.

"That's not true," said Gram, tears starting in his eyes. Inwardly though, he felt keenly the kernel of truth behind the words. "It wasn't like that."

"Stop thinking with your privates! I didn't raise you to be some randy, lust-addled, half-wit fighting in the streets over some slut!"

"No!" shouted Gram. "Don't you dare speak of Alyssa that way!" He was trembling now.

"Or what?" challenged Rose. "You'll strike me down? Is that how you solve all your problems now?"

"No." Gram clamped his mouth shut, trying to control himself. It felt as though his chest might explode.

Rose watched him, her own face red, and then she took a deep breath. "I'm sorry. I shouldn't have said that," she told him. "I don't think I've ever been so hurt in my life."

"I wasn't trying to hurt you, Mother."

"Well, you did! I've never been so disappointed, no—disgusted. Do you think your father would have wanted you to behave this way?"

"No."

"Who taught you to fight like that?" she asked then, but she spoke again before he could reply. "Never mind, I already know the answer to that. I heard you address Cyhan out there. That's plain enough.

"I'd have the brute strung up for it if I had my way," she muttered. "Unfortunately, that's not an option," she added, talking now to herself before looking at her son once again. "Is that what you want? Do you think that's what your father wants?"

"That doesn't matter," said Gram softly.

"What?"

"I said, 'That doesn't matter'!" he repeated loudly. "I am not Dorian Thornbear and I won't ever be. It isn't his life to live, it's mine! I don't care what you want, or what he wanted. I want to be *me,* Gram Thornbear!" The words sounded blasphemous to his own ears, but he felt them earnestly, down to the bottom of his soul.

Lady Rose Thornbear went still, staring at her son with wide eyes. After a moment it became too much and she turned away to stare out the small narrow window.

Gram watched her, his anger fading to be replaced by an unnamed dread. His mother's shoulders were moving, though no sound came from her. He had said what shouldn't have been said, and now he couldn't take it back.

"Fine," she said, her voice thick with emotion.

"Mother…"

"You're right," she continued in a quiet voice. "It's your life, and I have no right to try and live it for you."

He took a step forward, trying to close the gap, to bridge the distance that was growing between them.

"This is my fault. I've tried too hard to protect you, to keep you from the things that would hurt you. Your father wouldn't have wanted this. He was sick at heart, near the end, but he would have trained you. I chose to interpret his words to suit myself. I didn't want to lose you."

"You won't lose me, Mother."

"I already have," she said in a small voice. "Where is your father? Where are your grandfathers? Have you noticed that all the men in our family are dead?" She rose and left the room, returning only moments later. When Gram saw her face it tore at his heart, her eyes were red and her face streaked with tears. Worse, in her hands she held the replica of Thorn that he and Matthew had hung on her wall.

"This is what killed them," she said. "Every single one of them, my father, your father, your father's father; they all died fighting." She thrust the weapon into his hands. "Take it. It's yours. You'll start training tomorrow."

Gram's cheeks were wet as he took the sword, the sword he had already stolen, though she didn't know it. "I won't die. There are no wars these days…"

"There are always wars," she told him. "Men find ways to make them, for good or ill. One day you will find your own war."

"I won't…"

Rose pressed her finger to his lips. "Hush. I've made up my mind, and I'll say no more, but to give you one piece of wisdom, the knowledge that your father learned before he died. War is death, whether it kills you or not. Kill or be killed, whether you die or whether you slay your enemies by the thousands, it leaves you dead inside. Every life you take will lay a price on your soul, so weigh it carefully. Never pay it unless the gain is worth the loss."

"I will make you proud, Mother."

She seemed to curl in on herself, even as his arms went around her, trying to comfort her. "I am already proud, a proud daughter, a proud widow, and a proud mother. Pride is all I have, and as I enter the autumn of my life it is a poor substitute for family."

They cried together, until she pushed him away. "I'm done," she said then. "No more weeping, if you are to be a knight, then be the best." She left him standing alone.

He heard Carissa's voice in the other room, "Momma, what's wrong?"

His grandmother entered and hugged him. "I told her it would come to this."

"I'm sorry, Nana," he replied. "I think I've broken her heart."

"Shhh," she soothed. "Women's hearts are not so weak as that. She will mend."

Thornbear

Chapter 24

Gram joined the other young men on the training field the next day.

Robert Lethy was the first to greet him when he approached, "Hello Gram."

"I'm sorry, Robert," was all Gram could say.

"It's alright," said Robert, ever forgiving.

Perry simply offered his hand, which Gram shook wordlessly. They had already made their peace.

He had apologized to everyone that had been involved in the incident at the ball, but he had yet to speak to Sir Cyhan directly.

"Gram will be joining us from today onward," announced Cyhan. His announcement elicited curious looks from the others but he ignored them. "Step aside with me for a moment," he added, pointing at Gram.

They walked a short distance apart from the others.

"Please forgive me, Zaihair," said Gram.

"For what?"

"For fighting at the ball, for injuring your squires. I've dishonored your…"

"Shut up," said Cyhan, interrupting him. "You will only address me as 'zaihair' when we train in private. As for apologizing, I will tell you when you must do so."

"But, the other day…?"

"Your fights with other men are none of my concern, boy."

"I was wrong to start a fight in the hall, though," insisted Gram.

"I'm not your father, nor your judge. It's for your mother and the Count to decide the right and wrong of your actions. I only intervened when it was necessary, to prevent you killing that young fool," said Cyhan.

"We've settled our differences."

"Good, you aren't ready to kill yet."

"Begging your pardon, sir, but what?" Gram was thoroughly confused.

"Did you think I stopped you to protect my squire? He made his choice when he insulted you. I would hate to lose him but I'm not here to coddle idiots. I stopped you because it would have set your progress back, or even ruined you. Like your father, you're tender hearted. Killing him would have damaged your resolve, your heart."

"So you wouldn't have cared?"

Cyhan grimaced, "I told you, boy. Most fight with their bodies, some with their minds, and a few, the crazy ones, like you, with their hearts. Killing someone in anger at this stage would have damaged you—here!" He struck Gram's chest with his palm. "When you're ready, when you have defeated yourself, then you can make your own choices about whether or not to kill."

"And you don't care who I kill?"

"I trust you to make your own decisions. I have my own oaths, people I've sworn to obey and protect. If you find yourself at cross-purposes with me, then you have a problem, for I am the one person you will probably never be able to beat."

Gram thought about his words. "Why not?"

"Because I'm your teacher. That's why you folded up when I cuffed you the other day. You're already good enough that you'd be a hard fight—if I was a stranger. Soon you'll be better than that, but raising your hand against the one that taught you is next to impossible. Could you strike your mother?"

"Never!"

"Exactly. And that is why you won't ever be able to beat me, but I'll damn well make sure you're a match for anyone else," said the old knight.

"Is there anyone you can't beat?" asked Gram.

"Not any longer," said Cyhan.

"What about your teacher?"

"He's dead." The knight turned away then, and began walking back to the others.

"What happened to him?"

"No more questions."

***

Gram had another surprise waiting for him when he returned home later in the day.

He was tired, all the way down to his bones. The morning's training had been physically exhausting. Sparring in heavy mail followed by a long run had tested his endurance, and then, after lunch, he had gone to face another session alone with Cyhan. Despite his teacher's assurance that he didn't need to apologize, Cyhan had made certain that Gram didn't walk away without quite a few bruises.

Returning to his family's apartments, he had hoped for a brief rest and perhaps a chance to wash before heading to the great hall. Instead he found that the front room had been rearranged. The smaller table had been removed and a larger one brought in. It appeared to be set for five.

"What's this?" he asked.

"Momma wants to have a private dinner," said Carissa as she finished helping one of the kitchen maids set the table.

They had done as much in the past, but only rarely. Rose preferred to eat amongst her peers. She had often lectured Gram on the importance of being seen, both to maintain social bonds and to reassure those who served them.

"There's a fifth seat," he pointed out. The fourth was likely for their grandmother, but the fifth was a mystery to him.

"We are having a guest," answered his sister, giving him a sly smile.

Rose entered then, carrying a decanter. Setting it on the table she looked at him before making a face and sniffing. "Go clean up, you stink of rust and sweat."

He gathered a fresh tunic and went to do as she asked. When he was returning some half an hour later, he found that his grandmother had just arrived and was standing in the hall. He hurried to open the door for her. "Do you know who is coming for dinner?" he asked.

Elise winked at him, "You'll see in a few minutes."

When the knock came a little later, he rushed to open the door. Alyssa stood outside. "It's you," he said in surprise.

She smiled nervously, "It's me."

"Do come in."

She stepped inside, and Gram ushered her to a seat at the table, while Rose sent the maid to tell the kitchen that they were ready. They all sat then, and Rose nodded to Carissa. She stood and lifting the decanter set out already, began to pour.

"Would you like some wine?" his sister asked their guest.

"Please, thank you."

Gram followed her example and took some as well, his eyes darting back and forth as he watched the women of his family. *What is this all about?* he wondered.

They began to chat then, small talk about the weather and similar nonsense. When the food came a short time later, Gram found himself relieved. Despite his mother's best efforts, he had never learned to enjoy such empty conversations. He was grateful for something to do with his hands.

As they finished their food and the meal came to a close he began to feel a sense of trepidation. His mother was very traditional, and he knew that her true reason for the invitation would soon become clear. Once they had eaten, and only then, would she reveal her purpose.

"I have to thank you for caring for my son in my absence," said Lady Rose after the empty platters were taken away. "In particular for stitching his wounds."

"It was a small thing," replied Alyssa. "Lady Thornbear would have done it if I hadn't been there."

Elise leaned forward, "Even so, it was neatly done. I like a woman that isn't afraid to do what must be done."

"I think he likes having scars," put in Carissa.

They laughed at that, and then Gram spoke, directing his words to Alyssa, "I'd like to apologize for spoiling the ball, especially right after your song."

"Anytime would have been a bad time," said Rose, remonstrating him.

"Did you like my singing?" asked the young woman.

"It was amazing!" enthused Carissa. "You have the loveliest voice."

"Thank you."

"Your talent is rare and exceptional," agreed Rose, "but I have a more important matter to discuss with you. May I speak frankly?"

Alyssa dipped her head respectfully, "I am honored to be invited into your home. Please ask me whatever you wish."

"My son is in love with you."

Gram choked on his wine and began coughing uncontrollably. Everyone ignored him, though. Elise and Carissa were watching his mother and Alyssa with keen eyes.

Alyssa remained still, showing no sign of shock, though she didn't reply immediately. After a minute she blinked and it was then that Gram realized that she had not done so for almost a full minute.

"You'll forgive me for startling you, I hope," added Rose.

"He's completely besotted," agreed Carissa.

Gram glared at his sister, finally finding his voice, "I am not drunk."

"That's not what I mean," said Carissa.

Elise shushed her, putting a hand on the girl's arm, "Let them talk."

"I didn't expect that," admitted Alyssa.

"But you already knew," said Rose. "Don't play coy."

"Yes, Lady Rose."

"Just Rose," answered his mother. "If we're to be family then we can drop the titles."

"Family?! But...," Alyssa had finally lost her composure, she started to rise from her chair but Elise put a hand on her shoulder, pushing her back down.

"Sit down, girl."

Gram had his face in his hands by then, uttering a low groan.

Rose studied the young woman across from her, "Do you love my son?"

Gram opened spread his fingers so that he could see through them, unable to look away. He felt as though he had entered some terrible play, but he desperately wanted to see how it ended, no matter how painful it was to watch. Alyssa's head was down, staring at the table in front of her.

Seeing that, his heart fell. *She can't say it, or maybe she doesn't believe it.*

A small voice caught the silence, "Beyond hope and despite all reason, I do. I love him."

Carissa let out a long sigh; she had been holding her breath. "Whew."

Gram felt much the same, "May I say something?"

Three women and one girl answered as one, "No."

"I cannot marry him, though," announced Alyssa. "My father won't allow it."

"Then why would he foster you out?" asked Elise.

"That was my mother's idea, but Father has other plans for me."

Rose looked at her with one brow raised, "Let me worry about that."

"There's nothing you can do," protested Alyssa.

"I have already sent a letter to your family, requesting permission to visit them in the spring. We can discuss it then."

Alyssa's face showed terror then, and she stood abruptly, "No! You can't do that."

"I can and have. Trust me, girl, I can be very persuasive," said Rose.

Elise chuckled and Carissa moved to stand behind Alyssa, patting her shoulder calmly.

"Don't worry," said Gram's sister. "Momma will fix it. Your father doesn't stand a chance."

Alyssa looked at Gram, a single tear rolling down her cheek, "I do love you."

The others took it as a hopeful sign, but Gram felt a deep sorrow in her gaze. The words meant one thing, but behind them was another message, and it felt like a good-bye. He rose and embraced her, unable to remain at a distance from her any longer.

His mother spoke then, "Also, I must ask that you refrain from sleeping with my son anymore, at least until after we've spoken to your father."

Gram whirled on her, "By all the dead gods! Is there anything you won't say?"

Carissa was pointing at him, one hand over her mouth, "You didn't!"

Elise began to cackle, venting her laughter like an old crone while Alyssa buried her face against Gram's back.

"Yes, ma'am," she said into the space between his shoulders.

Chapter 25

Two days later Gram found himself riding across the fields beyond Washbrook with Alyssa beside him. It was still morning, but just barely. The sun was rising close to its apex for the day, and soon the folks at the castle would be gathering for lunch. The two lovers had other plans, however, and the saddlebags on their mounts were packed for a pleasant picnic.

Gram had already gotten permission from Cyhan to skip his afternoon session and he was looking forward to spending some time alone with Alyssa.

"Not here," she told him when he suggested they stop in a pleasant spot bordering the forest. "Let's find a shady glen." She turned her horse toward the woods.

"Sure," he said agreeably and soon they were picking their way along shady forest lanes. Twenty minutes later they were far from any human habitation, or prying eyes.

They unpacked in a grassy spot, where the trees opened up enough to provide the earth with warm sunshine. Alyssa had brought a large blanket, which she spread on the ground to provide a place for their meal.

The cups and a jug of wine came out first, and Gram poured them each a little.

She drank hers down in a long swallow, making him raise his eyebrows, and then she set it aside, leaning in for a kiss.

He responded in kind, but pulled away a moment later. "We haven't eaten yet."

"That can wait." Her eyes held an unspoken urgency.

"They asked us not to…"

She kissed him again, and he reconsidered his opinion.

It had been some time since they had been alone together, and despite his best intentions, he found himself reaching a conclusion far sooner than he might have liked. He began to pull away, but she held onto him tightly.

"No, don't stop."

"I'm too close," he told her, panting.

She twined her legs around his hips, urging him deeper. "I don't care. I want this."

"But…"

"Just this once," she whispered into his ear. "Just today, please…"

He looked into her eyes, and a growl rose in his throat. Pressing her down he gave free rein to the primal beast within, and soon enough they were both crying out, mad with the passion of youth.

Afterward they ate some of the food she had packed, though there was far too much for the two of them to consume.

"I can't eat all of this," he admitted.

The expression on her face was one of terrible sadness. "I know. I think I overdid it."

"Why the long face?"

She studied the ground, "I can't explain it."

"Try."

"I love you, Gram, but I know this will come to ruin."

"Is your father really that bad?"

A light breeze plucked at her hair. "His intentions are good, but his methods are...," she stopped. "I don't want to talk about it."

He sighed, "I think I can understand that." Leaning over, he brushed his lips across the back of her neck, sending a thrill down her spine.

"This is the last time for us," she said bleakly.

"What does that mean?"

"We can't be together anymore, this is the last time."

He thought about her promise to his mother, the one they had just broken. "I guess you're right. We shouldn't do this anymore. But it's just temporary, until we get your father's permission to wed. How long before you have to be back at the castle?"

"Not until dinner time."

"Then let's make it count for something," he said, and then he used his lips to express himself more directly, kissing her cheek and then tracing her jawline.

Moments later she met them with a hungry ferocity that both surprised and delighted him, and they spent the rest of the afternoon exploring the limits of their strength.

The sun was low on the horizon when they relented at last and began packing the scattered remains of their picnic back into the saddlebags. Alyssa put the food into hers.

"I'll keep this," she said. "I'm going to skip dinner this evening."

Gram was disappointed, "Why?"

"I'm writing a letter to my father. I need some time alone," she answered, though something about her tone rang false with him.

He decided not to press her on the issue and together they rode slowly out of the forest. When they emerged again into the open field she paused, "You go ahead. It's best if they don't see us returning together. Tongues will wag."

"I don't want to leave you alone," said Gram. "What if there's another hungry cat out there?"

She smiled, "I'm on a horse. Even a starving panther wouldn't chance that."

"Are you sure?"

She gave him a fierce expression, "The entire world is my weapon, what have I to fear?"

Gram frowned, *it was the same phrase Cyhan had once told him.* "Where did you hear that?"

Alyssa's eyes widened for a second before relaxing again, "It's something my uncle used to say. Why?"

"I just thought it was interesting. I'll see you in the morning," he replied.

She nodded and they split up there, taking different paths toward the castle. They could still see each other for some time, and he waved at her frequently, but eventually distance and the rolling terrain occluded his sight of her.

***

Morning came, but Alyssa was not at breakfast. He asked Moira about her absence.

She looked at him as if he were mad. "She's in Arundel, remember?"

"No. What are you talking about?" Gram's heart was beating faster.

"You escorted her yesterday."

"No, Moira, I didn't." he replied in alarm.

"I saw you ride out with her," she insisted.

"Why did you think she was going to Arundel?"

"She told me so. She said Elaine invited her to stay with them for a week. Wait! Where are you going?!"

Gram was running for the stables.

There were no grooms present when he got there. They were still eating breakfast, but he didn't need them to tell him that Alyssa's horse wasn't in its stall.

"Dammit, no!" he cursed, before launching into a long line of invective. He went to the tack room while he swore, taking his saddle and carrying it to Pebble. He saddled her, continuing to curse, though eventually he stopped. The mare could sense his agitation.

He rode out without a word to anyone, ignoring the friendly call from one of the gate guards. Pebble could sense his urgency and she picked a fast pace, cantering down the street through Washbrook. Once they had passed beyond the town gate he nudged her sides and she broke into a gallop.

Together, man and horse raced through the open countryside until he found the last place he was sure he had seen her, before she had passed from view. Dismounting, he began to search the area, while Pebble blew loudly, trying to recover her wind. He led the mare behind him while he searched.

The ground was soft, but he found no tracks. Forcing himself to be calm, he left Pebble and began to move in slow circles, working his way outward until at last he spotted a faint half circle impression. *There.* He went back to Pebble, and taking her reins in hand, walked with her to the spot.

He stood there for a while, letting his eyes take in the scenery, trying to get a feel for it. Following a half-day old trace through an open field wouldn't be easy, even when it involved something as heavy as a horse. He found several more tracks before the ground became too hard to have taken a good print.

From there it was half intuition and half experience. *Look for what isn't there.* In places the grass was bent, but he could never be completely sure it wasn't something else that had caused it. He pushed his doubts aside and kept pressing on. At one point he lost sight of any trace of her, but he came to a small stream shortly after. Walking along one side of it, he eventually found the place they had crossed, where deep hoof prints scored the thick mud.

He crossed there and picked up the trail on the other side, but it didn't become any easier after that. He struggled with his patience, knowing that haste would cause him to lose any hope of following her, but all the while in the back of his mind, he knew she was moving ever farther away. He couldn't possibly track her as quickly as she would be moving, even if she chose a casual pace.

The day wore on, but he refused to give up. The horse's path led him into the valley, leaving the road behind and meandering into the lush grass that sloped gently down toward the Glenmae River. Her course made little sense. It didn't lead toward Arundel or Lancaster. In places it circled and it appeared as though the horse had stopped for long periods.

It was late afternoon when he spotted the horse. It was walking slowly, moving in his direction.

Alyssa was nowhere to be seen.

She abandoned the horse.

Despair seized his heart. At some point she had separated from the animal, leaving it to create a false trail for her. "Probably when she crossed the road," he said to himself. Her light feet would have left little sign there, and the horse would have been tempted by the thick grass leading to the river. Otherwise it might have turned back for home sooner, possibly giving her away or raising an alarm when it returned rider-less.

Ignoring the horse he mounted Pebble and urged her into a gallop, riding back to where the trail had crossed the Arundel-Lancaster road. Once there he continued in the direction of Arundel. Alyssa was from Gododdin, and if she had intended to go home, that would be the only direction to take.

He had no hope of tracking her on the hard packed earth of the road, so he rode swiftly, silently, hoping he wouldn't pass some sign of her as he went. He had already lost a lot of time.

Gram followed the road throughout the rest of the afternoon and into the evening. Hoping that she hadn't abandoned the road and taken a cross country route. He would miss her then.

Darkness fell and he resumed walking, leading Pebble behind him. He stayed quiet, and the only sound was that of Pebble's shod hooves striking the dry ground. His only hope was that he might see a light in the darkness, or catch some sound of her if she had made camp.

There was no moon that night, and only the light of the stars served to provide enough illumination for him to keep to the road. He walked on, refusing to give up, and when the sun rose again in the morning, it found him still plodding along, weary and worn. He was past Arundel now, and the road turned north to cross the Glenmae River and enter the mountains on its way to Gododdin.

With the return of the sun he mounted again and rode Pebble at an easy pace. They stopped at the river and he gave the mare some time to drink there before moving on. He reached the mountains before dark and stopped.

This is ridiculous. She was well ahead of him, assuming he had even chosen the correct direction. It was also quite clear that she had planned her disappearance. Her words the day before had been very clear. He just hadn't been listening.

She had even packed extra food to start the journey. There had been enough left to last her a few days if she ate sparingly. In contrast to that, he had no food at all, and Pebble, though willing, had had nothing but a few short minutes to graze throughout the day.

If he wished to pursue her further he would have to graze his horse, or find a farmer willing to spare him some grain. He would also need food.

"There are no farmers in the mountains," he told himself. While he had never made the crossing into

Gododdin he knew that the journey took a day and a half before reaching the lowlands on the farside.

He would have to turn back to get supplies, and that probably meant going to Arundel at the very least.

"Why!?" he shouted, listening to his voice echo back faintly from the rocky hills ahead.

Tired, frustrated, and angry, he turned Pebble around and began the long ride back to Castle Cameron. They plodded through the night, and a few hours after the sun had set he spotted a campfire beside the road.

Suddenly hopeful he hurried forward, but he soon discovered that it wasn't Alyssa. Perry Draper and two guardsmen from Cameron were preparing a late supper. Fire-blind they were startled to see him emerge from the black night.

"Hello," he greeted them.

"No luck eh?" said Perry.

"No."

Perry gave him a sincere look, "I'm sorry, Gram. There's still some hope, though. We sent out several search parties, to Arundel, Lancaster, and even the valley farms."

"That's good," said Gram, but deep down he knew they wouldn't find her. It was quite clear to him that she knew exactly what she was doing, and she was sufficiently skilled to make certain no one would find her.

The entire world is my weapon, what have I to fear? He remembered her words clearly, and looking at Perry he recalled how she had handled him during the festival. She had taken him down with such casual competence, and made it look as if he had fallen.

Her uncle taught her a lot more than just that phrase. He was sure of that.

Chapter 26

They returned to Castle Cameron the next day.

As he had expected, the other search parties had found no sign of her, though her horse was discovered grazing in one of the pastures not far from Washbrook. The sympathetic stares he had to endure upon entering the castle yard were almost more than Gram could take. If anyone had been unaware of his romance with Alyssa, they all knew by now. The story of her flight and Gram's frantic chase were the talk of the castle, and most likely the town as well.

Returning home, he shut himself in his room. It was bad enough facing his mother's stare as he entered, his sister's worried look was more than he could bear. Going to his bookcase, he took out his father's heart-stone and held it tightly. From his window he watched the afternoon sun wane until darkness reclaimed the world.

Slipping out of his clothes he climbed into bed, still holding the red gemstone. In the blackened room he could almost imagine she was there beside him, sleeping perhaps. The pain in his heart was beyond anything he had imagined it could be, like a physical wound. Clutching the stone tightly he buried his face in his pillows, hoping they would muffle any sound he might make.

Alone in the dark no one could hear him cry.

Morning came, unwelcome, bringing with it the misery of a new day. He didn't want to wake. Waking meant facing the future, a future that didn't include

Alyssa. A knock at the door heralded the arrival of his first visitor.

"Go away," he said, raising his voice.

The door opened anyway. His sister entered and closed it behind her.

"I think you misunderstood me."

"I'm sorry," she said, quietly approaching the bed.

"Did mother send you?"

"No. She said you probably wanted to be left alone."

"So she plans to wait a while before telling me what a great fool I am. That's wonderful," he responded bitterly.

"That isn't fair," said Carissa. "None of us are happy about this; we liked her, mother included."

"Doesn't change the fact of my stupidity, though."

"Being smart isn't everything," she told him. "We would probably argue a lot more if you weren't so dumb."

He couldn't help but laugh at that, but the humor brought new tears. "Please go, Carissa. Mother was right, I need to be alone."

"I'll save some food, in case you get hungry later," she said, and then she left.

The rest of his morning was quiet. He finally rose sometime around mid-morning. True to her word he found a tray of cold meat and cheese outside his door. He satisfied his empty stomach with that before returning to sit on the side of his bed.

Another knock interrupted his dark thoughts not long after lunch.

"Go away."

Chapter 26

The door opened, only to be filled by the form of a very large man. Cyhan stood there. "It's time for your training. You missed the morning session."

"I don't feel like it today."

"Ask me if I care."

Gram glared at him. "I'm not in the mood old man."

"Too fucking bad. If you don't like it, you can *try* to take it out on me."

"I know what you're trying to do, and it won't work. I'm not leaving this room today," said Gram stubbornly.

"You ain't got no choice, boy. If you won't get up I'll just beat your ass right here. One way or another, you'll fight," Cyhan stepped into the room, exuding menace.

Gram leapt up from the bed, angrier than he had been since his fight with Perry. The stone was still in his hand and it seemed to pulse in his grip, filling him with a sense of power. He tossed it on the bed and looked at the other man. "Why don't you just try then?"

The old warrior moved forward, and Gram misread his feint. He almost put himself directly in the path of Cyhan's first jab, but he changed directions at the last second, narrowly avoiding the blow. A look of surprise was on his teacher's face as he struck back, hitting the big man hard in the chest, sending him flying backward.

"Not bad," said the old knight and then he moved forward with deliberation.

Gram was surprised by his lucky blow as well, and he felt his mind slipping into the empty space that it always did when they fought. The room turned into a battleground as they moved back and forth.

They were not evenly matched. Today Gram was faster, stronger, and meaner. He was as tall as Cyhan now, and while his frame was not quite as muscular yet, he had all the benefits of youthful speed and endurance. He pressed the big man back, forcing him into a defensive posture.

Within seconds he saw his opening, and moving to one side he caught his teacher off-balance, twisting to throw the older man back toward his bed frame. Cyhan crashed into with a sound like thunder, causing one of the heavy posts to splinter and lean to one side.

Gram turned to press his advantage but Cyhan caught hold of the bed and used it for leverage as he avoided the younger man's sudden kick. Ripping the damaged bedpost free, he slammed it into Gram's back, sending him to the floor.

He lay there, stunned, staring upward at his teacher, and struggling to draw breath. Eventually he got the words out, "That was hardly fair."

"The world is my weapon, boy. Did your friend give you another magical boost?" Cyhan was panting.

"No," said Gram. "I was just mad as hell."

"Mad is good, as long as it doesn't make you stupid," said his teacher, "but that was more than just mad. I've been training you for months now. You were faster than normal today."

Rose looked in on them from the doorway. "I started to call for the guard, but once I saw the two of you, I thought the better of it. We can't afford to lose good men."

Gram stared at his mother. *Was that a joke?* He often had trouble figuring out her dry sense of humor.

Cyhan laughed, still holding the bedpost.

Elise Thornbear looked over Rose's shoulder, "I see he decided to use your favorite weapon, Rose."

Is everyone in the castle in my room today? wondered Gram. "Weapon?"

"Your mother once used a bedpost to brain your grandfather Duncan," said the old woman. "It's a wonder she didn't kill him."

He had never heard *that* story.

"Not now, Elise," said Rose, giving his grandmother an irritated look.

"Actually, I think this would be a perfect time," observed Gram.

Cyhan interrupted, "That will have to wait for later, ladies. This young lion has to finish his training for the day." Dropping the bedpost on the mattress he began ushering Gram out of the room.

"Still?" protested Gram. "I thought we settled that already."

The knight gave him a frightening grin, "Should we have another conversation?"

"I'm moving. No need to make threats."

***

Cyhan focused Gram's training that afternoon primarily on physical exercises and balance, forgoing any further sparring. He never admitted it but when

Gram thought about it later he suspected that it might have been for personal reasons. Despite his considerable prowess, the big man had probably taken quite a few bruises. Gram had been far from gentle.

The realization resulted in a mixture of emotions in Gram, both guilt and pride.

As they ended and began walking back to Cameron Castle, Cyhan held his hand out toward his student. "I think this is yours." A large red ruby lay in his palm.

Gram took it. "How did you get this?"

"You dropped it on the bed when we went at it," said Cyhan. "I had a feeling you didn't want your mother seeing it when she came in."

He nodded.

"That was part of your father, wasn't it?"

Gram slipped the stone into his belt pouch, nodding again. He didn't trust himself to speak.

"How long had you been holding it before I came in?"

Embarrassed, Gram didn't want to admit that he'd been clutching the stone for most of the night. "Several hours."

"Do you feel anything from it?"

"Sometimes it feels warm, but it might just be my body heat," said Gram. "Other times, when I think about Dad, or when I feel…" He stopped, unable to continue along those lines. "I like to think there's something of him in it. It makes me feel better."

"How often do you do that?" asked Cyhan.

"A lot when I was little," said Gram, "but not much anymore. It had been months since the last time I looked at it. Yesterday was rough…"

"This morning you fought like a demon, almost like you'd taken an earth-bond," noted the warrior. "Have any of the wizards seen it?"

Gram shook his head. "I picked it up right after— it happened. I never showed anyone."

"I won't tell you your business, but you probably should," advised his teacher.

He said no more after that and the two finished their walk back. Gram was still upset but he was starving from his exertions and when the time came for dinner, his hunger outweighed his anxiety at facing his friends.

Everyone was glad to see him at the table, his mother in particular, though she avoided addressing him directly so as not to draw attention to him. Carissa rose and hugged him, not caring whether it embarrassed him. Matthew and Moira were happy as well, but they waited for the noise to resume before talking to him.

"I'm really sorry," said Matthew. "It was a big surprise. None of us thought she would disappear like that."

"Thanks. I'd rather not talk about it, though," said Gram.

Matthew nodded, content to leave the topic, but Moira looked as if she had something to say. Gram ignored her.

"Actually Matt, if you don't mind, I'd like to talk to you about something else after we eat," said Gram.

"Sure, want to go to the workshop with me? I have more to show you anyway."

Gram nodded.

"I need to talk to you, Gram," said Moira.

"I know you mean well, Moira, but I don't really feel like being cheered up right now."

"I understand," she said. "I just need to give you something." Her face held an emphatic expression.

"Alright," he told her, "I'll come by after I talk to Matt."

***

"Stand against the wall there," ordered Matthew once they had gone inside the workshop.

"Huh?" Gram had only wanted to show his friend the stone.

"I need to measure you."

"Oh, fine." He stood by the wall, expecting his friend to bring out a measuring tape. When he was suddenly engulfed in blue light he yelped in surprise. "What are you doing?"

"Just hold still, or it's going to look all wonky," cautioned the young wizard. "Are you ready?"

Gram took a deep breath, "I guess." He held still, but then decided to ask another question, "Why don't you tell me what you're doing?"

Matthew sighed, "Now look what you've done."

Standing beside Gram was what appeared to be a perfect duplicate of him, almost. The doppelganger's face was distorted and blurred in a disturbing manner. "What is that?!" Gram leapt to one side, putting some distance between himself and his clone.

"Relax," said the young wizard, "It's just an illusion." He moved forward and using a silver stylus he traced several lines on the floor. "There, all done."

"It's hideous," said Gram.

"That's because you started talking when I made the impression. If anything, I've improved on your natural ugly," said Matthew sarcastically. "Doesn't matter, though, the face doesn't need to be accurate."

"What's it for?" asked Gram, ignoring the insult.

"I'll show you in a second. Close your eyes."

"Why?" asked Gram suspiciously.

"Trust me."

Fighting down his irritation, Gram did as he was asked.

Matthew turned away and took Thorn out of a large wooden case. He spoke a few words quietly and it vanished, returning to its storage place in the pocket dimension. "I just didn't want you to see it before you called it," he said. "You can open your eyes."

Gram did, giving Matthew a questioning look. "Now what?"

"Call it."

"You just had it, you could have handed it to me," said Gram.

"Where's the fun in that?" said Matthew. "You've been spending too much time with Sir Cyhan. I swear you're turning into an old man before my very eyes. Call the sword."

Gram tried to remember the sensation from when they had practiced it before. It only took him a second and then the sword was in his hand. His arms tensed as they took the sudden weight, despite its size though, the great sword only weighed a little over eight pounds.

"Oh!" he said, stunned. The broken sword was no longer broken. He put his other hand on the hilt, moving the six foot great sword carefully through the air in front of him. "It looks amazing."

Matthew smiled, "Damn right it does. Now repeat after me, '*klardit*'."

"Clar-what?"

"Klardit," repeated the wizard. "It will help if you imagine it the way that it used to be when you say it."

"This is the way it used to be."

"I mean when it was broken."

"Oh," said Gram. "Klardit." Nothing happened.

"You have to do both at the same time. It's like calling it. Picture the old Thorn, say the word, and imagine a tiny bit of aythar flowing from yourself into the hilt."

"You should have told me all that to begin with."

"A very—grumpy—old—man," observed Matthew. "Just do it."

Gram did and to his surprise the sword blurred, flowing in his hands. A moment later he held what appeared to be the broken sword, as it had been before Matthew remade it. "Wow."

"Now you can store it on the wall and your mother will never know we did anything to it," said Matthew proudly.

"About that," began Gram, "Mother actually gave me the sword. I don't need to hide it from her anymore."

"Well, shit-damn!" said Matthew. "Why didn't you tell me? Do you know how much time I wasted making this form? It's not as easy as it looks!"

"It was just the other day."

Matthew took a deep breath, "I guess it wouldn't have mattered then. Still, I spent a lot of time on that."

"It's kind of nice, though," said Gram trying to mollify him. "Sort of like a tribute to the past."

"Yeah, whatever," said Matthew. "Put it back for me."

Gram concentrated and the sword vanished.

"No, I meant on the table."

"You really need to work on your communication," groused Gram. He called the sword back and placed it on the work surface. He noted that when it returned it was in the form he had sent it away in. "Is it finished now?"

Matthew gave him an enigmatic smile, "Not by far. Make sure you don't try to call it again until I give you the go ahead."

"I won't."

"So what did you want to talk about? Is it something to do with—her?"

Gram shook his head before pulling the large ruby out of his pocket. He held it up for the young wizard's inspection.

"What's...?" Matthew paused, glancing up at Gram with wide eyes. "Is that—what I think it is?"

"It's from that day, the World Road Gate..." The day his father had been crushed alive. "I think it's his heart."

"They never found it when they went back to collect the remains," said Matthew in a hushed tone.

"I picked it up, before anyone noticed." He briefly explained his experiences with it as well as Cyhan's observations.

"It doesn't look magical," said Matthew. "Otherwise someone would have noticed back then."

"Are you sure?"

"Let me examine it for a minute." The young wizard took it from his hand and held it, closing his eyes and focusing his attention, while Gram held his breath. He frowned. "There's something here, but it's very faint."

"Could his spirit be in there?"

"No," said Matthew immediately, but then he retracted his statement. "I mean, I don't know. I doubt it. A living person, even a normal one, possesses a far greater amount of aythar than this stone does. It's barely showing anything above what one would expect for a bit of inanimate rock."

"But there's something?"

Matthew gave his friend a sad look. "I'm sorry. It's probably just some sort of leftover energy from before he died." He held the stone out to Gram.

As Gram reached for it Matthew's eyes widened.

"What was that?" said the wizard.

"What?"

"Hand it back."

Gram did and Matthew looked at it once more. "Maybe I imagined it. Here." As soon as Gram's hand touched the stone Matthew exclaimed again, "There!" He took it from Gram once more and then handed it back. "Every time you touch it there's a flare, like a tiny spark."

"What does that mean?"

"I don't know. Try thinking of your father, or whatever it was that made it feel warm before your fight this morning," suggested Matthew.

Gram closed his eyes and imagined his father again, trying to recapture the feeling he had had the night before. The stone warmed in his hand and Matthew hissed through his teeth.

"It's glowing! Damn, look at that!"

Gram opened his eyes but they showed him nothing unusual. "It looks the same."

"No, it's brilliant, the aythar is streaming out of it. How is it doing that?" said his friend.

"It just feels warm to me," said Gram.

"That's because your body is absorbing the aythar. It's like you have a bond with... Oh!" Matthew stopped, thinking furiously. "That's his aystrylin, or what's left of it!"

"His what? It was his heart, if that's the word you're looking for."

"No, well yes, that's one way to put it, but it wasn't literally his physical heart. When he transformed his wellspring, the center of his being, his life, became the ruby. It's kind of like a heart, but it's more important than just some bit of flesh pumping blood."

Gram looked at him, "And...?"

"The earth bond is still there," finished Matthew. "But that doesn't make sense. Normally when someone is transformed they become part of the earth, the bond ceases to exist. Then again, your dad was a stoic. That's why he kept changing back, according to my father anyway." He was talking to himself now, trying to understand what he was seeing.

He looked at Gram. "That's his aystrylin, but it wouldn't be absorbed. It remained separate, and the earth-bond your father took is still attached to it."

"What does that mean?"

"That you're holding a source of power, if we can just figure out how to use it," said his friend.

Chapter 27

Gram left the stone with Matthew after some debate, and when he returned, he was so preoccupied with his thoughts that he almost forgot about Moira's request.

A small bear outside of his family's apartments reminded him. "She's still waiting for you," said Grace.

He hadn't even noticed her standing there. "Oh!"

Scooping up the bear, he headed down the hall and turned the corner. The guard outside the outer door to the Illeniel living area nodded at him as he passed. Past that was the antechamber, followed by another door.

The second door was the true entrance to the Count's home. If he opened it himself, it would lead him into an empty, but carefully furnished family apartment. Built into the frame was a cleverly concealed magical gate enchantment. The magic was only active while the door was closed and intact. When opened by a stranger, it silently shut off, leaving a perfectly normal entrance into a normal apartment.

When it was opened by the right people, however—primarily the members of the Illeniel family—the portal stayed active, and the doorway led to a hidden cottage deep in the Elentir Mountains. The purpose of having it remain active while closed was so that servants and others could knock on the door and be heard by the family.

Gram knocked.

Moira answered immediately, looking anxious and slightly annoyed. "What took so long?"

"We had a lot to talk about."

She stepped out into the antechamber, closing the door behind her. I found something. She held out a carefully folded envelope. It was marked with an ornate 'A' stamped onto a red wax seal.

"What's this?" he asked her.

"Turn it over."

On the back, written in a careful and ornate hand, was his name.

"Where did you get this?"

"It was in a box on her dressing table. I searched the room right after you ran off the other day but I didn't get a chance to give it to you until today." She seemed ready to explode with pent up energy.

"What does it say?"

"I don't know! It had your name on it!" she barked. "Are you going to open it?"

She was obviously dying of curiosity but Gram couldn't help but be impressed with her resolve. Not many would have resisted the urge to look at the letter. Especially a wizard who could very likely replace the seal with him being none the wiser.

He didn't suspect her of such a thing, though. She was dying to find out what it said and he knew her better anyway. "Thank you."

"Are you going to let me see what it says?" she asked.

"Let me read it first." Turning away he broke the seal, and with trembling fingers he withdrew a small sheet of parchment. Only a few short words were written inside.

A letter waits at the shepherd's cottage.

He stared at it, a faint hope blooming in his chest.

Moira's voice came over his shoulder, "Which shepherd?"

Gram frowned at her, "You didn't even wait for me to say it was alright."

"I'm sorry! She was my friend too! Which cottage? Do you know where she means?"

"No idea," he lied.

She told him as much, "Don't give me that! You do know!"

"It's personal," he told her.

"I'll just follow you then," she warned him.

Gram realized he had tensed, and he blew out a great lungful of air. "Listen, Moira, this is something she didn't want anyone else to read. Otherwise she wouldn't have made this note so cryptic. She knew there was a good chance someone else would read it first."

"It isn't that cryptic," the young woman shot back. "There aren't *that* many shepherds in the vicinity."

"Please Moira," he said sincerely. "I doubt I could fool you. Please just let me get the letter and keep it private. If it isn't too embarrassing, I might share it, but I can't promise."

"I'm not *that* insensitive," she protested. "I didn't open *this* letter after all."

"Thank you."

She pursed her lips. "What if there's something dangerous in the letter? Will you tell someone then, or go charging off on your own again?"

"Trust me to use my own judgment," he told her.

"Only if you promise to tell me if you decide to go off chasing her again," she said, crossing her arms.

Grace was standing near and she nodded, adding her agreement.

"Fine," he said. "I promise not to leave without talking to you first. Is that good enough?"

Moira hugged him.

"What's that for?" he asked.

"To make me feel better," she told him.

***

Fifteen minutes later he was riding across the darkened fields outside of Washbrook. Fortunately the moon had finally decided to make an appearance, though it was still only a quarter of its full size. It provided enough light to make finding his way relatively easy once his eyes had adjusted.

He found shepherd McDermott's home without incident and he knocked on the door as politely as he could, given the fact that it was the middle of the night.

"Alan, it's me, Gram Thornbear!" he called, guessing that the shepherd might be understandably reluctant to answer the door at such an hour. "Please open up!"

After a minute a reply came from inside, "Hold on! Give me a second." The shepherd's voice sounded thick and sleepy. A light appeared through the cracks in the door and then it opened. Alan stood with a small tin lamp in hand.

"I apologize for coming at such an hour," said Gram.

"She didn't tell me you'd be bangin' on the door in the wee hours of the mornin'," said the shepherd.

The man obviously hadn't been in to town, or he'd have heard the news already. "She vanished, day before yesterday," explained Gram.

"I thought she was jus' leavin' a secret lover's letter," replied the other man. "Here, give me a minute." He went back inside before returning a moment later. "This is it."

"Thank you," Gram told him gratefully. Like the previous letter, this one was sealed with red wax. Breaking it open he tried to read, but the moonlight was insufficient. "Can I borrow your lamp for a minute?"

"Sure'n that's fine," said Alan, handing him the small lamp.

Holding the letter in one hand and the lamp in the other, Gram stepped away and started to read. A presence nearby made him pause. The shepherd was staring over his shoulder. Gram stared at the man, raising one brow in a silent question.

"Don' mind me, sir. I can't read," said the shepherd.

"Then why try to look over my shoulder?"

"Jus' curious. An' I've always thought letters were a bit mysterious," said the old man. "She's got a fine hand don't she, sir."

Gram was struck with a simultaneous feeling of kinship and irritation. Part of him wanted the comfort of someone friendly close by, and part of him wanted to rebuke the shepherd. The strong smell of sheep and sweat made his decision for him. "I'd prefer it if you gave me some privacy," he said mildly.

"Ah that's fine then," said the shepherd, moving a short step away.

Gram added several steps of his own before studying the letter in his hand:

Dear Gram,

This is my farewell. I write those words first, so that you will not think that hope lies further on in this letter. I have hurt you enough already with false hope. We will never meet again.

I am sure by now that you have discovered that much of what you thought about me was a lie. I cannot apologize for my deception, for it was deliberate and purposeful. I spoke with the intent to deceive, from beginning to end. For that I deserve no forgiveness; though I believe my actions were done in service to a just cause—I would not expect you to agree.

The only consolation I can offer you is this: In hurting you, I have hurt myself. The only truth of our time together, is that I fell well and truly in love with you; something I never intended to happen. You were my finest mistake. Your love, and the strength of your unwavering trust, tore asunder the gates guarding my heart. I have never felt such a thing before, nor do I expect to again.

In your eyes I became a new woman, and that woman loved you dearly. If it were possible, I would prefer that you remember me as I was with you. If I could choose my life, it would be with you. I would have married you and been the woman you thought I was, but that was never to be.

Do not look for me. The woman you loved exists only in the fiction of our hearts. Seeking her will only prolong your pain.

Love,
Alyssa

He held the letter in numb fingers, rereading it in disbelief. It must not be true, it couldn't be true. There was no promise for the future, no misunderstanding to be repaired. The words held only bleak disappointment.

"You don't look so good, lad."

Gram nodded and handed Alan the lamp. Folding the letter up carefully before backing away, he mounted Pebble. His throat felt tight, but he managed a quick, "Thank you," before turning the mare's head toward Castle Cameron.

Once there he found a certain bear waiting inside the main door. Grace held out her arms to him, and he lifted her up, cradling her in one arm.

"Well?" she asked.

"It was just a good-bye," he managed after a short walk. "Nothing more."

She patted his cheek with one soft paw and then hugged his neck. "I'm sorry."

When he reached the door to the Thornbear apartment, he set her back down. "Tell Moira for me. I'd rather she not ask me about it, or tell anyone else."

Entering the front room he found his mother sitting up, drinking tea. He was surprised. It was unusual for her to stay up later than a couple of hours after dinner. She gestured to him, indicating the chair beside her.

He took it, but didn't say anything for a long time. When she didn't speak, he eventually took the initiative. "You're awake."

Rose set her teacup down, gazing at him with tired eyes. "What mother could rest while her child is in pain, wandering the night?"

"It isn't your fault."

"Fault is of no concern in matters of the heart," she answered.

"I've been a fool."

"Love is often foolish, but it does not make you a fool. The wise know that there are few things of true value in the world, but love is one of them. That is why we risk so much for its sake."

"Only a fool would love someone that doesn't return that love."

His mother sipped at her tea once more, raising her brow at his response. "Is that what you think? That she did not love you?"

The letter still burned against his chest, where it lay couched, but he nodded a silent 'yes'.

"She was a consummate actress, I will give her that much," said Rose, "but even *she* could not blind these eyes. She spoke the truth when she came to dinner with us."

He had expected a different response. He himself had been sure of Alyssa before, when she had doubted herself, but now that he had seen the letter, he found his belief in her love to be faltering. To find his mother inadvertently confirming the message in Alyssa's secret letter...

"How can you say that?"

Rose chuckled ruefully, "I don't know, Gram. For all my logic and reason, there are some things I know without truly understanding *how* I know them. Some women would claim it was intuition, but my experience has been that often other people use the word 'intuition' simply to support what they wish to believe. I loathe the word because of that, but in this case, I can offer no better explanation."

"I don't know what to do."

His mother rubbed her eyes, but she remained silent.

A dozen things ran through Gram's mind, thoughts and emotions twisted and twined together. His mind was torn, and his body felt the need to be up and about, to *do* something. The frustration, the pain, the *sadness*, made him want to curl up in his mother's lap, as he had when he was a small boy. But he could not voice his feelings, nor could he seek the solace of childhood. Those days were gone.

"It hurts Momma. I have to do something. What would you do?" he asked, his voice cracking despite his best efforts.

"There's no good advice," she admitted. "Patience, certainly, but that won't help you regain what you have lost, it will only minimize the turmoil. Do you really want me to tell you what to do?"

"Only if it means I'll get her back," he replied.

Rose laughed, "At least you're honest. Most ask for advice, and then get angry when it doesn't match their desires. If I could have you do as I wished, I would tell you to forget her, but that isn't very practical is it?"

He shook his head.

"Eat, sleep, and exercise your patience. Life continues, and so must we."

Chapter 28

The next day was hard, as was the following one. Gram returned to training, but he found it brought him little joy. It served only to keep his body occupied, but his mind drifted and it was difficult to maintain proper focus. During his sparring sessions with Cyhan, it seemed as if he had lost ground. The harder he tried, the worse he did.

Meals were better, but nothing tasted good. Food was something necessary to fill the belly, but it gave him no pleasure.

Gram was depressed.

A week passed, and then another, before his mood improved. Slowly but surely he returned to himself. Training became an opportunity to vent his frustration and he enjoyed not only mastering the sword techniques that Cyhan taught the others, but in demonstrating his superiority upon his fellow trainees.

Gram was big; something that training with Cyhan alone had not allowed him to appreciate before. His mother was tall and he was told his father had been similar to Cyhan in size, but now that he was allowed to train with the other young men, it was far more obvious to him. Gram was over six feet in height now and his shoulders were broad. He had always been strong, but constant exercise had added considerable muscle to his frame.

His aggressiveness during training had begun to make the other trainees leery of practicing with him. When sparring he fought hard, and though they used wooden swords and wore armor, his blows left painful bruises.

To keep him from demoralizing the others, Cyhan and Captain Draper removed him from the training class and had him train with the regulars. Gram fared just as well there, and the number of men available to practice with, allowed him to switch his partners frequently. No one wanted to face him more than once.

Eventually Captain Draper took him aside, after one particularly brutal sparring match.

"Gram, what are you doing?"

"What you told me to do, sir," he answered bluntly.

"You're making my job difficult," said the Captain. "These men don't come out here every day to provide themselves to you as training dummies. They aren't out here for you to beat them half to death."

"Have I broken the rules, sir? You told us to fight as if it were real."

"Until the opponent yields."

"Trell didn't yield, sir."

"He couldn't! He was unconscious from the first blow, yet you felt the need to strike him three more times before he could finish falling down!" said the captain, raising his voice. "You may have broken his arm!"

Gram frowned, "The sword hit his rerebrace, sir. It shouldn't have broken anything."

"If you hit a man hard enough, things break, armor or no armor! Even if it isn't broken, the bruising will likely keep him from training for a week. I won't have any guardsmen left to defend the keep if you keep sending them to the infirmary! Do you understand?"

"Yes, sir."

"Let me talk to him," offered Cyhan. He motioned to Gram and the two of them walked apart. Once they were out of earshot he stopped. "It's time to stop fighting and start teaching."

Gram frowned.

"You've learned as much as you can from sparring, and most of what you're doing with me now is just practice, but you can still improve," said the older warrior.

"How, Zaihair?"

"In the past, I told you to take each bout seriously, and that's good advice, but there comes a point where you won't find a challenge practicing against most men. You've reached that point, though far sooner than I expected."

"I still can't beat you, Zaihair," said Gram.

Cyhan smiled, "And you won't, but even I can't afford to spar with you as much as you need. For one thing, my body simply can't take that much abuse day in and day out. You're going to have to lighten up."

"If I don't work as hard as I can then I won't get better."

"There's another way," replied his teacher. "You teach." The big man watched Gram's face—searching for understanding—but when he failed to find it, he went on. "Teaching something, *anything*, to someone else, will improve your understanding. Your body knows what you've learned, and your mind has tuned itself to the unspoken world; practicing harder now won't help you."

"You want me to teach someone Zan-zei?"

"No. Save that for later, someday when you're older. No, I mean teach them what you've learned about the sword. Captain Draper and I have taught you a lot of techniques, and you've mastered them far better than any man on the field here. For example, poor Trell, instead of proving your knowledge by pounding him into jelly, try to teach him, to help him master what you already know."

"I don't think he'll be back for a few days," observed Gram.

Cyhan growled, "Don't play stupid, boy. From now on, they aren't you're opponents anymore, they're your students. Use what you've learned to instruct them—without killing them."

"Are you planning to place me above the others?"

"That would create problems. No, you'll have to learn to teach indirectly. Show some mercy on the field, and help your sparring partners correct their errors, instead of just punishing them."

"And that will make me better?" Gram was having difficulty believing it.

"It's far harder than you think. Teaching is the hardest thing you will ever do."

***

Rose Thornbear was composing another letter, this one was a report for the Queen, when a messenger entered. She was sitting at a desk, using the Cameron library, when the man came in holding a small envelope.

"Milady, a letter has just arrived for you."

Rose stood and stretched, feeling the ache in her back from being too long in the chair. Reaching out, she accepted the envelope and dismissed the servant. "Thank you, Tom. You may go."

Tom left and she stared at the address on the outside of the envelope. It was from John Conradt, the Baron of Conradt, in Gododdin. She broke the seal and opened it, holding it before her in the light that streamed in from the windows.

Dearest Rose,

I was surprised to receive your correspondence. Though it has been many years since last we spoke, I have always remembered those days fondly. I was also pleased to hear of your son's health and well-being. I am sure he has become a fine young gentleman.

I am troubled by the content of your letter, though, for my daughter Alyssa still has not been fostered out. I fear you have been misled, and I wish to make it clear that my daughter has never visited Cameron...

Lady Rose finished the letter and then gently folded it, showing little outward sign of her agitation. *I knew it.* She worried about Gram's reaction when she told him the news. She was also concerned about the imposter's purpose. *Why was she here? Did she gain what she sought, or did she flee beforehand, fearing discovery?*

The letter had created a new tension in her but Rose was nothing if not disciplined. She wrote a quick reply, thanking Marie Conradt for her response and apologizing for the confusion. She kept the reason for the confusion deliberately vague out of necessity, since she herself didn't know much more than her friend living in Gododdin.

Once she had finished, she sealed it and wrote out the address. Then she headed for the door to the Illeniel's home, handing the letter to a servant by the door as she left the library. "Please see this posted with the first courier heading that way."

It turned out that Penny was in Washbrook, discussing certain procurements for the winter with Joe McDaniel, but Peter, the Count's chamberlain, was at the door and he ushered her inside. "The Count is here, Lady Rose, if you'd like to see him instead," he offered courteously.

Ordinarily she might have scolded him for undue formality. She had been the one to originally hire Peter Tucker and his sister Lilly years before and they had all been through a lot together. Today she didn't bother. "Where is he?" she asked curtly.

"In his workshop, milady."

She brushed past him and made for the stairs. The house was built on a steep incline against a mountain. The entrance from Castle Cameron came in on the upper level of the cottage, where the living areas and kitchen were. Mordecai's workshop and some of the more practical parts of the house were on the lower level, with another doorway exiting onto a meadow.

She rapped on the door to the workshop twice, and then waited. If he had been in any other part of the house, save the bedroom perhaps, she might have simply entered without waiting. Things were sometimes dangerous in the shop, though, so caution was the order of the day.

"Come in, Rose," he called to her. As usual his magesight had identified her long before she reached the door. In fact, he had probably taken note of her the moment she entered the house. It was one of the more unsettling things about living in close proximity with wizards, but she had long since grown used to it.

She launched into her subject without preamble, "I've received a letter from the Barony of Conradt." She paused as she looked at the workbench. "What is that?"

"It's *supposed* to be a self-heating teapot," explained Mordecai, "but mostly it's a steam-bomb."

She gave him an odd look.

"It has some problems still."

"Steam-bomb?"

Mordecai shrugged, "I'm making it for Penny, so she can make tea without having to fire up the stove. It seemed like a good idea for a present, but it keeps heating too quickly, with violent results."

"It's still in one piece," she observed.

"This is the third one."

Rose chuckled, "Well, if you get it perfected I would love one too, so long as it won't kill me."

"Sure," said Mordecai. "So, what was in this letter?"

"It seems that our guest, Alyssa, was an imposter. Marie Conradt assures me that her daughter is still with them and has yet to be fostered out."

"Have you told Gram yet?" he asked.

"Not yet. I wanted to notify you first. We need to figure out what her goal was," she stated. "I dread telling Gram. He's just beginning to get over this."

"I don't envy you that," said Mordecai. "I'm just grateful that mine haven't shown any interest in the opposite sex yet."

"They're almost seventeen; you need to think about fostering them out. The Queen would take them, and they would have many opportunities to meet the right sorts of potential marriage partners in the capital."

The Count growled softly, "They aren't ready yet." Walking over to one wall, he removed the apron that protected his clothes, hanging it on a wall peg.

"*They* aren't, or *you* aren't?" asked Rose, pointedly. Then her eyes focused on his chest, "Is that blood on your shirt?"

Mordecai looked down, "Hmmm." He wiped at the red stain with one finger, and then brought it to his mouth, tasting it. "Nope, jam."

Rose shuddered involuntarily as she watched him. "How did it get there?" she asked, but then she saw him use the hem of his tunic to wipe his hands. "Never mind, I think I've figured it out. How Penny puts up with you, I'll never understand."

"We grew up in similar circumstances," he reminded her.

"She has adapted to society far better than you have."

Mordecai grinned, "I'm a slow learner. Back to our mysterious visitor, though. I don't see what anyone would have had to gain by sending a spy here."

"There are multiple possibilities," said Rose. "Assassination or information gathering for a foreign state are the first two that come to mind."

"No one is dead."

"Yet," corrected Rose. "Or it could be that she was forced to leave before completing her assignment. Her entanglement with my son became a liability for her when I returned. She knew of my letter to Marie Conradt."

"I haven't been politically involved in years," noted the Count.

"A foreign state might not know that, or care," said Rose. "As far as I have been able to discover, she didn't spend much time asking questions, though. Did she ever visit your family here?"

Mordecai shook his head, "No. Penny kept the socializing to the castle."

"Then we know very little."

"Welcome to my world," he replied.

"I'll send inquiries out, but I don't expect to learn anything," said Rose, studying his features. Mordecai was still an attractive man, despite the years. Then her eyes lit on a spot on his cheek. "Oh for heaven's sake," she exclaimed, exasperated. Drawing out her handkerchief, she put the corner in her mouth before leaning forward to clean the jam from the Count's face.

"Thank you, Rose." His blue eyes seemed to sparkle and Rose stepped back, keeping her face neutral; only age and experience saved her from a telling blush.

"You're welcome," she told him. *I've been alone too long.* She left then, going in search of Penny.

Chapter 29

Autumn slowly gave way to winter, and while Gram knew he would never forget Alyssa, she came to dominate his thoughts less frequently. He devoted himself to his training, and just as Cyhan had predicted, he found helping his fellow soldiers improve was a rewarding challenge.

With time his reputation amongst the men improved, and now most looked forward to a chance to spar with him. His private sessions with Cyhan grew less frequent, but he filled the extra time by haunting the woodlands around Cameron and Washbrook with Chad Grayson.

Spring eventually returned and as the first green buds began to appear on the trees, Rose called him aside one morning after breakfast.

"Gram, I need to talk to you."

"Yes, mother?" he said, looking down at her. Rose was tall for a woman, but Gram stood several inches over six feet now.

"You'll turn seventeen later this year, and though it pains me to say it, I think you should consider going abroad."

Her words both excited him, and filled him with trepidation. Leaving Cameron would mean leaving his teacher, but that wasn't what bothered him. Cyhan had already taught him what he could; his development relied on practice and self-discipline now. Deep down, it was his secret hope that Alyssa might return somehow. He was anchored by the fact that subconsciously, he was still waiting for her.

"Why?"

Rose reached up, putting one hand on his cheek before letting it fall to rest on his solid shoulder. *He's so big,* she thought, remembering the small boy who had once followed her endlessly. "Sir Harold, in Albamarl, sent a missive to me. He's looking for a new squire, and Sir Cyhan recommended you to him."

Gram looked away, feeling uncertain. It was a marvelous opportunity, but still he was reluctant, "I don't think I'm ready."

"Ready?" she said incredulously. "You are already the best man on the field here. You have little to gain by staying. If you truly wish to be a knight you must look to your future. Sir Cyhan already has two squires. In the capital you could advance, and there are other matters to think of as well."

"I'm not interested in matchmaking, Mother," he told her stubbornly.

Rose Thornbear had learned a hard lesson in pushing her friend to seek a new husband years ago. She wouldn't repeat it again. "That wasn't my intention. You need to meet your peers, develop friendships with other young noblemen. Someday my father's mantle will fall on your shoulders, as well as the title of Thornbear. You must be acquainted with your fellow lords. Friendships are hard to come by in your later years, now is the time to make them."

Gram pressed his lips together in a firm line, uncertain what to say. He knew she was right, but his feelings dictated a different course of action.

She patted him once more before folding her hands demurely before her. "You don't need to give me an answer immediately. The Count has been invited to visit King Darogen of Dunbar. He's asked me to come with him, to offer advice. You can give me your decision when I return."

He frowned, "How long will you be gone?"

"It would be a journey of many weeks, but Mordecai will take us in that abominable flying contraption of his. We should make Surencia within a day, but we will stop to visit King Nicholas there for a week before proceeding on to Dunbar. That visit will take another week in all likelihood, possibly longer. We may not be back for three to four weeks."

"Us?"

"The Count, Penelope, myself, and the twins," she replied.

"What of guards? You cannot go without an escort."

She smiled, "I'll be traveling with no less than three wizards. I doubt anything could endanger us, but you are correct, it would be unseemly to go without at least a token guard. Sir Cyhan will also come, along with a detachment of three guardsmen."

"Can he fit so many in his flying machine?"

"It will be tight, but the inconvenience is far less than spending weeks on horseback."

Gram nodded, "It sounds as if you have everything planned out."

"Of course, though I'll need you to take care of Carissa while I'm away."

He laughed, "More likely she'll take care of me."

***

Gram was in the courtyard three days later. The morning air was chilly, a remembrance of a cold winter. Carissa stood beside him as they said their farewells, watching the adult portion of the Illeniel family, along with their mother and the guards squeeze into the mostly invisible flying machine. Mordecai was the last to board.

"Peter Tucker will be in charge of the day to day affairs while I am gone, and Captain Draper will handle the defense of the castle, but I will feel better knowing you're here to keep an eye on Conall and Irene."

Gram gave a modest bow, "I will see that they are safe, milord."

Mordecai chuckled, "Don't give me that 'milord' crap; you're practically one of my own children." He embraced Gram quickly. "Gods, boy! You've gotten as big as an ox."

"It's the food Cook prepares. It's a wonder I'm not fat," joked Gram.

The Count patted his own incipient belly, "If I'm not careful, I will be. Elaine will be checking on things every so often and she'll be able to contact me if something turns up."

"Everything will be fine, sir."

Matthew gestured at him through the transparent wall of the flying machine, patting his own forearm and giving Gram a negative shake of his head. It was a reminder that he shouldn't try to summon Thorn.

Chapter 29

Despite the long winter, Matthew was still making improvements. He nodded to let Matt know he understood.

A moment later they rose slowly from the ground and then began to speed away, heading north for the capital of Gododdin.

***

Life was quieter with the Count and the twins gone.

Gram continued his routine with Captain Draper and the men each morning, but he spent his afternoons with Carissa and the two younger Illeniel children, Conall and Irene. He and Carissa stayed at the Illeniel home in the mountains at night, along with Lilly Tucker, who was normally in charge of Irene and Conall. They were old enough now that neither of them needed much looking after but they were too young to leave alone.

A week after the Count's departure, Gram sat outside the Illeniel cottage, playing chess with Irene while Carissa watched. It was all his sister could do to restrain herself from helping him. She was a far better player than he was and Irene was methodically destroying his defense.

"Nooo," moaned his sister slowly as his fingers left the knight. Clearly he had made another mistake, though he couldn't see it.

Irene smiled and moved her bishop to pin it. She would have him in checkmate in a few more moves. "Muahahaha," she said, affecting an evil laugh.

"Ahhh," he said, gradually beginning to realize his mistake.

Irene clapped with joy as she saw understanding on his face. Gracefully admitting defeat, Gram tilted his king and resigned. "You'll have to play Carissa now. I can't offer you a good challenge anymore."

They switched seats, and he watched them play, but his mind was elsewhere, wandering. A cold wind was sneaking down the neck of his doublet, but it was balanced by the warmth of the spring sun. Despite the pleasant weather, he felt uneasy.

"Try not to look so sour about losing," advised his sister.

"No, it isn't that," he replied. "Something feels odd."

"Perhaps you're starting to develop your magesight," suggested Irene.

"Neither of us have a wizard for a parent, Rennie," reminded Carissa. "There's little chance of that happening."

"Oh, yeah," said the younger girl.

They continued to play but his feeling remained. When they finished he looked at the sun, "It's almost time to eat. We should go back to the castle."

The girls nodded and began packing up the board and pieces. They found Lilly and Conall in the house, and the five of them returned to Castle Cameron. As they walked, Gram finally figured out what had been bothering him.

The birdsong disappeared. Their chirping was normally omnipresent during the daylight hours in the mountains. *There must have been a predator close by.*

He resolved to have his bow close at hand the next time they went out.

***

They were in the middle of dinner when the messenger arrived, along with one of the guards that had been stationed at the gatehouse.

"Arundel is under attack!" he shouted as he entered the hall.

The hall exploded with surprised shouting as everyone stood and began talking at once, but Captain Draper quickly quelled the chaos, "Sit down and shut up!"

Peter Tucker and the captain took the messenger aside and spoke briefly, before returning to speak to the gathered people.

"It appears that a small band of raiders has attacked some farms near Arundel, looting and burning," said Peter, addressing them. "Finish your food quickly. Captain Draper will double the guard tonight, and patrols will be sent out to search and scout. We will make sure that the bandits are not taking refuge in these lands."

The captain was already striding purposefully from the hall and Peter moved to Gram's side, "I'd like you to take Irene and Conall back to their home and stay with them."

"Lilly will be there," said Gram. "I could do more good in the patrols. I know more woodcraft than most of the men here."

"Absolutely not," said the chamberlain. "Until I know the extent of the threat I have to take every precaution, and that means making certain that the Count's children are safe, not to mention your sister and yourself."

Gram leaned close, speaking softly, "You know damn well the Count's home is a hundred miles from here. They will be perfectly safe without me."

Lilly Tucker already had Irene and Carissa in tow, and Conall followed behind them with a look of disappointment.

Peter looked at him sternly, "I know nothing of the sort, but in any case my instructions are clear."

Conall came back, "Gram, are you coming with us?" The look on his face made it clear he didn't relish the thought of being penned up with nothing but girls for company.

Gram looked from him to the chamberlain and back again, "Yeah, go ahead. I'll be there shortly."

Conall rewarded him with a grateful expression and ran to catch up with the others. Gram pursed his lips and headed for the Thornbear apartments. If he was going to be stuck 'guarding' the children, he might as well claim the mail and sword his mother had given him recently. The sword was new, but the chain was an inheritance from his father. Dorian had stopped wearing it after Mordecai had given him enchanted plate, but it was far better than normal mail. It wouldn't stop a crushing blow but it was enchanted to prevent anything from piercing it.

He walked slowly along the corridor, his mind on dark thoughts.

He was halfway there when he remembered the silence of the birds. Cold fear ran down his spine. *What if the raid on Arundel was merely a distraction, to keep our attention elsewhere?* It was well timed, with all the older Illeniels being absent. Few enemies could hope to threaten Arundel seriously, not while Walter Prathion and his children lived there.

Gram changed directions and broke into a run. He heard the screaming before he got there.

One of the door guards at the Illeniel's door was down already, his blood pooling around him. The other was nowhere to be seen. Gram ducked through the outer door and beheld a scene straight from some terrible nightmare.

The second guard was still alive, barely, his body half wedged in the inner door that led to the Illeniel's secret home. He was clinging to the doorframe with all his strength, trying to prevent the men inside from shutting the door. Once it was closed, no one left inside the castle would be able to reach them. The only ones still at Cameron with the ability to do so were already inside, Lilly Tucker and the two children.

A black clad figure within drew back the door, only to slam it again, crushing the guard's arm and leg. He started to pull it inward again, preparing to slam it once more when Gram crashed into it, using his body like a battering ram.

The door flew open momentarily and Gram bounced sideways, falling into a coat tree and narrowly avoiding a spear thrust. Five men stood within, one with the spear and the others wielding black wooden truncheons and dark steel daggers. Lilly and the children were nowhere to be seen, but he could hear the sound of screams further within the house.

Gram's mind went blank as he fell, disappearing into the void. Grabbing the coat tree as he fell, he rolled with it, using his momentum to get clear of the spearman. A sharp pain along his ribs told him that he might already be wounded, but he had no time to spare for that.

Lying on the floor was not the ideal position from which to start a fight with five armed opponents.

Trusting his comrades to deal with the intruder, the spearman turned and used his spear to push the wounded guard back through the door before slamming it shut. Meanwhile, two of the men with truncheons moved to dispatch Gram. The remaining two scuttled to the sides, ready to assist if necessary; the entry hall made it difficult for them all to reach him at the same time.

The coat tree caught one of them in the legs, knocking him from his feet, though the second man managed to leap over it. His only weapon tangled up in the first man's legs, Gram abandoned it and leapt to his feet before the other recovered from his evasive maneuver. One of those that had held back advanced on his rear, swinging his truncheon at Gram's undefended skull.

With uncanny awareness Gram stepped backward, letting the club swing past in front of his face as he caught the man's arm in his, twisting and flinging his assailant into the other that was coming at him from the front.

Moving sideways, he narrowly avoided a thrust from the spearman that had been aimed at his kidney. Snatching up a small side table he brought it up just in time to stop a swing from one of the truncheons, bending at the waist simultaneously to avoid the dagger thrust that followed it from a low angle.

Taking the table by two legs he swung sideways, flooring the spearman before he could recover and using the momentum of the strike to bring it back into line for the third enemy's truncheon swing. It shattered in his hands under the force of the blow, leaving him with two table legs and a bit of loose tabletop dangling from one of them.

Gram smiled fiercely, advancing with the two wooden posts in his hands.

Their faces were hidden by black cloth, but the invader's eyes widened as he came on, whipping the two table legs about with deadly precision. The spearman never had a chance to rise as one of the heavy pieces of wood connected, making a sickening thud against his skull.

The ensuing battle was short and ugly. Wielding his two makeshift clubs Gram blocked their attacks, moving forward and then to the right to unbalance their defensive position. Before the man on the left could flank him he had brought the one on the right down and he forced the center man to wheel, to keep him in his line of sight.

Feinting, Gram sent one man's attacks too far to the left, and he rewarded him with a double strike to the arm and ribs before dropping down to avoid the third's swing at his head. From below he took out that one's legs, finishing him as he fell.

The last man ran, seeking to escape, or perhaps warn the others. Gram threw one of his wooden legs, and felt a sense of satisfaction when it caught the escaping enemy in the back, throwing him off balance. He launched the second club at the man's legs, leaping up to follow it.

That one knocked the man down, and before he could rise, Gram was on him. The man had lost his truncheon in the fall, but he still held the dagger and the two of them wrestled for control of it. The ending was a foregone conclusion. He outweighed the assassin by more than fifty pounds, and as the men on the training field knew, Gram's strength was something to be feared.

Using his weight, Gram slowly forced the knife hand downward, until he felt it reach the man's chest. A final push and it was in, sliding in with sickening ease. His opponent's desperate yell for help became a gurgling cough.

Wasting no time, Gram untangled himself and stood, claiming the man's truncheon for his own. He hefted it carefully before bringing it down brutally, rendering his enemy unconscious, if not killing him instantly. He strode back down the corridor and made sure the others wouldn't get back up before he let himself relax.

The immediate danger past, his thoughts returned and he stared at the carnage in the hallway. Blood, brains, and even bits of bone littered the hall and spattered the walls. Five men were dead. *Not wounded, dead,* he thought. *I did that.* His mind replayed the scene and he saw himself again, smashing the heads of those who had been rendered helpless.

Gram's stomach grew tight, and he felt his insides begin to heave. *What have I done?*

A cry from deeper within the house brought him back to his senses. There was more yet to be done.

Thornbear

Chapter 30

The sound wrenched him back to the present and Gram straightened up. Casting about, he found another of the men's truncheons and with one in each hand he moved on. With the men at the door dead, there was a chance that the others in the house might not know he was there.

The scream had come from the kitchen, and as he got closer he could hear the sounds of a scuffle within. Not daring to wait he flung the door open and entered.

His eyes found Carissa first; she was standing beside Conall, the two of them backed into a corner by the stove. Four men were in the room, while two more were in the connected dining room, dragging Irene's lifeless body between them.

One of the four was struggling with Lilly Tucker, blood was running from her scalp, but she showed no sign of surrendering yet. The second stood back, laughing as he enjoyed the spectacle while the other two were slowly approaching the children, being careful not to give them a chance to run past and escape.

"Don't kill the woman, we can enjoy her on the trip back," said the one watching.

Another voice yelled from the other room, a woman's voice, "Leave her, we're here for the children!"

Carissa's eyes found Gram's, and he could see hope blossom in them. Before the intruders realized he was there he had cracked one's head with a truncheon. The other two turned to face him and the battle grew serious. Lilly began to struggle even harder against the third attacker who was holding her down.

The two that faced him knew their business; they circled the small table that occupied the center of the kitchen, flanking him from either side. It took everything he had just to keep them at bay. A terrible shrieking cry came from Lilly and the third man stood back up, a bloody dagger in his hand. Laughing, he threw it at Gram.

Dodging to one side to avoid the dagger, he was forced into the line of one of the men's truncheon blows and the heavy weighted club glanced across the top of his head. The pain blinded him for a moment and Gram reeled, trying to maintain his equilibrium. Falling in the other direction he stumbled into the other man.

He knew the next blow would take him from behind.

Clutching the man he had fallen into, he twisted and used his momentum to turn his opponent into a human shield. It was a ploy that worked better than he expected, the man in his arms went limp as his comrade's club rendered him unconscious.

Still staggered, Gram thrust the limp body away and then stepped into something slippery. His leg went out from under him and he fell. He rolled as he hit the floor, using the table as cover. A hasty swipe from one of them caught the back of his shoulder but he kept rolling, taking him from that one's reach and knocking the feet out from under the one that had stabbed Lilly.

The man fell, grappling with Gram as he came down, but Gram was ready for him. Dropping the truncheon he struck the invader with a heavy throat punch. He knew *that* fight was already won, but he struggled to free himself as the man clutched at his clothing. His other opponent was coming at him, weapon in hand. He tried to flip over, to interpose the body of the one holding onto him, but he didn't have the leverage.

He was dead if he couldn't move.

Desperate, he shoved the one holding him, driving his head into the hard iron stove, but he knew it was too late. A high pitched scream behind him cut the air.

Carissa had retrieved the dagger that had been used to kill Lilly and she stood behind the last man. As he screamed he turned and battered the small girl aside, his truncheon hitting her solidly in the chest. Carissa fell back, crashing into one of the cabinets.

The man in black was still screaming, clawing at his back, trying to withdraw the dagger that she had plunged into his kidney. It was a mortal wound, but he wasn't dead yet. Furious he raised his club to finish the girl that had slain him.

Gram caught his arm, wrenching it back, around and then up, pushing until the shoulder joint popped. Then he removed the dagger and drove it in again, higher up, between the shoulder blades. Not content to let him fall, he slammed his foe into the stone floor.

Carissa threw her arms around him and Conall stood beside them, holding an iron pot. The boy's arms were shaking and his eyes were wide.

Gram stroked Carissa's hair for a moment, "Are you alright?"

She looked at him, tears of anger and pain in her eyes, "I told Momma I would take care of you."

The words brought a brief smile to his lips, "You certainly did." It reminded him of something his mother had once said, while talking about his father, *No sane person threatens those a Thornbear protects.*

"They killed Rennie and Lilly," said Conall, his eyes dark and empty. He wasn't crying but Gram suspected he was going into shock.

He took the boy by the hand, shaking him to get his attention, "You have to get Carissa out of here, back to the castle. It isn't safe here. I'll take care of the rest."

Conall's eyes focused on him, and then he nodded.

"Can you walk?" he asked, looking at Carissa. A strong smell of wood smoke was coming from somewhere.

"Something's broken," she told him, "but my legs work fine."

"Go then," he said, rising and urging them toward the door. He checked the hall again before they entered.

"There are dead men by the door to the castle, ignore them and go get help. I have to get Rennie and then I'll follow you."

The two children nodded and ran for the door. Gram returned to the kitchen and picked up one of the truncheons. The dining area was empty, but two black clad forms were in the main room beyond it. One was lifting Irene's limp body, casting it over a broad shoulder before going down the stairs that led to the lower level. The smaller one turned to face him.

"Leave the girl and I will let you live," Gram warned.

The small assassin ignored him, advancing lightly while holding two short wooden rods, one in either hand. She wove them in and out, in a pattern that kept them sometimes parallel and at other times crossing.

It's a woman, he realized then. The dark clothing had hidden the fact from him at first.

Pushing that thought aside, he moved into range; Irene came before any qualms he had about fighting women.

He deflected several of her attacks but the weighted truncheon was slower than the light rods and she wielded them with blinding speed. Within moments he found himself on the defensive, giving ground and forced to maneuver around the furniture to keep her at bay. Her movements were so fast that he was unable to stop them all and he took several sharp raps to his arms and legs, reserving his defense for the more serious thrusts at his sternum and throat.

She kicked out, sending a chair flying backward and blocking his retreat. Shifting his stance, he was forced to advance and he took several hard strikes to one arm before she realized her mistake. Ignoring what was likely to be a hard blow to the side of his head he drove the truncheon forward in a stop-thrust maneuver. He knew already that she wasn't likely to hit hard enough to do more than daze him and the strike to her sternum would take her out of the fight.

What happened next shocked him.

She altered her flow and instead of taking the easy shot at his head, she bent her legs and arched her back, springing into a back flip that took her across the room and out of his range. She had anticipated his ploy and given herself space with a startling display of gymnastics.

How did she know? The fact that she had seen through his sacrificial maneuver surprised him more than the flip had. *If Cyhan were a woman, this is what he would be like,* he thought silently. His confidence slipped for a moment. *One mistake and she'll kill me.*

The thought of Irene being carried ever farther away erased any thoughts he had of retreat. *Relax,* he told himself and then he shut down his mind, surrendering his conscious thought and falling deeper into the empty place that his teacher had drilled into him. His eyes took in the room, marking the furniture and other obstacles. Then he stepped forward.

He outweighed her by at least seventy pounds or more, but she held the advantage in speed and weapons. He needed to get close.

They circled the room for a minute or more before he got within range. He took several more hard blows to his arms, but he drove her back, forcing her into the corner. A low table there limited her options for escape, but she let him maneuver her there anyway. When he closed for the finishing blow, he knew what would happen.

She saw the attack coming and once again her lithe form took flight as she dropped her weapons and flowed sideways into a handspring. His truncheon took her in the stomach and she crashed to one side, hitting the wall.

He gave her no chance to recover, kicking the table upward to slam into her as she rose from the floor.

If his weapon had connected with the spot below her sternum she wouldn't have recovered, but it had landed too low, hitting the abdominals rather than her diaphragm. The table bruised her but she still reached her feet and moved into his towering charge.

Lightning fast, a kick sent his weapon hand up, the truncheon flying away and then she punished his torso with three hard jabs. Her knee came up and Gram narrowly avoided having his manhood badly bruised.

Still, barehanded he was nearly as fast; his size and strength made the outcome inevitable. Finding his balance, he blocked her next punches and for a few seconds the two of them traded rapid fire jabs and blocks. Calm and implacable, his right hand struck her head and he tried to catch her by the hair. Once he had a grip on her it would be over.

She dipped down, trying to avoid the grab, and her hood came away in his fingers.

A familiar face lay underneath. It was Alyssa.

Gram froze, but she wasn't suffering from the same shock. Rocketing upward her open palm struck his chin, sending his head back and knocking him from his feet.

"I really wish you hadn't done that," she told him. Her hair was tied into a tight bun on top of her head and reaching up she tugged at it, pulling it free to cascade down around her while Gram scrambled backward, trying to clear his head.

"Why?" he asked, gaping at her with pain in his eyes.

She approached as he stood, his legs like jelly beneath him. Falling into a crouch she tried to sweep his unsteady legs out from under him but he stumbled back, just managing to get away. Leaping back up, Alyssa lunged at him. It was a poor choice on her part and reflexively he caught her by the wrist, yanking her in close.

She struggled with him, but his strength was too great. He felt a sharp pain in his wrist but he ignored it as he twisted her arm back and forced her to the floor, one forearm hard against the back of her neck. He had her helpless now, his weight on her back and one arm pinned painfully.

"Why?" he repeated. "Why would you do this?"

A strange numbness was traveling up his arm and he saw something small fall from her hand as he pressed harder on her arm.

"Answer me!"

"You fought well," she said, "but this fight is mine."

His mind went back, and he remembered her undoing her hair a moment before. A foolish move in a fight, but she had had a reason for it. The long bloody needle she had dropped was poisoned.

Growling he tried to push harder but the arm she had pricked was weaker and his chest felt strange. "Traitor," he cursed, but the word came out slurred. His eyes cast about, seeking a weapon he could use before his strength vanished but there was nothing close.

The needle, he thought, but his fingers scrabbled awkwardly as he tried to grab it. Her arm was free now and levering herself up with it and one leg, she sent him falling to one side.

His arm was rigid now and his breathing labored. A cold pain crept through his body as his muscles contracted painfully, rendering him impotent, helpless. She crouched over him, looking down with sad eyes.

"You're dying," she said. "The poison causes a state like tetany, causing the voluntary muscles to lock up first, but your breathing will stop soon. You have to fight hard, focus on your breathing."

His eyes were the only thing that would move now, bulging as he fought to draw breath. He saw her hands, working quickly to untie a pouch at her waist. She drew out a small vial and then she rolled his head, fighting against his rigid muscles to get the back of his head against the floor and pry his stubborn lips apart. Unstopping the vial she poured a thick liquid into his mouth. Some of it dribbled away, but more seeped in around his tightly clenched teeth.

"This is the antidote. But it will take time to work. You won't be able to move for hours, and when you do, your body will feel as though you've been beaten and bruised from head to toe." Standing up she took hold of his feet and began to drag him toward the stairs. The smell of smoke was getting stronger.

The next fifteen minutes were painful as she dragged him feet first down the wooden stairs, his head hitting against each step as they descended.

"They've set fire to the house," she informed him. "It will destroy everything, including the gate back to the castle. Once you recover you'll have to make your way back on foot."

He stared at her, willing his thoughts at her, wishing she could hear him. *Why are you doing this!?* She was oblivious however, and she left him inside the house, near the door that led outside. He could hear her talking to someone there, but the sound of crackling flames and burning timbers from above drowned out her words. A few minutes later she returned and began to drag him outside.

"I told them I was checking the house, to make sure the gate would be disabled. They think you're dead already," she said. "I never wanted it to happen like this. No one was supposed to get hurt."

His eyes glared at her accusingly as he struggled to breathe.

"The antidote has an unfortunate side effect as well. It will make you very sleepy, but you mustn't fall asleep. If you do, your breathing will stop and you won't wake up. You have to stay awake long enough for it to counter the poison." Her eyes were wet. "Please."

Gram was furious inside. He couldn't imagine falling asleep; all he wanted was the use of his body again. If he had had the power of his arms he would have throttled her.

"They won't hurt her," she added. "Our purpose was to take her, not kill her. Irene will be well treated. I promise you."

She dragged him farther, pulling him away from the house until he was sheltered by a rocky outcrop. "You should be safe here. Just don't let yourself sleep.

I will never sleep again, he thought, *not until I've choked the life out of you with my bare hands.* His eyes rolled from side to side as he tried to take in his surroundings.

Alyssa studied him, her eyes glimmering with unshed tears. "I'm so sorry, Gram. I didn't want it to happen like this. I would have preferred never to see you again, and to leave our memories together untouched. With Celior's mercy, we will never meet again." She stood and looked down on him.

"You should know, you were the best I've ever fought, and the only one I've ever loved—but duty comes first."

Then she was gone. Gram was left staring at the uncaring sky, watching clouds float by while he fought for each breath.

Thornbear

Chapter 31

Lying in a mountainside meadow in spring might have been a pleasant experience under different circumstances. Aside from his emotional turmoil, the most obvious unpleasantness was the cold. In spring the mountain never got much past something that might be called mildly warm and being in the shadow of the rocks meant that he was cold.

Paralysis, while distressing, was something his long afternoons with Cyhan had made tolerable; he was pretty used to spending long periods without being able to scratch his nose. Physical discomfort he could deal with.

Slowly suffocating, struggling to draw each breath, while alone and trying to resist alternate bouts of drowsiness and stark terror—that was something new. Gram didn't think there was a name for the feeling of this new experience, it would probably require a new word, but he didn't have time to think of one.

He was too busy trying to stay alive.

His heart was pounding and his eyes flew open as he frantically forced his lungs to draw air again. He had drifted off once more. The worst part of it was how peaceful it was; the numbness of the poison blunted much of his body's natural response to suffocation. When the drowsiness closed his eyes the only thing that served to wake him was the beating of his heart, and even that seemed muted.

I can't die yet.

In his mind's eye he saw Irene once more being carried away, limp across a stranger's shoulder. She had trusted him. If he had gone with them immediately, rather than try to fetch his things first, it might have gone differently. Maybe he would have delayed their attackers long enough for all of them to escape. If he had paid attention to his earlier observation, the silence of the birds, he might have kept them from this situation altogether.

They were waiting then, gathering around the house. They probably had a set time, so that they could time their attack after the raid in Arundel, when they knew any defenders would be drawn away. *And they knew how to find the house because I told them. Because I told her.*

Gram knew this was his fault and he burned with equal parts shame and outrage. But he was tired, so very tired. Blackness passed over him again, like a warm blanket that could protect him from the cold of the ground beneath him.

"Gram! Gram!"

Something was hitting his face. He opened his eyes, annoyed, and drew another deep breath. His heart was pounding again, a sure sign he had stopped breathing. The fuzzy features of a small bear loomed into view. Grace was there, beating at his cheeks with her small paws.

He wanted to tell her to leave him alone, but his mouth didn't work. Nothing worked. Only his eyes, and when he remembered, his lungs.

"What's wrong with you? Talk to me!" she said, sounding worried and desperate.

The bear moved out of view as she examined his body from head to toe. When she came into view again he could see that her cloth body was scorched and dirty. *She must have come through the house,* he noted.

"You have a long shallow cut along your ribs, but it's not very big. It has already stopped bleeding. Why can't you move?"

She checked his arms.

"There's a small spot near your wrist, but it might not even be a wound. Looks more like a bug bite," she announced.

She waited beside him, tapping him with small paws whenever his eyes closed. What might have been an hour passed, but she never left. Eventually she grew bored and began to talk again.

"Conall and your sister got out safely. They nearly ran over me in the hallway. That's how I knew what was going on. Conall told me that you were still in the house. He also said that...Irene was..." She stopped then, unable to continue.

She's not dead, Gram wanted to shout.

"I should have been here," said Grace woefully. "This was my job. I was supposed to protect the family. If I had been here, instead of running about the castle, none of this would have happened."

Gram wanted to laugh. The thought of a stuffed animal protecting them was ridiculous, but the pain in Grace's voice was real.

"If they hadn't already been dead when I got here, I would have killed them all," she growled, her small voice sounding fierce. "But *you* did that didn't you? You were there when I should have been."

There was nothing you could do, thought Gram. He wanted to hug her, to give her some small comfort.

"I found Lilly," she said, her voice flat. "She was going to be married. Did you know?"

He had not known that. It was the sort of thing that had probably been talked about but he wouldn't have paid much attention. *Carissa probably knew.*

"All those years, she spent the best part of her youth taking care of the family. She hardly took any time for herself, but she had found someone, someone patient enough to wait for her. Now she's dead because I was too busy satisfying my own selfish curiosity instead of being here." Grace buried her head against his chest. "David—I can't imagine how much this will hurt him, and Peter. Poor Peter, he doted on his sister."

Peter Tucker, Lilly's brother, was the chamberlain of Castle Cameron, but Gram wasn't certain which David she meant. *David Summerland?* He was about the right age, and he was in the castle often enough to know Lilly. He was a tailor in Washbrook. Gram hardly knew him. He was a quiet, gentle man, just the sort to love someone like Lilly. *They would have made a good pair.*

His hand twitched, responding to his impulse to stroke the small bear.

"Your hand moved!"

It had. It also hurt like hell. With the return of that tiny bit of mobility had come some sensation. His hand ached, and as feeling returned to his arm, the pain spread. His arms and legs felt as though he had been tied down and beaten with clubs. His torso joined the chorus of misery soon after.

"Ohh," he groaned.

Grace patted him, sending waves of agony through him. "You're getting better. What happened? Can you talk?" She shook him and although her small body couldn't move him much, it was enough to make him want to scream.

"By all the dead gods! Please stop!" he tried to yell, but all that came out was a garbled mess. Gram's ribs spasmed as he tried to talk and his mouth gaped.

She continued to shake and pat him, making the next quarter of an hour a painful experience. Eventually he regained enough motor control to tell her, "Schtop, pleashh. It hurtsh. Don tousch me."

"Oh! Sorry." Grace stopped. "What did they do to you?"

"Poishun," he managed, lifting his wrist briefly to indicate the spot she had found before. The movement sent fiery waves along his arm. "Uhnn!" he gasped. *That was a mistake,* he told himself.

The rest of the day was nothing but torture and it was almost nightfall before Gram was able to sit up on his own. Everything hurt. Everything.

The house had burned until nothing was left of it but ash and a few smoldering timbers. The gate to Castle Cameron was gone and Gram knew that he and Grace were stranded at least a hundred miles from home. Not that he had any intention of returning home.

He had something more important to attend to, a rescue, and if it proved possible, revenge. He described what had happened to Grace while he recuperated. To put it mildly, the small bear was incensed.

"I'll kill that bitch," she swore.

Such language seemed out of place for her, but Gram couldn't fault her for it. "No, Grace. Leave her to me."

"Look what she did to you already."

Gram nodded tiredly, "I won't allow her that opportunity again, but I want you to promise not to hurt her." He couldn't help but wonder how the bear thought she would effect her revenge.

"Why?" said Grace fiercely.

"Because I still love her, despite everything. I don't know why she's done this, and I will see Irene returned, but in the end she kept me alive rather than kill me. If anyone kills her, it will be me." His anger had faded to a dull glow as the day waned. Gram had more questions than answers and he wanted the truth before he decided Alyssa's fate.

"What about Lilly?" rebuked Grace.

Gram winced again, remembering her bloodied form. "There will be a reckoning to pay for that, but I don't think Alyssa wanted that. In fact, I don't think she was in charge of this, but she still must bear some responsibility for it."

"You're a fool, Gram. Nothing good will come from showing mercy to that treacherous slattern," hissed Grace venomously.

"Slattern?" said Gram curiously. "Really Grace, you have to stop reading those books."

"Don't try to make light of this!"

"How am I supposed to take you seriously when you use words like 'slattern'?"

"It's a good word," she insisted.

"For my grandfather to use. Those books are turning your brain to fluff."

"It's already fluff and it works fine. Besides, I can't help it. Romance novels speak to me."

"If I didn't know better, I'd accuse you of reading them for the naughty bits," he observed.

"That's Moira. I read them for the adventure and emotional enlightenment."

Gram chuckled, though it sent slivers of pain throughout his body, "Emotional enlightenment? You are a very peculiar bear."

She sniffed, "I prefer to think of myself as 'sophisticated'."

"In either case, we may have gotten just what you always wanted."

"That isn't funny, Gram. I never wanted this."

He levered himself slowly up, and managed to stand, though his body made every effort to convince him it was a very bad idea. "Think of it from the outside. Put a little distance between yourself and the situation and it looks very much like something out of one of your books. We have love, betrayal, mysterious villains, a fool that needs to atone, and a damsel in distress."

"I am not in distress," huffed the bear.

"I meant Irene," he corrected. *Technically you aren't really a damsel either,* he thought, but he wouldn't have dared to say that.

"If anything, I'm the fool that needs to atone. I should have been here."

"That's me," said Gram. "I'm the one that trusted her, that gave away the location of this house."

"Don't be ridiculous."

"What would you call me then?"

Grace straightened up before announcing with great gravity, "You are my bumbling but faithful sidekick. The comic relief of our sordid tale."

He stared at the blackened and dirty stuffed animal. She made her pronouncement with such earnest sincerity that he began to laugh despite himself. And then he lost his already unsteady footing and fell over. The pain served to bring his laughter to an abrupt halt. "Ow! Damn! That hurts."

She patted his head, "One can't help but love the bumbling but faithful companion."

He laughed again, even as the pain brought tears to his eyes, "Please stop, Grace. It hurts too much to laugh."

"Such is your lot, poor wight," she told him.

"If you are the hero of our tale, who gets the girl in the end?"

Grace glared at him, "Don't even suggest it. If anyone kisses that trollop, it will be me."

"Huh?"

"It won't be a pleasant thing, dear. You haven't seen my teeth yet," she assured him.

Gram couldn't make sense of that remark, but he decided not to pursue the matter. Easing himself back to his feet he began to walk.

"Where are you going?"

"Nowhere yet. We need to survey what's left, to see if there's anything we can use," he explained.

She followed him as he walked gingerly around the outskirts of the burned husk that remained of the Illeniel cottage. With every step he groaned at the soreness that pervaded every muscle, but he refused to stop. By the time night had fallen he had accepted the fact that there was almost nothing they could use. If there was anything worthwhile left in the ruin it was far too hot for them to recover. The embers of the burned house would probably stay hot for days.

"Well there's one bright side," Gram told her.

"Such as?"

"We don't have to worry about making a fire tonight."

Grace chuckled, but his statement was a practical one. Even in spring, the mountain air would be dangerously chilly as the night progressed. They could easily stay warm by remaining close to the ruined home.

"The heat may last us for several nights," she suggested.

"We won't be here tomorrow night," said Gram.

"I think you should rest before we try to get home," said the bear.

"I'm not going home."

Grace punched his leg, though it had little effect. It served to punctuate her anger. "Idiot! You're half dead. You'll be lucky to survive the trip back down the valley without proper food and clothing, and you think you can chase after them?"

He shrugged.

"They have at least a half day's head start already, a full day by morning. They probably have horses, and allies, and supplies—and who knows what else?! And you think you can go off by yourself, chasing them through the mountains? How would you even find them, much less catch up to them?!"

He nodded, acknowledging her points. "That's true, up to a point, but I will find them. The rocky terrain isn't ideal, but there are at least three of them, if you count Irene. As you say, they probably have more waiting with horses or mules to carry their supplies, and that will make it far easier for me to track them."

"Oh, so you're a tracker now?!"

"What do you think I've been doing with Master Grayson in the mornings?"

"Drinking and lazing about in the woods, knowing that drunkard," she groused.

Gram sighed, "No. He's the finest tracker and the best archer in all of Washbrook."

"And how will you survive? You've no food, no supplies, not even a coat!"

"I have you."

"And that's what you're going to take?"

Gram smiled, "Just the 'bear' essentials."

Grace groaned at the pun, "You're not even fit to be the comic relief."

Chapter 32

Despite the easy warmth of the ruined house, Gram had difficulty sleeping. The aftereffects of the poison left his body aching in places that he hadn't even been aware that he had muscles. The catatonia that the drug had induced had forced every muscle he possessed into a state of maximum tension until it had worn off. It was similar to the pain that followed overexertion and extreme exercise, except that it included virtually all of his muscles.

Morning found him hungry and exhausted.

"Are you still sure about this?" asked Grace.

Deep down he wanted to give up. He knew she was right. Attempting to follow the kidnappers in his current condition, with no food, supplies, or proper clothing, was a fool's errand. Still, something inside him wouldn't allow it.

"This is my only option."

"No," she argued. "We talked about it yesterday, you have at least one other truly sensible option…"

"For *me,* this is the only option," he stressed, and then he began walking. Grace followed in his wake. "Do you want me to carry you?" he asked.

She laughed, "You can barely walk straight."

"You don't weigh much."

"I'll wait until you're better. I can keep up with any pace you can set currently."

He couldn't help but agree with that. He thought of mentioning the fact that she would get dirty, but a simple glance reminded him that she was already as filthy as a cloth bear could get. Instead he turned his attention to the surrounding landscape.

He had made a note of the direction they had gone the day before while he had been surveying the area. Of course, there really weren't many directions they could go from there. Down was the primary option. The house had been situated on the northern facing side of a mountain, just within the upper end of the tree line. The slope was wooded, with occasional meadows and open areas.

Near the bottom, where it met the base of the next mountain, was a stone gully that marked the source of the Glenmae River. From there, the logical course would be to follow the river fifty miles through the mountains, until it reached Shepherd's Rest, a small valley that bordered the main valley of Cameron and Lancaster.

Gram hoped that was the course they had taken, for it would be the easiest. The only other routes would be to follow a narrow northern pass into the Northern Wastes, or to head south, deeper into the Elentirs. East wasn't an option at all, for while it led eventually into the western plains of Dunbar, it was guarded by a truly massive rise of interlocking mountains.

They won't follow the river, he thought, *for that will take them closer to Cameron and Lancaster and they can't be certain how much time they have.* Carissa and Conall would have alerted those at the castle to the kidnapping and once a message reached the Count, he would return at speed. Gram wasn't sure how fast they could get back, but if they could make a teleportation circle, the speed would be practically instantaneous.

But they knew that. That's why they made sure he was far away, so that it would take time to notify him. They probably hoped to accomplish the kidnapping without alerting anyone for at least a day. If Conall and his sister hadn't escaped, no one would have known for days. They might have knocked on the door and wondered, but no one would have known for sure.

So they planned ahead, and they hoped to be far enough away to evade capture by the time Mordecai got here.

If that was the case then it wouldn't matter if the Count was warned half a day sooner. The captors would be far enough away that it would be impossible to find them. The Elentir Mountains were vast, thousands and thousands of square miles. Even a mage would be hard pressed to find a small group of people in it, once they were far enough away from their last known location.

But the Count is smart; he'll probably think to search the most likely routes that people on foot can take. The route to Shepherd's Rest would cost him at least a half a day to search, even flying.

"What are you thinking about?" asked Grace.

"Terrain," he said curtly.

"Are you even sure they came this way?"

He nodded. "They have to go downhill until they reach the river."

"Is that just a guess or can you really see a trail?"

Gram sighed, "Half of tracking is anticipating what the quarry will do; the signs just help by confirming that you haven't taken a wrong turn. If you go too far without one, you have to reconsider."

"But have you actually *seen* any signs?" she insisted.

"Yes," he told her. "Look over there, see that pine?"

"Uh huh."

"The bark has been knocked loose on this side, leaving a darker color exposed. Someone probably brushed up against it."

"Or a moose did," she offered.

"I haven't seen any moose, but I do know that several people came this way in a hurry yesterday, and I've spotted a number of similar marks as we came down."

"But you could be following a moose."

Gram took a deep breath. "Theoretically, I suppose that's possible, but only if it were several moose."

"Why several?"

"The sheer number of signs. See there? Those leaves have been disturbed. I can't say for certain *what* did that, but whatever large animal did it, it was likely several or there would be fewer places for me to notice."

"So it could be a herd of mooses," she said, stifling a giggle.

"The plural of moose is moose," he corrected.

Grace agreed, "I knew that would bother you."

Stopping, Gram pulled up a small weedy looking bush with white flowers and slender leaves. Resuming his walk he began plucking the leaves and flowers off, eating them as they went.

"Is that good to eat?"

Gram made a face. "Yarrow," he told her. "It tastes awful by itself but you can eat it. It's better as a tea or added to a stew."

"It doesn't look like enough to keep you going, though," she commented in a worried voice.

"It isn't," he admitted, continuing to chew the bitter leaves. "But every little bit helps. If I can't eat all of it, I can use the rest on my skin. It keeps mosquitos off."

"I guess you really weren't getting drunk and lazing about all those mornings."

"Did you really think that?"

She had known better, but that wasn't really the point of her conversation. Grace was deeply worried about Gram's chances of survival. She knew she couldn't talk him out of his current decision, but she had a feeling that if she didn't keep his spirits up he would eventually succumb to despair.

"Oh I didn't," she protested, "but your mother will be very relieved to hear that you were actually doing something practical. She and your sister had begun to wonder if you were developing unnatural tendencies with some of the sheep."

"What?!" he exclaimed, before giving her a rueful stare. "Now I know you're making things up. Carissa doesn't even know about such things."

"I wouldn't be so sure. She's been asking a lot of questions about boys lately."

He growled, "What boys?" The thought of boys, in conjunction with his baby sister, was a touchy topic for him.

Grace laughed, "I'll never tell."

***

They reached the bottom by mid-morning. It was easier going there, except for the occasional boulder or other obstacle. Gram gathered more plants that he found growing in a low meadow near the small trickle that would eventually become the Glenmae River.

"Does that one taste better than the yarrow?"

Gram smiled, "Much better." He held up a plant he had just pulled from the ground, the roots showed pink through the earth clinging to them. "This is amaranth. It's a shame they don't have seeds yet, those are a good enough to survive on. The leaves are passable as greens, but they won't be enough by themselves."

"The hunter taught you that?"

"Actually I learned about this from Nana, she used to have me gather them for her. She had a taste for it. She said where she grew up they actually cultivated it for food."

"Will we really be able to find enough for you to eat?"

He grimaced. "The hard part will be collecting enough without stopping. I can probably find pin cherries, dandelions, maybe even some gooseberries, but none of that will be enough. Eventually we'll have to get meat or fish. This stuff is only going to delay starvation."

"You don't have hooks, netting, or a bow."

Gram had already thought about that. "I don't have time to fish or hunt properly anyway."

"But you have a plan?" asked Grace. "Right?"

He bent down and picked up a solid stone. It was half the size of his fist. Placing it in his pouch he kept walking. "I have a pretty good arm, and there are lots of small animals. I'll have to eat whatever I'm lucky enough to kill or find. Snake, lizard, squirrel, something will turn up."

She shuddered, "I don't have any experience with eating, but none of that sounds very appetizing."

Wait till she realizes that since we have no way to make a fire, I'll have to eat it raw. He tried to ignore the queasiness that that thought invoked. *Another day without real food and maybe I won't care.*

The shallow wash that they were following split. Ahead the water continued on, heading west where it would eventually emerge into Shepherd's Rest, to the north a dry streambed meandered away in the direction that led to the Northern Wastes. Gram stopped.

"Did you spot some sign?"

"No, but this is where they *could* change course. I'll have to work my way around the area until I can determine for certain which way they went," he explained.

He focused on the northern route first, since he feared they planned to go in that direction, and his suspicion was soon proved correct. It was less than a quarter of an hour before he found the signs of a camp, as well as a few hoof marks. Grace watched him as he turned over several rocks.

"They were here?"

"Maybe," said Gram. "This camp is more than a day old. See the blackening on the rocks? They made a small fire and scattered it afterward. They turned these over to hide the fire marks. At a guess I would say this was where they stopped when they were coming in. Some of them waited here to meet those that went to attack the house after they were done."

"You found the camp easily enough," observed Grace. "Wouldn't they have been more careful?"

"It isn't as easy as it sounds, and they didn't really have to bother. They didn't think anyone would be tracking them immediately afterward. It should have been at least two or three days before anyone got here, if not longer. I only found it because of the hoof prints in the sand over there. One or two rains and I doubt I would have seen anything.

"I can't be sure how many were here. Definitely they had several pack animals, donkeys maybe. I killed about nine at the house, but there were probably more waiting here with the animals."

They began following the dry wash, letting it take them north. Gram kept his eyes open for more signs, as well as for small animals. He hadn't eaten solid food for almost a full day now and his stomach was beginning to hurt.

Unfortunately he saw neither, and as the afternoon sun waned he began to feel shaky. A light rain began to fall.

"Shit."

"This is going to destroy the trail, isn't it?" she said.

"It will obscure some signs," he admitted. "But we are less than a day behind them I hope, so we will probably be alright. Rain is a bigger problem for scent tracking, if you're using dogs. Mostly I'm concerned about getting wet."

Grace didn't like the sound of that. She had been watching Gram all day and he was far from his best. His gait was unsteady and he looked pale. The rain might not be too bad while the sun held out, but once night fell the air would turn cold.

He kept moving rather than stop. There wasn't much in the way of potential shelter anyway. Making a lean-to from the meager deadwood in the area would have taken considerable time and provided little relief from the rain. Taking advantage of some of the rocky overhangs would have been better, but he already worried that they were losing ground.

"Gram," said Grace quietly. He didn't answer. "Gram!" she hissed, "There's something ahead."

He paused, looking at her. "I don't see anything."

"It's not in view yet. It's past those rocks," she pointed, indicating several large boulders a few hundred yards ahead.

"How can you see past the rocks?"

"I don't see the same way you do," she explained, patting her eye buttons. "These are just buttons. I see the same way wizards do, magesight."

"That's handy to know," said Gram.

"My range isn't nearly as good as theirs, and this is at my limit..." She stopped, a growing feeling of fear sweeping over her. Whatever she was sensing was powerful, and it was coming close. "This isn't good. I think it sees us. It can probably see farther than I can. We have to run!"

"That isn't likely to happen," observed Gram. "Can we hide?"

"No, we stand out like torches in the dark. This thing sees aythar, like I do," she finished with a low groan. "It's too late."

The bear collapsed, falling prone onto the bare ground. "Grace, are you alright? What's wrong?" Gram was beginning to feel something, as though the air itself was growing heavy. It weighed on him, a pressure on his mind.

A figure appeared in the distance, a man, perhaps, but then it unfurled golden wings and took to the air. It was flying toward him. Gram's body began to shake as he fought to stand. It was as if a giant hand rested on his shoulders, pushing him toward the ground.

The world grew dim as the creature descended on his location. It wasn't dark, and his eyes still worked but there was an invisible brilliance around him, an unseen light that blinded his mind, making it difficult to think. "What is this?" he ground out through clenched teeth.

"What have we here?" said a voice of heartbreaking beauty. It was a male voice, matched by a muscular body of unearthly grace. "A human, traveling with a spell-beast. How unusual."

Gram tried to keep his eyes on the man, but his gaze went to the ground instead. *He's too beautiful.* It was too painful to look at him. Tears leaked from the corners of his eyes and a feeling of unbearable sadness threatened to overwhelm him.

His life was meaningless. He could see that now, faced with the celestial being before him, his own humanity seemed dirty and squalid. Gram's knees buckled and he fell before what could only be one of the gods.

A light burned through his mind, examining every inch of his soul while he cringed inwardly. He knew he was unworthy.

"Gram Thornbear," mused the deity, letting the words roll gently from his lips. "How fascinating. Such a pathetic creature you are, nothing like your father at all."

Gram's thoughts crystallized then, at the mention of his father. He was filled with questions. The light sorted through his thoughts.

"Dorian is dead. Such a shame, I would have loved to kill him. Your father was a far more substantial being than you, manling. I should weep for your family to see how far the Thornbears have devolved. Dorian was one of the few men that could stand before me without quivering in fear."

Celior. He remembered now. Celior was the only one of the shining gods to escape, the only one that hadn't been destroyed. Gram wanted to cry to think of the destruction of such a transcendent being.

"You love me, don't you boy? Just like your mother. She felt my touch once, and shivered in ecstasy. Your father hated me for that, but despite his best efforts, she never forgot me. I gave her more pleasure with a single kiss than he could give her in his entire life."

The god's words struck a chord within him, but he couldn't give voice to it. Despite the blinding light in his mind he still felt the scorn. *How could anyone deny him?*

"Such a lovely sister you have," commented Celior. "When this is over perhaps I will make her one of my acolytes. I will show her the love her father could never give her."

A spark lit in Gram's mind then, a rage that would not be ignored, despite the gut wrenching fear that controlled him. "No."

"How interesting. The pup shows his teeth. Is it the thought of your sister that instills such defiance in you?" Celior leaned down, stroking Gram's chin with one finger. The contact sent waves of pleasure through him, threatening to blot every thought from his mind.

"I wouldn't hurt her, manling. She would welcome me."

Gram's rage burned through the empty pleasure. "No."

"It is your sister. The thought of my hand on her inspires—jealousy? What a sad incestuous creature you are. You should be happy for her. What of your mother? We could be a happy family together. Mother, son, daughter, and of course I would be your father. Imagine the joy."

With the words, Celior sent images into Gram's mind, of his mother and sister, naked. Obscene visions that made him want to vomit in horror. The god touched his chin again, obliterating the revulsion with overwhelming passion.

"I could even share them with you, manling. Is that what you'd like? Or perhaps you'd prefer to experience a father's love more directly?" The visions changed.

"You—are—not—my—father," Gram managed, choking out the words.

"Such a disobedient child you are," said Celior. "Very well, I will give you a gift out of respect for the dead lump of flesh you call your father. Those you seek are yet ahead of you, but weak and feeble as you are, you have no hope of catching them. If you do reach them they will kill you."

Is he going to release us? Gram didn't dare to hope.

"I am not here to stop you," answered the god. "I am here to kill the wizard when he comes, rushing to save his lost child. To you I will grant freedom, and with it, the finest of torments—hope."

A sense of shame washed over Gram, though some part of him knew it came from the outside. *I am not even worth killing.*

"Pray that your enemies slay you, child," said the shining god, bestowing a serene smile on him. Its glow flowed over him like the sun. "For if you survive, I will make the visions I have shown you come to pass. I will have you cry to me in gratitude as you lick your family's heart-blood from my heels."

Something warm and wet splashed onto his head and back, filling him with vitality and a sense of well-being. The stench of urine filled his nose.

"Take this blessing and go, child," laughed the shining god.

The impulse to run rose within him, an overpowering urge. Leaping to his feet Gram snatched up the cowering bear and ran, following the dry gorge and bounding over whatever rocks or other obstacles barred his path. He ran with the grace of a deer and his heart pounded in his chest, ringing with energy.

Inside he cried for shame.

Chapter 33

They traveled perhaps a mile before the desire to run faded, though neither of them spoke when he slowed.

Gram's face burned with humiliation. Nothing in his short life could have prepared him for such an encounter and he flinched inwardly whenever his mind showed him flashes of what Celior had described. He felt his gorge rise, but his body was too healthy to vomit.

An hour passed before Grace finally spoke, "It wasn't really urine."

The rain had stopped and his clothes seemed clean, but he remembered the smell. "I don't think there's any doubt about what it was." The wound in his side was gone, and his muscles no longer ached and trembled, but his pride was wounded beyond repair.

"That thing, it can't pee any more than I can eat. It healed you, that's all. He wanted you to feel humiliated."

"What makes you such an expert?"

Grace's voice was rich with anguish, "Because we're the same. He called me a spell-beast, but in reality that's all Celior is as well. We don't eat, and neither do we—excrete."

The simulated urination was the least of Gram's problems, though. The god's intrusion into his mind had left him feeling dirty, soiled. The illusions he had been forced to witness hadn't been his own, but they had felt real. Celior had violated him more thoroughly than any rapist could hope to accomplish.

And he did the same to my mother. Anger threatened to rob him of what little sanity he had left. *No wonder she never spoke of it.*

His father hadn't bowed, though. He knew that much. Dorian Thornbear hadn't fallen to his knees in fearful obeisance. *Dorian was one of the few men that could stand before me without quivering in fear.*

"I'm a coward," muttered Gram.

"Don't give him what he wants," said Grace. "That thing we met is just a twisted bully. He's been around so long that the only thing left that gives him any pleasure is messing around in people's heads."

"My father was able to face him."

"Dorian was a stoic! Celior couldn't get inside his head, Gram. Just because you're not like him in that regard, doesn't make you any less brave. What you did back at the house took courage. You have two parents, and both of them faced that monster. Your mother wasn't a stoic, but she didn't let it stop her. She went through something similar, but afterward she picked herself up and kept going."

"I'm not as smart as Mother."

"Being a genius isn't everything, Gram, and it certainly isn't what got her through it. You owe a lot of who you are to her, things that perhaps you don't see, but you aren't her, and you aren't Dorian. You..." she poked him with one paw, "... are Gram Thornbear. Your story starts here. That thing may have knocked you down, but getting up is your choice. A Thornbear gets back up."

He thought of his mother, sitting in her chair and sipping at her morning tea. Her quiet presence had been a constant in his life. She watched the world with eyes that saw things that even magesight couldn't reveal. Despite her calm demeanor, her keen perception and powerful confidence had always intimidated him. What would she have done if she had been with them a few minutes ago? What had she done after *her* encounter with the filth and depravity that was Celior?

He knew the answer.

Gram picked Grace back up, squeezing her gently. "Thanks Grace."

"Don't thank me. You're the one that decided we had to go after Irene," said the bear. "And I still think you're a terrible failure at certain things."

He looked at her curiously, "What things?"

"You're the worst comedic sidekick I've ever had."

That brought a smile to his lips, "You aren't doing so good as the tragic hero either."

"Don't let my small size fool you. In the end, I will get the girl," she answered.

***

They traveled on, and the going was much easier now. Celior's 'blessing', while disgusting, had been real. Gram's body felt strong and sure. The aching of his muscles was gone, and also the shakiness he had felt. He was still hungry, but it wasn't the same painful emptiness now, it felt more as if he had merely skipped breakfast.

The cut in his side was gone, along with every other bruise or abrasion he had gotten. *We have a chance now,* he thought to himself. *While they're traveling with pack animals and a prisoner, I'm alone and unencumbered.* He could catch up to them, so long as he didn't lose the trail.

Food was still a concern, though. Gram walked quickly, using his newfound energy to keep up a brisk pace, but while his eyes caught the occasional sign of their enemy's passage, he saw no animals. The stone he held in his hand went unused.

Darkness fell, but he didn't stop.

"Aren't you going to rest?" asked Grace.

"Not until I get tired," he told her. "Even if we make camp, we have no fire or blankets. Walking keeps me warm."

"You won't be able to see in the dark."

The world had already become a monochrome scene of shadows and grey. The moon was up but it was hidden behind one of the mountains. His eyes had adjusted, but with only starlight he could barely see more than the ground immediately before him. "I can see enough to walk and your vision will keep us going in the right direction."

"How far does your special sight reach?" he asked her.

"About two hundred yards," she answered, "but I don't know how to track."

"That won't be a problem until we reach the rise I saw before the sun went down. Until then they don't have any options, and if they've stopped to camp in the trees along the west side of this gully you will be able to see them, fire or no fire," said Gram. The eastern side of the wash was steep and craggy, so there was no chance of anyone camping there. "We'll keep going until it splits and then stop for the night."

They continued their trek, moving slowly as he picked his way in and around massive boulders that had long ago fallen from the rocky eastern side of the gully. The mountain that would eventually interrupt their path at the northern end had seemed only a few hours distant in the light of day, but in the dark it never seemed to get any closer.

Sometime near midnight Grace poked his cheek, "There are two men ahead, at the limits of my sight," she whispered.

That was far enough away that being seen wasn't a concern, but sounds traveled a long way in the rocky valley. His eyes strained against the darkness, but he could see nothing ahead of them but dim grey stone and dark shadows. It was probably a cold camp; if the men had built a fire it would have been easily visible. "Describe their position."

"They are tucked into a low place above a big overhang on the right hand side. I don't think you would be able to see them even if the sun was up."

It sounded like a perfect position for an ambush. "What are they doing?"

"Lying down, with their backs on the rock. They have their bedrolls beneath them. They might even be asleep. They aren't moving but they have bows next to them."

"Let's wait a while," said Gram. "I want to make sure they're asleep before we move."

"It's a sorry ambush if they're sleeping," commented Grace.

"People don't travel at night. If you weren't here I would have stopped a while back," Gram told her. "The bows are useless in the dark too. They were probably left behind to kill or delay anyone following the others. The rock you described would be a good place to pick people off with a bow."

"It would be a useless tactic if one of the wizards was with us," she said.

"But none of them are, and Celior is waiting for them if they come. This is just a precaution I think, and a lucky one for us," said Gram.

"Lucky?"

"Look at my shoes." Gram had left the castle wearing soft cloth shoes. They were well suited to smooth stone corridors but they were quickly disintegrating on the sharp, rocky terrain. Another day and his feet would be essentially bare.

"Two men are waiting to kill you and you want to steal their shoes?"

"A bedroll, food, heavy clothing, and a bow would be welcome too," he added.

She thought about it for a moment, realizing he was right. "Let me do it," she offered.

The thought of a small stuffed bear attacking two grown men threatened to make him lose control and laugh out loud. He squeezed her for a second, "No, this is a job for your comic companion."

"Let me help then," she insisted.

"What can you do?"

A lot more than you realize, she thought. "I can choose how I sound, for one thing," she told him. "I can sound like a real bear. They might run if they thought a brown bear was coming after them."

"Hmmm," said Gram thinking. "That gives me an excellent idea." He began outlining his plan.

They waited another quarter of an hour before they moved, making sure that the men were truly asleep. When it was clear that the men weren't just pretending they began to move, Grace guiding him slowly and carefully up and over the rocks on the right hand side. Despite their care there were still several scary moments when a rock was displaced or unnoticed dead leaves rustled underfoot.

Each time they made a noise they would stop and wait, making sure they hadn't alerted their prey. It took nearly an hour before Gram was in position, crouching silently some thirty feet from where the strangers slept.

He would have liked to get closer. Ideally he would have preferred to be able to attack them in their sleep, but one of the men had woken, alerted by the sound of a rock falling. The intervening distance was open and sparsely covered with dry grass and rocks. Once he left the cover of the rock that hid him he would be easily seen, even in the dim starlight, and the ground ahead was sure to make noise.

Grace separated from him then, moving down the rocks and working her way along the gully before climbing up again on the other side. Her soft lightweight body made stealth easy, but her short limbs were a serious hindrance. Some places were simply impossible for her to climb over. She was forced to take a long circuitous route. It was another hour before she had picked her way around to a position on the other side of the men, sixty or seventy feet on the other side of their camp.

The one that had woken was already asleep again, but she doubted Gram knew that, and fortunately their plan didn't require such knowledge. She began with a low growl that mounted in volume until it was a frightening roar.

Gram had been waiting patiently for that signal but he didn't start forward until he saw the blurry shadows of the men begin to move. They were scrambling in alarm, sitting up and staring into the darkness in Grace's direction.

The noise she made only grew louder, and she didn't pause. They needed to make sure it would cover any sound his approach would make.

"We have to move!" said one of the men. "It's getting closer."

"I can't see anything," hissed his companion. They were snatching up their bedrolls and packs, gathering everything into their arms as they prepared to make a hasty retreat. "What is that?"

"It's a fuckin' bear, idiot. Grab your bow," said the other. "No, don't try to string it. That'd just piss it off. We have to run."

Unfortunately one of them spotted Gram as he ran forward. Frightened by the sound of the bear he dropped everything in his arms as he saw the dark figure charging at him from the darkness. His friend stumbled and fell sideways, unsure what was going on.

Gram's knife took that one in the back, and then he was after the one that had just dropped his gear.

The man had already put his sword belt on, though, and while the rest of his belongings were scattered around him he retained the wit to draw his blade. Shaking with fear and adrenaline he pointed it in Gram's direction. "You ain't no bear!"

Grace continued to roar from the darkness behind him, but the man ignored it and leapt forward, thrusting at Gram with his weapon.

Shit, thought Gram, retreating hastily to avoid being skewered. He held only a four inch knife, and while one of the men was down for good, he was at a serious disadvantage. Worse, the shadow of the rock overhanging the men's camp made it even harder to see.

Stepping on a rock he stumbled, but rather than try to keep his feet he let himself fall. He remembered the stone from his advance a moment before, even though he had failed to take it into account during his withdrawal. It was a modest stone, about a foot across. He fell over it and rolled into a crouch beside it as his opponent came on.

Dropping his knife he hefted the stone with all the speed his muscles could provide. It might have weighed thirty or forty pounds, but he flung it up and forward as though it weighed nothing, striking the swordsman in the legs.

The other man stumbled, but didn't fall, his sword arm shooting out to his right in case he had to catch himself. Gram surged up and into him as the sword went out of line, striking the man in the chin with the top of his head and driving him from his feet.

They struggled in the darkness for a few seconds, but Gram was already on top of his foe and once he had his hands on the man's face he shoved it downward, slamming his skull into the stony ground. He repeated the brutal action several more times, until his enemy's body had gone limp and the back of his head had become a soft wet ruin.

The stillness of the night returned and Gram stared at the man underneath him. *A few minutes ago he was sleeping peacefully.* His hands were wet and sticky. A sudden noise to his right made him realize that the man he had stabbed was still alive.

Standing, he walked over, looking down on the one that had taken his knife in the back. The wound had been high up, but the blade hadn't struck his heart. From the wet sound of the fellow's labored breathing it had probably punctured one of his lungs. He was a dead man, but he might last for hours.

I'm sorry.

That's what he wanted to say, but the words wouldn't come out. The man he was looking at had been planning to kill him, or whoever followed. He was part of the band that had taken Irene, that had killed Lilly. He didn't deserve an apology, and yet, watching him die made Gram's stomach twist.

"Why?" he asked, addressing the dying man. "Why did you do it?"

The man's eyes rolled in his head, staring fearfully at Gram. He knew he was dying, but he yet feared the final blow. His lips opened and he struggled to speak, but the words came out wet and garbled. Something dark ran from his mouth. In the daylight Gram was sure it would have been red.

Is this what he felt? Gram thought of his father. *How many times did he experience this?* Dorian Thornbear was said to have killed hundreds, if not more, in both times of war, and in smaller personal conflicts. *It should have driven him mad—unless, he enjoyed it.*

But Gram's memories of his father didn't depict a madman. His father had been kind and patient. His mother had said so as well. Gram wished his father was alive, so he could ask him. *How do you get past this pain, this guilt? There is blood on my hands now.*

The man on the ground tried to speak again, and this time his words were clear enough to understand, "They paid—me."

He was a mercenary soldier. Had he had a family? Were there people waiting for him to return?

"You picked the wrong job, my friend," said Gram. "Who paid you?" The words sounded calm, almost casual coming from his lips. *Who is this passionless killer?* thought Gram, *it can't be me.*

But it was.

"Please…" begged the mercenary, unable to finish his sentence.

Gram went back to the other and retrieved the sword. It would be easier to use. The knife was too close, too personal. Standing over the dying man again he held the sword up, trying to decide the best place to put the blade, to end his suffering. The man's eyes bored into his own, begging and accusing with the same stare.

He dropped the weapon. It was too cold. If he was going to do this, he would take the full weight of it. He took out his knife instead, and knelt beside the figure. "I'm sorry," he said then, and plunged the blade into the man's heart.

The stranger jerked once, and then died, a last wet breath leaving his mouth. His eyes never left Gram's.

Though his stomach was empty, Gram began to heave, vomiting onto the ground. A small amount of fluid came up, and after that it only dry heaves that shook him. Grace stood close by now, gently patting his back, but she said nothing.

Chapter 34

Gram moved the bodies, dragging them some twenty yards from the camp before stripping both of them of their clothing and boots. In the dark it was hard to say what might fit and what wouldn't. The tunic and coat of the one he had stabbed were ruined, but his boots, belt and trousers were probably still good. The belongings of the one whose head he had smashed were probably fine. He would sort through them in the morning.

Laying one bedroll on top of the other he curled up inside it and hoped he could get warm. He didn't expect sleep. His conscience wouldn't allow that, surely, but when he closed his eyes and opened them again he found the morning sun shining down on him. His body's exhaustion had taken precedence over his moral confusion.

He lay quietly for a few minutes, enjoying the sound of birdsong and the play of sunlight on the rocks nearby. His mind was still, at peace. He had done terrible things the night before, but he was careful not to look at them directly. In the light of day they seemed like nightmares, terrible indeed, but unreal.

"You're awake," noted Grace.

"Seems like it," he replied, sitting up.

"How do you feel?"

"Later," he told her. "There are things to be done." He stood and began sifting through the chaotic remains of the camp, making a small pile of the things he would keep.

There were two packs and within them were enough bread, dried meat, and hard cheese to last the two men for several days. He ate a modest breakfast and packed the rest of the food into one of the packs. He rolled up one of the bedrolls and tied it onto the pack as well and then he examined the clothing.

Most of it was too small, and his own doublet and trousers were far better, despite being made for a more civilized environment. He counted himself fortunate that one of the men had had big feet, his boots were a bit tight, but they fit. Gram made two small cuts in them, in the front and along the outer edge, giving his feet enough room to be more comfortable. He couldn't afford blisters.

He belted on one of the sword belts and chose the better of the two swords, then he did the same with the bows, pulling them to a full draw to test their strength. He collected the arrows from both their quivers and counted them. *Twenty three.*

Glancing at the sun he decided it was probably close to nine o'clock. Picking up Grace, he put her on his shoulder and began picking his way down.

"Focus on the sides, in case there are any other ambushes set," he told her. "I'll worry about finding their trail."

"Sure," said Grace. "How are you…?"

"Later," he interrupted. "Much later."

"Alright," she said, accepting his reluctance.

They reached the rising ground that formed the base of the mountain that divided the wash by noon. Gram was far from anything he was remotely familiar with now and he couldn't be sure of the merits of either path, so he had no way to judge which direction their quarry might have gone. Either way might lead to a dead end, or both might be viable.

He spent an hour checking the eastern side without luck before he tried the western path. Within minutes he discovered several signs, a bit of disturbed soil and some trampled grass. The clincher was a small piece of leather, probably a bit of harness that someone had trimmed for some reason.

They traveled along, climbing over and around increasingly difficult terrain. Gram might have worried that the way would become completely impassable but he knew that those he followed had taken their pack animals through once already and they had to have mapped their route beforehand. He kept his eyes on the ground, trusting Grace to alert them if there were any hidden traps.

A strange noise began growing in his ears sometime around midafternoon. It wasn't a sound he was familiar with, a distant rushing sound, as if there were river rapids nearby. But there was no water. The low rocky valley they followed was dry, and the sound seemed to come from above, as if the sky itself was making the sound.

"What is that?" he wondered aloud.

"I don't know."

The mountain to their left was dipping low and a gentle slope led to a ridge there. "Let's climb up," suggested Gram, "maybe we can see something from there."

Half an hour later they were close to the ridgeline. Gram stayed low as they crested it, not wanting to alert their enemies. Anyone traveling below would be able to see them from miles away if they stood there.

The sound had reached new heights, but Gram still couldn't understand its source. There was nothing like a river in view and the open sky was clear, except for a small dot to the west. He figured that it must be a bird, but it was too indistinct for him to identify.

Then he realized it was moving, but not in the fashion that one would expect of a bird. It passed through a cloud and he knew then that it was much farther distant than he had thought, and consequently traveling much faster as well.

"What is that?" he wondered.

"I can't see anything," said Grace. "My vision is wonderful for things within a few hundred yards, but I can't see anything beyond that."

"There's something flying, a long way off, to the west of us," explained Gram. "It's big enough that I thought it was a bird at first, but now I don't know what it is."

"Could it be the Count's flying machine?" suggested Grace.

"It never made a sound like this," said Gram. "And there would be several people visible, or a larger dark spot, maybe. I'm not sure what it would look like at this distance."

Whatever it was, was taking a path that angled past them. It wouldn't fly directly over them, but as they watched, he figured it would pass within a couple of miles. *Probably over that peak there,* he thought, mentally marking a mountaintop in the distance. As it grew nearer he thought he could make out some discernible features.

"It's a man," he declared. "I can make out his arms and legs now. He's flying along like an arrow from a bow, headfirst."

"That has to be the Count then."

"Can he fly like that?" asked Gram.

"He did during the last great battle," said Grace, "right before he fought Mal'goroth. Moira told me about it."

"But he was some sort of shiggreth monster god-demon then," said Gram.

"I bet he remembers how," she said, "but I doubt it's safe."

An attack on his family might just drive him to take such a risk, thought Gram, as the figure passed over the mountaintop he had noted before. The Count's path was perpendicular to them, and though he was still a few miles distant, Gram could see he was moving at an unbelievable speed.

A booming roar, like thunder, struck him then, a sound so powerful it felt like a physical blow, and Gram and Grace both fell flat onto the rocks.

"What was that?!"

"I don't know," said Grace. "It felt like something just shook the world."

"It even rattled my teeth." *How fast was he flying?* The stories he had heard from the battle with Mal'goroth mentioned something similar, when Mordecai had flown with such speed that it seemed as if the sky exploded, but he had assumed the story was exaggerated.

"He must have gotten word from Elaine," said Grace. "There was no circle at the house, so he must have just taken off and flown straight for it."

"Celior is waiting for him."

"I feel sorry for the god," said Grace smugly.

"It isn't good, Grace. Celior was afraid to come out in the open before. He fought Mordecai once and lost, and since then the Count defeated the other shining gods as well, along with most of the dark gods."

"So he'll have no trouble giving that arrogant bastard a good thrashing then."

"Maybe," said Gram, "but Celior is expecting him. He's drawn him out, unprepared, away from his allies and any traps he might have prepared in Cameron. And the Count isn't as powerful, or immortal for that matter, as he was when he fought the others."

"I don't think he was any of that the first time he fought Celior," said Grace. "He'll win."

Gram thought of Celior's threats regarding his mother and sister. *He's got to win.* "Let's go," he told Grace. "We can't do anything about it, one way or another, so let's do what we can."

They descended again and resumed their course, following the occasional signs that indicated a group of several men and their animals had gone in the same direction. *I'm coming for you, Rennie.*

They traveled onward, watching the sun set behind the mountains. The air grew cold with the disappearance of the sun, but once again Gram kept them going, not wanting to stop until they came to another place that their quarry might have had a choice of directions.

Several hours after dark the lights began.

"What was that flash?" he asked.

"I didn't see anything," said Grace, "but if it came from far off I wouldn't."

A moment later a rolling boom reached their ears. "It sounded like thunder," noted Gram. The sky overhead was clear, full of brilliant stars set against a velvety black firmament. Another flash of light split the darkness.

"Do you think a storm is coming?" wondered Grace.

"I'm not sure." The wind was starting to pick up, but there were still no clouds. The next flash caused the entire sky to glow, casting the world around them into stark white and black contrast. A steady golden light was flickering and shimmering beyond the mountains to the south of them now, as if a monstrously huge bonfire had been lit. The night was punctuated with an unending staccato of resounding booms.

"They're fighting," stated Grace.

"Remind me never to piss off Matt's dad," said Gram, trying to make a joke, but inwardly he was worried. *If he falls, we're doomed.*

"I'm sure Mal'goroth wished he had known that before he did the same," observed Grace.

But Celior did know better, noted Gram, *better than anyone.*

The wind had become a raging tempest, and while there still weren't any clouds, the sky was continually shattered by dazzling curtains of lightning that stretched from one horizon to the next. The peals of thunder were so deep they seemed to shake the mountains themselves.

"We should keep moving," said Gram. "I have a feeling the show is only going to make Irene's captors hurry faster." He left unspoken the fact that he wanted to be as far away as possible in case the wrong one emerged as the victor.

They continued on while the sky changed colors, sometimes illuminating the ground before them as if it was daytime, and then leaving them in utter blackness. A new star had risen in the sky to the south; a brilliant flame that flared and burned. Gouts of fire issued from it, striking the mountains below while curtains of lighting seemed to envelop it at frequent intervals.

Gram couldn't even begin to guess which was which.

They ran when the light was strong and stopped when it vanished, their eyes no longer adjusted to see by mere starlight. The bizarre battle continued behind them for almost a quarter of an hour before it stopped, ending with a frightening sound. Gram fell as the earth beneath him jumped, throwing him from his feet and slapping him hard as he hit the rocks. The world shook and the sky grew red before fading away into soft darkness.

Silence reigned and the star that had burned in the sky was gone.

"Is it over?" asked Grace, whispering as though she feared the combatants might hear them despite the intervening miles.

A booming laughter rolled over the land, as if to answer her question. The burning star rose into the sky again and Gram knew that Celior was still free. He had won. The earth shook once more, and then the world was silent, while the star flew south, eventually dwindling into the distance.

"I think he's dead," said Gram in a dull voice, numb with shock.

"Don't say that."

"That was Celior's laugh. That was him flying away."

The bear hadn't been able to see the flying star, but she refused to give in to despair. "They thought he was dead and lost before, but it was never so. I won't believe it," she said.

Gram picked her up and resumed walking. He didn't reply to her hopeful declaration.

"You believe me, right?" insisted the bear.

Gram didn't answer. The darkness had closed around them and despite her presence, he felt more alone than ever. The man that had become his second father was dead, or worse. He trudged on. *We still have Matt, and Moira. They'll set it right, and by all the dead gods, I'll do everything I can to help them.*

Thornbear

Chapter 35

It was close to midnight when Gram finally decided to rest. He ate more of the cheese and dried meat they had taken from the ambushers and then he laid out the bedroll and slept. Once again, despite his fears and worries, his body's exhaustion took matters into its own hands and he sank into an empty oblivion. If he dreamt, he didn't remember it.

He woke with the morning sun and after a quick breakfast, they set out again.

"Grace," he said.

"Yes."

"Something occurred to me when I was going to sleep last night."

"What?" she asked.

"You once told me that you need Moira to restore your magic every few days, but today is the third day we've been out. How much longer will you…?"

She patted his cheek to reassure him. "I should have told you before. Whenever Moira is going to be away for a while she stores extra aythar for me. See these buttons?" She pointed to a row of three buttons along the front of her body.

"Yes."

"Each one holds enough aythar to sustain me for roughly four days. I'm fine."

"Oh." He did a quick mental tally. The Count's family had been gone a week before the attack and they had been traveling for three days. The three buttons would last sixteen days, and she could manage three on her own. He didn't like the result. "It's been ten days, that only leaves five more."

"I know," she answered calmly. "I can stretch it a bit if I'm careful."

"The Count was planning to be gone three to four weeks, that wouldn't have been enough time even if none of this had happened."

"There was a stasis box in Moira's room. If I ran short, I would have climbed inside and waited for her to get back," she explained.

"But that's gone now…"

"Since the Count came rushing back, I'm sure the twins will be returning home at speed too," she replied.

"Except that we aren't in Cameron, Grace. We're in the middle of the mountains. Even if we turn around now it will take almost three days to get back to where the house *was,* but we need to be in Cameron. There's no telling how long it will take us to get there!"

"Gram," said Grace gently. "We all make choices. You and Irene are my choice."

His eyes blurred with sudden tears. The events of the last few days had been terrible, but it was the thought of losing Grace that finally broke down the barrier he had been holding between the present and the pain of it all. "Why didn't you tell me?! We should have headed straight for the castle."

"You wanted to save Irene, and so did I. The only reason I counseled you against it was because I feared for your safety, Gram. When it was apparent that you wouldn't be dissuaded, I decided to do everything I could to help. I didn't tell you because I didn't want you to worry. There's nothing to be done about it," she said with finality.

He wiped at his cheeks. "Dammitt."

"Don't cry," she told him. "You're supposed to be my bumbling but faithful sidekick, remember? Keeping us cheered up is your job."

He laughed but his eyes wouldn't stop watering. "I'm not very good at my job."

"I have high hopes that you will improve," she told him.

He nodded, not trusting himself to speak. *She really is the tragic hero of this tale.*

***

That afternoon they reached the end of the mountains. The low valley they were following opened up gradually and Gram could see the beginnings of the Northern Wastes ahead.

The signs of their quarry's passage had become more frequent and were far newer now, giving him hope that they were close behind Irene and her captors. He could only hope they caught up soon. Tracking them through the rough desolate terrain of the wastes would be even more difficult without the mountains to funnel them along more predictable routes.

He broke into a trot, loping forward at a ground eating pace. If they were going to catch them it needed to be soon.

As the land smoothed out he spotted a small group of people in the distance, no more than a couple of miles ahead. He began to run.

"Do you see something?" asked Grace, wishing again that her vision extended farther than a few hundred yards.

"Yes," he panted as he ran. "They're a mile or so ahead of us."

"How many?"

"Four, no five of them," he answered, "plus two donkeys."

"Can they see us?"

"Definitely. They're trying to hurry now. It looks like Irene is on one of the donkeys. The other four are walking." Gram focused on his breathing. He needed to catch up to them, but more than that, he needed to be able to fight once he did.

They ran a bizarre race for ten minutes, while he steadily gained on them. With four people afoot and two pack animals, Irene's captors had no hope of getting away from him. They were only a hundred yards distant now and by some undetermined signal they stopped, turning to face him.

He could see Alyssa now, standing beside the donkey on which Irene rode, while three other men stood in front of them, blocking his path. One of the three was clearly the leader; he smiled and gestured to the other two who spread out to the sides, taking out bows and stringing them.

"They have bows, Grace," he warned her.

"Turn around!" she exclaimed. "They'll turn you into pin cushion."

"It's too late for that."

"Put me down. I'll stop them," she told him.

Gram ran on, cutting to the left to avoid the first of the arrows. "Do you really have some secret power?"

"I'm a spell-beast. Their arrows won't hurt me," she said.

"They might hurt Irene if they think they're in danger," panted Gram. "I'll get close and keep their attention. If I get a chance I'll throw you to Rennie." He ducked to the right and felt an arrow graze his cheek. They were still fifty yards distant.

"They'll kill you, Gram! Let me do this," shouted Grace.

"Not a chance," he told her. "We're in this together."

Zigzagging, he drew closer, but as the archers drew their bows back once more the leader held up a hand, ordering them to hold their fire. Looking at Alyssa he barked an order and she stepped away from Irene, moving to stand in front of him. The leader took the reins to Irene's donkey and Alyssa drew her sword.

Gram pulled up ten feet short of her.

The man behind her spoke then, "You are a tenacious brat, I'll give you that."

"Let Irene go," Gram said, trying to catch his breath.

The leader was a stout looking man. He wore a leather vest, leaving his muscular arms bare and his head was hairless, though whether from baldness or shaving, Gram couldn't be sure. He stood close to six foot in height, but his shoulders were broader than any

Gram had ever seen. He reminded Gram of a bull for some reason. "What's your name, boy?"

"Thornbear," he responded, hurling the name at the man like a curse.

"Oh, you're Jasmine's latest toy, aren't you? She thought you died in the fire," said the bald man. Gesturing to the woman that Gram had known as Alyssa he added, "Come here girl."

Alyssa turned and stood before the man.

Striking as swiftly as a snake the bald man's open hand struck her hard, sending her head snapping to one side. "Never lie to me again, bitch."

"Leave her alone!" shouted Irene, still tied to the donkey. The girl was furious.

"Forgive me, Zaihair," responded Jasmine with no inflection in her voice.

Gram started forward, sword in hand, but the bald man held up a hand, "Stop!" Snapping his fingers he indicated the archers. "If he comes any closer, shoot the girl." They turned their bows to point at Irene.

The bald man smiled as Gram obeyed. "Let's not skip the introductions, Thornbear."

In his mind Gram was replaying what she had just said. *Zaihair, he's her teacher.* His worst fears crystallized. *Is this her uncle?* If the man he was facing was a master of the unnamed path, then his hope of success was far smaller than he had dreamed.

"Jasmine said your name was Gram and that you were being taught by my brother, the traitor. Is that true, boy?"

Brother? Is he saying he's Cyhan's brother? His eyes widened in shock. The resemblance, now that he

408

was looking for it, was unmistakable. *If this man was Cyhan's brother...* He looked at Alyssa. *No, her name is Jasmine,* he corrected himself. The similarity in her features was there as well. *Is Cyhan her uncle as well or something more?* "What is your name?" he asked the bald man.

"You didn't answer my question. Is Arzam your teacher?"

"I don't know anyone named Arzam."

Jasmine spoke then, "He goes by the name 'Cyhan' now, Zaihair."

The bald man smiled again, "Then you are the traitor's student."

"Sir Cyhan is no traitor," growled Gram.

"My brother became a traitor the day he left our people. Who would have raised this poor girl if I hadn't taken responsibility for her? Not him, he betrayed not only his people, but his own blood."

"What?" Gram stared at him in shock, and his only comfort was the sight of Jasmine's expression. Her visage had been expressionless until then, but now her surprise was written clearly there. *She didn't know either.*

"Arzam is my fath...?" began Jasmine.

"Silence!" barked the bald man. "You speak only when I give you leave."

"What is your name?" asked Gram, repeating his previous question.

The leader lifted his chin, "I am T'lar Darzin, last of the eleven masters of Zan-zei. Does that mean anything to you?"

"Not especially," said Gram. "Should it?"

T'lar laughed, "It means that your teaching is poorly done. Arzam should have taught you the names of the masters, their predecessors and students. He and I are the only two left."

Behind T'lar, Gram could see a large body of men approaching in the distance. The Wastes were a flat cold desert and they were still miles away, but he knew he had little time. The men were on horseback and the miles between them wouldn't last long.

"Our escort is close at hand, boy. You have lost," said T'lar.

Gram felt a calm slide down over him. "You won't leave here with her."

"I'll give you one choice, child. Surrender to me and I will make you my student. I will teach you the things that my brother has obviously not seen fit to entrust to you," said T'lar. "You like my student don't you? You already know how skillful she is in bed. Join me and she can be yours."

"Alys—she isn't your property."

"Oh but she is, boy. You heard her call me 'zaihair' didn't you? Surely you know what that means. I hold her life in my hand. All that she is, is mine to dispose of as I wish. I taught her to fight, and I taught her to fuck. Come with me, and I will make you my heir."

"That isn't true."

"Jasmine," said T'lar. "Have I spoken truth?"

Her eyes were downcast, but her voice was firm, "Yes, Zaihair."

"If I give you to this man, what will you do?"

"Anything he wishes, Zaihair."

"If I tell you to cut your heart out, what will you do?"

She drew her dagger, holding it over her heart.

"Wait," said T'lar, and then he looked at Gram again. "What do you say? This is the best offer you will get. If you reject it, your life will be short."

Gram held the cheap sword he had taken from the ambushers before him in both hands, the point directed at the sky. "My name is Gram Thornbear and I swear to you, on my family's honor, that you will not leave this place with her. I will see you dead this day."

"Even if you could do such a thing, the wizard-child would die," said T'lar. "Is that what you want?"

Gram's eyes narrowed, his gaze burning into Jasmine. "Better that than for her to be taken as your slave." Grace gasped at his pronouncement.

"Very well. Jasmine, kill him."

The woman that Gram loved raised her head and looked at him with dead eyes, with a sword in one hand and a dagger in the other she ran at him.

He met her without flinching; drawing his smaller feast knife to use in his off-hand, the two of them began to fence. Grace had dropped from his shoulder and stood close by. She was hoping for a chance to reach Irene without being noticed but there were too many eyes. She was forced to wait.

The calm Gram had felt before grew deeper as he slipped into the void, the empty place where his body fought without hindrances or compassion. He faced Jasmine on equal footing now, with similar weapons and no obstacles. She was fast but he was far stronger and his reach was greater, his blows drove her guard out of line with each attack and she was forced to retreat before him.

They fought in a blur of steel, their swords reacting to cues too subtle for the conscious mind to even see, but as their battle progressed they both felt the inevitable outcome. Gram was winning, and soon his sword would have her blood.

She backed and circled, and then her foot lashed out, not in the hope of reaching him, but rather to send a spray of dirt and sand toward his face. Gram had anticipated her, though, and his eyes closed before her foot had even left the ground. He fought blind, his pace never faltering, and when his eyes opened again he saw the fear in her face.

No, not fear, it's something else. The thoughts passed through the emptiness of his mind, but his body had not time to listen. Jasmine feinted to his right but he moved left and his sword was there before her, beating down on her main hand while his left, still holding the knife, struck her in the chin, rocking her head and sending her flying back with brutal force. If he had used the blade she would have died.

She was stretched out, unconscious.

"I really wish you had accepted my offer," said T'lar. "You would have been a wonderful successor." Moving forward the man drew his sword, but left his other hand empty. He engaged Gram without giving the younger man a moment to pause.

Gram still held an advantage in reach, but T'lar's wide body held incredible strength. He matched Gram blow for blow and gradually he forced his younger opponent back. Using only the sword he intercepted every attack with a grace that seemed almost supernatural. T'lar's breathing was even and his body relaxed as he forced Gram to retreat in a small circle.

The bald man's free hand darted forward, slapping Gram in the chest in a move that surprised him. T'lar smiled, "I could have killed you just now, boy."

Gram struck back but his sword found only air and then he was off-balance. T'lar's sword struck him in the face, but it was the flat of the blade that hit. Bruised and dazed Gram fell backward. From the corner of his eye he saw Grace sidling closer to where Irene was tied to the donkey.

Gram rolled as he hit the ground, attempting to gain some space to recover, but T'lar was on him again. Gram's sword went flying as T'lar disarmed him. Gram's knife hand almost found a home in T'lar's belly but the bald man caught it and twisted his arm around and back. Seconds later Gram was in a tight grapple, with one arm locked painfully behind him.

T'lar applied firm pressure, until Gram felt sure his arm would break and he cried out in pain. Then he saw Jasmine had risen from the ground, dagger in hand.

"Come here, girl," said T'lar. "Kill this fool." He pulled back on Gram's head, forcing his chest outward to expose his unguarded stomach. "Stick that knife in him and all will be forgiven."

Jasmine stared into Gram's eyes, and he saw something there. Not fear, as he had thought before, but love, and resignation. Knowing T'lar couldn't see his face he mouthed his last words silently to her. *I trust you.*

She turned and ran for Irene, while everyone watched her in shock. Slashing with the blade she cut the girl's bindings and helped her to the ground as Grace ran toward them.

T'lar was the first to react. "Shoot!" he screamed. "Shoot the girl! Shoot them both!" The archers loosed and both arrows flew toward Irene Illeniel.

"No!" cried Grace, but she was still ten feet away.

The world seemed to freeze as the arrows struck home, not into their intended target, but into Jasmine instead. She had knocked Irene prone and thrown herself between the girl and the archers. Two arrows stood out from her, one in her back and another from her ribs. She fell forward, wrapping Irene within her arms, hoping to shield her from any more arrows.

The small bear exploded, and where it had been emerged a raging beast, a bear formed seemingly out of red and blue coruscating energy. Grace roared as she ran, passing the fallen woman and girl and flinging herself at the closest of the two archers. The man's scream was short-lived as glowing jaws clamped down, crushing his shoulder.

Gram had closed his eyes. *Please, Matt, please tell me you put it back,* he thought. T'lar's grip on him had loosened as Jasmine had run for Irene.

"Klardit," whispered Gram, willing the sword to appear as he pitched forward, pulling his adversary off balance. The two men fell forward, Gram on his stomach while T'lar landed on his back, crushing him to the ground.

"What?" said T'lar, confused. He released Gram and rolled off, his stomach tearing open as he pulled away from the broken sword. Gram held Thorn reversed in his hand, with its broken end pointing upward. He stood slowly, looking down on his enemy. T'lar was struggling to hold his entrails in with both hands, and then he looked up at Gram in horror, "How?"

Gram swept Thorn across, using the foreshortened blade to sweep T'lar's head from his shoulders. "You don't deserve an explanation," he said coldly.

Thornbear

Chapter 36

Gram wasted no time on the man he had just slain.

Grace had finished the second archer and now stood protectively over Jasmine and Irene and her appearance was a shock. Her form was that of a massive bear, but one that had been constructed of brilliant red and blue energies, as though the light itself had taken solid form.

What lay under her watchful eyes concerned him more.

Jasmine held Irene tightly in her arms, but the arrows that had pierced her looked bad. One was protruding from the right side of her back, just beneath the shoulder blade, while the other had lodged between her ribs about six inches under her left arm. There was surprisingly little blood visible, but Gram knew that was not necessarily a good sign.

"I'm sorry," said the woman he had loved.

Irene looked over her shoulder, "She's hurt bad, Gram." The girl had tears in her eyes. "She's not like the others. She took care of me... before this."

"I know, Rennie," said Gram. "Can you breathe?" he asked the wounded woman.

"I think my lungs are intact," she replied, cutting directly to his concern. "But...that just means I'll live a little longer."

"Jasmine," he said, experimenting with the sound of her name in his mouth.

"No," she protested. "I don't want that name, not anymore. I want to be Alyssa. That other name, it belonged to a life that I regret. If you remember me as anyone…"

"I won't be remembering you," insisted Gram. "You're coming with us. The wizards can fix this. You just have to hold on long enough."

She smiled sadly, "You still want to save me? After everything I've done to you?"

Gram knelt beside her. "Yes. I'm a fool, just like my grandfather, but I still love you."

"I was going to kill you," she replied. "I hated myself, but I would have done it."

"Why didn't you?"

"Your eyes," she said softly. "Those beautiful eyes—when T'lar held you, when he told me to kill you, and you looked at me with those eyes. How could you say that you trusted me?"

"I don't know," he told her. "But it was the truth, and if it wasn't, then I didn't want to live any longer."

"My heart broke when you looked at me and said that, and I knew I couldn't be the woman I had been. Jasmine died. I want to be Alyssa for what little time I have left, though I don't deserve even that."

"You can spend your life making it up to me," said Gram. Dismissing Thorn, he reached out to her.

"What are you doing?" asked Alyssa.

"I'm going to carry you away from here," he answered.

"Gram," said Grace, "We have to move quickly. The riders will be here soon."

"Can you carry Irene on your back?" he asked the bear. He carefully broke the larger portion of each arrow off as he spoke, leaving only the point inside

Alyssa, along with an inch of the shaft protruding from her.

"Of course," said Grace. "You'll have to hold on tightly, Rennie. Can you do that?"

Irene nodded, climbing onto the bear's broad back.

Gram slipped one arm beneath Alyssa's right arm, sliding it around her shoulders, careful to avoid the arrows. The other he slipped under her legs, and then he began to lift.

"Stop, Gram," she protested. "You can't run with me. I'm too heavy..." Her words ended in a painful hiss as he took her weight. "I'm dead already. Just leave me," she finished.

"Shut up," he told her gently, and then he began to walk.

Grace watched him worriedly, but said nothing. She moved at a rapid pace and Gram struggled to keep up. After a hundred yards he was falling behind. She stopped and waited. "How far away are they?" she asked.

Glancing over his shoulder Gram gauged the distance. "Maybe a mile."

"We aren't going to make it," stated the bear.

"Put me down," begged Alyssa.

"Go on," Gram told Grace. "Run. Get Irene back home."

"I can't do it without you, Gram," said Grace.

"I won't leave her!" he said desperately. "Save Irene. You can move faster without me."

"I can't," said Grace. "I don't have long. The journey back will take days."

"You've got five days left, right?"

The bear shook her head in a strangely human gesture, "Not anymore. My transformation used up the last of my aythar—in a few hours I will fade." Her voice held a sad sense of finality.

"Dammit Grace! Don't make me choose!" he shouted in frustration.

"I'm dying, Gram. Let me go," said Alyssa.

Looking down he could see that he was covered in blood. The motion and strain of being carried had caused her wounds to bleed freely. His vision grew blurry and finally he accepted the inevitable. Setting her down carefully, he felt hot tears streaking the dirt on his cheeks.

"Leave me a sword," said Alyssa. "If I am able, I will delay them."

He nodded wordlessly and drew out the cheap blade he had stolen, placing it in her hands. "I love you."

"And I you," she answered. "If such things are possible, I will find you in the next life."

He kissed her and stood, putting his back to her. Irene watched them from Grace's back, and her face was a terrible thing to behold. *If she looks like that, what must I look like?* Gram wondered.

Grace began to run and Gram followed, letting his long legs stretch out as he tried to match her pace. Looking back he could see Alyssa sitting up, a lonely figure in the stony desert. The sword was point down in the ground in front of her and she held the hilt with both hands, using it to keep herself upright.

They ran on, trying for as much speed as was possible. Gram suspected that Grace was restraining herself, loping easily along on her four legs. He tried not to think about what she had said before. Losing Alyssa was hard enough; losing Grace would be too much to bear.

Glancing over his shoulder again he saw that the riders were only a quarter mile away now. They would reach Alyssa soon, but she was no longer sitting up. Her body had slumped, and she lay awkwardly on the hard ground. She had lost consciousness—or worse.

Gritting his teeth, Gram ran on. The wind stung his eyes but he hardly cared.

Five minutes passed and they reached the gap in the mountains where they had emerged originally, but they could feel the thunder of the horses behind them. "Run, Grace! Give it everything you have!" he shouted.

"You run faster!" she growled back.

"This is everything I've got! Keep going!" The effort of his sprint made it difficult to talk.

"Take Rennie," she shouted, "I'll hold them at that outcropping."

She was talking about a spot some twenty yards ahead. It wasn't a true choke point, the rocks blocked the right hand side with a steep overhang while the rough ground sloped upward to the left, but it would make it possible to delay the riders some. They could ride around the place, but it would force them to cover more difficult terrain. It was far more likely they would choose to simply ride down whoever tried to hold the open gap at the bottom.

"I can't run fast enough," he told her.

"Worst sidekick ever," she yelled back. "You win Gram, but I won't forgive you for this." Grace's body stretched out and her loping run sped up. As Gram has suspected, she could run much faster than she had been.

Gram slowed and came to a stop at the narrow spot, staying close to the overhanging boulder. The horsemen were close, no more than twenty yards behind and he could see their leering grins as they closed on him, riding at a full gallop. There were at least fifty riders, some with spears while others carried sabers and small bucklers.

He thought of Dorian one last time. *I won't disappoint you Father. They'll soon know what a Thornbear can do.*

He faced them open-handed and unarmed as the lead rider barreled down on him, spear pointed at his chest. When the onrushing horse was no more than fifteen feet distant he called Thorn, this time in its full form, a six foot great sword, with a massive ruby set in its hilt. He noted the ruby with some surprise. *Nice touch, Matt,* but he had no time to appreciate it.

With a surge of strength Gram dodged to the right at the last second, taking the side the rider was least likely to expect. A right hander would normally have gone left, to be able to swing more effectively with such a large weapon, not that the rider had been given a chance to realize his prey was now armed.

The spear missed him and Thorn's blade neatly removed the horse's forelegs, sending the rider into a deadly crashing fall, but Gram didn't pause. Sweeping forward with the great blade again he whirled to strike upward, taking the second rider's mount in the throat. The steel passed cleanly through the right side of the horse's neck before continuing on to take its rider in the chest.

Within seconds the area had become an abattoir of blood and screaming horses. The riders behind had slowed, to avoid plowing into their now dying comrades. Gram didn't need such restraint—he was just getting started.

Running among them he lashed out with Thorn, cutting man and beast, hewing a bloody carcass-strewn path as he went. Spears stabbed at him but he dodged each with uncanny grace and when a buckler was raised to stop his sword, he ignored it. Thorn sliced through flesh, bone, and even steel shields with equal ease.

Thorn burned in his grip and the longer Gram fought, the more powerful he became. Feverish energy coursed from the red stone in its hilt and soon he was moving with unbelievable speed. Gram strode through enemies that seemed to move far too slowly, and he carried death in his hands.

Time passed slowly as he walked among them. Men wept and died while the ground was soaked with their blood. He shattered swords, battered men from their saddles, and when they cried for mercy their words fell on deaf ears.

After an unknown period the battle halted. The riders that remained were withdrawing, pulling away in fear and terror from the demon that had slaughtered so many. Behind them, some fifty yards distant rode an armored man, picking his way casually forward.

Their leader's aspect was black, not just in the color of his mount, or his armor, but as though the light of the sun itself could not touch him. He was a dark stain against the horizon, and he exuded an ominous power that seemed to weigh on Gram's shoulders.

The dark rider held a black staff and he leveled it at Gram as if it were a spear. Something unseen flowed from it, pressing down on him. His knees grew weak and he felt the rider's will, like a heavy blanket, smothering his defiance. Still thirty yards away, the rider whispered, but Gram heard his voice clearly, "Kneel."

Trembling, Gram struggled to stay on his feet, but his strength was waning.

Thorn blazed in his hand and he heard his father's voice, *"No."* In his mind's eye Gram saw his father once more, standing behind him, large hands clasped over his own, supporting the blade and giving him strength—embracing him. *"Stand, Son."*

He lifted his chin and straightened his back. The pressure remained, but he held himself upright.

The rider watched him for a moment, and then lifted his staff higher, pointing it at something above Gram's head. A burst of amaranthine light emerged, ripping through the air to pass above him. It left a vivid afterimage and Gram wondered for a second why the stranger had deliberately aimed to miss. Looking back over his shoulder he immediately realized why.

A dragon was falling from the sky.

Could it be the Queen? Gram dismissed that thought; it was too small to be Ariadne's dragon, Carwyn. That creature had grown to enormous proportions in the years after she had received it, while this one looked to be no more than ten feet in length, from nose to tail-tip. It carried a rider, and the two of them were spiraling downward. If their fall wasn't checked, they would soon hit the ground within a short distance of where Gram stood.

The Countess had been given a dragon, Gram knew that because it had gifted her with strength and speed, but no one had yet seen it. He didn't think this was it, though, the rider was a man.

The dark rider was aiming again, preparing to finish them.

Gram sprang forward, charging at his unknown enemy. Whoever rode the dragon was a friend; of that much he was certain.

His foe glanced at him, marking his advance, and then dismissed him. Despite his speed Gram couldn't reach him in time, nor did the rider seem particularly worried. Knowing he would be too late, Gram ran for a large rock that interrupted the ground before him and with a short hop he was atop it. Using his considerable momentum he leapt again, putting as much strength into the jump as he could.

A second bolt of amaranthine power blazed forth, and Gram intersected its path, holding Thorn before him as though he would cut light itself.

Gram's world fractured and he was flung back. The purple beam had struck Thorn and detonated, shattering the sword and sending him tumbling backward in a parabolic arc. He still held the sword's hilt, but a shimmering cloud of spinning steel fragments surrounded him.

No!

Gram didn't have the breath to scream, but his heart cried at the sight of his ruined weapon. He hit the ground hard, pain erupting in his side from the impact, but the damage to Thorn mattered more to him than his bruised and battered ribs. He struggled to rise, but his body refused to cooperate. Gram's clothing was scorched and burned but the blast had done remarkably little damage to him personally.

As he watched, the sword began to reform. The pieces that had flown apart now coalesced again, fitting together like pieces of some insanely complex puzzle and where they joined, he could see no lines to indicate they had ever been separate. Gram stared at Thorn in wonder, managing to sit up even as he gasped to draw air into his battered chest.

Boots crunched in the gravel behind him. Matthew Illeniel stood close at hand.

"Cool isn't it," he said mildly, indicating the sword with his hand.

Gram gaped at him, but he didn't have enough wind to speak.

The dark rider dismounted and began to walk toward them, "So the spawn of Illeniel has come at last. Your father will regret sending children to fight his battles for him."

The pressure that Gram had felt before intensified, and Matthew grimaced, a look of concentration on his face. Reaching into a pouch, he withdrew a handful of something that looked like salt and then tossed it into the air. The small crystals spread in the air, floating and spreading out around them. The pressure vanished and the young wizard's face relaxed, "That's better."

The dragon stood behind them, standing unsteadily on three legs. It held one of its forelegs away from the ground, and Gram could see that it was bleeding. "Fly Desacus," said Matthew. "You've done enough."

The beast didn't move and though Gram heard no response it must have made one, for his friend replied.

"Just go! Trust me."

Reluctantly the dragon backed away and then took wing.

Gram managed to get to his feet then. His back screamed at him in protest and it felt as though the damage to his side might be more serious than he had thought, but he could stand. Drawing a careful breath he spoke, "You certainly know how to make an entrance."

"It runs in the family."

The air around them flared with actinic light and Matthew's face took on an uncomfortable expression. The wizard looked at Gram, "You need to put on the armor. I can't shield us both like this for very long."

"Armor?"

"I thought I told you."

Gram growled at him in frustration. "Matt, you never tell me a damn thing! You love surprises like some men love strong drink."

"The word is 'tiersen', say it and focus your will. It's just like the other commands," said his friend, ignoring Gram's complaint.

Gram didn't bother arguing. "Tearsun," he said, hoping his pronunciation was close enough as he pushed his will at the tattoo on his arm in that peculiar way that Matthew had shown him before. New metal scales appeared, flowing from the air around the hilt of Thorn and streaming down his arms. They overlapped as they covered him in something that looked like scale mail, but unlike conventional armor they covered everything, wrapping over and around his body like a second skin. Seconds later it was done and looking down Gram could see he was enclosed in gleaming metal.

Touching his face he felt more metal scales there as well, but unlike those covering the rest of him, these were transparent.

"You have to admit that *that's* cool," insisted Matthew. The world around them flared again and fingers of magenta power coruscated around them, held back by an invisible barrier.

We're about to be killed by some crazed monster and all he can talk about is how amazing his latest creation is, thought Gram, feeling a desperate urgency. "Yes, Matt, it's goddamn awesome. Do you have a plan?"

The young wizard gestured and spoke a word and the rocky overhang that Gram had previously fought beside collapsed, burying the dark figure that was approaching. "Sure," he answered. "Run!" Without waiting, his friend turned and began pelting away, racing south, in the direction that Grace and Irene had gone.

Gram watched him run in amazement before belatedly following. Matthew had always been a naturally gifted runner, but he lacked a lot when it came to regular exercise. Gram overtook him in seconds, the energy from Thorn lending unnatural speed to his legs. "This is your plan?!" he yelled.

Matthew was already beginning to breathe hard, "Brilliant right?!"

We're going to die, thought Gram. But then, he had already been planning to face that only moments before. "Keep going," he told his friend. A crashing rumble behind them signaled their foe's emergence from the rock fall. "I'll try to distract him. Call the dragon back and get out of here!"

"I'm not done yet!" shouted his insane friend. Searching the path ahead of them desperately Matthew called out again. "See that bush ahead of us? The one next to the funny shaped boulder...?"

"Yes."

"Try to get him there. I have something that might work. It will take a minute to prepare, but when you hear me yell, get out of the way," said Matthew. "Got it?"

"Yeah," answered Gram. "What are you going to do?"

"Something new."

You and your stupid surprises! thought Gram. "What happens if I don't get out of the way in time?"

"Just make sure you do," yelled Matthew. "I don't want to have to try gluing you back together afterward." A new blast of light struck him then and the young wizard went tumbling forward.

Gram stopped and turned. Behind them came a creature from his nightmares. The dark rider had transformed as he emerged from the fallen rocks, growing into the shape of some grotesque, monstrous spider. It raced toward him on shining black legs some seven or eight feet in length. Red eyes glowed on its head and powerful mandibles were matched on each side by massive fangs.

By all the dead gods, Gram cursed mentally, *what is that thing?* Raising Thorn he prepared to meet its charge. A second bolt of power struck him and the world vanished in a flash of brilliant light. Gram fell, his arms going out to break his fall as he flew back. He feared losing Thorn, but the sword remained stubbornly in his hand as though it had been welded there. *The armor and the sword are one,* he realized. *I can't drop it.*

Rolling to his feet he felt more than saw the sweep of one of the creature's giant legs coming from one side. Striking sideways he tried to block it, and he felt Thorn hit something hard. Half of one of the spider's legs fell beside him and he whirled to bring the blade to bear on the creature's hard carapace.

The sword bit deep and grey ichor oozed from the wound. One of the monster's forelimbs struck him hard, batting Gram away and to the side. The blow threatened to jerk Thorn from his grip, but since the weapon was somehow attached to him, the force of the attack ripped the weapon free, tearing an even larger wound in the carapace as it came away.

"You dare to attack me, manling?" The alien voice issued from somewhere within the strange spider. "I am Chel'strathek, the Terror of the Night. Your weapon cannot harm me." The monster's carapace was healing even as he spoke and its damaged leg had nearly regained its former length.

Gram had recovered his balance and came back at the dark god with a vengeance. The stone in Thorn's hilt pulsed as it gave him strength. The great sword became a grey blur in his hands, as he cut at the creature, cutting away limbs and mandibles. Ichor flew as Gram's fury increased.

He had seen his father fight such creatures once before when he was young and helpless to aid him. It was *things* like this that had ultimately led to Dorian's death. He fought not only the monster before him, but the memory of his helplessness. A sweeping cut sent a giant fang sailing away as it ruined the thing's head and mandibles. Another leg swept toward him but Gram leapt, up and over it, in an arcing jump that sent him almost ten feet into the air.

Coming down he braced the sword in his hands, driving it point first directly into the spider's armored cephalothorax. Chel'strathek screamed in pain and bucked, pitching Gram to one side. The sword held him in place briefly before coming loose, and then he fell, unable to maintain his position on the giant arachnid.

Razor sharp legs battered him as he struggled to rise, but they could not pierce his armor. Gram felt himself repeatedly slammed into the ground, until he began to wonder if it would be better to simply stay down. The armor itself seemed impregnable, but the blows were punishing his body within it.

A strange pause in the attacks allowed him to regain some sense of the world around him, and then he saw the reason for it. Chel'strathek had drawn back, preparing another of his strange purple blasts. Scrambling to his feet, Gram narrowly avoided the first sizzling attack and the dreadful magic created a smoking crater in the place he had just been.

Dazed he tried to get his bearings. He had lost sight of the place he was supposed to be taking the monster. *There.* His eyes lit on the bush, but his momentary hesitation nearly cost him.

Amaranthine light enveloped him and his feet left the ground. The force of the blow nearly hammered him into unconsciousness and his armor shattered, flying into pieces just as the sword had when it was struck. His body was a microcosm of pain and his nostrils were filled with the smell of burnt hair and skin. He hardly felt his landing, though the rocks tore away both skin and clothing as he skidded across the rough ground on his back.

Stunned, and blind from pain, he rolled over, attempting to rise to his hands and knees. He could feel the armor reforming around him, but he wasn't sure it mattered. Another attack like the last and he wouldn't be able to move.

His right arm collapsed as he tried to put his weight on it. Something was broken there. Gram fell onto his shoulder and then rolled, desperately hoping it would help him avoid the next blast.

His vision cleared and he was dismayed to see that he had been sent flying in the wrong direction. Chel'strathek was more than thirty yards from the place Matthew had indicated, and he was between Gram and his goal. Worse, the dark god was about to launch another bolt of destructive force. Scrabbling to the left Gram managed to get behind a mule sized rock.

The stone exploded, deafening him as it was obliterated, but he had found his feet at last. Running forward he dragged Thorn behind him, still attached to his now useless right arm. He began changing directions as he charged, first left and then right, his legs pumping to drive him across the ragged ground.

Sprinting, he made it past the dark god and headed for the one place that still held hope.

Chel'strathek abandoned his attempts at hitting him with focused beams and as he passed close, the arachnoid god emitted a cone shaped pulse of intense energy, a broad attack that was impossible to dodge. Gram was lifted into the air once more and the world went black as he smashed into something far harder than he was.

"Get up!"

Gram heard the voice clearly, but he wasn't entirely certain whether it came from within or without. It sounded like his father's voice. He opened his eyes and immediately wished he hadn't.

Everything hurt, but more pressing was the fact that Chel'strathek was preparing to blast him to jelly. The wide cone-like attack had thrown him some twenty feet to the side, but it hadn't had the necessary power to shatter his armor. Now that Gram was no longer moving the dark god was preparing to remedy that problem.

Pushing off with his left hand he managed to get up and to one side in time to avoid the attack before it came. Seeing more of the terrain reduced to smoking gravel no longer had quite the effect on him that it had had before. Fatigue, injuries, and sheer exhaustion were beginning to take their toll on his reactions. The damned spider was no closer to where he needed it to be, and Gram doubted he could get there before he was completely incapacitated.

Then he had an idea.

It wasn't his best idea; he would readily have admitted that, if he had had the mental energy to devote to such analysis. Regret would have to come later.

He began running once more, this time instead of heading for the target area, he angled his route to pass between it and Chel'strathek's current position. He made sure to get close enough that the monster would try his wide cone attack again.

This is going to hurt.

It felt a lot like he imagined it would be if one were to be struck by a charging bull. Once again he was sent into a soaring arc, but this time he landed close to where they wanted Chel'strathek.

He rolled to a stop ten feet past the spot he hoped to get his enemy to, but that would have to do. Movement was no longer a viable option. It hurt just to breathe and he was fairly sure that his left leg was broken. Gram didn't even bother with attempting to escape, he lay completely still.

I'm helpless now. Come and get me.

As he waited he realized the flaw in his plan. Chel'strathek might choose to finish him without approaching. *Shit.* He no longer had any options. *Surely he'll get closer since I'm not moving.*

Seconds ticked by with glacial slowness, until finally he heard the tell-tale sound of chitinous legs on stone. The beast was coming closer. He didn't turn his head to look, fearing that any sign of consciousness might make the arachnid rethink his approach.

A shadow fell over him and he saw a thick black leg appear next to his face. *No, not that close. Stand over there!* The damned spider was directly above him now.

His head was facing the correct direction to see Matthew stand, some hundred yards distant, holding his arms wide and moving his lips. Something dark appeared between his outstretched hands and it began to slowly turn in the air.

The spider laughed. "Foolish wizard! Do you think to strike me with such a slow and clumsy attack?" His legs bent, as he prepared to leap away.

Gram reached across his body, taking Thorn into his left hand and sweeping it across in a wide stroke, clipping the ends from two of Chel'strathek's legs. The arachnid stumbled and then Matthew released his attack.

Four black triangles, connected at one central point and spanning a space of four or five feet, flew through the air parallel to the ground. It was spinning as it came and when it reached Chel'strathek, it passed through the dark god's body as though it were nothing more than illusion.

With a strange detachment Gram noted that it passed partly through the bush that stood between them and where the black triangles went, wood and leaves simply vanished.

As the strange triangle blades emerged from the other side of the arachnid's main body, it shivered and then erupted. The air went white and a giant hand crushed Gram's body into the ground.

Chapter 37

"Wake up," said an insistent and increasingly irritating voice. Gram ignored it. *I'm dead, go away.*

"You have to wake up," it said again, and then something pushed against his shoulder. Sharp pains lanced through Gram's body. He began to rethink his 'dead' hypothesis. Being dead wasn't supposed to hurt so much.

Another rough jolt made his mind up for him. "Goddammit, stop!" he hissed.

"You're alive!" It was Matthew's voice.

"Not for long if you keep beating on me like that," Gram complained. He paused briefly and then asked, "How bad is it?"

"I can't tell. You need to dismiss the armor so I can see your body."

"I thought you had magic eyes."

"Magesight won't penetrate this armor. If it could, you'd have died from the first one of those blasts," said Matthew.

"That would be some pretty shitty armor then," agreed Gram.

"Thanks for the compliment," said Matthew dryly.

"How do I dismiss it?"

"It's the same command word."

Gram started to comply but then a thought occurred to him. "It might be better if I leave it on."

"Why?" asked the young wizard.

"It might be the only thing holding me together."

"If it was that bad you'd be dead already, but you could be bleeding in there. I need to see you so I can make sure you don't die."

"You're always a ray of sunshine, aren't you?" noted Gram. Doing as he had been told, he dismissed the armor. He was rewarded with a worried intake of breath when Matthew saw him.

"Oooh damn!" said his friend.

"I'll dismiss the sword too, hold on," said Gram.

"No! Don't!"

"Why not?"

"I think it's keeping you alive," said Matthew, a sound of wonder in his voice.

"What?!" Gram struggled to lift his head.

"Don't move!"

"Why?!" Gram was growing more panicked with each warning.

"Just shut up. It's bad, really bad. If you move… oh gods! Just be still. Let me do what I can," Matthew sounded close to panic himself.

"Can't we wait for your sister? You didn't do such a great job last time you worked on me," observed Gram.

"We split up before I found you. She's taking Irene and Grace back to Cameron. You don't have that much time," said Matthew. "You'll have to settle for me."

"Fuck."

"Don't worry. I did some practicing after last time. Moira told Dad and he wasn't too pleased. He wanted to make sure I would be better prepared in the future." Matthew's voice was calm now.

"If you had made armor that didn't fly apart every time something hit it then this wouldn't *be* the next time," argued Gram.

"It doesn't, Gram," said Matthew. "That armor only does that when something catastrophically powerful hits it. From what Dad told me once, Karenth hit Dorian with one of those purple bolts and it destroyed his armor completely. You got hit *twice,* and then again twice more by those broad cone attacks— and you still have armor."

Gram didn't say anything; he was torn between irritation and the logic that told him he should be grateful. Silence was his best compromise.

"Well?" asked Matthew.

"Well what?"

"You still haven't told me how cool you think the armor is…"

"Really?!" growled Gram. "Couldn't this wait? Don't you have something more important to do right now?"

"I figured I should get your feedback now, in case…" Matthew's sentence trailed off.

"In case what?! I die?" Gram said, raising his voice. He wanted to shout but his lungs didn't seem to have the strength for it. "Honestly, Matt, you're unbelievable. I'm dying and you want to know if I liked the shiny armor."

"There," said Matthew, letting out a long sigh and beginning to laugh.

Gram stared at him in dismay.

"You should see your face," said Matthew.

"This isn't funny, Matt. I'm dying."

"Not anymore," said his friend.

"Huh?"

"I'm done with the worst of it," said Matthew. "The large vein in your left leg was torn. I've fixed that and fused the bone back together, but the scariest part was the piece of rib that had lodged in your heart."

"I didn't feel anything. When did you start?" *Did he say my rib went through my heart?*

"I started as soon as you removed the armor," replied his friend. "That's why your body is numb. Dad made me memorize all the major nerves."

Gram took a moment to process that, noting with some surprise that his body was indeed numb. *How did I not notice that? Was that why he kept talking? To distract me?*

"If a rib went into my heart I'd have died before you got here," said Gram blankly.

"That's why I told you not to dismiss the sword. There was a line of power running from the ruby stone to your heart and lungs. Somehow it kept the blood flowing and your lungs working until I could fix it." Matthew was staring down at him with red eyes.

"Are you going to cry?" Gram asked in alarm. Matthew wasn't known for emotional displays.

"No," said his friend, wiping at his face. "Shut up. You're my best friend. I thought you were dying."

Gram mumbled something unintelligible. His throat was thick and made it difficult to speak.

"What?" asked Matthew.

He swallowed and tried again, "I said, 'the armor is really cool'."

Matthew laughed, "Yeah, it is, isn't it? Your plan to lure Chel'strathek over here by letting him blast you at close range was pretty cool too."

"Now you're just being a smartass."

"Yeah," said his friend with a smile. "I am. That was the stupidest thing I think I've ever seen."

Gram wanted to laugh too, but his body wasn't quite up for it. "Can I sit up now?"

"Not yet. Your right arm is still dislocated and you have torn muscles in several places. Let me fix those and then maybe I'll let you have the use of your body again."

***

Matthew called his dragon, Desacus, back and healed his leg before they mounted to leave. Gram looked at him skeptically.

"The two of us will be too much for him," he said. The dragon didn't look capable of carrying more than one rider.

Matthew put a hand on his shoulder, "I'll make us lighter, don't worry."

"Every time you say 'don't worry' I later decide that I should have worried," said Gram.

"You sound like an old woman."

There's a reason old women live to be old, thought Gram, but he refrained from arguing further. Soon they were winging their way back toward Cameron Castle.

"You said Moira was with Grace and Irene…"

"When Dad got Elaine's message, he left immediately. Moira and I brought the others back in the flying machine, but it took us longer. Once we reached the castle we had nothing to do, and Dad hadn't come back, so we took matters into our own hands."

"I didn't know he had given you the dragons," said Gram.

Matthew smiled. "He hadn't. But he had shown them to us. He was planning to wait until we were much older."

"Then how?"

"We broke in," said his friend. "Mom was attuned for the door to the egg chamber and I already knew the key to the stasis lock."

Gram just shook his head.

"After that, we took the dragons and flew to the house, but there was no one there and the house itself was nothing but charred timbers. We split up and began searching. Moira found Grace and sent me a message, so I headed for the same area, but instead of them I found you. Mom is probably still searching, since she couldn't hear Moira's message." He tapped his temple.

"The night before this," said Gram, "I saw your father fighting Celior."

"Then maybe he's already back at the castle," said Matthew.

"I don't think he won."

"Dad wouldn't lose," said the young wizard. "He's beaten far worse."

"Celior was waiting for him. I think he caught him by surprise."

"He wouldn't lose, Gram."

"But..."

"Just shut up," said Matthew. "He'll be there when we get back."

I hope so, thought Gram.

***

When they arrived at Cameron, many hours later, they found that neither the Count nor the Countess was there. Moira had returned with Grace and Irene and was waiting worriedly for them.

Gram's family was glad to see him.

Rose's hand covered her mouth when she saw what he looked like.

Carissa was more direct, "What happened to you?!" She ran to him, flinging her arms around him and sending shocks of pain through him from his recently abused ribs.

"Easy," he answered, patting her head. "I got pretty banged up."

His mother touched his face gingerly, "You have no idea how worried we've been." She glanced at Carissa, "Go fetch your grandmother, quickly."

They fussed over him, and put him to bed almost immediately. Moira came and double checked her brother's handiwork, but she found little to complain about. Elise Thornbear brewed him a foul tasting tea, 'to ease the swelling' she had said.

Gram accepted their efforts without complaint, though he almost gagged drinking his grandmother's foul concoction. Soon after that, he fell asleep.

Chapter 38

Gram slept a long time, but his rest wasn't easy. His dreams were haunted by the events of the past week. He saw again the faces of the men he had slain and when he managed to escape those memories, Alyssa came to haunt him, dying repeatedly in his arms. It was almost a relief when he finally awoke.

"How long have I been in bed?" he asked his grandmother. She sat on a soft chair, close at hand.

"All last night and most of today," she replied. "The sun is going back down now."

He was surprised. He had thought perhaps it was morning. "Has the Count returned?"

"The Countess came back late last night. She left again this morning, to search for him again, but he has not been back," said Elise.

"But you think he will be back?" he asked hopefully.

Elise sighed, taking a cloth from a washbasin she approached the bed. "Since you're awake you can help." She handed him the wet rag.

He looked at her curiously.

"Use it to clean yourself up. I doubt you want your old grandmother doing it."

Looking beneath the sheet he could tell that someone had already cleaned most of the blood off. He was glad he hadn't been awake for that. "He will be back, right?" he repeated.

"I'm an old woman, Gram," said Elise. "I've sat beside many sickbeds and waited through a hundred long nights, waiting and hoping. Later, when you're up and around, they'll talk and make optimistic predictions, but I've given up such things."

"But…"

"Mordecai has cheated death many times over," she continued. "He might return, but I won't hold out hope for it. I'm grateful enough for what fate has already returned to me."

"What's that?"

"My grandson," she said simply.

They didn't talk for a while after that. Gram sat up and Elise let him dress himself, but only in loose trousers and a soft tunic. His body was bruised and swollen from head to toe. His mother came in a short while later.

She studied him with a serious gaze before speaking, "I cannot begin to tell you how proud I am."

Those hadn't been the words he expected. "Momma I…"

"Shhh," she said, hushing him. "Let me talk for a bit. Grace has been talking while you slept. She repeated much of what you already told us, though she had a decidedly different point of view."

Gram grew worried. He could only imagine what Grace might have said.

"Matthew told me about your fight with Chel'strathek, and Irene told me even more. Especially concerning Alyssa and your fight with her master," said Rose.

He nodded.

"They're calling you a hero in the great hall," she added, "but you mustn't let such things go to your head."

"Yes, Mother."

"Let me see it."

"See what?"

"The sword," she said simply.

"Ah…" he answered uncertainly, realizing that Matthew had probably had to relay that part while telling his own story.

"I'm not angry, Gram," said his mother. "I'm well past that, and I've given you the sword, though I now know you had already taken it. Let me see it with my own eyes."

Gram stood and uttered the command that would summon Thorn, calling it out in its broken form.

"Show me the rest," she said.

He used another command and the great sword reformed, becoming whole once more, a dark ruby set in the pommel.

"Is that what I think?" she asked, gesturing toward the red stone.

He nodded, his heart aching as he saw her eyes begin to water. "I picked it up after he died."

"I never dreamed…" she said softly. "And you never told me."

"I'm sorry."

"It's long past time for apologies, Son," she answered. "You're a man now, no more excuses. Show me the armor."

"Tiersen," he said and the silver scales appeared, flowing over his body and encasing him once more.

Her eyes widened, tears brimming. Rose stumbled, but Elise caught her.

Gram dismissed the armor and put his arms around her.

"You looked just like him," mumbled Rose.

***

Gram's family encouraged him to stay in that evening, rather than eat in the great hall, but he declined. He wasn't looking forward to the stares and attention he might face, but he figured he might as well get it over with.

When he stepped into the hall the wide room fell silent. Heads turned and people gawked at him. Everyone knew him already, of course, but they stared at him as if he had become a new thing.

Gram ignored the looks and headed for his customary seat, hoping they would return to their conversations quickly, but that was not to be. Someone stood at one of the lower tables, the one where the majority of the guardsmen sat, Perry Draper.

"Hail the champion of Cameron Castle!" he said in a loud voice.

Gram watched him in horror, wondering if it was a joke of some sort, but the rest of the guardsmen stood, quickly, one after another. Perry raised his cup high, "Three cheers for Thornbear!"

The entire room came to its collective feet then and cheers rang out, followed by clapping and more rousing cries.

Gram was forced to stand, since it seemed rude to do otherwise, but his mouth refused to give him an adequate response. He stared about him, feeling his face grow hot.

Lady Rose came to her son's rescue. "Thank you, everyone. My son is honored by your cheers, but I fear he is still fatigued from his ordeal. Please sit. Let him eat in peace."

There were nods and a few more cheers but the crowd finally settled and people took their seats again. Gram looked at the seats around him. Of the Count's family, only Conall was present. Moira and Matthew had left early, along with the Countess, to search for their father. He wasn't sure where Irene was, but he imagined she had probably elected to dine in the family apartments, to avoid the same attention.

Carissa gave him a sympathetic look from the same seat that Alyssa had once used. "Bear up, Gram. It won't last forever, but you deserve the praise."

A second silence fell over the room and people began to stand again. Penelope Illeniel stood in the doorway, flanked by her two oldest children.

It was customary to stand until the Count and Countess had taken their seats, but Penny seemed disinclined to do so. Instead she moved to stand in front of the center of the high table, as though she would address the gathering. Matthew and Moira moved to stand on either side of her.

All three of them had obviously just returned. The twins wore supple riding leathers, while the Countess herself was still armored, wearing the enchanted mail her husband had long ago crafted for her. Her sword was still belted at her side, which was even more unusual. She removed the metal cap from her head and set it heavily on the table behind her.

She was sweaty and red from a day in the sun, and her braids had fallen to frame her face, making her look like some poet's version of a warrior-princess. She waved her hand at him, "Gram Thornbear, come stand before me."

Shit.

He did as he was told, feeling awkward as he rose from his chair and walked across to stand where she had indicated. "Yes, Your Excellency?"

The Countess raised her eyes, taking in the room as she spoke, "I have spent the day searching, and when I was not involved in that endeavor, I was with my daughter, making sure she would recover. Because of that, I have not had time to talk to you regarding your actions over the past week."

She wants to talk about it? Here?!

"Your Excellency, if you like, I would be happy to answer any questions you have, but I would prefer not to…"

"Silence," she commanded. "You will speak when I have finished."

"Yes, milady." Gram heard light laughter coming from the crowd.

"My youngest daughter has spoken highly of you regarding her rescue. I have also taken counsel with my oldest son and daughter, and both of them agree that you behaved in a fashion that has made you worthy of high honor here in this hall. Even more telling was the story relayed by my daughter's companion,

Grace." Penny stepped forward then, placing her hands on his shoulders and looking into his eyes. She leaned close and kissed him once on each cheek.

"Thank you, Gram, from the bottom of my heart, thank you. If it weren't for you I would have lost my daughter. That is a debt I will never be able to repay. If my husband was here he would thank you as well."

She embraced him then, while Gram stared wildly at Matthew and Moira, uncertain what he should do.

The Countess pushed him back then, holding him at arm's length before releasing him. "Kneel, Thornbear."

What? Gram's confusion was growing, but he did as he was told. He watched in horror as she drew her sword and he realized what she was about to do. "Wait! I'm not old enough. I haven't even..."

Penny gave him a stern glance and Gram closed his mouth.

"For your service, your loyalty, and your bravery, I will see you knighted. Do you object?"

He kept his gaze on the floor, "I am not worthy, Your Excellency."

She smiled, "Fortunately, it is not your place to judge."

Matthew leaned in and whispered something in his mother's ear. She nodded and sheathed her sword again.

Matthew addressed Gram, holding out his hands, "Your sword, please."

"I don't have... oh." Gram called Thorn, making certain to summon it in its whole form. He offered the great sword's hilt to his friend. Matthew then passed it to his mother.

Penny spoke once more, holding Thorn with its point toward the ceiling, "The sword is a symbol of a knight's troth and trust, of his enduring fealty to his liege. The Knights of Stone were created to serve both this house, and the best interests of humanity itself. Will you swear fealty to me and my husband, the Count di' Cameron?"

"I so swear, Your Excellency," answered Gram.

"Then by the power I hold in trust as Lady of Cameron, Countess and servant of the Queen of Lothion, I dub thee knight," said Penelope. She brought the tip of the sword down to rest on one shoulder before lifting it and touching the other. "Rise Sir Gram and take up your sword." She reversed the blade and held Thorn's hilt toward him.

As he took it, she continued, "You father would be proud of you, Sir Gram, and his father as well, whose name you carry. May you ever wield Thorn in justice and for the protection of the weak."

Gram placed the point against the floor, holding the great sword by the ricasso, just below the quillons. "I will spend my life for that purpose, my lady."

A large hand descended on his shoulders. "Stand, Sir Gram." Cyhan was behind him, dressed in his armor and formal regalia, as Grandmaster of the Order of Stone. It was something Gram had rarely seen, and he hadn't even noticed the big knight's approach.

Sir Cyhan bent down behind him, buckling gilt spurs onto Gram's boots, the final symbol of knighthood. Then he stood and delivered a powerful blow to Gram's shoulders, the traditional 'buffet'. "Welcome brother knight," said Cyhan before embracing him.

The hug, coming from a man that never showed emotion, undid him. Unable to help himself, Gram wept, while the hall cheered once more.

The Countess wasn't finished, however. "Sir Gram, your service has left me in your debt. Is there anything you would ask of me? I will grant any boon, if I am able."

Wiping at his eyes Gram thought for a moment. In his mind, being knighted was more than enough of a reward, but there was one thing that had weighed on his mind. "If it isn't too much, I would like to recover Alyssa's body."

Penelope nodded, "Tomorrow you will ride with me. Layla will take us."

"Layla?"

"My dragon."

Thornbear

Chapter 39

Cyhan stayed close to him when he left the hall after the meal. It was obvious he wanted to talk, but it was a while before Gram could escape from the numerous well-wishers who followed him. It seemed as though everyone in the castle wanted to shake his hand, or give him advice.

"Excuse our newest knight," said Cyhan, "but I need to discuss some matters with him."

He cut through the crowd like a ship through a storm, extracting a grateful Gram from their well-meaning chatter.

"Let's get some air," suggested the older warrior.

The breeze in the courtyard was cool. The sun had already retired, leaving the moon to provide most of their illumination. They walked to the gatehouse and ascended to the walls. The parapets provided an excellent walkway, showing the town of Washbrook beneath them in monochrome hues.

Without preamble the senior knight began, "Grace told me that their leader's name was 'T'lar'."

"There's more," said Gram. "Did she tell you what else he said?"

"That he claimed to know me," replied Cyhan.

"He said your name was Arzam, and that he was your brother."

"Grace told me that much," responded Cyhan in a neutral tone.

Gram watched his face, hoping for some sign of confirmation, or denial, but there was nothing. "He also said you were a traitor."

There was a flicker then, but it was gone so quickly Gram almost wondered if he had imagined it. "Tell me the rest."

"Alyssa, her name turned out to be Jasmine, she called him 'zaihair'. He said he was her teacher, and he offered to take me as his student. He said some other things too…" Gram had difficulty figuring out how to frame the rest.

"What?"

"He said she was your daughter."

Cyhan's response was immediate, "I have never fathered a child."

There was no hesitation there, but he didn't bother to deny being called a traitor, noted Gram. "She seemed surprised when he said that," added Gram. "When she was here before, she told me that she had an uncle that abused her. T'lar said you had abandoned her."

"I have no children," said the big warrior once more, but his eyes were thoughtful.

"Maybe he lied."

"T'lar was many things, but he would not lie."

Gram's stomach churned at the thought that T'lar had been completely honest. Some of the things he had said about Alyssa…

"Ruth," said Cyhan at last. "It could only have been her. She hid it from me."

"Can you find her? To ask…"

"She's dead," said Cyhan, cutting him off. "She died at the hands of the shiggreth, while kidnapping the Countess."

"Oh." Gram remembered the story. His father had tried to save her and been taken prisoner along with the Countess. Little had been said about the woman that led the abductors, but now it seemed she had been one of Cyhan's lovers. *What do I say to a man whose brother, daughter, and previous lover all were involved in kidnapping attempts against the Count's family? What kind of place does he come from?*

"You killed T'lar," stated Cyhan, looking directly at Gram.

"Yes, Zaihair."

"Tell me how."

Gram described the fight, how T'lar had beaten him without killing him, how he had asked Alyssa to kill him instead, and how Gram had used Thorn to take him by surprise. At the end he included the fact that he had beheaded the dying man.

"My brother was a fool," said Cyhan simply. "You were kind to kill him swiftly."

Gram was feeling uncomfortable. *I just told him I slew his brother and he thanked me.*

"You worry that I will bear a grudge?" suggested Cyhan, reading his face. "I will not. T'lar made his own choices. If I had been there, I would have done the same."

"Could you kill your own brother?" The words slipped out before Gram realized what he was saying.

"I have done worse," answered Cyhan. "T'lar was right to hate me. He had good cause to call me 'traitor'."

"Why?"

"You did not tell me everything T'lar said to you," said Cyhan bluntly, ignoring the question. "But I do not wish to hear it. You said that he was my daughter's teacher and I know what that means. I am glad that you killed him."

T'lar's words echoed in Gram's mind, *'I taught her to fight, and I taught her to fuck'.* He also remembered Alyssa's words regarding her early life, *'I was twelve'.* The thoughts made him clench his fists.

Cyhan watched his face and then continued, "My teacher had three students. I was the oldest and my brother T'lar was his second student. The third…" The big man's voice caught in his throat for a second.

"The third?"

"The third was my sister. She was five years younger than me, and her name was Jasmine. I killed my master when I was seventeen."

Gram stared at the older knight, his mouth falling open. *And T'lar named your daughter Jasmine as well… That's sick!* "I'm… that's…"

The old warrior looked away, turning his back to hide his face. "I will not mourn my brother's death."

"Did your sister survive?" asked Gram.

"She was killed, as a lesson to me, for interfering."

And then you killed your teacher, thought Gram. He was curious about the details, but the nature of the story was too awful for him to pry.

They walked for a while longer, bound together by silence. They stopped when they had reached the side that faced away from Washbrook, looking instead down on a wide field that stretched away to the forest beyond. The wind and moonlight on the tall grass created the illusion that they were looking over a wide body of water.

"Tell me about my daughter," said Cyhan quietly.

"You met her while she was here..."

"I paid little attention. I barely marked her presence. I have lost many things in my life. Now I have lost something without even knowing it." There was a rough sound to his voice.

"She was strong," said Gram. "That was the first thing I noticed. She was practical, confident, and strong."

"What did she look like?"

"You saw her."

"But I didn't *look*," growled Cyhan with emphasis. "I hardly remember her face. Tell me what you saw."

"She had smooth skin, darker than mine, but not quite your tone. Her eyes were dark, soft around the edges, and they always held a certain light, as though she was looking at the world and seeing something I had missed..." Gram talked for a while, until he could no longer continue, and then they watched the grass in silence.

***

The next morning Gram rose early and immediately after breakfast he joined the Countess, walking with her to the courtyard. She stopped them there and they waited.

"Is she coming?" asked Gram.

Penny nodded, "Yes."

"How do you talk to her?"

"It takes some getting used to. I hear her inside here," she tapped her temple.

"Matthew and Moira can do that too," said Gram.

"It's almost natural for them," said Penny. "They've been doing it since they gained their powers. I still find it disconcerting."

"They can talk to their dragons that way now as well," commented Gram. "I wonder if it gets confusing, having so many voices in their heads."

"They can talk to Layla too," said Penny, "not just their own."

"I think I'd go crazy."

"Moira tells me that it's a matter of attention. They don't hear or project to each other unless they do so on purpose."

That made sense to Gram. "What does Matt say?"

The Countess frowned, "He doesn't describe things like that very often. If I ask he's likely to just say, 'it's fine Mom'."

Layla's shadow fell over them then, and a moment later the massive dragon had descended, sending up gusts of dust and wind as her wings beat the air. She bent her forelegs and lowered her body to make it easier for them to climb up.

Gram hesitated, causing the Countess to look at him curiously. "Are you coming?"

"I'm a little nervous," he admitted.

"You rode home with Matthew. This is no different."

He had been half dead then. Falling from the back of a dragon had almost seemed like a welcome thought. Now he was merely stiff, sore, and bruised. He very much wanted to live. "Shouldn't there be a saddle or something?" he asked.

Penny smiled. "Mort kept saying he wanted to wait until she had finished growing. There's not much help for it now. Sit behind me and hold on. Layla will be careful with us."

Gram thought about Matthew and Desacus, spiraling down from the sky after Chel'strathek's attack. Neither he nor the Countess were wizards, and he doubted they would be able to recover from such a fall. Sighing he climbed up and put his hands around her waist. Layla's wings began beating powerfully and he closed his eyes.

A few minutes later he reopened them and immediately regretted it. *That was a mistake,* he thought as his stomach flipped over. The ground was far beneath them, moving by with a slowness that belied their actual speed.

It was hours before they reached the place where he had left Alyssa, but where he had expected to find a body, there was nothing. The sword he had given her lay discarded on the ground. T'lar's body still lay where he had fallen, a hundred yards or more in the distance. Buzzards circled and hopped around his carcass.

"Could she have walked?" asked Penny.

"No," said Gram.

"Perhaps she wasn't as badly wounded as she seemed."

"She had two arrows in her. She could barely sit," he replied. "The last time I looked she had fallen over. Let me look around."

The ground had been churned up by the horsemen's passage when they had been chasing Gram and Irene, but he knew some of them had returned after their fight with him. Ten or fifteen of them had survived, at the very least. After Chel'strathek had been destroyed, he and Matthew had gone directly to Castle Cameron but the last of the riders had to have returned this way.

He spotted some tracks that indicated horses going the other direction, confirming what he already knew. *They left T'lar and his archers, but they took Alyssa. Why?*

Had she still been alive? If that had been the case, she would surely have died soon after, being jostled around on horseback. *Maybe they thought she would live. If so, they probably dumped her body somewhere out there in the Northern Waste, after she died.*

Layla carried them along what he thought would be their route of escape, but while she flew as low as she could, Gram spotted nothing. At his request she circled, moving outward in a slow spiral, but after a few hours he still found no sign.

"Can you leave me where her body was?" he asked.

"Why?" said Penny.

"I can't track from the air. It's been a few days, but I might be able to follow their course across the waste," he said.

"Gram—*Sir* Gram," she corrected for emphasis, "I understand your desire to find her body, but we have larger concerns. Cameron is without its lord and I am without my husband, who is presumably still alive."

Gram grimaced, *he probably didn't survive either.*

She sensed his doubt, "Even should I fail to find him, I have a duty to my people, and a duty to the crown."

"But I…"

She held up a hand to forestall him, "I didn't knight you as a ceremonial reward. Your duty is to me now, and to the people that depend on us."

He clenched his jaw before dipping his head, "Yes, my lady."

They flew back, but not on a direct course to Cameron and Washbrook, instead they followed the stony valley in the direction of Penny's former home. "You said you saw Mordecai pass by. Can you direct me to the area you think he fought in?"

"I think so," he answered.

They flew on and he directed her to stop when they reached the low ridge where he and Grace had watched the Count fly over. Taking to the air again, they made their way to where he had spent the night and he tried to gauge the direction he had seen the lights coming from during the battle with Celior. Using those two references, they flew toward the area he thought represented the site of the battle.

At first it seemed that they would find no sign. The mountains and surrounding tree cover showed nothing to indicate the titanic battle he had witnessed, but then they crossed another mountain and found the valley beyond marked by the evidence of a colossal explosion. The trees were flattened in every direction, as though a powerful force had emanated from the center of the valley floor. The rocks had been scattered and boulders shattered. Lightning had left black scorch marks on the trees where they had fallen.

"This must be it," said Gram.

"I've seen Mort's work too often to think it anything else," said Penny.

"You and the Count went through a lot of this back then, didn't you?"

She chuckled, "Ha! You think this is bad? I have to clean up after him at home."

Gram laughed at that, but he couldn't help but wonder at her calm. As they dropped down to survey the central point he said as much, "How can you stay so composed?"

Layla landed and they climbed down before she answered, "I gave up on him once, and I've regretted it ever since. I won't make that mistake again, not until I see his body with my own eyes—and maybe not even then. But don't mistake my self-control; inside I am anything but composed.

"Practicality was a lesson I learned from your mother," she said after a minute, while they were searching. "When I was younger I was wild, but Rose taught me a lot about the power of a level-head."

Their search proved fruitless. The broken ground held no clues that Gram could read and there was no sign of a body. Celior had taken to the air when he left. They had no trail to follow.

As the shadows lengthened in the afternoon they climbed onto Layla's back and headed home.

"What will you do now?" asked Gram.

"What I must," said the Countess. "Care for my people, protect my family, and prepare for war."

"We don't even know who is responsible."

"We will," said Penny. "Your mother is already working on it. All we need is patience."

Thornbear

Chapter 40

That evening Gram went looking for Grace. He hadn't seen her since they parted in the mountains, and although he had been told that Moira had brought her back, he had yet to see her with his own eyes.

The Illeniel family was actually living in the castle now; the rooms that had been a decoy were now in use. There were four guards posted on the door, rather than the usual two, but they recognized Gram.

"Sir Gram," said one, dipping his head in respect.

That's going to take some getting used to, thought Gram. He nodded in return and passed through the door into the antechamber. Peter Tucker answered the inner door, ushering Gram inside.

"I'd like to offer my condolences," said Gram. "About…"

The chamberlain held up a hand, "I understand. You did what you could. Lilly would have been grateful to you for saving the children." His face was a study in controlled pain. Peter Tucker was a bachelor, and for most of his life he and his sister had been a team, working for the Illeniel family.

Gram couldn't begin to understand what he might be feeling.

"The Countess is with your mother in the library upstairs. Matthew is in his workshop, but Moira, Conall and Irene are here," said Peter, summing up the current occupancy for Gram.

"Thank you." Gram went through the door and found Moira and the others in the large front room.

"I was hoping you'd come," said Moira.

Irene was more direct, running to him and throwing her arms around his waist. She didn't say anything, but she squeezed him with all the strength in her slender arms.

Gram stroked her hair, feeling awkward. "It's alright, Rennie."

The girl shook her head, "No, no it's not. I'm so sorry."

"None of it is your fault," said Gram. "All we can do is live our lives the best we can."

Moira peeled her sister away from him, "We all miss Lilly, Rennie."

Irene nodded, "It's not just that, though. Alyssa is gone too."

"She's the one that made this mess," said Conall harshly.

"She didn't want to," insisted Irene. "She was kind to me. Of all of them, she was the one that made sure I was alright. She was just doing what she was told."

"Lilly's dead and Father is gone too," growled Conall. "I'm glad she's dead. In fact, I wish she was still alive, so we could kill her all over again." The boy stood and left.

Moira gave Gram a helpless look.

"He doesn't understand," said Irene. "She saved my life. You were there, Gram, you saw it, right?"

"I saw, Rennie. I know. I loved her," answered Gram, fighting to control his own emotions. Looking up at Moira he asked, "How is Grace?"

Moira's expression changed, becoming smooth. "Rennie, I'm going to take Gram out. I need to talk to him. Do you mind?"

Irene shook her head and Moira led him out into the hall. Gram was growing steadily more alarmed. *Don't tell me we've lost Grace too. Please, don't say that.*

"Let's go find Matthew," she said.

"Is Grace alright?"

She gave him a strange look. "She's different now."

"What does that mean?!"

"She will be glad to see you Gram, but Matthew wants to be there too—when you meet her."

"Is she alright? Dammitt, Moira, don't play games. You're pissing me off!" said Gram angrily.

"I understand," she said calmly. "Trust me, though. Be patient and we'll take you to see her."

He glared at her but followed anyway. She hadn't given him any choice. They walked downstairs and went out to the workshop. Matthew had been locking himself in every evening after they finished searching for their father.

Moira knocked on the door, "Matt, it's me."

"Go away. I'm busy," came her brother's voice.

"Gram wants to see Grace."

A heavy clunking sound passed through the door, followed by the sound of breaking pottery. "Shit." After a minute Matthew opened the door. He stepped outside and locked it behind him before they could see inside.

"What are you doing in there?" asked his sister.

"Mind your own business."

Gram sighed heavily. Matthew had a long stubborn streak when it came to his sister, a stubborn streak matched only by her temper. He held up a hand, "Can you two wait to argue until after I visit Grace? Please?"

"What's this?" said Moira angrily, pulling up her brother's loose sleeve. The skin on his arm was lined with small cuts.

Matthew jerked his arm free, "That's from the jar I just broke."

"Liar," she accused. "You broke that thing as an excuse. You were working on that trans-dimensional enchantment again!"

"Just stay out of it Moira," growled her brother. "And it's a spell, *not* an enchantment."

Gram was completely lost. "Can you two do this later?"

"The dragons are already coming," said Moira matter-of-factly, before adding, "Did you know he cut his arm off yesterday?!"

"What?!" exclaimed Gram.

"I did not!" barked Matthew. "It was still attached."

"If Father was here he wouldn't want you working on that thing," she rebuked him, getting red in the face.

Matthew's eyes were tense, a sure sign he was about to lose his temper. Moira started to say something else but Gram put his hand over her mouth. "Enough. Let me talk." Turning back to Matthew he asked, "What are you working on?"

"Remember our fight with Chel'strathek?"

Gram nodded.

"You nearly died because it took me so long to create the 'death blossom', so I've been working on it. I'm trying to get it down so that I can use it spontaneously."

"Death blossom?"

"That's his stupid name for it," groused Moira. "He nearly killed himself yesterday."

"No I didn't!" yelled Matthew. "I stopped the bleeding."

"But I had to reattach your arm! What if Mama heard about that? How do you think she would feel?"

"She'd be fine," said Matthew. "Because my arm is fine, and besides, you aren't going to tell her."

Moira's eyes narrowed and Gram could see she was preparing her next verbal attack. "Would you just explain what this 'death blossom' is, please?"

"Remember what I told you about 'translation'?" asked Matthew.

"You said it was like teleporting, but between dimensions, right?"

"Yeah," said Matthew. "The spell I used yesterday is similar, except it creates three triangular dimensional interfaces, joined at a point of congruence. They act like blades that will cut through anything."

"Like arms," said Moira pointedly.

Matthew ignored her, "The one I used on Chel'strathek hit him close to dead center, and it cut through the spell-weave that sustained him. It worked, just like I thought it would." His eyes were lit with a feverish enthusiasm.

"So you cast a spell and killed him," agreed Gram. "You very nearly killed me too."

"That was the explosive backlash from the release of his aythar," said Matthew. "The important thing is that I destroyed a spell-weave with just a spell."

"So?" As far as Gram was concerned the two things might as well be the same.

"He's excited because no one has ever been able to do that before," explained Moira in a bland tone.

"If we find Celior, I'm going to have to do it again," said Matthew.

The beat of dragon wings drowned out her reply, as Desacus and Moira's dragon, Cassandra, descended.

"Are we going to have to fly?" asked Gram.

Both of them nodded at him in unison.

Shit.

***

They flew south, with Gram riding double behind Matthew. He kept his eyes open this time, rather than closing them at the start. It made it easier to adjust as the ground grew slowly farther away.

"Relax," said Matthew. "The spell I used to make you lighter will last a while. Even if you fell, you'd fall softly enough that you probably wouldn't even hurt yourself."

Gram's stomach turned over at the thought. "Please stop talking," he begged.

They flew for a quarter of an hour, until they had reached the line of mountains that ran to the south of Cameron and Lancaster. Dropping down, they landed on a large ledge that opened into an unnaturally large and smooth cave.

"What is this?" asked Gram.

"Dad and Gareth Gaelyn made it to keep the dragons," explained Moira. "The tunnel goes back in a long way, to the egg chamber. There are side chambers for the dragons that have already hatched."

Now Gram understood. The Count had never explained where the dragons stayed, or where he had hidden the other eggs, for obvious reasons. They followed a huge corridor deeper into the mountain, passing vast side arches.

"That's where Layla stays," said Moira, indicating the first arch on the left. "The next one on the right is Desacus'. Cassandra's is farther on, to the left. The rest after that are still unclaimed."

They continued walking, until Gram was certain they had gone more than a mile into the mountainside. At the end was a massive iron door, covered in strange symbols. Matthew stepped up and put his hand on the door, uttering a quiet word.

The door opened silently, a surprise for such a massive construction. Inside Gram saw a long room, occupied by stone benches arranged in rows. Atop each one was a wooden box, bound with iron straps.

"Those are the eggs?" asked Gram.

They nodded, walking forward to a box on the right hand side. The iron bands that sealed it had been cut already. Matthew reached out and pulled the lid aside. Moira lifted a large, rose-colored egg from within.

"What are you doing?"

She offered it to Gram, "Here."

"That's not for me. Your father is the one that's supposed to choose."

Matthew broke in, "He didn't create the dragons by himself, you know. He had help from Gareth Gaelyn and Moira. I even helped with some of it."

Gram took a step back, "I don't even like flying."

"This wasn't our choice, Gram," added Moira. "Father chose the Queen's dragon, Matt and I chose our own, but this one is special. This one chose you."

"How? I've never met any of them." He had heard that Moira created the animus for each of the dragon eggs, but he hadn't been present when it was done.

"Put your hand on the egg," she replied. "Introduce yourself."

"Trust us," said Matthew.

Gram glared at his friend, "You know how I feel about you saying that."

Moira sighed, "Just do it."

He knew better than to argue any further. Gram had secretly dreamed that one day the Count might offer him one of the eggs, but he hadn't imagined it would happen like this. His two friends had essentially stolen their dragons, albeit with their mother's help. The Count was missing now but it still... Gram closed off that train of thought. Putting his hand out, he placed it on top of the egg in Moira's hands.

It felt warm to the touch; firm, though soft as well, like boiled leather. "Hello," he said.

Gram?

The reply was purely mental, but the voice in his mind was familiar. It felt feminine.

"Yes," he answered. "This is Gram."

I've missed you. How is Rennie?

"Grace?!"

Of course.

"But you're a bear!" he blurted out. The twins were watching him with knowing smirks on their faces.

No, she replied, *I am, or rather I was, a spell-beast. I'm a little different now. The world is full of textures and sensations. I never knew what a joy skin could be.*

"Skin? You're an egg."

I'm inside the egg, but I have a true body now. I can already feel new things.

"I was so worried about you, Grace…"

You don't have to talk out loud, she told him. *You'll embarrass me if you say too much in front of everyone.*

"I'm sorr…" he stopped himself. *I'm sorry. This is all new to me.*

We can learn together, said Grace. *You still haven't answered my question.*

I forgot what it was, he admitted.

How is Rennie?

I think she's doing well.

Good, came the response from the egg. *How are you?*

There's nothing wrong with me, said Gram.

Aside from a broken heart and suffering a terrible loss, she answered. *Mourning is natural; don't pretend you aren't hurting.*

I am, he agreed, *but having you back helps a lot.*

The three of them walked back out, Gram cradling the egg against his chest. The air felt warmer and the smell of the stone in the cave was sharper. As they emerged into the dusky evening, he couldn't help but note how much brighter the world seemed. "Was it this light out when we went in?"

Matthew chuckled, "Dragons will do that to you."

"This is just starlight, Gram," said Moira. "You won't have any problems seeing, even if there's hardly any light at all."

Desacus and Cassandra were waiting for them. Matthew climbed up and offered a hand to Gram.

He shook his head, "I think I'll walk back, Matt."

"You can't climb down *and* carry that egg," said his friend. "And even if you could, it would take half the night to get back on foot."

Gram looked over the edge at the steep mountainside. "Dammitt."

We'll get to fly together soon, said Grace in his head.

Epilogue

Rose Thornbear sat at the writing table in the upstairs library. Finishing yet another letter, she folded it and then addressed it before adding sealing wax and stamping it with her seal. Once that was done, she arched her back, stretching. Sitting in the hard chair for hours on end was painful, but she wasn't finished.

The door behind her opened and Penny strode in, still wearing her armor. Rose couldn't recall seeing her without it since the news of the attack on the Illeniel family. "Are you still at it?" asked the Countess.

"Waiting isn't easy," said Rose. "Whenever I think I've sent the last letter, another idea springs to mind, and there's nothing for it but to send another inquiry. It will get worse once the responses start arriving. Don't you get tired of wearing all that metal?"

Penny sat heavily in a chair at one of the reading tables. "Yes. It isn't as easy as it once was, but I don't feel comfortable without it."

"It seems we each have our own ways of dealing with a difficult situation," commented Rose.

"At least yours is truly helpful," said Penny. "The armor makes me feel better, but it gets us no closer to discovering who this enemy is."

Rose rubbed her eyes. "Mordecai would feel better knowing you wear it, ready to protect your children."

"I wish I could think that," said Penny. "But in reality, they protected themselves this time. Without Gram, I might have lost my daughter forever."

"Don't forget the twins," said Rose.

"I haven't. They scare me more than anything."

"Because they're coming into their own?"

"Because they *think* they can protect themselves," corrected Penny. "I, *you*—we both know how deceptive the illusion of safety can be, but they're too young to understand danger."

"It doesn't do any good to try to protect them," said Rose. "I made that mistake with Gram. You've done much better with yours."

"I'm not so sure about that. Moira has been very cross with her brother lately, and George said some very unsettling things when I talked to him yesterday."

That got Rose's attention, "Explain what you mean."

"Matthew had just explained to him what he did to stop Chel'strathek. George expressed some disbelief at what he heard, while Moira became rather agitated. Neither of them liked what he said. George almost called him a liar, but I think he simply didn't understand. Moira on the other hand, knew the truth, which is probably why she was so angry. She's scared for her brother's safety."

"Did she tell you what she was worried about?" asked Rose.

Penny frowned, "No. She's hiding her concerns from me. They both want to protect me."

"They learned that from their parents," noted Rose.

"It's frustrating," agreed Penny. "Both of them think they know better than the rest of us. I talked to George afterward, alone, and he seemed rather troubled. He admitted that he didn't really understand what Matthew did, but that it shouldn't have been possible for a simple spell to destroy the magic that held one of the dark gods together."

Rose pursed her lips. "Mordecai is the only one who really understands the things that boy works on."

"And he isn't here."

"Maybe you should try to keep him busy," suggested Rose.

"How?"

"Have you seen the armor that he made for Gram? It appears from thin air and disappears just as quickly. You wouldn't have to wear that chain all day long."

"He said that took him a half a year to finish," observed Penny.

"Exactly."

Penny chuckled, "I don't think I will be able to pin him down that easily. He's very stubborn, and he has his own ideas about what should be a priority."

"Much like his father," noted Rose.

The Countess placed her steel cap on the table in front of her. "It's been almost four days, Rose. He should have sent a message by now or communicated in some other way—if he could."

"If he were alive. Is that what you mean?"

Penny nodded.

Rose looked away, "I'm the last person you should talk to for reassurance. You know I don't believe in miracles."

"This isn't the first time I've been through this," Penny reminded her. "I'm just trying to figure out where to go from here, if I can't find him—if he doesn't return."

"There are no easy solutions," said Rose. "We do what we can, and once we know where to lay the blame, we'll decide what our options are."

"How long do you think we should wait to announce it?"

"That Mordecai is missing?" asked Rose, pausing.

"Yes."

"As long as possible," she answered. "We have no body, so he can't be declared dead for some time anyway. The longer his absence is left unannounced, the longer our enemies will wonder, and the less time they will have to plan based on that information."

"Unless they already know," suggested Penny.

"We have many different enemies; only a few of them would know. You still gain an advantage keeping the others in the dark," advised Rose.

"As always, you see the clearest of us all," observed the Countess. "I don't know how I would manage without you, Rose."

***

'Four' felt something unusual ahead. She was called 'Four' because her creator hadn't had much time for more personalized names.

She crept across the rocky hillside as quietly as possible, keeping her body low to the ground. Four was small to begin with, her cat-like body standing only a foot tall on her four legs, but she crouched even lower now, hoping to avoid notice.

Four wasn't very smart though, or she might have considered the fact that she would stand out to magesight no matter how she tried to conceal her physical presence, her aythar glowed like a light in the dark. Creeping forward, she approached the dark opening that seemed to hold a strange presence.

In her mind, Four remembered what she was looking for; a man, tall, dark hair, and with aythar that had a particular flavor to it. It was a memory implanted in her mind by her creator, to enable her to identify him when she found him. *Mordecai.* There was a hint of aythar ahead that seemed to be his, hidden beneath a shadowed overhang. A deeper recession there indicated the beginning of a cave.

Something else was there as well, a darker thing, a powerful thing.

Four hadn't been given much capacity when it came to emotions. She was particularly lacking when it came to fear or a sense of self-preservation. Such things were pretty useless when you weren't expected to live for more than a few days. Entering the cave, Four gained a clearer view.

Mordecai was there, lying prone on the rocky floor, but she felt his eyes, or perhaps his attention, fall on her. There was a sense of recognition. *He knows my creator; he must sense a hint of her in me,* thought Four.

"Run," he managed to say with some difficulty, but it was too late.

The thing that stood over him stretched out a strangely fluid limb in Four's direction. Power flowed from it, and she began to dissolve, a momentary pain flashing through her body.

Moira! Four's cry went out as loudly as she could manage, but she knew it was futile, her creator was too far away. She would not hear her warning. *I will not make it to the meeting place,* thought the dying spell-beast, and then she was gone.

Coming Early in 2015:

The Silent Tempest

The story of Tyrion Illeniel and the events that began the war between the remnants of humanity and the She'Har continues with the second installment in the Embers of Illeniel series.

Coming in the Summer of 2015:

Centyr Dominance

The tale begun in Thornbear continues as Moira Illeniel begins a quest to find and rescue her father while learning the darker secrets of the Centyr legacy.

For more information about the Mageborn series check out the author's Facebook page:

https://www.facebook.com/MagebornAuthor

You can also find interesting discussions and information at the Mageborn forums or the Mageborn Wiki:

http://www.illenielsdoom.com/

http://magebornwiki.com/index.php/Main_Page

8411919R00268

Printed in Great Britain
by Amazon.co.uk, Ltd.,
Marston Gate.